Fall of Thanes

BY BRIAN RUCKLEY

The Godless World
Winterbirth
Bloodheir
Fall of Thanes

BRIAN RUCKLEY
Fall of Thanes

THE
GODLESS
WORLD
—
BOOK THREE

www.orbitbooks.net

ORBIT

First published in Great Britain in 2009 by Orbit

A CIP catalogue record for this book
is available from the British Library.

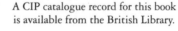

ISBN (hardback) 978-1-84149-440-1
ISBN (C format) 978-1-84149-787-7

Typeset in Garamond by M Rules
Printed and bound in Great Britain by
Clays Ltd, St Ives plc

Papers used by Orbit are natural, renewable and
recyclable products sourced from well-managed forests and certified in
accordance with the rules of the Forest Stewardship Council.

Mixed Sources
Product group from well-managed
forests and other controlled sources
www.fsc.org Cert no. SGS-COC-004081
© 1996 Forest Stewardship Council
FSC

Orbit
An imprint of
Little, Brown Book Group
100 Victoria Embankment
London EC4Y 0DY

An Hachette UK Company
www.hachette.co.uk

www.orbitbooks.net

For you,
and all the other readers who have followed the story
to its conclusion

Acknowledgements

Thanks to

Tim Holman and all the others at Orbit who have helped to make this trilogy happen, and helped to get it into the hands of readers once it did happen.

Tina, my agent.

My parents, whose support and encouragement I will never tire of acknowledging.

And Fleur.

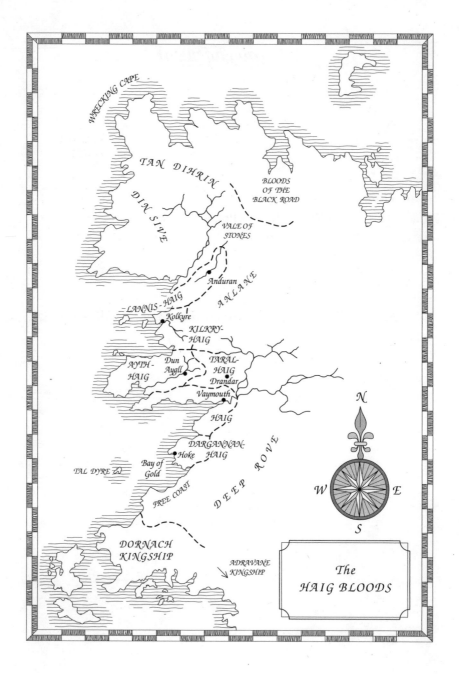

The
HAIG BLOODS

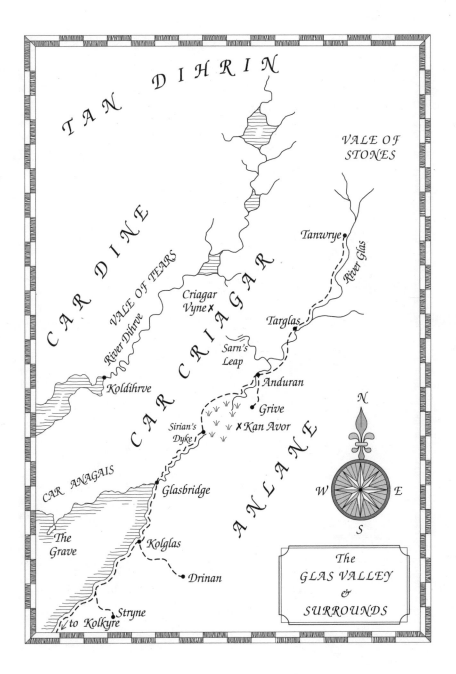

TAN DIHRIN

VALE OF STONES

CARDINE

VALE OF TEARS

CAR CRIAGAR

Criagar Vyne ✗

Tanwrye •

River Glas

River Dihrve

Targlas •

Sarn's Leap

Koldihrve •

Anduran •

Grive •

ANLANE

Sirian's Dyke

✗ Kan Avor

CAR ANAGAIS

Glasbridge •

The Grave •

Kolglas •

Drinan •

Stryne •

to Kolkyre

N

W   E

S

The
GLAS VALLEY
&
SURROUNDS

to Kolglas

Stryne

Hommen

IL
ANARON

Skeil
Anchor

In Cyr

Kolkyre

K A R K Y R E   P E A K S

Hent

Highfast

Anaron's
Bay

Donnish

Ive

River Kyre

VEILED
WOODS

VARE
WASTE

Stone

Kyresource
Lakes

Kilvale

to
Dun Aygll

N

W   E

S

LANDS OF THE
KILKRY-HAIG
BLOOD

Contents

What Has Gone Before

Orisian oc Lannis-Haig is now Thane of his Blood, but he is a Thane exiled from his lands, for the Glas Valley where he and his family dwelled lies under the brutal control of the Bloods of the Black Road.

Orisian has escaped from the pursuing forces of the Black Road to Kolkyre, the capital of the Kilkry Blood, long a close friend and ally to his own. With him have come Yvane and Hammarn, *na'kyrim* from the north, Ess'yr and Varryn, Kyrinin of the Fox clan, his shieldman Rothe and his sister Anyara.

Others have also converged upon Kolkyre, however, and Orisian finds himself the object of unwelcome attention from Mordyn Jerain, the Shadowhand, Chancellor to the Haig Blood, and Aewult, Bloodheir to the High Thane, Gryvan oc Haig. Their intent is to ensure the primacy of Haig in the efforts to turn back the Black Road. Frustrated by the machinations of these supposed allies, Orisian dispatches Taim Narran, his Blood's most accomplished warrior, with their meagre remaining forces northwards, hoping to delay or turn back the Black Road's advance. Orisian himself, concerned that a greater threat than even the armies of the Black Road is being overlooked, travels to Highfast, where a number of *na'kyrim* maintain a library.

The threat that so troubles Orisian is Aeglyss, a *na'kyrim* who has been crucified by the White Owl Kyrinin, but rather than dying,

descends from their Breaking Stone imbued with a rare and powerful ability to make use of the powers some *na'kyrim* can draw
from the Shared. Aeglyss first asserts control over the White Owl
clan, and then the Black Road army itself. He is the first *na'kyrim*
in centuries with the ability to bind another wholly and unre-
servedly to his will, and chooses to exercise this power over Wain
nan Horin-Gyre, sister of the Thane Kanin, to Kanin's increasingly desperate dismay.

In the course of his ascent, Aeglyss wins the allegiance of
Shraeve, a Battle Inkallim. He completes his rise to power when
Shraeve champions him in single combat against the senior war
leader of the Battle Inkall, Fiallic. With Aeglyss' subtle inter-
vention, Shraeve is victorious, assumes command of the Battle
Inkall's army and immediately pledges it to Aeglyss.

At Highfast, Orisian discovers that many of the *na'kyrim* there
can feel the alarming changes taking place in the Shared, and the
stirring of the Anain. He also finds Eshenna, who tells him that
Aeglyss is searching for a *na'kyrim* called K'rina, his foster mother
in his childhood. Believing he can be of more use in such a task
than trying to lead an army in the war, Orisian leaves Highfast
with a small company of warriors led by Torcaill, crosses the
Karkyre Peaks and descends into the Veiled Woods, where
Eshenna is certain K'rina can be found. They do indeed discover
the *na'kyrim*, but she has been mysteriously and disturbingly
transformed by the Anain, and in the course of capturing her,
Rothe, Orisian's shieldman and in some ways his closest surviving friend, is slain in battle with White Owl Kyrinin.

Orisian and the other survivors are driven by pursuing White
Owls back over the Karkyre Peaks. In their absence, Aeglyss
invades Highfast by possessing the body of Tyn, a *na'kyrim*
known as the Dreamer. When the other *na'kyrim* there refuse to
offer him any aid, Aeglyss destroys their library and kills many of
them. He also discovers Mordyn Jerain, the Shadowhand, who

lies injured after being attacked while he travelled there in pursuit of Orisian. The Shadowhand is carried away by Aeglyss' forces, and brought to Kan Avor in the Glas Valley, where the *na'kyrim* now resides. Aeglyss reluctantly resolves that the Shadowhand would be more valuable to him than Wain nan Horin-Gyre. He releases Wain from her binding, but has Shraeve kill her rather than let her go free. He then binds Mordyn Jerain, and sends him south to return to the Vaymouth, the capital of the Haig Bloods.

Taim Narran, leading the remaining forces of the Lannis Blood, is caught up in a great battle near Glasbridge. There, due to the pride and inexperience of Aewult nan Haig, the Black Road wins a major victory, and the armies of the True Bloods fall back in disarray to Kolkyre, where Aewult nan Haig accuses Taim Narran of treachery and imprisons him. He also takes hostage Anyara, Orisian's sister. She reluctantly remains in Kolkyre when Orisian sets out for Highfast, and there witnesses the assassination of Lheanor, the Kilkry Thane, by a member of the Hunt Inkall. As a result, Lheanor's son Roaric, a tempestuous young man, rises to the Thaneship of the Kilkry Blood. Aewult sends Anyara south to Vaymouth and the court of the Thane of Thanes.

The Black Road army descends upon Kolkyre and there, with the aid of Aeglyss' immense power, inflicts a further crippling defeat upon Aewult's forces. Escaping in the chaos, Taim Narran flees before the disaster now engulfing the lands of the Kilkry Blood. On the road to Ive, a small town south of Kolkyre, he is reunited with Orisian.

1

Ruins

Loss alone is but the wounding of a heart; it is memory that makes it our ruin.

A proverb of the Aygll Kingship

Pay no heed to grief. It is only weakness leaving your heart.

A saying of the Battle Inkall

I

The movement of birds. That was what told Orisian oc Lannis-Haig that they were coming. Wood pigeons, half a dozen, took flight from the leafless treetops, their wingtips cracking like a rattle of drums. He saw them arrowing away over the canopy, and knew that in their flight they told a tale of what lay beneath. Somewhere there, down amidst the dank greys and browns of the tree trunks and undergrowth, the enemy were coming: men, and likely women, he meant to see dead before the pale, sinking sun touched the horizon.

The woodlands were not large, not compared to the great tracts of forest Orisian had seen on the flanks of the Car Criagar or beyond the Karkyre Peaks. He shied away from that latter thought. His mind refused to approach too closely any memory of the Veiled Woods, and of what had happened there. If once he turned over that rock, what he uncovered might break him.

These woods were tame, as docile as any horse broken to the saddle and bit. Their oaks grew straight and tall above thickets of coppiced hazel. They lay amidst vast swathes of farmland and pasture on the gentle slopes west of Ive, and were just as much shaped by human hand as were those surrounding fields. Charcoal burners and timber merchants had laid out nets of pathways and clearings and campsites through them. Now, Orisian knew, one of those trails was being followed not by woodsmen but by the wolves of the Black Road.

He glanced at the warrior Torcaill, who was crouched along-side him amongst the rocks at the top of the slope.

'You saw?'

'Yes, sire. It won't be long. Will you come away now? Back behind the crest, at least?'

'No,' murmured Orisian. 'I'll see what's done in my name.'

He looked up, briefly, towards the west. There were clouds there: great dark masses that would muffle the sun before it set. More snow to come. The last fall had been almost a week ago, and light enough that no trace of it now remained.

'Let me bring up your horse, at least, sire,' Torcaill said.

'So I can flee more easily? No. Leave it where it is.'

The warrior frowned, his displeasure unconcealed.

'Go to your men,' Orisian told him. 'Make sure they're mounted and ready. If Taim needs you, it'll be soon.'

Torcaill went, scrambling back over the rocks. He had two dozen men waiting just out of sight. Orisian knew they would already be fully prepared. They were as eager as anyone to spill Black Road blood, and needed no encouragement from Torcaill to ready themselves for the task, but he found the warrior's concern for his safety unsettling. Troubling.

Only Ess'yr and Varryn remained with him. The two

Kyrinin were nestled down in the shadow of a boulder, paying no heed to the events unfolding around them. Ess'yr was smoothing the flights of her arrows one after another, a picture of perfect, absorbed attention. Her brother sat staring fixedly at the patch of grass between his feet. Neither had spoken since they settled into their place of concealment. They seldom did now, and perhaps that was why Orisian found their company easier than most. He craved silence, sought it as a friend and ally.

Three figures emerged from the woods: hunters from Ive, who today were bait in the trap. They trotted along the faint path that led up the slope. They were almost casual in their demeanour, but their backward glances hinted at tension. Orisian narrowed his eyes, trying to unpick the thick tapestry of the woodland edge, searching for the pursuit that – if all was happening as intended – should be close behind. He could detect no sign of it yet.

He noted that Ess'yr had set her quiver down. She wiped her right hand down the flank of her hide jacket, from the faint rise of her breast to her hip, and with her left took up her bow. She would willingly use it to kill on his behalf, Orisian knew. Varryn he was less sure of. The Kyrinin warrior had become the most reluctant of allies ever since they left the Veiled Woods; ever since Orisian had refused to free Ess'yr of any obligation to him, or send her away.

Rothe's absence stabbed at him afresh then, the anguish as pointed and wounding as ever. Each time he remembered that he could not turn his head and see the big, bluff shieldman there, an arm's length away, the thought strangled the breath in his throat and pinched at his eyes. It always brought the insistent memory, contemptuous of his every effort to dispel it, of his hand over the wound in Rothe's neck. Of the thick blood pulsing out between his fingers.

He blinked twice, knowing that the image would never be so

easily dismissed. The sounds of slaughter saved him. Cries were rising from the woods. He heard people crashing through the thickets, blades clattering against one another. The noise rescued him, for now, from the grasp of his memories.

The three Kilkry-Haig huntsmen had turned and were heading back to join the fight. Ess'yr stood up, shaking her hair away from her face with a feline flick of her head. Orisian could see movement in the gloom beneath the closest trees: figures struggling back and forth. Taim Narran's mixed company of Lannis and Kilkry men had closed with its prey. Black Road bands were ranging widely across the territory of the Kilkry Blood, raiding, scouting, seeking pillage or simple bloodshed. This was the second such group to come within reach of Ive in the last week; the second they had lured into ambush.

Men spilled out from amongst the trees, stumbling and struggling and hacking. Orisian rose. The shield was heavy on his left arm. He drew his sword, rhythmically tightening and easing his fingers about its hilt. It felt much more familiar in his grasp than once it had. Familiar but not yet natural, not good. Never good, perhaps.

'Friend or foe?'

Ess'yr stood perfectly still, bowstring drawn back almost to touch her lips.

'What?' Orisian asked.

'Is that one friend or foe?' she asked.

Orisian looked down the slope. One man had broken free from the battle and was labouring up towards them. His head was low, his attention consumed by the task of keeping his footing on the wet, slick grass. He wore a jerkin of hide and fur, carried a lumber axe in one hand. He had thick, dark hair. A heavy beard.

'Foe, I think,' Orisian said quietly, and before the sound of his words had died the arrow was gone, cutting through the cold air. He watched it, skimming out and down, struck by its elegant precision and the soft whisper of its flight, as it went unerringly to its warm home.

They entered Ive without ceremony, the last light of the day at their backs. What relief there was at their return was muted. They had killed twenty or more Black Roaders, and brought another back with them as prisoner, but such small victories brought little and brief comfort. There were, everyone knew, thousands more to take the place of those enemies felled today.

Torcaill and Taim rode on either side of Orisian. Varryn and Ess'yr walked a few paces behind them. When they had first arrived here with Orisian, the Kyrinin had been met everywhere they went in Ive by hostility and suspicion. They attracted little attention now. The town's inhabitants recognised them as members of Orisian's retinue, and accepted them – if reluctantly – as such. Orisian's Blood had long been allied to their own, and its Thane could keep what company he saw fit, no matter how strange and ill-advised such company might be.

As they made their way through Ive's darkening streets, they found their path blocked by a great mass of cattle, jostling and barging along beneath the switches of cowherds. In the failing light, the beasts all but merged into a single roiling creature, lowing and steaming as it rumbled into the town's heart, its flanks turned yellow by firelight spilling from windows. Men shouted at the cowherds to clear the roadway. Orisian rode on regardless, ploughing through the fringes of the herd. His company of warriors strung out behind him. Many of the Kilkry men amongst them drifted off down side streets, making for the homes they had been summoned from that morning, or to take their turn at sentry duty on the town's outskirts.

The cattle and their herders were only the latest of many to come seeking sanctuary in Ive, hoping for refuge from the chaos sweeping across the Kilkry Blood. Every time another family arrived, they brought tales of horror and disaster: wild Tarbain tribesmen burning and looting villages; companies of Inkallim appearing suddenly out of the night, intent upon slaughter. Donnish, the coastal town a day or two's ride west of Ive, had already fallen, abandoned by the tattered remnants of the Haig armies all but destroyed by the Black Road's remorseless advance. Further north, Kolkyre, where Roaric the Kilkry Thane languished, was cut off by a besieging host, and accessible only by sea. His Blood was on its knees.

Still, it was not yet as utterly ruined as was Orisian's own Blood. The sixty or so Lannis warriors at his back as he dismounted in the courtyard of Ive's Guard barracks were all that remained to him of his inheritance as Thane. He bore the title but in truth was master of nothing more than whatever strength rode with him. What respect was shown to him – and there was a good deal of it, from both his own followers and the people of Ive – felt, as often as not, undeserved and unearned.

Weariness took him as he entered the barracks. It was crowded inside, full of Guardsmen and townsfolk alike. And outsiders, too: those who had fled here with nothing but what they could carry, reliant upon the town's Guard for shelter or sustenance; warriors who had found their way here after defeat, and now slept on the floorboards of these draughty halls, dreaming perhaps of the chance to redeem themselves.

Orisian ignored them all. He met no one's eyes as he made his way to the stairs. When they recognised him, people here sometimes came begging for favours or aid. He helped them when he could – though that was seldom – but he was too exhausted for such exchanges tonight.

'I'll eat in my room,' he murmured to Taim, and climbed away from the hubbub.

He ate without enthusiasm. The food that was brought to him was good, the best the town had to offer, but he seldom had much of an appetite now. It was as if his mind and body could accommodate only so many hungers, and that for food was crowded out by less corporeal longings: for his sister's safety, for the undoing of so much that had been done to those he knew and loved. For some reason to be given for all the deaths.

After pushing aside the half-finished meal, Orisian closed his eyes and allowed his head to sink down onto his chest. He let time pass, consciously clearing his thoughts. It was a struggle, for he had barely more mastery over them than over the Blood he was supposed to lead, but he managed it. He dozed, until something – he did not know whether it was a sound from outside, or perhaps the determined, ungovernable stirring of his own mind – roused him.

He went sluggishly towards the window. He halted an arm's length back from it, keeping to the dark. He did not want to be seen if he could help it, and he was close enough to look down upon the little orchard, bounded by high stone walls, that lay behind the barracks. The ancient, crooked apple trees clenched up like wizened hands, half-lit by lamps burning in the kitchens. Almost beyond the reach of that light, in the heart of the grove, Ess'yr and Varryn had made shelters from stakes and hides.

Orisian could see the two Kyrinin now, moving amongst the trees. They drifted through the winter's dark, unhurried. They were gathering sticks for a fire. Orisian held himself quite still. Even his breathing grew shallow and soft. He did not know if they could see him from down there amongst the shadows, but they might. Their eyes were more than human, after all.

Ess'yr squatted down on her haunches to build the fire. Her hair slipped forward to hide her face. Orisian watched her hands instead. They were pale, indistinct shapes, but still their movements had grace and ease. Done with her preparations, she reached for some small bag or pouch and scattered something from it on a flat stone at the fireside. Food, Orisian knew. He had seen this many times since that first night with her in the forests far north of here. She left morsels for the restless dead.

He found himself wishing Ess'yr would look up, and turn her

face towards him. He both wanted her to know that he was watching her, and feared it. Perhaps she already knew. Perhaps she knew that he was constantly aware of her presence; that wherever they were, whoever he was talking to, if she was near there was always a portion of his attention claimed by her.

He could hear voices, softened and blurred, from the rooms below, and, more distant, the lowing of cattle, penned up in some yard or barn. Sparks flared amongst the sleeping apple trees. Once, twice, Ess'yr struck glimmers of fire from a flint. One must have taken, for she delicately raised the little bundle of kindling in her cupped hands and blew upon it. In moments, a tiny flame was born. Orisian could see her face then; see a faint line of firelight reflected on her hair. He smiled.

There were footsteps in the passageway outside. Taim Narran was calling for him. Orisian turned away from the window, feeling as he did so suddenly and terribly sad.

'You wanted to be informed, sire, if the prisoner was saying anything of interest,' Taim said when Orisian opened the door.

'Wait a moment while I get a cloak,' Orisian murmured.

'I can tell you what he's saying. If you would prefer to stay here. There is no need . . .'

'Do you think it's too cold for me outside?' Orisian asked gently as he settled the cloak about his shoulders. 'Or that I should not see what happens to prisoners in Ive?'

His Captain made no reply.

'It's all right, Taim. Whatever was fragile in me was broken long ago. Lead the way.'

II

The room clenched about him like a tight, hot fist. The heat of half a dozen small braziers was gathered by the rock walls, concentrated, blasted back to make the air thick and suffocating.

Within a couple of paces Orisian could feel sweat on his fore-head. The orange-red heart of each brazier almost seemed to pulse, so intense was the light and heat being hammered out into the cramped space.

The prisoner was tied to the far wall. His arms were stretched up and apart, bound to iron rings set in the stonework. He had slumped down and his own weight had tautened the muscles in his arms and shoulders. He was naked to the waist, his skin over-laid with a film of sweat. Fresh burns pockmarked his chest, red and brown and raw. The man who had inflicted them was stand-ing to one side, stocky, black-bearded. Orisian vaguely recognised him: he had seen him around the barracks once or twice before. One of the town's Guard. He wore massive leather gloves, and was watching the hilt of a knife sunk into the bra-zier. He did not even look up when Orisian and the others entered. There was no room in his attention for anything save that knife, buried in the fire, collecting into its metal the savage heat.

One of the several Kilkry warriors gathered there grasped the prisoner's hair and lifted his head up. His nose was broken and bent. The blood from it might be what crusted the man's lips, or his mouth might be shattered as well. Orisian winced momentarily at the sight of him. His own jaw and cheek gave a single aching beat, remembering the ruin visited upon them by the haft of a Kyrinin spear. A thread of mixed saliva and blood hung from the man's chin. Some remembered instinct made Orisian want to turn away. It was the stirring of the person he no longer quite was. It lacked conviction. He chose to look.

'Speak,' someone hissed at the broken Black Roader. 'Let's hear your poison again.'

Orisian glanced at Taim. His Captain's face was fixed and grim. Was there the slightest disapproving tightening around his eyes? A faint disgusted curl at the edge of his mouth?

Orisian could not be sure. Perhaps he wanted to see those things there, and allowed that desire to imagine them for him. He wanted to find in Taim some disgust and revulsion that he could borrow for himself; to be as horrified by this sight as he would have been just a few weeks ago.

The man's voice was stronger than Orisian would have expected. Uneven but clear despite the distortion of his heavy northern accent.

'You're finished. Your time's done. It's *his* time now. The Black Road's time. The Kall. He'll cast you all down into ruin and wreck, and lead us to the mastery of the world, and open the path for the Gods to return.'

'Who will?' the interrogator demanded, shaking the man's head so violently he pulled a fistful of hair from his scalp. He took hold again and twisted the prisoner's face toward Orisian.

Orisian watched those battered lips stretching into a snarling smile.

'The halfbreed. The Fisherwoman's heir. Fate works through him.'

'His name?' Orisian asked quietly.

'Not to be named. The *na'kyrim*. In Kan Avor. That is enough.'

'Aeglyss?' Orisian demanded, but the prisoner only grinned at him through blood. There was a madness in his eyes. A sort of mad joy, Orisian thought, a delight at the descent of the world into savagery.

'Keep him alive,' Orisian said, and left the choking heat of that deep chamber without another word. He climbed up the steps and out into the bitter night air. Tiny flecks of snow were darting down out of the darkness, dancing in the cauldron of the courtyard. He felt them falling on his cheeks and lips: points of numbing cold.

'It's as you thought,' Taim said behind him. 'As your *na'kyrim* have been saying. Whether in his own right, or as someone else's tool, the halfbreed's worked his way to the heart of things.'

Orisian looked up into the black sky, blinking against the grainy snow.

'They're not my *na'kyrim*,' he said.

In Eshenna's half-human eyes, Orisian saw very human things: exhaustion and a haunted, hunted unease. When first he met this *na'kyrim* in Highfast, he had found her determined, firm. That vigour was gone, or at least buried by the debris of what she had seen since then.

'Where's Yvane?' Orisian asked her.

'With K'rina.' She spoke that name with obvious reluctance. Another of the petty, cruel tricks the world was working upon its inhabitants in these troubled times: it had been Eshenna who insisted most determinedly that K'rina might be a weapon in the struggle against Aeglyss, yet the cost of finding her, and her condition when they did, had shaken Eshenna to her core. She had not been as well prepared as she imagined for what lay outside the walls of Highfast.

Orisian pitied her, but it was a detached kind of pity. Few had been ready for what had happened since Winterbirth. Many suffered. More than most, Eshenna had at least made some kind of choice in the path her life had taken in recent weeks.

That path had led here, to a simple, bare house just outside Ive's Guard compound. Erval, the town's Captain – and a good man as far as Orisian could tell, though as deeply unsettled as anyone by the course of recent events – had made it available to Eshenna and Yvane without hesitation or demur. Judging by its dilapidated and damp state, Orisian suspected it had been empty for some time. Still, it served the purpose asked of it now: a place for the *na'kyrim* to shelter away from prying eyes, small enough that it could easily be watched over by the men Taim Narran had set to the task. Whether the more important role of those guards was to ensure no misguided townspeople caused trouble for Yvane and Eshenna, or to protect those townspeople from K'rina if necessary, Orisian did not know. No one did.

'K'rina still will not come inside?' he asked Eshenna.

She shook her head. 'If we try to move her from the goat shed, she thrashes about. Howls.'

'But does not speak.'

'No. She never speaks.'

'You don't look well,' Orisian murmured.

Eshenna gave a short, bitter laugh. She was feeding wood to a little fire. As she bent, and sparkling embers swirled up in front of her face, the gauntness of her features was apparent. Since leaving Highfast, she had thinned and her skin had grown paler, almost as if the Kyrinin half of her mixed heritage was asserting itself.

'If there's anything I – anyone – can do for you, tell me,' Orisian said. 'I'll help if I can.'

'I know,' Eshenna sighed. She held a stubby chunk of wood in her hand, gazing down at it, running her long fingers over its flaking bark. 'I need sleep. And I need the voices, and the storms, in the Shared to quieten. You can't do that, can you?'

'No. I can't.'

Eshenna threw the log into the flames and crossed her arms, staring blankly into the heart of the fire.

'Yvane will be a while yet. She spends a lot of time with K'rina.'

Orisian nodded silently and left the *na'kyrim* to her dark contemplations.

Behind the run-down house, stone walls enclosed a long, thin yard. Half of it was given over to dark, bare soil, which the inhabitants must once have cultivated. Snow was speckling the earth now. The rest was cobbled, running down a gentle slope to a ramshackle shed against the furthest wall. Orisian walked towards it, brushing snow from his hair as he went. He could hear the low voices of two of Taim's guards coming from beyond the wall and the rumble of the slowly rising wind as it blustered about Ive's roofs, but there was no sound from within the shed.

He pulled the door open and peered in. The stink of goats assailed him. The animals were long gone. The only light within came from a single tallow candle Yvane must have brought with her. K'rina was curled in the corner of the shed, on old straw, facing the wall. Yvane knelt beside her, sitting back on her heels. Neither of the *na'kyrim* stirred at Orisian's arrival. He stepped inside.

'No change?'

'No,' said Yvane without looking round.

'You shouldn't be in here alone,' Orisian said. 'What if she attacked you? What if she tried to escape again?'

Yvane rose to her feet. There was just a hint of stiffness, the slightest unsteadiness, in the movement. Perhaps her years weighed a little more heavily on her now. Perhaps sleepless nights were taking their toll on her, as they did on so many others.

'She's not some wild animal,' Yvane said softly. 'Nor a prisoner, as far as I recall.'

'Maybe not, but we've paid a high price to bring her here. If we lose her, that price was for nothing. She's tried to slip away once already.'

Yvane hunched forward a little to brush straw and dirt from her hide dress. She gave the task more attention than it merited.

'What?' asked Orisian.

'You're wounded,' the *na'kyrim* muttered.

Orisian put a hand to the side of his face, tracing the great welt that ran up his cheek, feeling the yielding gap left by lost teeth. That was not what she meant, though. He knew the shape of her concerns, and it had nothing to do with the punishment his body had taken.

'Some wounds grow thick scars,' she said. 'Enough wounds, enough scars, and you can hardly recognise the one who bears them. Ends up being someone completely different.'

Orisian grimaced and stared down at the flagstone floor. He did not want to hear this. It achieved nothing, ploughing over and over the same small field of Yvane's preoccupations.

'When I first met you . . .' the *na'kyrim* began.

'When you first met me, all of this had only just started. I hadn't seen then what I've seen now.'

Yvane sniffed and rubbed at her nose with the back of a grubby finger.

'None of us had, I don't suppose,' she said. 'I could see why Inurian had taken to you, back then. I could see a little something of what he must have seen in you. He always prized gentleness, thoughtfulness. Compassion.'

'There are other things I need – we need – more now.'

'Are there? You think Inurian would agree, if he was still here? You think he would find you as worthy of his affection now as he did . . .'

'Don't,' Orisian snapped. He glared at her, and met those impassive, piercing eyes with a resilience he would once have thought impossible. He had much deeper reserves of anger to draw upon now, and it could armour him against even Yvane's fierce gaze.

She smiled, a gesture that started sad and became something much darker and colder before it faded away. She looked down at K'rina.

'None of us had any idea how far all of this would go,' she muttered. 'Except perhaps Inurian. He looked into Aeglyss' heart back then and saw the poison in it.'

'We've got a prisoner. He talks of Aeglyss as a leader. A ruler, almost, in Kan Avor. As if they all follow him now.'

'Oh?' Yvane sounded barely interested.

'It makes K'rina more important.'

'As what? A club to beat Aeglyss with?'

'Or a key in a lock,' Orisian said, exasperated. 'I don't know. Something. It was you and Eshenna who told me she mattered in the first place. I didn't want to find her like this. None of us did. But now we know the White Owls – Aeglyss – were seeking her. We can see that something, whatever it is, has been done to her. She's important. Don't blame me for wanting to understand how, and why. For wanting to know that there was a reason for my warriors to die finding her.'

Yvane held out a placatory hand. 'We'll disturb her,' she said, with a glance down at the prostrate woman in the straw. She bent and picked up the little candle. The flame died between her finger and thumb. For a moment there was only darkness and the wind rattling the roof shingles.

'Let's go back to the house,' Yvane said.

They barred the door of the shed behind them.

'I need to know, Yvane,' Orisian said as they walked. 'We all do. There's no time left to be gentle, or cautious. Things are falling apart. If K'rina is to mean anything . . .'

'Mean anything?' Yvane snapped, coming to a sudden halt and jabbing Orisian in the chest. 'She *means* as much as I do. Or you. That is precisely what she *means*. Or do you think a mere halfbreed must work harder than that to have meaning?'

'You know that's not—' Orisian protested.

'Something's been done to her,' Yvane rushed on, uninterested in anything he might have to say. 'That's what you said. Well, she didn't do it to herself. The Anain have scraped out her mind, as best we can tell. As if she was nothing, as if whatever thoughts and feelings were in there before mattered not at all. She's a victim in all of this, as surely as anyone is. As surely as Inurian was, or Cerys or any of the others at Highfast.'

She hung her head. The two of them stood there in the dark yard, the wind rumbling overhead.

'Nevertheless,' murmured Orisian.

'Nevertheless,' said Yvane dully. 'There's always a nevertheless. But not tonight. Tonight, I'm going to try to sleep.' She turned and walked away from him, towards the pale flame of a candle burning in the window of the house.

Orisian stalked back to his bedchamber with a familiar, imprecise anger churning in him. It was always there, always ready to fill any spaces in his thoughts if given the chance. Yvane would say it was the wake Aeglyss left as he moved through the Shared, discolouring everything – every mind – it washed up against. Orisian did not know. It felt like his own thing, crafted from his own experience, but he did not doubt that such a sense might be deceptive. It hardly mattered. It was there, in his heart and his mind, and he must deal with it, whatever its source.

Before taking to his bed he looked down on the orchard once more. The fire was still burning, a little beacon beneath the creaking and swaying apple trees. There was no sign of Ess'yr and Varryn. They had probably retired to the shelters they had made for themselves.

He laid himself out on the mattress and closed his eyes. He no longer expected any night to bring easy rest, for they were always full of frightening dreams and sudden wakings. Still, he could hope.

III

Orisian broke his fast the next morning in the main hall. The trestle tables were lined with Guardsmen, and with the homeless and destitute given shelter in the barracks. Orisian sat with Taim and Torcaill and the rest of the Lannis warriors.

The hall was filled with cacophonous activity. Plates clattered; arguments raged; cooks and servants rushed back and forth. Orisian's head ached, and he winced at each crash of a falling tray and each shouted insult. The night had not, in the end, been restful. Several times he had woken with a heart set racing by the horror of some forgotten dream. The wind had raged all through the hours of darkness, shaking the building.

'Two dead sentries on the edge of town last night,' Taim said between mouthfuls of salted porridge.

'No one saw anything?' asked Orisian.

Taim shook his head. 'But one of them was savaged. Had his hand almost torn off, and his throat bitten out. Dogs, it looked like.'

'Hunt Inkallim,' said Torcaill. He looked as weary as Orisian felt.

'Seems likely,' agreed Taim. 'There's a good chance one or more of them got inside the town. Not a good sign.'

'I don't mean to be chased out of here yet,' said Orisian quickly. Best, he thought, to anticipate the suggestion he could already imagine Taim formulating.

The warrior regarded his Thane for a moment or two, and Orisian could see his disagreement clearly in his expression, but when Taim spoke it was mildly: 'The Hunt'd only be creeping around in here for two reasons I can think of. Either they meant to kill someone – you, most likely, if they know you're here – or they're scouting the place out for an attack. Neither choice bodes well for us.'

'I know,' Orisian said.

Although Ive was a substantial town, one of the Kilkry Blood's biggest, it was ill prepared to stand against an assault. It had long been remote from any disputed land or battlefield; it had no castle, and the wall that once ringed it had long ago been dismantled, its stones turned to more peaceful use in the skeletons of barns and farmhouses.

For days now, labourers had been toiling all around the edge of town, trying to encircle it with a ditch and timber palisade. Until that work was completed, Ive's only defence was the flesh and steel of the warriors gathered there, the Guard and the poorly armed townsfolk themselves. In all there were perhaps a thousand trained fighting men, and another two thousand untrained but willing and able to fight. More than enough to master the savage but disorganised raiding bands they had faced so far; too few to last long if the Black Road's full might descended upon them.

'There might still be time to get to Kilvale,' Torcaill said, sounding almost hopeful. 'For every score that turn up in Ive each day, there's a dozen leaving and heading south. They think the road's still open.'

'But they don't know,' Orisian said. 'Nobody knows who's in control anywhere, not really. It'd take . . . what, two days to get there? If we're caught on the road, we'd be finished. And there's nowhere the Black Road will want more than Kilvale. It's their birthplace. If we did reach Kilvale, and it falls, where do we run to then? Dun Aygll? Vaymouth, even? What kind of a Thane would that make me?'

He glared questioningly at Torcaill. The warrior studied his bowl, stirring the porridge within it carefully.

Taim Narran was less reticent. 'A living one, at least,' he murmured.

Orisian looked at the older warrior, an angry retort boiling up towards his lips. But the momentary fury passed. He breathed deeply.

'I'm sorry,' he said. He pressed finger and thumb to his temple, willing the throbbing in his skull to subside. 'I just think . . . I think we lack the strength to make any difference in whatever struggles are to come between Haig and the Black Road. And we – you most of all, Taim – could hardly expect a warm welcome from Aewult, in any case.'

'It's true Haig has no need of our few swords,' Taim acknowledged. 'Gryvan must wake to the danger now. Once he rouses himself and his people from sloth, the Black Road's ascendancy will be at an end, Aeglyss or no Aeglyss. But we – you – still

need to survive long enough to see that day. I'd not choose Ive to
make a stand, if that's . . .'

Erval, the leader of Ive's Guard, came hurrying down between
the lines of tables. He stumbled over a sword someone had rested
against a bench, but rushed on regardless. He was red-faced,
plainly agitated. Heads turned to follow his progress. He came
to a rather disorderly halt behind Orisian and dipped into a
hasty bow.

'There are messengers come in search of you, sire. I've got
them waiting in the courtyard.'

'Who sent them?' Orisian asked.

The Guard Captain looked apologetic. 'Aewult nan Haig, sire.
They claim his authority, and through him that of his father, for
the message they bear.'

'Let them freeze the rest of the day in the yard, then,' Torcaill
muttered.

'I think they may have left their patience behind when they
set out on their journey,' said Erval.

Orisian sighed and swung a leg out over the bench.

'There's no point in delaying,' he said as he rose.

'It might be best,' Erval agreed, relief plain in his voice.
'There's a fierce mood in the town, and word's already spreading that there're Haig men here. You know how that will taste
to people. The sooner they've said their piece and gone, the
better.'

Torcaill and Taim were getting to their feet to follow Orisian.

'Not you, Taim,' he said.

The warrior frowned.

Orisian smiled at him. 'You're an escaped prisoner, aren't you?
A fugitive from Aewult's version of justice?'

Taim sank heavily back onto the bench.

'I don't want any trouble if I can avoid it,' said Orisian. 'No
more than we've already got, anyway.'

'Take a few of the other men, at least,' Taim said. 'Let them

think you've got some swords at your back. And remember they
have your sister.'

'That's not something I'm likely to forget.'

Torcaill quickly assembled a little escort party, and Erval led
them all out of the hall. The place was silent as they left.

The wide courtyard was dusted with snow. Most of it had
been swept up by the overnight wind, and packed into corners
and crevices. There was no wind now, but it was bitterly cold. As
Orisian and the others emerged onto the cobblestones, the nearest of the messengers was clapping his gloved hands together to
warm them.

The Haig Bloodheir had sent ten men. Six of them were warriors, standing back and watching over the party's horses. The
other four were less martially attired, clad in fur capes, wearing
gauntlets of what looked like velvet rather than leather. The one
who stepped forward to greet Orisian had a gold clasp holding
his cloak around his neck.

The man bowed more deeply and respectfully than Orisian
might have expected from one of Aewult's household. Any
appearance of respect was quickly dispelled once that formal gesture had been completed, however.

'This man,' the messenger said with a jab of his chin in Erval's
direction, 'seems to think our business is best conducted out
here in the cold. Perhaps you could prevail upon him to change
his mind, Thane?'

And in that one instant Orisian was vividly transported back
to Kolkyre, to the entirely uncomfortable company of Aewult
and Gryvan's Chancellor Mordyn Jerain. Evidently disdain and
casual self-importance were traits shared by all ranks within the
Haig Blood. Back in Kolkyre, he had been somewhat cowed by
it. Now, his mood merely soured, and his headache asserted
itself.

'I imagine the Captain anticipated your desire to be back on
the road south as quickly as possible,' he said. 'You seem to

know my name, so perhaps you could allow me the same privilege.'

The messenger stood a good head taller than Orisian, but the reprimand narrowed his shoulders slightly, put the faintest hint of submission into his posture.

'I am Gorred Mant dar Haig, sire. Emissary of Aewult nan Haig. These men are—'

He gestured towards his companions, but Orisian cut him off. It was indeed cold out here beneath the cloudless winter sky. For that and other reasons, brevity appealed greatly to him.

'You came seeking me, did you?' he asked.

'Indeed, sire.' Gorred had recovered a little of his composure now. He stood straight once more and Orisian suspected that beneath that voluminous cloak his chest swelled. 'Rumours reached Kilvale mere days ago that you were here in Ive. There was great relief, of course. People have been concerned for your safety since you left Kolkyre.'

'You may report that I am in good health, then.'

'Indeed.' Gorred extended an arm, flapping his hand. One of the other Haig men stepped forward, hurriedly dragging out two scroll cases from some hidden pocket or bag and passing them over.

'I bear two messages, sire,' Gorred said, proffering the two tubes to Orisian.

'Just tell me,' Orisian said.

'I do need to hand them over, sire.' That welcome trace of discomfiture was back in the emissary's voice. 'I will not be deemed to have discharged my duty if I don't put them in your hand.'

Orisian took the cases from him, and passed them at once to Torcaill, who casually tucked them under his belt.

'Tell me,' Orisian said again.

There was an abrupt flurry of noise from beyond the open gate. Loud but indistinct voices were battling one another in the street beyond. Gorred glanced over his shoulder in irritation.

Several of Erval's Guards were clustered in the gateway, in animated discussion, gesticulating towards something out in the street. Gorred turned back to Orisian.

'These are delicate matters, sire. Perhaps best discussed in a more private setting.'

'The sooner we are done, the sooner you can be on your way back to Kilvale. You'll know better than I that the roads grow more dangerous with every passing day. Every hour, even.'

Gorred looked distinctly unhappy but did not press the point any further.

'Very well. First an assurance as to the well-being of your sister, who is protected from all harm within the walls of Vaymouth itself, under the attentive care of—'

'Move on,' barked Orisian. It was a struggle – one in which he was not entirely successful – to keep the anger that welled up within him out of his voice. The mere mention of Anyara, especially in the mouth of one whose master had made her a virtual captive, or hostage, was enough to shake his precariously maintained balance.

Gorred blinked. 'Ah. Well, the substance of the first message is an invitation to join with the Bloodheir at Kilvale. It is his hope that you and he could then discuss the possibility of your attendance upon the High Thane in Vaymouth. You would thus be able to satisfy yourself as to your sister's . . .'

Another surge of agitated cries disturbed the messenger's flow. Gorred grunted in irritation. Everyone looked towards the gate, for the voices drifting in from the street unmistakably now carried an undercurrent of violence and anger.

'Forgive me,' Erval murmured in Orisian's ear. 'I should see what's happening.'

Orisian nodded, and the Captain of the Guard went trotting over to join his men at the gate.

'What's your second message?' Orisian asked, before Gorred could resume.

'It was hoped you might be able to accompany us on our return to Kilvale, sire. The Bloodheir was very hopeful of that.'

'I am needed here for a little while yet,' Orisian said. 'I will have to follow after you when I can. If I can. What's the second message?'

Gorred's eyes flicked momentarily away from Orisian, scanning Torcaill and the other warriors behind him. There was clear unease in the glance.

'It is understood that you have Taim Narran here with you. Is that true?'

Orisian put a hand to his brow, fending off the aching beat in his skull. His hands were so chilled that he barely felt the touch of skin to skin. He envied Gorred his fine gloves. But he made no reply to the messenger's question.

'I was instructed to ask after Taim Narran's presence, you see,' Gorred persisted, 'because certain charges were raised against him during the period of your absence. The Bloodheir requires—'

'Requires?' echoed Orisian. 'Taim Narran is my man, not Aewult's.'

'Nevertheless,' Gorred said. 'Nevertheless.' There was a dogged, somewhat glum determination about his manner now. As if he had at last resigned himself to abandoning any pretence at courteous discourse; as if he accepted the futility of clothing hard words in fine silks. 'No command was issued to release him; rather, you might say, Taim Narran chose to bestow freedom upon himself. And he fled from battle.'

Torcaill and the other Lannis warriors stirred at that. Orisian bit back his own instinctive contempt for Gorred's accusations.

Erval was returning hurriedly from the gate. Behind him, Orisian could see a solid knot of Guardsmen now barring the entrance to the courtyard. There were other figures moving beyond them, rushing up and down the street. Something dark, which at first Orisian thought must be a bird, darted over the heads of the Guards. The object arced down and broke apart on the yard's cobbles, a clod of muddy earth.

'Trouble,' Erval hissed into Orisian's ear. 'There's a crowd gathering. They know who's in here. Haig's little better liked than Gyre these days.'

Gorred was watching them, frowning. Orisian turned his head enough to hide his lips from the emissary.

'Can you quieten it all down, if we keep them out of sight?'

'Not sure, sire,' Erval whispered. 'There's more folk arriving every moment, and I've not seen a bloodier mood on them in years. Not ever. Could easily go bad, this. My men . . . it could be difficult if I ask them to fight their own people in defence of Haig.'

Orisian looked back to Gorred. The messenger raised questioning eyebrows. Orisian came to a decision.

'We're done,' he said, as clearly and firmly as he could. 'For your own safety, emissary, you must leave at once. Erval here will have his men escort you out of Ive, and see you a way down the road.'

'Sire? We have not finished our discussions, surely? If I am to return to the Bloodheir with nothing more than this, I must of necessity make an honest report of how I was received and treated.'

'Report as you like,' snapped Orisian. 'Dead men make no reports, and that's what you'll likely be if you tarry here.'

Gorred smirked, as if Orisian's words were preposterous. 'Messengers are protected, sire. They are not to be harmed, on pain of death. Everyone knows as much.'

Orisian pointed at the gate. 'Does that not sound to you like ignorance, then? Do you really think such laws are what govern hearts today? I'm *trying* to protect you.'

Gorred looked from Orisian to the gateway. Some of the Guards were dragging a man into the compound and beating him with their clubs. Another of them was on his knees, pressing his hand to a bloody scalp wound. Aewult nan Haig's messenger pondered for the space of a few heartbeats, and the fight leached out of him.

'Very well,' he said curtly. At a single, sharp gesture his companions and escorts began to mount their horses. He glanced almost dismissively at Orisian. 'You have the messages, Thane. The Bloodheir will anticipate an early reply, to both of them. Or better yet, your presence, and that of Taim Narran.'

The ten horses clattered over the cobblestones towards the gate. Erval ran ahead of them, shouting at his Guards to clear a path for the Haig party. Orisian and his men followed more slowly in their wake. It all felt unpleasantly like disaster to Orisian. A chasm was opening up between the Haig Blood and those of Lannis and Kilkry, yawning ever wider with each defeat and humiliation visited upon them by the Black Road.

The Guardsmen pushed out into the street, and Orisian saw for the first time just how large and frenzied a crowd of townsfolk had assembled. There were scores of them, of every age and kind. They choked the street. They fell back before the determined advance of Erval's men, but it was only the crowd reshaping itself, yielding in one place to thicken in another. Not a retreat. More figures came rushing from side streets and houses, like bees plunging in to join a furious swarm.

The Haig riders ventured out onto the muddy roadway. Their horses were skittish, catching the feral mood of the throng. People were falling, crushed between the lines of Guardsmen and the mass of townsfolk surging up, howling abuse at Gorred and the others. On every face Orisian saw visceral hatred, an instinctive yearning for bloodshed.

'Gods,' he heard Erval muttering at his side, 'it's bad.'

A stick came tumbling end over end through the air, blurring past Gorred's shoulder. The envoy ducked and scowled. His horse tossed its head. Slowly, edgily, the beleaguered company moved down the street.

'You need more men,' Orisian said to Erval. The Captain of the Guard looked bewildered, almost lost, in the face of the savagery that had taken hold of his town and his people.

'Send for more men!' Orisian shouted at him, and this shook Erval from his daze. One of the nearest Guardsmen was dispatched to find reinforcements.

It was too late. The townsfolk of Ive were possessed by a terrible fury, one that would brook no restraint and had purged them of any doubt or sense. Events rushed, like avalanching snow, towards their conclusion, as if that very conclusion had reached back and dragged everything irresistibly into its hungry maw.

One of the Guardsmen facing the multitude was knocked down. The space around Gorred and the others was abruptly constricted. Someone flailed at one of the Haig messengers with a hoe. A flurry of missiles came tumbling in: sticks, earth, stones, even a clattering pot. A Haig warrior was struck and reeled in his saddle, almost falling. His horse lurched sideways. Its mass ruptured the protective ring of Guardsmen. Townsfolk boiled into the gaps.

'Stop them!' Orisian shouted at Erval. The Captain was shaking his head, not in denial but impotence. He took two leaden paces out into the street and shouted angry commands. His voice was drowned in the flood of rage-bloated cries and howls.

The mob thickened around the horses. Here and there, like helpless flotsam on a surging sea, Guardsmen struggled against the crowd, but they were too few, and the ire of the townsfolk was far too fierce to be dampened by half-hearted blows from clubs or staves. The horses were rearing, their riders now slashing about them with swords and spears. Stones and chunks of wood were raining down on them.

A couple of men had climbed onto the roof of one of the houses and were stripping its tiles; the slate squares sliced through the air, spinning straight and true. Even as Orisian watched, one hammered into the forehead of Gorred's horse. The animal screamed and staggered. As it stumbled, eager hands reached up from the crowd and grabbed its mane, clawed at the rider's legs, tore at the saddle. Man and horse went crashing down and were instantly swallowed up.

Orisian started forward, but Torcaill held him back.

'If they kill them, Aewult will blame us!' Orisian cried. 'Lannis, Kilkry, all of us.'

'I know,' Torcaill said, 'but we can't stop it now. Look at them. It's not safe to even try.'

Horrified, Orisian turned back to the street in time to see one of the Haig men leaning low to jab his spear into a youth's belly, and then in his turn being hooked out of his saddle and dragged down. The riderless horse went charging off through the mob, battering a path clear, trampling bodies as it went.

Torcaill was pulling Orisian back from the gateway. A stunned Erval retreated alongside them. Someone was screaming amidst the chaos. It was a raw, unrestrained sound. Another horse, its saddle empty, came pounding back into the courtyard, wild-eyed and bleeding from cuts to its neck. It ran in great circles, shaking.

It did not take long, once that peak of violence had been reached. The awful sounds surged and merged and then gradually fell away. Men spilled out from the barracks in some numbers, too late: Guards, and warriors, and Orisian's own men, with Taim Narran at their head. Careful, cautious, they advanced out into the street, and found there only the dead and the injured and the debris. And shocked and shivering townsfolk, left feeble by the ebbing of their fury, staring at their bloody handiwork, murmuring in unsteady voices, trying to drag the wounded away to shelter or aid.

Orisian and Torcaill and Taim walked numbly among the bodies. The corpses of the Haig party were easy enough to find. Fur cloaks were bloodied and soiled and trampled, velvet gloves torn.

Torcaill prodded Gorred's body with the toe of his boot. The messenger's head rolled to one side. His face was broken in, the cheekbone and orbit of his eye shattered. The one eye that remained intact stared up at Orisian. He felt the cold, accusatory weight of that dead gaze, and turned away.

'The day's hardly begun, and already it's decided to be a bad one,' Taim said. 'Our troubles breed faster than mice.'

Torcaill stood looking up and down the street, his gaze drifting over the dead and the dazed. 'I count eight Haig dead. Two short. They must have broken out. This'll foster no friendship for us if word reaches Aewult,' he said.

'Soon we'll have nothing but enemies left,' murmured Orisian.

IV

Kanin oc Horin-Gyre ran. The snow was thick on the ground here on the western fringe of the Karkyre Peaks, but still he ran, and took a bitter pleasure in the burning of his lungs and the aching of his legs. He pounded through the drifts, not caring whether his warriors kept pace with him, barely even remembering that they were there behind him somewhere. Past and future were gone from his mind, and only this momentary present existed for him; only the straining of his muscles, the heaving of his chest. And that small group of fleeing figures just ahead: the men he meant to kill.

One of them glanced back and staggered to a halt, shouting something Kanin could not make out. Several of the men kept running, but as many stopped and turned. It must mean, of course, that Kanin had left his Shield behind. These Kilkry peasants thought they had him outnumbered. Outmatched. He rushed on. They did not know him; did not know what cold passion burned in him. They could not see the embracing shadow of death that he felt all about him now, in his every waking moment.

He brushed aside a spearpoint with the face of his shield, slashed an arm with his sword. Snow sprayed up. Shouts crowded the still air. It was only noise, without meaning, to Kanin. Figures closed upon him. He did not see faces, only bodies to be cut at, dark forms to be broken. A second went down beneath his blade. A spear thrust glanced harmlessly off his mailed shoulder. His opponents seemed slow and clumsy to him. He, by contrast, rode a cresting wave of death-hunger. It sped his limbs, sharpened his eyes and mind. It made sense of the senseless world for him.

A man whose brown hair was speckled with the silver of age came towards him, gesturing ineffectually with an old sword. Kanin could see that the blade was notched and had no edge. He ran to greet it, unhindered by the snow that tugged at his ankles. He killed the man, and then another, and rejoiced in the shedding of their blood. And soon there were only bodies about him, and he could hear his warriors coming up behind him.

Kanin stood still and straight for a few moments, panting out great gouts of misting breath. Sword and shield hung slack on either side of him.

'Half a dozen must have escaped us, sire,' Igris said.

'So?' Kanin growled. 'Send someone after them, if you wish. I'm done with it.'

'These'll not be hunting any more of our scouts, at least,' Igris said, surveying the corpses laid out around his master.

'They're nothing,' grunted Kanin, sheathing his sword. 'Look at them. Farmers. Old warriors, perhaps, who've not lifted a blade for years. There's none left north of Kilvale that are worth fighting.'

'Except those shut up in Kolkyre with their Thane,' the shieldman suggested.

Kanin shook his head, not in denial but frustration. He strode away, back down the trail of trampled snow the pursuit had created. Whatever warriors Roaric oc Kilkry-Haig had at his side behind Kolkyre's walls were beyond reach. They could not venture out without risking destruction, but nor were the investing forces of the Black Road strong enough to storm the place. Not without a firm guiding hand to muster them all together and drive them into an assault, at least, and it seemed there was no such hand at work any more. Things had passed far beyond that. Forces more ferocious and unthinking held sway.

Kanin slipped and slithered down the rocky slope they had ascended to outflank the Kilkry bandits. He went recklessly, letting his feet stutter over slick stones, taking a slide of loose snow and pebbles with him. He hit the ground at the foot of the incline hard, punching his knees up into his chest. The cold-looking men who had been left to guard the horses watched in silence. Kanin ignored them and went straight to his mount. He hung his shield from the saddle and brushed dirt and grit from his elbows.

The urgency of the chase and the slaughter was leaving him, retreating like a slack tide. It left the familiar hollowness behind. Only violence seemed to fill him now; without it he had only an empty kind of longing. So it had been since his sister's death. So, he knew, it would remain until Aeglyss was dead too.

There were a dozen or more tents around the huge farmhouse Kanin had slept in for the last couple of nights. Horin warriors were scattered amongst them, tending fires, clearing snow, sharpening blades. Three were deep in discussion with a band of Tarbains who had come up to the edge of the camp; negotiating, Kanin guessed, a trade of booty or food. Kilkry lands were thick with such roving companies of looters and raiders and scavengers. The army of the Black Road had once, briefly, been mighty and vast. Triumphant. That had changed since their crushing defeat of the Haig forces outside Kolkyre. Great fragments of the army had splintered off, becoming a thousand ravening wolf packs, uncontrolled and uncontrollable, seething back and forth across the land, almost delirious in their desire for blood.

He reined his horse in outside the stables and left it to a stable boy to feed and water the animal. It was the third mount Kanin had had since marching out from Castle Hakkan in the far north all those months ago. The first, he had felt some affection for, but it, and the second, had been killed beneath him. This one would no doubt suffer the same fate soon. He felt nothing for it.

Icicles bearded the eaves of the farmhouse. Kanin heard laughter from within: a brief outburst in response to some jest or mishap. It was like hearing a language he did not know. Beyond the building, a column of men and women trudged through the shallow snow. They were folk of the Kilkry Blood, pressed into service as pack animals by their captors. Each carried a deep, wide-mouthed basket strapped to his or her back. They bore firewood and grain down towards the sprawling Black Road camps on the plain around Kolkyre.

Their escort looked to be mostly Wyn-Gyre warriors, but there were several overseers who carried no weapons at all save stubby whips. One of these men was standing off to the side of the column, flailing away at some fallen victim. Kanin paused to watch. The whip cracked back and forth. None of the other guards so much as glanced at the scene. Many of the passing prisoners did, but their burdens were heavy and they could spare no more than a moment's attention for fear of losing their footing on the path of hard-packed snow. No matter their age, Kanin thought, they all looked old: bent and ragged and gaunt. The badge of defeat.

He found himself becoming irritated. The blows from the whip were having no effect on the prostrate form at the overseer's feet, yet the man went on and on, his exertions becoming wilder and more frenzied with every stroke. The futility of it angered Kanin.

He walked closer, approaching from the side to avoid the flailing whip. The man curled in the snow was folded down into a small, pathetic bundle like discarded sacking; unmoving beneath the increasingly savage blows. Kanin did not need to see his face to know that a whipping was not going to bring him back to his feet.

'Enough,' shouted Kanin. 'He's dead. You're wasting time.'

The overseer ignored him. He lashed the corpse again, and then again, each strike accompanied by a grunting snarl that took to the air in a cloud of mist. As the man drew back his arm once more, the whip curling around and out behind him, Kanin stepped forwards and seized his wrist.

'Enough, I said.'

The man spun about, his face contorted by rage. He shrugged off the Thane's grasp and stumbled back a few paces as if unbalanced by the ferocity of his emotions. Such ire burned in his eyes that Kanin could see nothing beyond it: there was no spark of recognition, no glimmer of anything other than animal fury. The man came forward. He raised his arm, the whip quivering with all the anger it inherited from its bearer.

Kanin arched his eyebrows in disbelief, but did not move aside or raise any defence against the imminent blow. Igris, his shieldman, was quicker. The warrior stepped in front of his Thane and, even as the whip began to snap forward, put his sword deep into the overseer's belly. The man fell to his knees. The whip snaked out feebly across the white snow. Igris pushed, tipping the man onto his back, then set a foot on his chest and pulled his blade free. The overseer gently placed his hands across the wound in his stomach, interlacing the fingers almost as if he were settling himself to sleep on a soft bed. He blinked and panted. Tears ran from the corners of his eyes. His blood trickled into the snow and stained it.

Kanin turned and walked away. The column had shuffled to a halt, both guards and bearers watching. Their interest was desultory, remote. Kanin ignored them. Igris came hurrying after him.

'Did you see his eyes?' Kanin asked.

'Yes, sire,' Igris answered.

'Nothing in him but bloodlust. Didn't even know me; blinded by it. That's what we've come to. We turn on each other, like starving dogs.'

'Perhaps you've some ale you could offer me, Thane?'

Kanin looked up from the platter of goat stew he was hunched over. Cannek was standing in the doorway of the farmhouse. Over the Hunt Inkallim's shoulder, Kanin could see snow falling. Cannek's cloak – a heavy, rustic garment more suited to an impoverished farmer – was smeared with melting flakes. The Inkallim was smiling. He smiled too much, Kanin thought, and without good reason.

'Or if not ale, a seat at least?'

Kanin nodded at the bench opposite his own. He took another mouthful of tasteless stew.

'No ale, though,' he said through it.

Cannek wrinkled his nose in disappointment as he shrugged the cloak from his shoulders. He spread it to dry on the floor in front of the fire.

'I looked for you down by the city.' He sat at the table, facing Kanin. 'You wearied of the siege, it seems.'

Kanin glared at the Inkallim from under a creased brow, and then returned his attention to the bowl of stew. But his appetite, meagre at the best of times, was gone.

'If so, I sympathise,' Cannek said. He unbuckled the knives that were always strapped to his forearms and laid them down on the uneven tabletop. Their dark wooden handles, Kanin noticed for the first time, had tiny ravens carved into them. Cannek rolled his shoulders and flexed his arms back. It was a lazy movement, like a wolf stretching.

'It's unpleasant down there,' the Inkallim said. 'A shortage of food, an excess of foul tempers and ready blades. The dead go unburied and unburned. Some of the Gyre levies have taken to Tarbain customs, by all accounts: making cups from the skulls of dead Kilkry farmers and suchlike. I am not surprised you took your leave.'

'There's a sickness abroad. Everything is falling into ruin. I want no part of it. Anyway, nothing will come of the siege.'

Cannek nodded. 'Kolkyre can't be starved into submission, since we've not got the ships to close their harbour. And it can't be stormed. Not unless Shraeve recalled every spear that's gone off south beyond Donnish.'

'Would they come?' Kanin asked darkly, pushing aside his plate. 'If Shraeve summoned them?'

Cannek scratched the side of his nose. 'Probably. The issue of command remains a little . . . unclear. There are plenty of companies from Gyre and the other Bloods milling about now, trying to assert themselves. Not wanting to miss out on all the glory to be won. But the Battle dominates, on the whole; and Shraeve is their Banner-captain. So yes, the armies might come and go at her call. Or that of Aeglyss, which amounts to the same thing. The masses seem willing to put a good deal of trust in him.'

'You are remarkably at ease with the thought.'

'I find our faith a great comfort in troubled times.' Cannek smiled again, sharp and fleeting. 'Things are as they are. If there's one thing the creed teaches us, it's that a man gains nothing by worrying about it. Not even when he hopes to be the agent of change.' The Inkallim looked pointedly around the empty room. 'I'd heard you'd developed a liking for solitude. Are we truly alone? No prying ears?'

'None,' said Kanin. He insisted that his meals and his rest

were undisturbed these days. Barring immediate need, not even his Shield were permitted to attend him. He and his thoughts occupied a world that every day seemed more distant from that inhabited by others; the two domains, he found, did not mix well.

Cannek nodded, satisfied. 'There's a council called at Hommen. The Battle, the Lore, some of the Captains from the Bloods. Aeglyss is coming down from Kan Avor.'

Kanin grimaced in surprise. 'I'd not heard.'

'You were not invited, Thane. You're thought to have . . . what's the phrase? Retired from the fray, I suppose. You've shown no great interest in the broad course of events. And it's Shraeve who is calling us together; she – or the halfbreed, I suppose we should say – is no great admirer of your talents. Or your preoccupations.'

'You're going?' Kanin asked.

'I, and one or two of my fellows.'

'You'll kill him?' said Kanin. The excitement he felt was not an elevating sentiment; there was nothing bright or warming about it.

'The opportunity may arise. It seems likely.' Cannek shrugged. 'What the outcome will be, I cannot say. That's for forces greater than you or I to determine.'

'How will you do it?' Kanin asked.

'Oh, best not to enquire too deeply into such things for now. We must preserve your innocence in these matters as far as we can, don't you think? Half the point of this is to protect you, and your Blood, from the consequences of what is happening. Comfort yourself with the thought that our reach was long enough to put an end to a Thane in his own feasting hall. Aeglyss is a good deal nearer at hand than Lheanor ever was.'

There was a dull thump from outside one of the shuttered windows. Cannek's eyes were drawn by the sound. His hand went to one of his knives, and had it halfway out of its sheath before Kanin could even draw breath.

'Snow,' the Thane said. 'It falls from the roof.'

'Of course.' Cannek relaxed a trifle, though his hand remained on the knife.

Kanin pushed back the bench on which he sat from the table, and rose. He began to stride back and forth. A rare vigour, such as he seldom felt now except when in battle, had taken hold of him.

'It's as well you came to tell me. I could not have waited much longer, whatever promises you dangled before me. It's eating me from the inside out. What must be done, must be done.'

'Patience is a virtue often rewarded by fate, Thane. Your restraint has been commendable, I'm sure. Still, I told you the Hunt would take this burden from you, and so we will, if fortune permits us. The Hunt does not make empty promises.'

'Does it not?' growled Kanin. He could think of more than one occasion when the Hunt Inkall had failed in its avowed intent – not least when the children of Kennet nan Lannis-Haig had slipped through its grasp in the Car Criagar – but now was not the time to pick fights with the one ally he had against Aeglyss. And there was as clear a sign as there could be of how misshapen everything had become: that he should look to the ranks of the Hunt for allies.

He sat heavily on a three-legged stool close by the fire. His limbs would not rest, though, and he was back on his feet in a moment.

'Does Goedellin concur in this?' he demanded. 'Does the Lore give its backing?'

Cannek sighed expressively. 'The Lore deals in fine judgements. The intricacies of the creed, teasing out the complexities of any case or cause: these are things we can leave to Goedellin. You and I, we can deal in more . . . direct explorations of fate's intent.'

'No, then,' said Kanin. 'The Lore will not take your side. Our side.'

'The Lore – or Goedellin, who *is* the Lore here and now – reserves its judgement,' said Cannek, spreading his arms. 'Let us leave it at that.'

'Can't he see?' cried Kanin in exasperation. 'Is he so slack-eyed he can't see an enemy when one stands before him?'

'It is possible to see too much, sometimes.' Cannek said. 'Too many possibilities, too many potential explanations. Success easily overturns old rules, old ways of thinking. Such are the victories we have gained, it is no surprise that some – many – see the glimmer of still greater, perhaps even final, glories on the horizon. For such a prize, they are willing to keep the most surprising company.

'But in any case, I do not think of Aeglyss as my enemy, Thane. I will try to kill him, but not out of malice. I simply mistrust the notion that he is fated to play so central a role in our affairs. I mistrust the notion that a halfbreed, and one whose adherence to the creed is at best questionable, should be the one to usher in the final triumph of our faith. Others find those notions more plausible than I. There is error, somewhere. My only intent is to remove any uncertainty over whose it is. Fate already knows the answer. Soon, we will too.'

And that is where our ways must part, thought Kanin. The vengeful, unambiguous passion that burned in him was something Cannek would never share. The Inkallim still framed everything in terms of the faith, of fate. Once Kanin might have thought in the same patterns, but such habits had flaked away from his mind like dead skin, day by day.

The door creaked open, caught by the cold wind. A flurry of snowflakes tumbled in and Kanin saw, sitting outside, one of Cannek's great dark, jowly hounds. As if sensing an invitation, the beast rose and took a couple of heavy paces towards the light and warmth. Cannek rose and went to the door, giving an animal hiss. The dog sank back onto its haunches as the Inkallim closed it out.

'I will come to Hommen,' Kanin said.

'Indeed,' said Cannek, going to stand by the fire, taking its heat into his back. 'Even uninvited, your presence could hardly be challenged. You are a Thane, after all.'

'I want to see him die.'

'I assumed you would.'

'We'll leave in the morning.'

'You do as you wish. I will be travelling through the night.' The Inkallim scooped his knives up from the table and began strapping them back onto his arms. 'It would be best if we did not arrive together. Our intimacies must remain secret, Thane, like any pair of illicit lovers.'

Kanin grimaced. 'It's not love we cultivate.'

V

A host of crows came raucously in under the clouds, like black fish shoaling in the shallow sky. They jostled and tumbled and rolled their way down into the naked trees on the edge of town, where they roosted. Orisian watched their tumultuous descent through the dusk, and in their voices heard the sound of Highfast, where he had watched their like playing violent games with the mountain wind. Highfast, of which neither Yvane nor Eshenna would willingly speak now, fearful of its meaning, of what they had felt happening there.

Only the vaguest of rumours had reached Ive regarding that remote stronghold's fate, but Orisian had access to other truths, ones he thought more reliable than the wild stories of terrified villagers. He believed what Yvane had told him before she fell into grim reticence on the subject: *na'kyrim* minds snuffed out like crushed candle flames, a torrent of death and destruction running through the Shared. Aeglyss. Aeglyss, the question to which he could find no answer. Perhaps there was none to be had, but he could not bring himself to stop looking.

Torcaill and a handful of his warriors walked at Orisian's back. They had been shadowing him for much of the day, disturbed by the violence visited upon Ive's sentries in the night, and upon the Haig messengers. Every raised voice, every figure moving in an alley or doorway, seemed a possible threat. A formless dread, an anticipation of imminent catastrophe, was in the air.

When they reached the house where Eshenna and Yvane sheltered, Orisian defied Torcaill's protests and left his escort on the street. It was not only that he found the poorly concealed unease of the warriors when in the company of *na'kyrim* distracting; there was also a deeper-rooted instinct to keep some portion of whatever incomplete and vague truths might emerge here hidden. There was too much in K'rina's plight, and in the things Yvane and Eshenna spoke of, that could point the way to despair.

Yvane and Eshenna were seated by the crackling fire. They had flatbreads spread on slates and propped up to cook in front of the flames.

'You heard what happened this morning?' Orisian asked as he entered. 'To Aewult's emissaries?'

Yvane nodded. 'We could hardly miss it. Noisier than rutting stags.'

'Every time we get word of what's going on out in the countryside, it's of some horror worse than the last,' Orisian said. 'Everything's falling apart. Everyone's going mad.'

'There's a fever in the world. The weak, the angry, the fearful, the bitter; they'll lose themselves to it first. And there's never been a shortage of those sentiments in the world, has there? But we could all follow. Every one of us, pure-blooded or not, knowing it or not, is touched by the Shared. Aeglyss will rot us all from the inside out. He may not even mean to.' She shrugged. 'I don't know. Whether by choice or not, he's potent enough to make his own sickness into everyone's. Or bring the sickness that's already there to the surface.'

She sounded tired, defeated, to Orisian. That was not the Yvane he needed.

'You talk like one of the Black Roaders. A sick world, ready to rot from the inside?'

Yvane sighed. 'Centuries of Huanin killing Kyrinin, True Blood killing Black Road. Sons killing fathers killing sons. Aeglyss is making nothing new; he's only releasing what's always there, under the surface.'

Orisian flicked a hand at her in irritation. 'There's more than that. We haven't lost yet.'

'Of course there's more than that,' Yvane said. 'But the Shared remembers all things. It makes memories of every sentiment, every thought, every desire. Believe me, a great many of them are dark.'

'Not all, though,' Orisian said stubbornly.

Yvane looked up at him. She had weary eyes.

'What do you want to do?' she asked him.

'That's what I have to decide. It's why I'm here.'

'We've told you all we can.'

'There's no time left, Yvane. The Black Road is winning. We'll be cut off, or worse, any day now. We can't remain here. But where we should go, what we should do . . . You can't tell me, but perhaps she can.' He pointed at the wall, and beyond it the yard and the shed and the mute, damaged *na'kyrim* within.

'We don't even know if she's got any secrets to reveal,' Yvane muttered stubbornly.

'I need to find out.' He could hear his voice rising, his frustration stretching it. 'Inurian could reach inside anyone and tell truth from lie, read the temper of their heart. You can find another *na'kyrim* wherever they are, and speak with them. I've seen you do it. Eshenna can find minds in the Shared. She led us to K'rina in the first place. I don't believe there's nothing more we can know. I need you to help me find an answer, in the Shared, in K'rina. Anywhere. Somehow. Please.'

Orisian felt guiltily as though he were accusing these two *na'kyrim* of something. That was not what he intended, but Yvane's intransigence bred a certain reckless desperation in him.

'You don't understand what you're asking,' Yvane said. 'The Shared's nothing but storm and misery and horror now. It's a darkness, haunted by beasts. By one beast in particular.'

'As is the world. That's why it matters. I know you never wanted to be a part of this, not any of it. I know that. But you've got to choose sides, Yvane. I can't understand, but still I ask. Who are you trying to protect? K'rina? Yourself?'

'I will do it.'

Orisian looked in surprise at Eshenna.

'Do what?' Yvane asked the other *na'kyrim* sharply.

'Reach out. Reach for her,' Eshenna said quietly, without looking up. 'I can't carry on like this. It's grinding me away, inside and out. When I wake, the first thing I feel is fear, as if it's been waiting there at the side of my bed while I slept. Like a black dog, waiting for me to come back to it. Hateful. I'm too tired to carry that weight all day, every day. I can hardly think straight; everything in my head that's mine is getting drowned out.'

'I know,' Yvane said. She looked as if she was about to say more, but pursed her lips. There was, Orisian recognised, a certain strain of sympathy and understanding that she could fall back upon – if she chose to – only when dealing with other *na'kyrim*. It remained, and she could still find it, even when her temper ran hot. It clouded her judgement too, he thought, when it came to K'rina.

'Perhaps I should never have left Highfast,' Eshenna sighed, 'but all of this would still have found me there. Perhaps worse. In any case, it won't stop.' She glanced up at Yvane, seeking confirmation. 'It's not going to stop, is it? Not unless Aeglyss chooses to stop it. Or someone kills him.'

'I doubt he could choose to stop this,' Yvane said. 'I doubt he can control anything about it, really.'

'Then someone has to kill him.'

'If you reach into the Shared, if you let even the smallest part of it into you . . . you risk letting him in too.' Yvane was sad rather than argumentative. 'You know that? It's his territory now. His hunting ground. You might come apart.'

'The first thing I feel when I wake up is fear,' Eshenna repeated in a flat voice. 'That is already breaking me apart.'

The three of them went together to the shed at the end of the yard, each carrying a candle that they had to shield against the shifting of the cold dusk air. They entered in silence, and set the lights down, and gathered about K'rina. She did not respond to their presence. She just lay there, curled on her bed of straw; perhaps asleep, perhaps not.

Yvane gently roused K'rina and lifted her onto her knees.

'Can you hear me?' Yvane asked quietly.

K'rina remained blank. Silent. Yvane backed away and Eshenna took her place, kneeling in front of K'rina.

'Be careful,' Yvane said. She was resigned now. 'Go no further, no deeper, than you must.'

'I know,' Eshenna replied as she reached up and brushed K'rina's hair away from her eyes. She laid one hand on the *na'kyrim*'s cheek, the other on her hand where it rested in her lap. In another place, between other people, it could have been a loving contact, Orisian thought. A gesture of affection.

'I'm sorry,' he said. The words came of their own accord. He suddenly felt guilty, even ashamed, that he had forced this. Yet it was necessary, his instincts insisted.

'Keep quiet,' Yvane said.

Eshenna closed her eyes, bowed her head a little. Her breath fluttered out of her. Her shoulders sagged. She might almost have been falling asleep. K'rina remained wholly impassive. The two of them sat thus, linked in their different, unnatural trances, for so long that Orisian's doubts began to reassert themselves.

'It's not working,' he whispered to Yvane. She splayed her hand at him, irritably demanding silence. She was frowning in concentration.

Somewhere outside, diminished by distance, Orisian thought he could just still hear the harsh calling of the crows. The sound seemed to him to have a hostile edge to it now, as if mocking his hopeless efforts to oppose forces that could not be opposed, or understood. He flailed about like a drowning man in a flood, he thought. Perhaps all he could hope for was that he did not drag too many others down with him. He caught himself before that despair took too firm a hold. Could he even trust it as wholly his own?

A faint hiss from Yvane brought him back from his dark, distracted reverie. Eshenna was gasping. Her jaw cracked open and shut, the joint creaking as her muscles spasmed. A blush was spreading through her cheeks and brow, brightening and deepening with every desperate breath.

Orisian looked at Yvane in concern. She narrowed her eyes.

'I don't know,' she said. 'I can't tell what's happening.'

Eshenna jerked, almost as if she was trying to pull away from K'rina, but she did not – or could not – release her grip. Her spine curved and flexed, snapping her head back then down again into her chest.

Orisian saw Yvane wincing, her brow creasing. She shrank away from the other two *na'kyrim*.

'What is it?' he asked her.

'Something . . .' she whispered, then shook her head sharply, as if beset by a host of biting flies.

Orisian could hear – or *feel* – a roaring, like a distant waterfall, or a storm blowing through trees. But it was inside his head, not outside, in the bone of his skull and the substance of his thoughts. It bled darkness from the edges of its sound, blurring shadows across his vision. The world was tumbling away from him, or he from it. The cramped shed around him swelled, rushing out to become a vertiginously immense space.

'Separate them,' he said, reeling at the dizzying sense of dislocation. He reached out and took hold of Eshenna's arm, trying to pull it away from K'rina. 'Help me,' he hissed at Yvane.

There was an instant of reluctance, a hesitant fear, and then Yvane too had hold of Eshenna, and was murmuring urgently to her.

'Come back, Eshenna. Come back. Can you hear me? Come back to yourself.'

Orisian could barely hear her above the rushing within his skull. The sensation of falling was sickening.

It was only with the greatest difficulty that they could part the two of them. K'rina slumped limply to the straw. Eshenna fell back into Orisian's arms. He laid her down as gently as he could. She was calm now, though tremors still inhabited her hands, and when her eyes struggled open, her gaze was unfocused. Orisian found himself cradling her head, and could feel the dampness of sweat in her hair. Her stone-grey eyes blinked up at him.

'She's empty,' Eshenna gasped. 'Nothing there, just a pit that falls away for ever. Into nothingness. It wanted to take hold of me, and I could not prevent it. But it didn't know me. That's the only thing that saved me. It's made for someone else, waiting for someone else, or I would have been lost. Swallowed up and caged in there for ever.'

She was crying, though whether it was from pain, or fear, or relief Orisian could not tell.

'Be still,' said Yvane. She spoke to Eshenna, but it was K'rina she was looking at, in the flickering light of the candles, and it was a look of suppressed horror or perhaps grief.

'Was it Aeglyss?' Orisian asked.

'No, no,' Eshenna said, casting a desolate glance towards the prostrate *na'kyrim*. 'It's what's in her; what's been made of her. She wasn't meant for us. We should never have taken her. We should never have interfered. We've ruined everything.'

There were voices outside in the yard. Footsteps on the paving stones, a muttered conversation, and then a rapping at the door that shook it on its old hinges.

'The Black Road, sire,' Torcaill shouted. 'They're on the road south of here, close enough to reach us tomorrow from the sound of it. Hundreds of them, maybe thousands.'

'All right,' called Orisian. Then, more softly: 'I'm coming.'

He cast a last worried glance at Eshenna and met her tear-filled eyes.

'I have to go,' he said.

'It's true, what I said before,' she breathed.

'What?'

'Someone has to kill him.'

VI

Kanin hated the sight of Hommen. This miserable and meek little town was where word of Wain's death had first reached him. It was here that he had watched Shraeve win leadership of the Battle in combat, and save Aeglyss' life in doing so. It was here that his life and his faith had been brought to ruin. And perhaps all the world with them. On his journey north, he had seen plentiful signs of the dereliction into which a once-noble enterprise was slipping.

He and his company had skirted the edge of the vast army sprawled around the landward walls of Kolkyre. Like ants teeming about a corpse too thick-skinned for their jaws to pierce, the forces of the Black Road had spread themselves across great swathes of farmland. A stench, of burning and death and animals, hung over the fields and camps. Riding through the fringes of this disorderly host, Kanin saw bodies lying bloated by the side of the track; men and women howling with glee as they mobbed together to beat a Tarbain tribesman; a warrior kneeling in the mud, weeping uncontrollably, hands resting limp and upturned on his thighs.

Beyond Kolkyre, they made camp for the night a short way from the road, and in the freezing darkness a band of looters, reckless or starving or mad, tried to steal their horses. They killed two of Kanin's guards before his warriors could be mustered to drive them off. His Shield took one alive, though only because Kanin intervened to preserve the man's life for a time. He questioned the prisoner himself, but got little sense from him. The man was of the Gaven-Gyre Blood, a carpenter from Whale Harbour. He would not, or could not, give his name, or that of any captain he followed. Nor could he explain how the faith and duty that led him to leave his home and march to battle had been corrupted into banditry and murder. Kanin cursed him, and struck him, and walked away. He heard Igris behead the carpenter as he stooped back into his tent.

As they followed the road along the bleak shoreline towards Hommen, they passed through a broken, almost deserted, land. Many of the farmsteads and hamlets bore the black scars of fires. Doors hung loose or had been torn away completely. Outside an isolated cottage, a dead child, a boy, was impaled on a stake. Frost had laid a crisp white veil over his face. Crows had taken his eyes and opened his nose and shredded his lips.

Waves lapped along a coast littered with broken-backed boats that had been thrown ashore after coming free of their moorings. There were sea-softened corpses that lay pale and fat on the pebbles. A pack of dogs was tearing at one such piece of the war's debris, surrounded by a patient audience of gulls and crows. A bone-thin grey hound tensed and growled when Kanin reined in his horse to watch.

There were few of the living left in this ruined land. A handful of sick Gyre warriors who had taken refuge to recover or die in a mill looked on with rheumy eyes as Kanin passed by. A solitary woman stumbled along beside his horse for a way, until she tripped and fell to her hands and knees in the snow. She said not a word, but laughed feverishly, desperately. In a field, a dozen or more enslaved villagers scrabbled in the snow and soil for half-rotted vegetables that should have been harvested long ago, watched over by grim-faced men who stared suspiciously at Kanin's company.

And Kyrinin. Three times Kanin saw woodwights. They roamed the higher ground inland from the coast, falling away behind the shelter of ridge lines almost as soon as he caught sight of them. Had they been closer, he might have led his warriors in pursuit of them, hunted them. When his father had agreed to the alliance between his Blood and the White Owls what felt like a lifetime ago, it had been meant to last only as long as did the Kyrinin's usefulness. That they still lingered, with impunity, in the lands the Black Road had reconquered was an insult. A corruption of what should have been. A sign of how thoroughly Aeglyss had twisted everything.

Amidst all this emptiness, Hommen itself was an island of life. As he drew near, Kanin could see the smoke of scores of cooking fires. There were countless tents amongst the houses, ranks of tethered horses being fed and watered, crowds of men and women from every Blood. And to Kanin it was still more hateful, and reeked still more pungently of death, than the desolation that surrounded it.

He left Igris to find shelter and food for his band of warriors and walked down through the crowds to the crude wooden quay. The masses of men and women who thronged Hommen's streets barely intruded upon his awareness. He recognised no one. He heard the babble of voices as the empty noise of birds. He felt no bonds of faith or purpose or intent with these people.

He stood on the planks of the quay, close to the spot he had been standing when the rumour of Wain's death first found him. He looked west, across the grey, dead expanse of the estuary towards the limitless sea. And so bright was the sinking sun that lay white and cold on the horizon, so piercing its light, that he had to close his eyes. He heard seagulls overhead, laughing.

'What happened to my sister, Shraeve? You were there, in Kan Avor, when she died. You must know what happened.'

'She was fortunate enough to leave this world. That is what happened. She will wake in a better one, and you will see her there, Thane.'

Shraeve and Kanin stood outside the little hall that lay beside the main road through Hommen. It was an island of comparative calm, the space in front of the hall's doors, for Shraeve's ravens had cleared it. Twenty of them stood in a wide half-circle, keeping back any who sought to draw near without permission. Onlookers were clustered beyond that silent cordon, eager to catch sight of the great and the powerful who were gathering here.

'Not good enough,' Kanin hissed. He took hold of the Inkallim's upper arm as she walked away from him. It was like grasping rock. He turned her to face him, and she met him with cold contempt.

'I am Banner-captain of the Battle Inkall, Thane,' Shraeve said softly. She glanced at his restraining hand, and he let it fall away from her; not through fear, or respect, but because his purposes would not be served by fighting with her today. Shraeve would have to die as well as Aeglyss, he realised with new clarity, but not now. Not yet.

'I want to know what happened to my sister,' he said. 'There is no shame in such a desire.'

'Shame? No, perhaps not. But it serves no purpose. Mourning is but self-pity. You know it as well as I do.'

Once he had known it. Now, it sounded like a hollow platitude, vindictively crafted by the lips of an enemy.

'Let the dead go, Thane,' Shraeve said. 'We will join them soon enough, in the better world.'

Men and women were filing past them into the hall. Leaders from the Gyre and Gaven and Fane Bloods; Lore Inkallim, led by the shuffling, hunched, black-lipped figure of Goedellin; Cannek, who studiously avoided Kanin's gaze as he settled his two hounds down to await his return from the council.

'It's time,' Shraeve said, and turned away from Kanin.

He followed her into the musty gloom of the hall. It was empty save for a single table at its centre, lined with chairs. Serving girls – whether brought from the north with the armies or prisoners pressed into service, Kanin could not say – were lighting torches along the walls and setting out beakers of wine and ale and plates. At the far end of the hall, standing by small doors that must lead to the kitchens or other antechambers, were White Owl Kyrinin. They were hateful in Kanin's sight, and he averted his eyes from them.

One or two of those already seated regarded him with curiosity, perhaps even suspicion, as he took his place at the table. He ignored them. They were nothing to him, these latecomers to the war his family had started. Not one of them had offered his father any support; not one of them had crossed the Stone Vale until they, or their masters, caught the scent of victories already won, and of spoils and glory to be claimed. He clasped his hands in his lap and stared fixedly down at them, watching his fingertips redden as the tension within him tightened its grip.

He heard the wide doors of the hall scrape shut. The last of the daylight was excluded and they were left with the yellow flamelight and the scent of smoke. The servants went out, one by one, past the woodwight sentinels, and a heavy silence descended.

'Where's the halfbreed?' a man asked at length. Kanin had

met him once or twice before, long ago: Talark, Captain of a castle on the southern borders of the Gyre Blood. A relative, by marriage, to Ragnor oc Gyre himself.

'He will join us shortly,' Shraeve said placidly. She had taken her twin swords from her back. They rested in their scabbards against the side of her chair. 'He is preparing himself.'

'For what, I wonder?' Cannek asked, almost mirthful, as if some unuttered jest was pleasing him.

Shraeve ignored the Hunt Inkallim. 'There are other matters to talk of first. Kilvale. Kolkyre.'

'Food, if you've any sense,' Talark muttered irritably. 'Half my warriors are starving. Most of my horses have gone into their bellies.'

'All the more reason to keep moving on. Conquest will feed our armies. Every town we take, every village, has stores laid in for winter. That promise, and the strength of their faith must keep them—'

'They have stores only if they don't burn them or empty them before we get there,' Talark interrupted her. 'And if the farmers and villagers who flee before us haven't already eaten them.'

'The Battle has arranged for supplies to be brought down through the Stone Vale,' Shraeve replied. 'A hundred mules, all fully laden, reached Anduran only two days ago.'

'Mules!' Talark scoffed. 'It's wagons we need, and oceans of them. Not a few mules.'

'Perhaps if the High Thane, your master, gave more than half his heart in support of us, you could have those wagons.'

The Gyre warrior glowered at Shraeve. 'It's difficult to get wagons across the Vale at this time of year. You know that.'

'Indeed. Yet you sit in the hall of a Kilkry-Haig town. It seems we – those who came before you, Talark – have already proved that even the impossible can sometimes be possible. If the will is there. The faith.'

One of the Gaven-Gyre warriors cut short the burgeoning

argument by rasping her chair back across the floor and rapping the back of her hand on the table.

'If it's conquest that concerns you, our time might have been better spent busying ourselves with that task instead of riding all the way back here to indulge in petty disputes. There's more than enough chaos already, without our absence to help it along.'

'She knows that,' Talark grunted. 'She's got her ravens out there taking charge of everything while we're dragged back here. This serves no purpose save that of the Children of the Hundred.'

'No purpose?' Shraeve snapped, anger colouring her voice for the first time. 'There is only one purpose in any of this. The service of the creed. Raising it up until all the world falls beneath its shadow. None who would dissent from that, none who doubt that the moment has come for all other concerns to be set aside, have any place in this endeavour. There must be unity. That is why we are gathered here now. Not to indulge in dispute, but to end it.'

'Don't question my faithfulness to the creed,' Talark said, though his tone lacked the steel of conviction.

'There must be unity,' Goedellin murmured. All looked towards him. To Kanin's eyes, the man looked more frail and weary than ever before. He spoke slowly, heavily, his seerstem-darkened lips sluggish. 'There must be unity, and certainty. Doubt is the enemy of faith. Yet these times are . . . confused. Few things seem as clear as once they did.'

'Success is clarity,' Shraeve said. 'It answers all questions.' She was firm, but her manner had shed its confrontational edge. It was good to see, Kanin thought, that the Battle's confidence and arrogance had not yet become bloated enough to crowd out some vestigial respect for an Inner Servant of the Lore.

'Indeed.' Goedellin nodded. 'Indeed.' And then: 'Perhaps.'

'When Kilvale falls, all doubt will be undone,' said Shraeve

with cold certainty. 'When we hold the Fisherwoman's birthplace, the birthplace of our creed, then the fire will burn
brightly in every heart. Nothing will quench it then. None will
be able to argue fate's intent.'

'Oh, there's always room for argument,' Cannek interjected
lightly. 'It's in our nature to be disputatious.'

Kanin groaned inwardly. Why taunt the woman? Why so
brazenly flaunt his opposition? But, of course, Cannek was one of
those who found such liberation in the Black Road that he feared
nothing, found nothing troubling. He would dare anything, and
greet the consequences of his daring with equanimity. Such sentiments, once familiar, were beyond Kanin's reach now.

At the far, gloomy end of the hall, the Kyrinin were moving.
One of the doors opened. Kanin held his breath, and sensed the
same sudden expectation taking hold of everyone else at the table.

The *na'kyrim* entered, and whatever feelings had been stirring
in Kanin turned to disgust at the sight of him. Aeglyss was a
wasted figure, emaciated and gaunt, coming unsteadily forward
on the arm of a tall woodwight. The halfbreed's colourless skin
was scabbed and slack. Kanin grimaced.

Yet when he looked about the faces of the others gathered
there, he saw entirely different emotions portrayed. A hint of
unease now and again, but fascination too. Even Talark watched
Aeglyss approach with a pathetic, wide-eyed touch of wonder.

There was an empty chair at Shraeve's side. Aeglyss settled
gingerly into it. He looked so small. Kanin imagined that the
halfbreed's neck would break with only the gentlest of twists.
The Kyrinin warrior who had escorted Aeglyss to his place
remained standing there, just behind him.

'Must we have woodwights in attendance?' asked Talark,
recovering a fragment of his previous antagonism.

'This is Hothyn,' Shraeve said. 'He is the son of the White
Owl Voice, and leader of the warband that accompanies Aeglyss.
His presence is a sign of our strength, not our weakness.'

Yet I saw these same White Owls killing one another in the streets of Glasbridge, Kanin thought. Even in them, Aeglyss could not command the unity you hope for. Not until those who contested it had been killed.

'Do not be distressed by my appearance,' Aeglyss suddenly said. His voice grated in his throat. 'I am engaged in a struggle, every day, to contain and to shape what burns within me. It takes its toll. Flesh and bone were not made to bear such burdens. A river that rises in its greatest flood will ruin and break its banks, and so it is with me. The flood is in me. Once I master it, I will repair its ravages.'

He smiled, and Kanin saw yellowing teeth, black veins of corruption and decay spreading from them through white gums. He imagined that were he close enough he would catch the stink of rot from that foul mouth. The smile faded, and Aeglyss closed his eyes.

'I can smell the spice-thick air of Adravane's Inner Court,' the *na'kyrim* murmured. 'I feel the sand beneath the hoofs of a Saolin running on the Din Sive shore. I remember the Whreinin; can reach out and know what it was to be of the wolfenkind. The Anain raised a forest to drown a city with trees, yet they flee from the shadow of my mind as I move through the Shared. But they cannot flee far enough, or fast enough. Even them I can taste. Their age, their thoughts running like blood through veins of leaf and bough. All of this flows through me, and I flow through all things.'

He shivered, as if a cold pleasure filled him. 'Your cause has found a servant in me, and the world has never seen my like. Such is the gift that fate, through me, bestows upon you. It is a terrible gift, but that is my burden. I will bear it and I will serve you.'

He looked around them all then, giving each of those at the table a brief moment of his undivided attention. His gaze brushed most briefly over Kanin, or so it seemed to Kanin himself. Even

that instant of contact was enough to feel the weight of what lay
behind the *na'kyrim*'s eyes. To Kanin, it was oppressive and invasive. To others, he saw as their turns came, one by one, it was
exhilarating.

'I am the answer you and your people have been seeking all
these years,' Aeglyss breathed at length.

And Kanin felt it. He felt it blooming in his breast and
spreading its warmth through his limbs. It lifted him, and for
the space of those few heartbeats there was nothing but the
utter delight of knowing that all was as it should, and must, be.
That all his hopes would be fulfilled, in their last and smallest
detail. That the world this *na'kyrim* could promise him was all
he could ever desire. Yet still, amidst it all, there was a hard
nugget marring the perfection of the sensation: a nugget of
hatred; the contradictory whisper that his truest, deepest
desire could not be fulfilled by this halfbreed, but only by his
death.

'All I ask is that you put your faith in me,' Aeglyss said. 'And
in the allies I bring to your cause. The White Owls. The force of
my own will. The Shadowhand.'

'It's true, then, that the Shadowhand is bound? That you have
done to him what Orlane did to Tarcene?' Goedellin's voice
broke the skin of the moment. Kanin found himself suddenly
breathing deeply, realising only now that he had been holding
his breath.

'To have such a weapon at our enemy's very heart . . .' whispered Talark.

'The Haig Chancellor is bound to our service—' Shraeve
began, but Aeglyss cut her short with a strange, strangled grunt.

'Some things should not be spoken of,' the *na'kyrim* said.
'Think instead of the gifts I shall bring you. Kolkyre, Kilvale.
Even unto Vaymouth itself, if that is your wish.'

'Still, Tarcene's binding hardly ended well. Not for the
Kingbinder himself, nor for the Kyrinin he served. Certainly not

for Tarcene,' murmured Cannek, but no one save Kanin seemed to even notice that he had spoken.

'There are things – aspects of what I have become – that none can understand,' Aeglyss continued. 'Burdens I must bear alone, in silence. Only my own kind could understand what I . . . but they are afraid. They fear my brightness will burn them. Only one . . . only she . . . She would understand.'

His head twitched and dipped to one side. His crab-like hand scraped rigidly across the surface of the table. His eyes lost their focus.

'But she's been stolen from me,' he rasped. 'I can't find her. She is gone.'

Goedellin was regarding the *na'kyrim* with consternation. Talark frowned uneasily. Yes, Kanin thought, you can see if you choose to; see his madness. This is the man you would make master of your hopes, your fates? This poisoned ruin of a man, whose thoughts trickle through his own fingers like so much grain? But the moment did not last. The doubts had no time to take root.

'We should eat,' Shraeve said, and at the sound of her voice Aeglyss recovered himself.

'Yes,' he sighed, straightening in his chair, drawing his hand back to press it against his chest. 'We should eat.'

The food was neither plentiful nor elegant. Bread and broth and a single haunch of mutton. They ate in silence. All save Aeglyss. He touched nothing, only watched.

A serving girl made her way around the table, pouring out wine from a clay jug. She came to Aeglyss last, and wiped the lip of the jug clean with a cloth before emptying the last of its contents into his cup. Aeglyss pushed away his plateful of neglected food. He lifted the cup to his lips and drank deeply. As he set it down again his hand gave a brief involuntary jerk, spilling wine on the table.

Kanin saw Cannek lay down a hunk of bread he had been

gnawing. The Inkallim was watching Aeglyss intently. Others caught the change in mood. Conversations died.

Aeglyss' face was white, paler even than it had been before. His eyes, the pupils dilated, were gleaming wetly. A muscle in his left cheek twitched, though his jaw was tight clenched. Otherwise, he was as motionless as a statue. Kanin looked around. Every eye was upon the halfbreed.

Still Aeglyss had not moved. His white fingernails were digging into the rough surface of the table. His eyes stared rigidly at Cannek. The Inkallim was quite calm.

'What have you done?' Shraeve said softly.

Abruptly Aeglyss retched, gripped by a convulsion that rose from deep in his midriff. He hunched forward and then straightened with a great gasp. The movement seemed to release all the tension from his body. He put one hand to his mouth and spat a small dark object into his palm. He held it out: a perfect orb of black matter the size of an eyeball, with strands of saliva still clinging to it.

'Yours, I think,' said Aeglyss thickly to Cannek. He set it down upon the table, where it rested like a dull, sodden marble a child had discarded. Cannek regarded it thoughtfully for a moment or two, his hands clasped together before him. The globule lost its form, slumping into a viscous stain.

'That's very clever,' Cannek murmured with a smile.

'What is this?' Goedellin asked, his voice all indignant puzzlement. 'Poison?'

Cannek's hands parted, and there was a blade in one of them. Shraeve's arm snapped up. One of her swords, still sheathed, came spinning across the table. Cannek ducked and swayed to one side, so that the sword went cartwheeling away off the side of his head. It was enough to spoil his own aim. His knife, sent darting out with a flick of his wrist, flashed past Aeglyss' shoulder. Shraeve followed her sword, vaulting the table, pivoting on one hand to drive a straight-legged kick into Cannek's chest.

The Hunt Inkallim went crashing back with his chair, rolling and rising smoothly to a crouch.

But Shraeve was too fast even for him. In the moment it took Cannek to recover his balance, she hit him with her full weight, wrapping an arm about his neck, splaying her other hand over his eyes. She took him backwards, tumbled the pair of them across the floor. And out of that blur of movement rose a clear, long cracking.

Shraeve stood. Cannek lay, eyes and mouth open, head tilted sideways on a broken neck. Shraeve brushed dust from her knees. The assembled warriors stared in a mixture of amazement and confusion at the dead Inkallim. Only Kanin turned back at once to Aeglyss. And found the *na'kyrim* watching him. Aeglyss wiped the back of his hand across his lips. He was breathing fast.

'Is that what you all require?' the halfbreed said loudly, and was at once the focus of all attention once more. 'That's the kind of answer you people demand, isn't it? There's fate for you. There's the choice made for you. I live.'

Kanin wondered if he was the only one to hear the contempt, the bitterness, that suffused Aeglyss' words. Silently, he raged against the immobility of his limbs, and against the impotence of his own anger. His sword was within reach – he imagined it calling out to him – but Aeglyss, the idea of Aeglyss, filled his field of vision: out of reach, untouchable, inviolable.

'You cannot kill me, for I am not as you are,' Aeglyss said. He slammed his bony fist down on the table. 'You think because I am flesh, I am weak. No, no. You must learn to think differently. You *will* learn. For all your hatred and your betrayals, I will raise you up. I will give you all that you want, feed all the hungers in your hearts, and those who turn against me will be cast down and ruined. There is no other way. No other truth.'

'As it is written,' Shraeve murmured as she picked up her sword and came back around the table to stand beside Hothyn. The two warriors, Inkallim and White Owl, flanked the *na'kyrim*. And no gaze would meet the challenge those three offered. No one could deny them the submission they demanded.

'Kill the girl who served me my wine,' Aeglyss said. 'And all the rest of the servants. All of them.'

He looked up at Shraeve and she nodded.

'You've uttered not a word, Thane,' Aeglyss said to Kanin. 'I've never known such silence from you. Have you nothing to say?'

'Nothing.' Kanin rose, horrified at the effort it took to turn away from Aeglyss, and at the yearning he felt to love the half-breed and all that he offered. But his hatred provided the one, thin sheen of armour he needed to resist that call. He spared a lingering moment for a last look at Cannek lying dead on the floor, and walked out. An absurd, half-formed smile had been locked into the Inkallim's lips by death.

Kanin waited outside, and the rest came soon after him, emerging blinking into the clear winter light. All were silent; some thoughtful, some shocked and shaken. In some faces he was sickened to see a sort of joy. This, he understood, was how it happened. There were some – many, perhaps – who found the horrors that Aeglyss embodied and offered not repellent but intoxicating. Once they caught their first scent of his corruption they wanted nothing more than to drink deep of it, to drown themselves in it.

When Goedellin appeared, Kanin stepped in front of the Lore Inkallim, forcing the old, bent man to stop.

'How many have to die, Goedellin? Before you will open your eyes to this madness?'

The Inner Servant rapped the heel of his walking stick on the ground but said nothing.

'My sister was the truest and most loyal follower of the creed, old man. Every beat of her heart was a promise of faith. Is she

owed nothing for that lifetime of fidelity? Did it earn her no
honour from the Lore?'

'Such matters are not straightforward, Thane,' Goedellin
grumbled. He shuffled sideways, trying to pass.

Kanin blocked his path. 'We had tutors when we were children,' he said quietly, insistently. 'Tutors from your Inkall.'

'I know. Wain told me.'

'Did she tell you that my father wanted to send them away?
After only a couple of seasons, he doubted his decision to bring
them to Hakkan. She changed so quickly, you see. She devoured
their teachings as if she had been starving until then, without
ever knowing it. My father was disturbed by it.'

The Inner Servant of the Lore angled his head a little, looking
up to meet Kanin's gaze just for a moment.

'We knew nothing of it until one day the tutors were simply
gone. Wain flew into such a rage.' Kanin smiled at the memory,
at the thought of that distant childhood, but knew it would
bring unbearable pain if he let it take too firm a hold. 'She
meant to have them back, and she did. A little girl, Goedellin,
bending a whole castle, the household of a Thane, to her will.
She sulked, and raged, and the tutors were recalled. That was
what it meant to her.'

The Inkallim was shaking his bowed head, though what the
gesture meant Kanin did not know.

'She should not have died,' Kanin whispered. 'You know this
is not as it should be. You know this is not fate.'

'What else is there, Thane?' Goedellin snapped. 'What else is
there?'

'Corruption! You think the warriors of the creed are fated to
fawn over that monstrous little creature in there? You think this
is what Tegric's Hundred died for? For us to submit ourselves to
the twisted delusions of that . . .?'

'Thane.'

Kanin turned. Shraeve was standing a few paces away in the

doorway, watching him with those dead eyes. Her swords lay once more across her back, their hilts framing her face.

'Aeglyss would talk with you,' she said.

In the instant of Kanin's distraction, Goedellin brushed unsteadily past him, hobbling after all the others.

'It's not fate,' Kanin hissed after the old man. 'It's something else.'

He turned back to Shraeve, his lip curled in contempt. 'Let your master talk to those who wish to hear.'

'You will wish to hear this, Thane.' She was unmoved by his bitter tone, as if what he felt or thought was of less consequence than the dance of a fly on a breeze. 'It is for no one else but you. It concerns your sister.'

And she turned and walked away. Like a hunter who knew her quarry was safely taken, needing and deserving no more of her attention. Kanin followed, heavy-footed, back into the hall, unable to do anything else. He wondered, with little interest, if he might be going to his death.

Behind him he heard startled, pitiful yelps. They were killing Cannek's hounds.

Aeglyss was alone in the hall, standing waiting for Kanin. Cannek's corpse was gone, along with Hothyn and the other woodwights who must have carried it away. So easily do we vanish from the world, Kanin thought. Our every intention and hope disappears in a moment, and counts for nothing.

Shraeve, at his side, drew Kanin to a halt three swords' lengths from Aeglyss. Feeling her touch, he turned to rebuke her, but the words died in his throat, smothered by the sound of Aeglyss' voice.

'You hate me, Thane. Don't trouble to deny it. I can taste your hatred of me, and that's a flavour I know well. It's been all around me through my whole life, the very air I breathe. There's nothing more to you than your desire to see me dead. And I understand. I do.'

The halfbreed's voice dripped with concern, with affection. A warm, comforting sense of sympathy enfolded Kanin, an almost physical sensation: a kind hand, taking him in its gentle grasp.

'Terrible things have happened,' Aeglyss whispered. 'You know but a fragment of it. I promise you, though, I promise you: I loved your sister just as dearly as you did.'

The truth of that was an unquestionable certainty, insinuating itself into Kanin's mind, entangling itself with the instinctive revulsion he felt at the thought. The bitter retorts that came boiling up towards his lips were snared and snuffed out.

'I can hardly tell any more what I remember, what I imagine, what memories I gather into me from the Shared,' Aeglyss rasped. 'But I know I loved her, and she loved me. She loved me as none has before. Only my mother . . . my mothers. But I was not strong enough to save her. Oh, I longed to. You cannot know . . .'

A tear, at the corner of the *na'kyrim*'s grey eye. Kanin could see nothing else but that perfect bead of moisture, a gleam of torch-light reflected in its smooth surface. It ran free, and Kanin watched its descent, felt his own vast grief carried along with it and growing, bursting up, swelling to merge with the still greater sorrow that filled the hall like a turbid mist. He trembled, overcome by the sense that there was nothing in all the world save loss and impotence.

'Nothing is as I wanted it to be,' Aeglyss said thickly. 'I never asked for all this death. Hers least of all. Don't you understand? What has happened is . . . I didn't choose this. Why can't you see that? Give me your forgiveness, Thane. Give me *her* forgiveness.'

'Forgive?' Kanin murmured. His thoughts were softening, losing their shape.

'It was my weakness.' Aeglyss hung his head. 'I could not sustain her love for me and still take hold of the Shadowhand. I would have done, if I could. Oh, nothing would have been sweeter. But I am too weak, too feeble; and I had to have the Shadowhand.' He looked suddenly at Shraeve, and then to Kanin, beseeching. 'We had to have the Shadowhand, did we not? We needed him? I gave up so much – Wain, K'rina – but the sacrifice was necessary, wasn't it?'

Kanin pitied the halfbreed in that moment, and could easily have reached out to him in comfort, offered the forgiveness and agreement that he craved. Yet nothing, no bewilderment of his mind, could wholly extinguish the murderous flame that persisted in the deepest, most fortified, refuge of his self. It flickered there still, and through all the fogs that beset him, its light remained a beacon he could follow.

'No path worth following is without sacrifice,' he heard Shraeve saying beside him.

'No,' whispered Aeglyss. 'No. And she knew that. Wain knew that.' He looked up, and there was a new chill in the gaze he laid upon Kanin. 'Others know it. Yet you do not, Thane. You are like ice, on which none of this can find purchase. There is something in you that resists me. Denies me.

'Why is it that you cannot share in this understanding? The Battle sees the shape of things, the Lore, and the White Owls. The Bloods fall in at my side, for they understand what it is I offer, what I can give to those who walk with me. All I ask for is loyalty. Trust. If those things had been there from the start – if *you* had offered them to me, Thane – none of this need have happened. Yet here we are. By choice or not, wondrous events begin to unfold, and I allow even those who have betrayed me to share in them. Why can you not be a part of this?'

Stubborn contempt rose within Kanin.

'Do you really not know?' he asked the halfbreed. 'Do you really understand so little of people?'

Aeglyss said nothing, but Kanin could see in his face genuine uncertainty, infantile hurt.

'If you wanted me to walk at your side,' Kanin said flatly, 'you should not have taken my sister from me.'

A twist of some violent emotion distorted Aeglyss' features for a moment. He bared his teeth.

'From you?' he hissed. 'You think the loss only yours? You don't know! What it cost me . . .'

He faltered. A tremor ran through his feeble frame, twisting his head to one side, tugging at his eyelids. Spittle bubbled out onto his chin.

The soft deadening of Kanin's senses abruptly cleared. He blinked. Aeglyss slumped down onto one knee, coughing. Sudden hope blossomed within Kanin. The halfbreed's head was bowed, jerking as he spat out phlegm from his lungs. Kanin's hand went to his sword. The blade began to sigh out of its scabbard. He stepped forward, possessed by a vision of what was about to happen, what he could do in the next moment.

And Shraeve lashed her forearm across his throat. He staggered, choking. Shraeve stepped in front of him, shielding Aeglyss from his sight, and his intent. She reached up and lightly grasped the hilts of the two swords sheathed across her back.

'It is my belief, Thane, that this man serves fate, and our creed. I do not know if you could harm him, but I will not permit the attempt.'

Kanin gasped for air, croaking incoherently, clasping a hand to his throat. He took hold once again of his own sword. Breath came at last, ragged and rough. Aeglyss was only now rising unsteadily to his feet. He was still enfeebled. Vulnerable. But there was Shraeve, quite still and calm.

'I would regret killing a Thane,' she said softly. 'It would be a fell deed. But the end of the world must be a time for fell deeds, if needed, don't you think?'

Kanin did not believe he could overcome her. Perhaps if Igris was here, the two of them together might have a chance against this raven, but Kanin knew what would happen if he challenged her alone. She was too fast, too skilled. He could hear, in his memory, the sound of Cannek's spine breaking. Once he had believed that fate could be generous to those who dared; now he was uncertain whether such laws still governed – had ever governed – the twisted world. Daring felt like recklessness, when the goal he sought was so all-consumingly crucial. He would be permitted only one attempt upon Aeglyss, and to fail in it would be to fail in everything, his entire life.

He coughed, and folded his arms across his chest.

'Your master seems unwell,' he said. 'Perhaps I should leave the two of you alone.'

He spun on his heel and walked briskly away, his heart racing, his cheeks burning with the backwash of tension and fear and anger that was now released in him. He could hear Aeglyss groaning, but did not look round. He went out into the light.

VII

Nyve's skin was old, with the hue of worn and faded hide. It had loosened as the years slackened the muscles beneath it and narrowed his shoulders. But still the First of the Battle had an air of resilient strength. There was enough breadth to him, and just enough firmness left in his skin, to give life to the raven tattoo that spread its wings across his shoulder blades. Theor, master of the Lore Inkallim, watched that black bird stir and ripple as a manservant drew a cloth slowly across Nyve's back.

The First of the Battle sat naked on a low stool in the centre of the stone wash-house floor. The servant went silently about his duties, pausing occasionally to rinse his cloth in a pail of hot water. Now and again Nyve grunted at the pressure of firm fingers on some sore joint, but he made no other complaint.

The servant carefully lifted the First's arm and stretched it out, and ran the cloth down it from shoulder to wrist. Drops of water pattered onto the stone tiles.

'I cannot undo what fate has decreed,' Nyve said softly.

'Of course,' said Theor. 'I would never ask such a thing. You know how much it pains me to even raise with you matters that are internal to the Battle.'

'Yet you do.' Theor could not see his friend's face, but heard the wry smile in Nyve's voice.

'I do. It cannot be avoided. Such are the tempestuous times in which we live. Don't pretend you don't share my concerns.'

Nyve lowered his arm. The servant charged the cloth with water and then twisted it into a tight cord above the First's head. Water splashed across his scalp and shoulders. It ran down over the great welt where his ear had once been.

'We set this horse running,' Nyve said. He gave his head a single dipping shake, scattering droplets. 'Too late to try to rein it in.'

'The Thane of Thanes disagrees,' Theor muttered. He walked round to the stone bench that ran along one wall of the wash house and tested its surface with the palm of his hand. It was warm: hot charcoal could be fed into a hidden compartment. Carefully, he settled himself onto the bench. The seductive warmth spread through his thighs and buttocks. Outside, the snow was knee-deep. Every stream ran beneath a skin of ice. Even down in the valley, in Kan Dredar, there had been no night without a hard frost, no day without at least some snow, for two weeks.

'When was the last time he agreed with us?' Nyve asked.

Theor rested his head back against the wall and closed his eyes. He truly was getting old, he thought, for how else to explain the intoxicating delight of such a simple thing? Luxuriant warmth in winter had never meant so much to him when he was young. Now, this warm stone bench filled his bones with delight, answering a need in them he had not known existed. Such were the seductions of comfort.

'If you need to sleep, we can always continue our discussions later,' Nyve said, a little louder this time.

Theor opened his eyes and winced apologetically at his friend. The old warrior was watching him, but there was no irritation or impatience in his gaze. Nyve would understand as well as anyone what it was to find the body ageing and faltering before the spirit within had prepared itself for the change. Nyve's hands were all but crippled, bunched into claws that would barely respond to their owner's command.

'I like this bench you've got here,' Theor observed.

'So do I.'

'I might have one made for myself.'

'Too indulgent for the Lore, surely?' Nyve grunted. 'I doubt your people would approve.'

'Seeking approval does not really accord with the precepts of the creed. In any case, I find myself less and less concerned with the approval of others as the years pass.'

'Indeed,' Nyve said, and then glanced at the manservant. 'Help me up.'

The First of the Battle rose, only a fraction unsteady, leaning on the servant's arm. Once he was securely on his feet he dismissed the attendant with a silent flick of his head.

'Pass me that robe, would you?' he said to Theor once they were alone in the warm, humid stone chamber. Theor hung the robe on his friend's shoulders and watched as Nyve made his careful way over to the heated bench.

Nyve settled onto the stone with a satisfied sigh. He stared at Theor. Those eyes, at least, were undimmed, unblunted. It was still the gaze of a fierce and potent warrior for the faith.

'You're tired,' Nyve said. 'You look sick, in fact.'

'I feel both. The world's as unsteady beneath my feet as a foundering boat. I am . . . lost, I suppose.' Theor knew he should feel shame that such words were on his lips. He was the First of the Lore, custodian of the creed. Keeper of the truth. He, of all people, should be resistant to the kind of uncertainty and confusion that assailed him. Yet there was no point in pretending things were other than they were. Not in front of Nyve, at least.

The First of the Battle grunted. 'Whisper such things softly, friend. There's danger in honesty.'

'It seems to me we are beset by dangers of many kinds,' Theor murmured. 'There are terrible temptations in success. It all too easily breeds pride, or error.'

'I see you are entirely determined to discuss Shraeve, no matter how it pains you to walk upon the Battle's ground,' smiled Nyve.

Theor shrugged regretfully. 'I must do as my heart and my faith bid me.'

'As I say, the horse is running. It is not our hands that guide it, but fate.'

'That is as it may be, but I fear Ragnor oc Gyre lays the blame for his Captain's death on our all too mortal shoulders. Temegrin the Eagle may not have been the most valued of the High Thane's servants, but neither was he entirely inconsequential. Ragnor sees our scheming, rather than fate's working, in the ascendancy of this halfbreed. In Shraeve's . . . accomplishments.'

'And you?' Nyve asked quietly. 'I care less than I should what our High Thane thinks. Tell me what you see.'

'I see nothing as clearly as I would wish. Fiallic was a good man. Measured. You told me yourself he was the finest Bannercaptain the Battle has had in our lifetimes. Shraeve is . . . more turbulent.' He spread his hands, an almost helpless gesture. 'This is not where any of us thought this track might lead. You cannot be as free of doubt as you pretend.'

Nyve grunted. 'Of course. If it was my choice, I'd have Fiallic back. If these bent hands could shape things, he would have killed Shraeve. But he didn't. No message I've had from the south, no rumour even, denies that she won her rank justly, by the will of fate.'

'And the halfbreed? She has drawn up your entire host, all the ranks of your ravens, at the side of some mongrel who was supposed to be nothing more than a tool in the hands of the Horin Blood. I find myself uncertain whose purposes are being served.'

Nyve regarded Theor pensively. He rested his hands, knuckles down, on the bench.

'I was never much given to deep thought on matters such as this; you know that.' He gestured, club-handed, at the lumpen scar across the side of his head. 'Had I spent much time thinking about it, I'd likely have taken flight. Let the hound that took my ear go hungry. But the path of my life was not written that way. It seems to me . . .'

He hesitated, narrowing his eyes as he searched for the right words. 'It seems to me that this is what we are for, you and I. Our lives have been very simple things: to serve the creed, to follow – and foster – the descent of this world to its inevitable ruin. We have been, in every sense that matters, meaningless except in our service to that purpose.

'So don't ask me to shed whatever little meaning I have had now, in the twilight of my life.' Nyve smiled, as if feeling the glow of that very twilight on his skin. 'The ascendancy of the creed is closer than ever before. By whatever means, however unexpectedly, Shraeve has restored us – the Inkalls – to heights we have not seen in many years. It is to us that the people look now for guidance, not the Thanes. If we pull back, hesitate, would we not make a lie of the long lives we have led? Would we not be denying the very purpose that has been our guide? I am too old to make such changes, friend. We both are. We've always been in the hands of fate. That the journey along the Road has become tortuous does not change that.'

Theor nodded. He understood. He felt it himself: the nagging sense that whatever doubts now assailed him were a betrayal of something precious and central to him. That if he surrendered to them, he would render himself, and the life he had lived, entirely empty. Still, those doubts were there. As was the insidious, all but heretical, fear that fate was somehow going astray from its proper path.

'Do you sleep well?' he asked Nyve. 'Are your dreams troubled?'

There was only the briefest moment of hesitation. 'I dream of violence. And of death. But I have always done so. They've been my sleep-companions as long as I can remember. And you? Is your rest uneasy?'

'It is.' Theor had to hold himself back. Some things he could not share, even with this oldest of friends. The waking dreams brought by seerstem belonged to the Lore, and only to the Lore. Yet a part of him wanted to tell Nyve how harsh and inhospitable the inner territories that seerstem opened up had become. The herb had blackened Theor's lips over the years: the smallest of prices to pay for the comfort and insight it had brought. But whatever it brought now, it was not comfort. Fear, sometimes. Doubt. It obscured where once it had clarified. The strange dreamlands that lay beyond the seerstem gate were bleak and unwelcoming. There was always the sensation of someone looking over his shoulder, or some movement just beyond the corner of his dreaming eye.

'I'm tired,' he murmured. 'Perhaps that's all it is. Perhaps I grow too old and weak to face the unfolding of fate's great plan.'

'You've a few years in you yet,' Nyve grunted.

'Perhaps. I am to meet with Ragnor oc Gyre. Down in Kan Dredar. He refuses to come to the Sanctuary, which is as sure a sign as you could wish for of his fraying patience. I thought perhaps you could provide me with an escort. I hear that there is unrest in the town. Riots. Killings.'

'You shall have as fine a guard of my ravens as you wish, First.' Nyve chuckled. 'It will do our High Thane good to see that all the Children of the Hundred stand shoulder to shoulder in this. And that the Battle still has enough swords here to put on a show.'

Theor smiled, and in smiling tried to pull taut the old, secure strands of his friendship with the master of the Battle. But there was a looseness in them that had never been there before, and he could not overcome it. The profound agreement of their instincts had always persisted without having to be spoken. Now, he felt it to be seamed with faint flaws that could not be patched with words, or with mere affection. He secretly and fearfully mourned the loss of its perfection.

VIII

Taim Narran cast an experienced eye over the host of the Black Road as it edged its way up the road towards Ive. Only a few hundred, he thought, yet the knowledge brought none of the relief he might have expected. Rather, he felt an empty despair at the prospect of inevitable slaughter, and the knowledge that victory or defeat today would bring no release for any save the dead. There must be light somewhere amidst this darkness, he thought, but he seemed to have lost the ability to detect its gleam.

'Move the horsemen out to the right flank,' he said quietly. 'They don't look to have any horses of their own. Perhaps we can get in behind them.'

He did not look round, but heard the riders galloping off to deliver his commands. Everyone, whether of Lannis or Kilkry stock, deferred willingly to him here. A certain martial fame – nothing he treasured or relished – had long ago attached itself to his name, and the people of Ive imagined him to be something he himself had struggled to recognise for some time: a great warrior and leader. They trusted in him to save them, and their town. It was a burden he bore without protest, but not gladly, and not lightly. Never lightly.

There were banners and standards from several of the Black Road Bloods scattered through the approaching army, yet Taim could see little sign of ordered companies or disciplined array. The northerners came on in a jostling mass, spreading out into a long, thick rank on either side of the road. There were no obvious Captains, just these hundreds of men and women come together into one huge blood-hungry crowd. And they bore a grim forest in their van: dozens of tall spears jostling for space against the grey sky, each topped with a severed head or bearing strips of flayed skin that stirred on the wind like pennants.

A woman, hands bound behind her back, legs hobbled, was dragged out in front of the seething army. She was wailing and struggling. Five warriors marched her a few paces forward and threw her down in the middle of the road. One of her captors spread his arms wide and bellowed wordless hatred at the ranks of Kilkry and Lannis men. Then he and the others beat the woman to death with clubs and staffs.

Taim turned away. She had looked to be much the same age as Maira, his daughter. He had never seen this from the Black Road before. This wanton, tribal brutality. It was not how battles were meant to be fought. Or perhaps it was, now.

The noise was new too. In all his years of facing the Black Road, he had grown used to the grim, almost unnatural, silence in which they often fought. This time, his ears rang to hate-filled roaring, like the baying of a thousand leashed hounds.

And then those leashes were slipped, and the dark wall of bodies and blades was rushing towards him. He drew his sword, cast one brief glance up towards the clouds scudding across the sky, not knowing what he hoped to see there, and heeled his horse into motion.

*

Ess'yr held out a flake of greasy squirrel meat to Orisian. He took it with a nod of gratitude. They ate in silence, warmed by the little fire, while the stubby twigs of the apple trees creaked in the breeze. Heavy clouds were racing overhead, but down in the orchard, amidst the aged protection of the trees, with the comforting flames, Orisian felt safe. Almost at ease.

Varryn would not join them, of course. He sat cross-legged some little distance away, cleaning the squirrel skin. He scraped away at the hide with his knife in silence, studiously ignoring Orisian and his sister. Ess'yr herself picked flecks of meat from a leg bone with precise finger and thumb. Orisian watched her, but when she looked at him he averted his eyes with a fleeting self-conscious smile.

He was faintly aware of the warriors loitering beyond the trees, at the back of the Guard barracks. Theirs was not an intrusive presence, though. They were sufficiently comforted by the high stone walls that enclosed the orchard, and sufficiently trusting now of these two Kyrinin, to permit Orisian some little privacy. It was a kind of wonder, he recognised, that a Thane of the Lannis Blood could sit alone in such company without his warriors imagining or expecting disaster. Those protective walls sheltered a moment, a scene, drawn from another world, another possibility, less scarred by bitter history. Though Orisian could not forget all that had happened, or the storms that raged beyond this island of calm, he could find here, in this company, a brief span of rest. Of stillness.

He licked his fingers clean. The fire was burning low, sinking into its bed of bright embers. He threw another couple of sticks onto it and listened to them crackle and hiss.

'There might be trouble coming,' he said pensively. Ess'yr said nothing. She was watching him, her eyes set like polished flints in the blue frame of her tattoos. Varryn's knife continued to rasp rhythmically across the skin.

'We think the Black Road has cut us off from the south,'

Orisian went on, unperturbed by their silence. 'Taim's gone to meet them. He wouldn't let me go with him.'

'You are precious to him,' Ess'yr said impassively.

'Yes.' Orisian flicked a sideways glance in her direction. Part of him longed to reach out to her, and lay a soft hand on her shoulder, her arm. 'Yes, perhaps. Though I don't know that I'm really any safer here than out there. I'm not sure such a thing as safety's possible any more.'

Ess'yr looked down, returning her attention to the little carcass.

'I would not . . .' Orisian began, but the sentence collapsed beneath the confused weight of his feelings. He tried again: 'I don't know quite why you have stayed here. I am − I am glad of it, but . . . If you want to go, you shouldn't stay because you think you owe me anything.'

He was aware that Varryn had stopped his work and was now staring at him. The cleaning knife rested point down on the warrior's knee.

'Owe you?' Ess'yr said. 'No. Not you.'

'Inurian?'

'It does not matter,' she said. A lie, Orisian thought; or at best a kind of truth his human understanding could not encompass.

'Our enemy makes alliance with your enemy,' Ess'yr placidly continued. 'We do not need to seek them out, for they come in search of you. Your fight is our fight.'

'Your brother does not agree,' Orisian said.

Ess'yr ignored him. Varryn returned to his task.

'It is only that I fear what may happen,' Orisian said. His mood was darkening once again, and he half-regretted speaking. If he had said nothing, just sat here and treasured the silent companionship, he might have preserved the illusion of closeness, of intimacy, a little longer. 'I see few paths that lead anywhere other than into shadow. I would regret it if you followed me that way when you did not need to. I just wanted you to know that.'

Ess'yr flicked bones into the fire. The trees above shivered in a momentary surge of wind.

'All paths lead to shadow in the end,' Ess'yr said.

'If we live through today,' said Orisian, watching the trembling flames, 'and through the next night, I mean to leave this place. I don't know what will happen, but the time is coming when all of this will end. One way or the other.'

He realised that he had lost their attention. The two Kyrinin lifted their heads, turned towards the west. Orisian saw the knife fall from Varryn's hand and his fingers dance into a blur of motion. Ess'yr made a grunting reply to whatever message her brother conveyed and rose to her feet.

'What is it?' Orisian asked softly, looking up at her. He could guess, in truth, for he had learned to read the code of their bodies and moods: in some sound or scent upon the air, some sign too subtle for meagre human senses, they had caught forewarning of danger.

Orisian twisted, a shout for his own warriors gathering in his throat, but Ess'yr was already moving. One pace, two, away from the fire. A stoop to sweep up her spear from where it rested against one of the apple trees. Her front foot stamped down. Her arm snapped forward. The spear flew.

And as that shaft left her hand, and darted across the darkening air between the ancient trees, there was movement atop the wall: a head, and then shoulders, just rising into sight. Orisian had time to register nothing more than a swirl of dark hair, the dull flash of a blade clasped in a gloved hand, before the spear thudded into the man's chest. He fell back silently and disappeared.

'There are more,' Ess'yr said, reaching for her bow.

But Orisian knew that for himself by then. He could hear the voices, the angry cries, the pounding feet. He leaped up and ran, shouting for his sword and shield as he went.

*

Taim Narran had abandoned any hope of imposing his will upon the battle. Slaughter swept across the fields and copses and stream beds. Like storm water, it went where it willed, its bloody extremities flowing down whatever channel the rise and fall of the land offered. No command could be given that would shape it or slow it. It was deaf to all save its own inner demands, which impelled it to consume and thrive and rage.

The men and women who acted upon its savage imperative forgot who they were and why they fought. They recognised neither friend nor foe, felt neither fear nor elation. There was within them only the burning need to kill. Each fought alone, subject to that need and only to that need.

Taim's horse had been hit by a crossbow bolt. It staggered down into a tiny gully and threw him. He splashed across the stream, seeing dark strands of blood threaded in the rushing water. Higher up the gully bodies were lying in the narrow channel. A woman was hacking feverishly at one of them with a long-bladed knife. Taim started towards her, to kill her, but a knot of men came suddenly tumbling down into his path, struggling and stabbing even as they fell and rolled in the stream.

Taim could confidently identify only one of them as an enemy: a massive mail-clad warrior who laboured to his feet, water cascading from his back and shoulders. Taim ducked behind his shield and barged into him, knocking him down. A single blow, with all of Taim's strength behind it, was enough to stave in the side of the man's helm. He began to convulse at once, thrashing about in the midst of the stream. Blood smeared out from his mouth; he had bitten through his tongue.

Taim was staggered sideways by two wrestling figures. He stumbled precariously over the smooth stones at the edge of the watercourse. The butt of a spear tripped him and in falling he punched his knee against a rock. The sharp, bone-shaking pain was like a lance of light, momentarily sharpening his senses, sending a beat of urgency and energy through him. Without it,

he might have been too slow to avoid the axe that slashed down
in search of his back. He rolled away through mud and spun
onto his feet in time to catch the second axe blow on his shield
and cut up into his assailant's crotch.

He scrambled up the bank of the gully, the soft turf smearing
beneath his feet. He emerged onto a field strewn with bodies and
with dropped or broken weapons. The thin grass had been trampled and torn. A woman went staggering past, her shattered arm
held tight to her side with a hand that was itself split and
bloody. A horse was lying on its flank close by, its legs stirring
faintly. Beyond it, a Kilkry warrior was fleeing from half a dozen
Tarbains, who pursued him with howls of mad fervour. Taim ran
to intervene, but his knee rebelled, and he faltered. The Tarbains
pulled down the warrior and fell on him like a pack of wolves
tearing at a deer.

A terrible hatred had hold of Taim, a formless thing that
began with no clear target or cause but willingly gathered those
Tarbain tribesmen in and made them its object. Overruling his
knee's protests, he rushed to them. So intent were they upon
their savage business that they were deaf and blind to his
approach until he was amongst them.

One went down, and then another. A club battered against
Taim's thigh, and he felt the bone blades that studded its head
punching through his skin, but there was no pain. He killed
another. The rest fled from him. The Kilkry man was long dead,
of course. The Tarbains had been trying to behead him.

There was no single battle happening here. There never had
been, from the first moments of contact between the opposing
forces. Instead, many brutal, separate little struggles were played
out across the fields, and on the slopes beyond. Many lonely
deaths. A hundred intimate horrors and cruelties.

Taim reeled from fight to fight. His mind and body were
exhausted but he drove himself on, possessed by the conviction
that the only way he could escape this waking nightmare was by

helping it towards its end, by killing everyone who could be killed. And in time he had done that, and he could find no more victims for his blade. The armies had drifted apart. There was no victory or defeat: the numbed survivors on both sides simply walked, or crawled, away, alone or in small bands. The cruel day had taken everything they had to give, and left them empty and trembling and lost, forgetful of themselves. They let weapons and banners fall and stumbled silently back the way they had come

Taim slumped to his hands and knees. He curled his fingers into the earth, making fists through the wiry grass. He was shivering, though he felt an almost feverish heat running through his skin. Blood was crusted all across his thigh where the Tarbain club had hit him. His guts were clenching, twisting. His stomach heaved and he retched and vomited up the morning's food. Once he was done, he rolled onto his back and lay there for a time, blindly watching the sky as it darkened, moment by moment, towards the gloom of dusk.

*

Ive quickly, almost enthusiastically, surrendered itself to violence. Chaos descended, and as it did so something rose up within the townsfolk to embrace it. Small bands of Black Road raiders burst in all along the western flank of the town, but they were few and disorganised, not enough to truly threaten Ive's safety. They were enough, though, to act as spark to the fire that had been on the brink of eruption for so many days.

The townspeople rushed from their homes, surging through the dusk in frantic search of enemies, whether real or imagined. In this great boiling cauldron the Black Roaders fought with savage abandon. They hurried from house to house, slaughtering all they found; they battled and died in narrow alleyways; they crept their way to the storehouses and the bakeries and the almshouses and set them afire. Smoke swirled in the yards and streets like acrid fog.

Consumed by their own ungovernable fear and fury, the people of Ive turned upon one another. Those who were not recognised were slain, hacked with kitchen knives and axes, beaten with hammers and impaled upon hay forks. The pillars of flame mounted higher and higher, turning the sky orange and rust-red. Horror was piled upon horror. Washed by the heat of a burning house, the family that had abandoned it was killed in the roadway before it. They cried out in vain to their killers, who had forgotten, in their madness, that they knew them. Some neighbours, armed with nothing more than clubs, hunted a Gyre warrior into a farrier's yard, cornered her there and battered her to death in the shadows; then, hurrying out, blundered into a company of Kilkry swordsmen, thought them foes, and died on the blades of their supposed protectors. The storm raged. Reason and restraint were rent apart.

Some few strove to hold firm against the beast that was running loose.

'We must keep the *na'kyrim* safe,' Orisian shouted at Torcaill. They ran together, with a handful of Torcaill's men behind them, out from the gate of the barracks.

There had been a sharp, vicious struggle in the orchard: invaders spilling over the walls, going down with Kyrinin arrows in throat or flank, stumbling in amongst the trees and running futilely onto human swords. Onto Orisian's sword. He had killed a man almost without knowing it, not recognising what was happening until the body was at his feet. Something in him rejoiced at the sight and something else recoiled. Both felt, in that moment, like a true reflection of who he was.

His heart pounded, his arms shook, so ferocious was his body's response to the sound and scent and feel of battle. Everything faded from his awareness save the overwhelming need to act, to move, to join the bloody dance. He had heard himself shouting as he ran from the orchard, through the courtyard of the barracks. He would have gone blindly and wildly out into the chaos but for the sudden sight of towering flames rising from some building on the far side of the town, and for the sudden burning in his nostrils and eyes as a hot wind blasted smoke into his face. With that bitter smell, he was returned for an instant to Castle Anduran on the night of Winterbirth; and the memory dampened rather than fed the sanguinary ardour that had burned within him.

There was no sign of the Lannis guards who should have been outside the little house where Yvane and Eshenna sheltered. Bursting in, ignoring Torcaill's anguished demands for caution, Orisian found no sign of the two *na'kyrim* within, either. He went, clumsy in his haste, knocking aside stools and chairs, out into the little walled yard behind the house.

There was a corpse there, sprawled across the cobblestones. One of his guards, Orisian thought, but he did not have the time to be certain. Half a dozen figures were clustered down by the goat shed. One or two held blazing torches aloft while others hauled at the door, trying to tear it open against faltering resistance from within. Orisian heard Yvane's voice, angry. Frightened.

'Get away!' Orisian shouted, leaping over the body.

Heads turned.

'There's halfbreeds in here,' one of them snapped at Orisian, as if that should explain everything to him. 'Wightborns!'

As if there was nothing more that could, or should, be said. It was not the words, though, that put a hollow kind of horror into the pit of Orisian's stomach, but the accent. These men were Ive townsfolk, not northerners.

'Stand aside,' he demanded, lifting his sword a little.

But the door came free then. Yvane came tumbling forward from within the shed, and Eshenna was crying out in fear inside. One of the men roared in triumph. Another threw his torch at Orisian and it came spinning towards him in a wreath of embers and flame. He ducked under it and ran at them.

His shield shook beneath some blow, he cut at legs, veered

away from a fist that darted at his head. And amidst all the chaos, he found a kind of clarity, centred upon the need to keep those within that shed alive. He fought as Taim Narran would have wished him to, with a cold determination. For the first time in his life, his mind and body united unquestioningly in the cause of killing. His sword broke an arm, and he heard the crack of the bone. He drove on, brought the blade down on the back of a man who was blocking the shed's doorway. He trampled the falling figure and turned to bar the entrance himself. And found Torcaill and the others, following in his wake, already ending the one-sided fight.

Orisian sat, legs splayed out on the cobblestones of the yard. Blood was running through the crevices all around him but he did not care. His warriors were dragging away the dead and the injured with little regard for which was which. Orisian unbuckled his shield and laid it flat across his knees.

'They'd have killed you if we hadn't come,' he said weakly. Even to speak seemed a terrible effort.

'They would,' agreed Yvane. He felt her hand touch his shoulder for a moment. 'Thank you.'

'They'd have killed you. And K'rina. Everything would have been for nothing.'

He laid his hands on the gently curving surface of his shield and watched his fingers tremble. It was almost dark now. Still rising into the sky, from all around, were cries of fury and fear, the scattered thunder of running feet, the audible death throes of buildings plunging into fiery ruin. The delirium, perhaps death, of the town.

'This can't go on,' he said. 'I'm killing Kilkry men now. That can't be right, can it? We have to find a way to end it. There has to be a way.'

'There is a way,' he heard Eshenna say behind him. She sounded utterly exhausted. 'Kill Aeglyss. This is his taint, his poison, at work. Use K'rina against him. It's the purpose the Anain meant for her, until we interfered.'

'Until Aeglyss grew too strong, perhaps,' Yvane said. 'Too strong for even the Anain to overcome.'

'Perhaps,' Eshenna acknowledged, empty and faint. 'Perhaps. But what other hope is there?'

Nobody spoke for a moment or two, and then Eshenna said again, 'What other hope is there?'

2

The City

This place, this city, shall henceforth be the seat of High Thanes; first amongst all cities, as we are now first amongst all Bloods. Vaymouth is mighty now, and shall be mightier still in years to come, for who can doubt that all the world will walk the road to its gates? All deeds of consequence, all acts of significance, shall be done here and nowhere else.

Memories of Tane will be dimmed and overshadowed. Kolkyre will be forgotten. The pride of those who dwell in distant Evaness will be blunted, their arrogant tongues stilled. We who call Vaymouth home shall live amidst the greatest power and the greatest glory this world has known since the Gods departed. Their radiant presence has passed, never to return, but see here what other lights a people may find amidst the darkness, what we may build with our own hands, and shape with our will: all the goods and coin of the world, flowing like tributary streams into the river of our streets and our marketplaces. Peace and prosperity and order. Great walls to shelter us, great towers to keep watch from. These are the stars by which we plot our course. These are the torches to light our path into the future.

The glories of the Gods are lost to us; if there are to be new glories we must fashion them for ourselves, carving them from the base matter of this abandoned world. This, the city, shall be their embodiment, and the place where they burn most brightly.

From Merwen's *Encomium*

I

The two young girls walked hand in hand, whispering as they went. Anyara did not need to hear what they said to know that they were beyond the reach of the world. They were followed, as they wandered idly through the bare garden, by maids who carried songbirds in gilded cages, but they might as well have been entirely alone. The girls were enclosed in the perfect privacy of their own realm: the place in childhood where nothing mattered save whatever thought had hold of them at that moment; where adults were but faint and inconvenient clouds on the horizon of their secret concerns.

Anyara could remember such a place, though she had inhabited it only briefly. She and Orisian and Fariel had shared it, in the days before the Heart Fever: a few precious years in which everything had been bright and exciting, and fashioned for them and them alone. She was exiled from that place by the passage of time, by deaths. And now by distance, for she sat on a marble bench in a terrace garden of Gryvan oc Haig's Moon Palace. These self-absorbed girls she watched were the children of some lady of the High Thane's court.

Anyara shrugged deeper into her fur coat. Winter had followed her southwards. All the way down from Kolkyre, through Ayth-Haig lands, across the moors and on through the farmlands of the Nar Vay shore, it had been an intangible, morose hound dogging every step her horse had taken, eating up the land in her wake. There was a faint mist on the air now. Around this palace in which she was a comfortable, imprisoned guest, Vaymouth sprawled beneath a dank grey blanket. All sound was deadened by the thick air. The birds in their cages did not sing.

'It must seem a silly affectation to you, this fashion for birdcages.'

Tara Jerain, the wife of the Haig Blood's infamous Chancellor, smiled down at Anyara.

'I hadn't given it any thought,' Anyara murmured.

Tara gave her another complicitous, almost conspiratorial, smile.

'It's kind of you to be so gentle with our foibles,' she said. 'I don't like them myself. The birds, I mean. May I join you?'

Without waiting for an answer, Tara settled herself on the bench. The many layers of fine fabric that enveloped her sighed and shifted over one another. Even in this dull light there were threads in there that shone and glimmered. The Chancellor's wife clasped her hands in her lap. The cuffs of her cape were trimmed with the white fur of snow hares.

'Nobody was interested in songbirds until Abeh oc Haig decided she liked them.' She leaned a little closer to Anyara as she spoke. 'Then, all of a sudden, every lady of the court – even the girls, intent upon being ladies one day – realised that they are the most fascinating and precious of things. Silly. Birds aren't meant to sing in the winter, but still everyone must have one.'

'Everyone except you,' Anyara grunted.

'Oh, no.' Tara shook her head lightly. 'I have one. Of course I do. Two, in fact. The best that money can buy, I'm told.'

Anyara wished this woman would leave her alone. She found more than enough that was hateful about her situation here in Vaymouth without being subjected to the babbling of the self-regarding butterflies who thronged the Moon Palace. She had heard of Tara Jerain, of course, even before she was brought here: the beautiful, cunning wife of the hated, still more cunning, Shadowhand. And Tara was indeed beautiful: eyes that even in this wintry light glittered like jewels, skin that bore a lustrous sheen of health. Her poise and confidence made Anyara feel like a child all over again.

'Those who think they know about such things tell me we'll have snow here in a few days,' Tara mused absently. 'Some years we have none at all, you know. I enjoy snow, myself. It makes everything look better than it really is, like fine furs and gems.'

Again, that warm smile. Anyara could think of no good reason why the Chancellor's wife should suddenly have decided to make this pretence at friendship. She had paid her no attention before now. No one in the Moon Palace had.

On the day of her arrival, Anyara – aching, tired and feeling entirely bedraggled – had endured a brief and rather strange audience with Gryvan oc Haig himself and his wife Abeh. They seemed more than a little bemused – in Abeh's case, offended – by her presence, as if she were an unexpected and unwanted guest they did not know what to do with. All of which served to irritate Anyara almost beyond concealment. She comforted herself by imagining that Aewult nan Haig might in due course learn precisely what the High Thane thought of sons who sent unsought hostages to their fathers.

Since that initial, clumsy welcome, Anyara had found herself all but ignored. She had fine chambers on the favoured south flank of the palace. She was given gifts of gowns and necklaces. Maidservants were assigned to her service. But almost no one spoke to her. She was given no reason or excuse to leave those fine chambers, and if she did so of her own accord, she found herself oppressively shadowed by those same, watchful maids, who would herd her back to her rooms as if she were a wayward, simple-minded sheep in need of penning. She had asked, once, to borrow horses so that she and Coinach could ride out towards the sea. She had not expected the request to be granted, and it was not.

'Your shieldman has been much remarked upon.'

Anyara glanced round. Coinach was standing a short distance away, by the gates that gave out onto these tidy gardens. He was rigidly straight-backed, staring ahead, steadfastly ignoring all the ladies and the servants and the children. It made Anyara smile, though she dipped her head to hide the expression from Tara Jerain. Coinach's determination to retain his dignity even in these disquieting circumstances had a touch of youthful pride and dogged loyalty about it that she found very pleasing.

'He's a striking man,' Tara observed. 'And it's so unusual for us here to see a woman with so . . . martial an attendant.'

'Things are a little different in the north these days,' Anyara said rather more sharply than she intended. She did not know whether it was Coinach or herself she was defending. 'Very different. Perhaps if all of you—'

Tara cut her short with a flourish of her smooth, ringed fingers.

'That's not what I wanted to discuss with you, in any case. Really, it's a little too cold to spend more time than is necessary out here, don't you think? I have a proposition for you. I thought you might find it more comfortable, more . . . well, more comfortable, if we found you different quarters.' Tara leaned in once more and whispered, 'Things can be so formal and tedious here, don't you find?'

'What have you got in mind?' Anyara asked cautiously.

'My own home, of course. We have a great many rooms that might find favour in your eyes, and I think you'll find it a good deal quieter. Much more calming.'

Anyara thought for a moment or two, and then looked sideways at Tara.

'Is this Gryvan's idea?' she asked. 'He doesn't know what to do with me, so tidies me away into your care. Am I so much of an embarrassment to him?'

Tara rolled her eyes in amused frustration. It was such a natural, relaxed gesture that Anyara found herself warming to the woman. She had to remind herself that this was the Shadowhand's wife, and by that measure unlikely to be a reliable friend.

'Really,' Tara said, 'is everyone of your Blood so blunt? It's refreshing, but there is no need to make quite such a close alliance with suspicion. Look –' confiding, companionable '– there's been some misunderstanding between your brother and Aewult. Or between Aewult and Taim Narran. I don't know; I don't follow these things closely. But it will all be cleared up before long, I'm sure, particularly now that Mordyn is coming back to us.'

'Your husband?' Anyara said in surprise. She knew the Shadowhand had been injured and then gone missing in the chaos consuming the Kilkry Blood. It had been one of the charges – or suspicions at least – laid against her, against Orisian, by Aewult nan Haig when he took her hostage.

'Oh, yes,' Tara said with such undisguised, apparently uncontrived delight that Anyara once again felt that questionable twinge of affection for her. 'Have you not heard? My husband is on his way south even now. He will be here very soon. And really, there's no need for you to be shut up in this marble tomb in the meantime. That is what I think, anyway, and the High Thane agrees.'

Anyara nodded thoughtfully. She did not dare to hope that all of this would really be so easily tidied away, but there was no denying that she hated the Moon Palace. If Gryvan oc Haig wanted her out of the way, for whatever reason, she was not inclined to resist.

The two girls she had been watching earlier had turned back to their maids. One of them was poking a stick through the golden bars of her birdcage, trying to make the prisoner within sing.

'All right,' Anyara said. 'I'd be grateful for your hospitality.'

'Do you find our new accommodation more to your taste?' Anyara asked Coinach.

The shieldman shrugged and wrinkled his nose.

'Each palace seems much like another to me. What colour it is makes little odds.' He stood uncomfortably in the doorway of

Anyara's new quarters in the Palace of Red Stone. His stiffness and formality amused her, for no obvious reason.

'It's porphyry,' she said. 'The red.'

'Is it?'

'Oh, don't try *so* hard to sound interested.' Anyara lifted the finely carved lid of a massive chest at the foot of the bed and peered in. Sheets and blankets: linen, wool, silk. Better, if she was any judge, than what she had slept amidst in the High Thane's palace.

'Sorry, my lady.'

'And don't start calling me that again,' Anyara said in mock irritation. She sniffed the bowl of water at the bedside. It had a strong scent. Roses, perhaps. 'There're more than enough ladies in this city already.'

Coinach made a non-committal noise that came surprisingly close to a grunt.

'Perhaps now that we're little a less closely watched, we can start some training again,' Anyara mused.

Since leaving Kolkyre, there had been almost no opportunities for Anyara to refine her still rudimentary skills with a blade. The constant supervision had made it all but impossible. If she was honest, she feared drawing ridicule down upon herself and – even more so – upon Coinach if they were observed.

'Perhaps,' Coinach acknowledged without notable enthusiasm.

The shieldman moved aside to allow a maidservant to enter, bearing fresh pillows for Anyara's bed. She was a short but graceful girl, much the same age as Anyara, with strikingly red hair. She gave a neat bobbing curtsy, and there was even a flicker of a smile on her face.

'What's your name?' Anyara asked, wondering how far the warmer welcome she was receiving here would go.

'Eleth, my lady.'

'I'm Anyara.'

'Oh yes. I know, my lady.'

'And this is Coinach.'

The maid blinked and cast a fleeting smile over her shoulder towards the warrior. Then, much to Anyara's surprise, she gave a little giggle. Coinach frowned, as darkly as if he had just heard someone impugning his honour.

Eleth energetically plumped the pillows and arrayed them upon the bed.

'The lady asked if you would join her,' she said as she worked. 'There are sweetmeats and warm wine prepared in the Tapestry Room.'

Anyara and Coinach followed their guide through the Palace of Red Stone. It felt entirely unlike Gryvan oc Haig's gargantuan Moon Palace. Whatever splendour the Moon Palace bought through crude size and ostentation, the Chancellor's abode matched through elegance. From its meticulously painted ceilings to its cool marble passageways, every element of its fabric spoke in refined and tasteful tones. There was a sweet, faint aroma on the air that Anyara could not quite place, though it reminded her of spice.

The Tapestry Room lived up to its name. Long tapestries covered three of its walls. In the fourth were set latticed windows, the light that fell from them diffused by shimmering, almost transparent curtains. Tara Jerain was already seated at a table bearing trays of tiny cakes and biscuits, and a jug of wine as darkly red as any Anyara had ever seen.

Coinach waited by the door, distancing himself slightly from the pair of serving girls who also stood there. Tara glanced at the shieldman as Anyara settled into a chair.

'Does he go everywhere with you, then?' she asked, without a trace of criticism or mockery.

'Not everywhere,' Anyara replied, slightly defensive. 'But most places.'

'Any why not?' Tara offered a platter laden with intricate,

absurd little confections. 'I am sure his presence must be of great comfort. In all manner of ways.'

Anyara wondered briefly if anything unseemly had been implied, but Tara was, as ever, smiling warmly. Whatever she said, it was always dressed in the livery of friendly, innocent banter.

'I hope your bedchamber is satisfactory,' Tara said.

Anyara nodded as the flavours of almond and apple suffused her mouth. Such wonderful delicacies were unknown in her homeland. Tara gestured to one of the servants, who came nimbly forward and poured wine into a pair of goblets.

'You must tell me at once if there's anything you require,' the Chancellor's wife went on. 'We will do whatever we can to make your stay here comfortable. Perhaps even pleasurable, I hope.'

'I would not want to cause you any inconvenience,' Anyara said. She tasted the wine. Its rich warmth eased down her throat.

Tara gave a little laugh. 'Believe me, you need not concern yourself over such things. You cannot imagine how tedious it becomes to see only the same people, day after day after day. You are a most refreshing change, I can assure you.'

'Perhaps one thing, then,' Anyara said, making a studied effort to sound casual and light-hearted. 'I hoped, when I was at the Moon Palace, that it might be possible to borrow some horses, and ride out to the sea. The opportunity never arose.'

'Of course.' Tara looked delighted by the suggestion. It was impossible to read the woman, Anyara thought. Or at least it was impossible to detect whatever calculation might lurk within her. Even Anyara's stubborn mistrust might be eroded by such meticulously crafted good humour.

'Yes,' Tara breezed on. 'We may have to wait a day or three for the weather to don a clement face, but it would be good to get out of the city for a little while. I'll go with you, if you will have me. I've a very fine bay horse that would be just right for you,

I'm sure. Although there's a grey, too, and he's a wonderfully gentle creature . . .'

Tara chattered on, outlining the merits of various possible mounts. Anyara's attention drifted as the soothing wine, Tara's graceful voice, the soft light spilling in through the curtains, all conspired to lull her into comfortable distraction. She allowed herself briefly to wonder what it must be like to live this easy life, so abundant in its comforts. She mentally shook herself, hardening her lazy thoughts. Slaughter was still being done, far from these marble halls. Orisian and Taim Narran and countless others were still adrift in that storm. Her people were drowning in blood.

She set down the cup of wine and pushed it carefully away from her. She was suddenly ashamed to be sitting here, in such company, amidst such grace, while others fought and died on fields that felt immeasurably distant.

II

When a clear morning at last arrived, and the horses were combed and saddled, it was a grand group that rode out from Vaymouth's southern Gold Gate. As well as Anyara and Coinach, Tara came with a pair of her maids, Eleth, three palace guards, the master of the stables and one of his boys. It was hardly the liberating solitude Anyara had half-hoped she and Coinach might be permitted, but it was movement, and change, and a brief escape from the encircling city walls, so she was determined to savour it.

They rode down the north bank of the River Vay, following a broad cobbled road through vast fields of stubble. Wagons and mule trains were brushed aside by the two guards who rode ahead, forced to the very edge of the road to make way for the riding party. Farmworkers and travellers and traders stood in the rough verge, watching with irritation or fascination or resentment, according to their disposition, as Tara Jerain and her retinue trotted splendidly past. Anyara paid little attention to all of this. She breathed deeply, and lifted her face to the breeze coming in from the west. The air had the sea on it, and that felt more like home than anything had in many days.

The fields were wide and flat, the sky ever-changing as rank after rank of long, twisted clouds processed overhead, the low sun winking in and out of sight behind them. They rode past a huge sprawl of jetties and quays and warehouses and inns. The tide was out, so beyond this mass of habitation and industry lay a prodigious expanse of dark mudflats, over which flocks of birds swept back and forth in coordinated precision.

On an open stretch of the shore, at the head of a beach of brown sand, was a cluster of trees and about it a short, green sward. Tara brought them to a halt there and dismounted. The maids unpacked bundles of cold meats and preserved fruits. Anyara went to stand with Coinach at the very edge of the grass. She could smell the strandline, the long-familiar but recently forgotten scent of rotting seaweed and brine and wet sand. She was pleased to see on Coinach's face the same sad pleasure as she herself felt. He looked, as he stood there staring out to the immense flat horizon of the sea, more at ease than he had done for a long time. It felt good, that moment of shared sentiment, but it did not last. Tara walked over to them, bearing food.

'We come hawking along here sometimes,' the Chancellor's wife said. 'Do you like hunting?'

'Not particularly,' Anyara said, knowing it sounded ill-humoured, but not caring.

'Ah, well. I can imagine how hard it must be to take much pleasure in that kind of thing at the moment. Believe me, since my husband left to go north, nothing has tasted good to me. It must have been still harder for you, to suffer the losses you have this winter, and now to know nothing of your brother's fate.'

Anyara grimaced. There was nothing she was less eager to discuss than Orisian, or anything that had happened since Winterbirth.

'I'm sorry,' Tara said at once, and she sounded entirely genuine, aghast at her own behaviour. 'Please forgive me. It is inexcusable to talk of such things without invitation. This sea air makes me foolish. That, and the promise of my husband's return. In seeking to offer comfort, I stumble about like an ignorant—'

'It's all right,' Anyara said to stanch the apologetic flow. 'I'm glad for you. You must have been greatly concerned for the Chancellor's safety.' And she found that she meant what she said. For all that Anyara disliked – detested – Mordyn Jerain, this woman's love for her husband was all too apparent. It felt churlish not to acknowledge such feelings.

Tara nodded. 'Oh, indeed. It was a misery, when so many terrible rumours were reaching us. I feel as though I am about to awaken from a bad dream. But what you and your family have suffered – my difficulties bear no comparison, especially now that they approach a happy resolution. Forgive me.'

'Look,' said Coinach quietly at Anyara's side.

Far off along the beach, back towards the harbour and dockyards, figures were running over the sand. They were so distant it was impossible to tell what was happening, and no sound could reach so far across the onshore wind, but it looked to be a pursuit of some kind. Something in the way the figures moved – their urgency, their effort – implied violence. They reached the line of breaking waves. Anyara could just make out the white speckling of spray bursting up as the first of them struggled through the shallow water.

'How odd,' Tara Jerain murmured.

Someone fell, and the figures became indistinct, crowding in together in a dark mass. Sharp, angular movements suggested a flurry of knees and elbows.

'They're killing him,' Coinach said.

'Surely not,' said Tara then, puzzled, doubtful: 'Perhaps they caught him thieving.'

'Perhaps you should send your guards to intervene,' Anyara suggested. There was something in the silent, savage scene she found unsettling. Even though it was safely distant, it had a simple brutality that felt as though it could all too easily reach across that stretch of sand. It soured the air.

'No, no,' Tara said. She was a little uneasy and distracted now herself. 'Best not to interfere. There's been a good deal of trouble recently, you know. I've heard that there has been much more . . . disturbance than is usual in the rougher parts of the city. As if some foul mood's taken hold of everyone at the same time. No, best to keep away from it. Perhaps we should make ready to return.'

In so far as she thought of it at all, Anyara had assumed that the Shadowhand's return would be marked by pomp, by ceremony or rejoicing, but it came suddenly and unheralded instead. She went, on the morning after their ride to the shore, to break her fast with Tara Jerain, as had quickly become their habit, and the Chancellor was simply there, sitting at the finely laid table. He was thinner than Anyara remembered. His skin had an ashen, bloodless quality.

Until now, these meals had been far more comfortable – almost pleasurable – occasions than Anyara would have expected. Tara was an easy companion, always ready to smooth the conversation along in gentle fashion. This morning was different, and from the moment of her first step into the room, Anyara sensed the change.

Mordyn was a deadening, darkening presence; nothing like the casually confident and eloquent man Anyara remembered from Kolkyre. He barely acknowledged her arrival at the table. His eyes flicked briefly in her direction and then sank back towards his food. He sat in a tight knot, his arms pressed close in at his side, his chin nestled down into his chest.

Tara Jerain said nothing. She greeted Anyara with a nod and a small smile, but they were frail tokens, the afterthoughts of a mind entirely elsewhere. In countless little ways, she betrayed her disquiet: snatched glances at her returned husband, the restless movement of her hands from platter to mouth to lap to table, the concern that pinched the skin at the corner of her eyes into nests of lines. Anyara was silenced by the oppressive unease. Even the serving girls moved quietly and hesitantly about their business.

There were a dozen questions Anyara could have asked. Longed to ask. She did not dare to utter any of them. Mordyn Jerain had always intimidated her, but this was different. Now the bleak silence he imposed simply felt too weighty to disturb.

She picked half-heartedly at the food before her. Her heart sank with the realisation that despite her determination to resist, she had come to believe the many subtle hints that once the Chancellor returned, all might be resolved in a satisfactory way. She had permitted a tentative blossoming of hope, seduced perhaps by Tara's companionship and the comforts of the Palace of Red Stone, and sloughed a few fragments of her caution and suspicion. Well, the Chancellor had returned, and he brought not relief but some strange shadow. Anyara glanced at him.

Mordyn Jerain was staring at her. For an instant his gaze was unguarded, piercing, then he appeared to realise she was watching him and his expression went blank, his eyelids fluttered and he lowered his head once more. But in that brief moment she had glimpsed such naked contempt, such loathing, that she was suddenly afraid.

Anyara spent that day in restless distraction. Eleth, the maid, sensed her mood and produced from somewhere materials and needles. She suggested she might show Anyara how to produce the patterns of decorative threadwork that had become popular in Vaymouth in the last year or two. It was a kind, sincere offer, but wholly impotent as a cure for Anyara's agitation.

She could not settle, could not sit still for more than a moment or two. She snapped irritably at Coinach without cause. He exiled himself to the passageway outside her rooms. Eleth came and went in an increasingly desperate attempt to provide some amusement. She fetched dainty cakes from the kitchens. Anyara dutifully ate them, and though she recognised that they were delicious, she found they gave her no pleasure. Eleth brought singing cagebirds. To the maid's consternation, Anyara only laughed bitterly at them, and bade her remove them.

At last, as the afternoon stumbled towards a grey dusk, Anyara sprang up from her chair with a sigh of frustration.

'There must be parts of this palace I haven't seen yet,' she said to Eleth. 'Show me something. Anything. I can't sit around here any more. I have to move.'

'Of course, my lady,' Eleth said promptly, evidently relieved. 'There must be somewhere . . .'

'Anywhere,' Anyara said, and stepped out into the corridor.

Coinach was waiting there. He was a touch startled by her sudden appearance, and gave her a somewhat anxious look, as if in anticipation of a scolding.

'Come,' said Anyara briskly. 'We're exploring. Or just wandering.'

Eleth led the way, walking with quick, small steps.

'Are you warm enough?' Coinach murmured at Anyara's side.

'I'm fine,' she said, which was not entirely true. Some of the passageways of the Chancellor's palace gathered and retained enough heat from the kitchens and bedchambers and communal rooms to remain comfortable all day, others – such as this one –

did not. She had left too hurriedly to think of bringing a cloak, but had no intention of turning back now.

As they rounded a corner, Eleth gave a soft gasp of surprise and drew to an abrupt halt. Anyara almost walked into her. Mordyn Jerain was there, standing motionless in the corridor ahead of them. His arms hung limp at his side. He was staring blankly at the wall. If he breathed, he did so soundlessly, and without discernible movement of his chest. He did not, Anyara realised after a moment or two's tense observation, blink. His eyes were glassy, unfocused.

She took a step forward, gently easing Eleth to one side. Coinach whispered something cautionary, but she ignored him. There was something eerily unreal about the scene. The Shadowhand looked like a man who had simply . . . stopped; as if his body had been unexpectedly abandoned by whatever enlivening force had once inhabited it.

'Chancellor?' Anyara said quietly as she took another pace closer. Here was an opportunity to undo her reticence of the morning, if Mordyn could be roused from whatever stupor had taken hold of him. Here was the chance to find out what he knew of Orisian; what role he might play in untangling her own uncomfortable situation. She firmly crushed the urge to slip away before this troubling man noticed her presence. If she was to be of any use at all to her brother, her Blood, herself, it would not be by hiding away, by giving in to the fears that flocked about her.

And then, slowly, he turned his head. She met his cold eyes, and was reminded of the predatory gaze of the hunting hawks her family had kept at Kolglas. It brought her to an instant halt. Yet he said nothing. He simply stared at her. In the space of a few heartbeats, the silence became so potent that she imagined she could feel its pressure upon her skin.

'Chancellor?' she said again, aware of the tremor in her voice. She quelled it. 'I wondered if I might speak with you?'

He tipped his head slightly to one side, narrowed those eyes a touch.

'You . . .' he said slowly, clumsily. 'You were in the forest. You were at Anduran.'

Anyara frowned. 'Anduran? Yes, yes, of course. Many times. Never . . . We met in Kolkyre, though, for the first time.'

'Indeed.' He fell silent once more, yet continued to stare at Anyara. There was nothing in his gaze now: no life, no interest. No hostility even. Just that dead regard.

Coinach came up beside Anyara. The Chancellor did not seem to notice him.

'Perhaps you should return to your chambers, lady,' Coinach murmured.

'I thought perhaps we might discuss my future,' Anyara said stubbornly to Mordyn. He would surely understand the absurdity of the circumstance they all found themselves in. Had he not been absent from Kolkyre at the crucial time, she doubted Aewult's idiocy would have been permitted to follow its mad course. 'I am sure this misunderstanding can be easily tidied away, now that you have returned. The High Thane will surely listen to you . . .'

'Yes,' said Mordyn. He still held his head at that strange angle, like a bird. 'He will. He already does. You are too late, though, to exert any influence upon what it is I choose to say to him. How unfortunate.'

He took a single step towards them. Coinach edged his shoulder in front of Anyara, and for once she did not find his protective instincts foolish or misplaced. There was something in the Shadowhand's manner so unnatural that it was impossible not to read threat into it. The corridor suddenly felt constricted: tight, like a trap.

'Things change too fast for you,' the Shadowhand said. 'You're nothing now. The struggle stopped being about you, your Blood, a long time ago.'

'Come away,' Anyara whispered to Coinach, tugging at his arm. There was, she now realised, nothing to be gained here. Quite the opposite, in fact: for the first time since she had arrived in this city, she sensed true danger rather than mere hostility or cold contempt, stirring in the shadows, in the edges. Drawing closer.

Coinach kept himself between her and the Chancellor as they walked away. Eleth was watching with a shocked expression, one hand lightly touching her lips as if in a forgotten attempt to hide her reaction. Anyara glanced back over her shoulder as they went. Still Mordyn Jerain was staring at her, leaning forward slightly, as if his own sudden, intense interest had overbalanced him.

'Hide,' he said. 'Hide away. It doesn't matter. What's coming will find you; find everyone.'

Anyara grimaced, filled with both detestation for the man and irritation at how deeply his words and his demeanour troubled her. She gathered in Eleth with an outstretched arm, and shepherded the alarmed maid away, back around the corner.

'Stay away from my table, lady,' she heard the Shadowhand saying behind them, out of sight. 'I will not break bread with you. Stay out of my sight, lest you draw my attention down upon you too soon.'

Anyara walked quickly away. She shivered as she did so.

III

Snow could conceal many shortcomings, but even its gentle blanket was insufficient to render Ash Pit appealing or graceful to the eye. Vaymouth's most ill-reputed ward stubbornly asserted its infamous character. The dilapidated houses remained grimy and tight-packed; whores still haunted shadowed doorways; rats still scurried brazenly through the debris of destitution; odious liquids still ran in the streets, cutting steaming channels in the snow.

Mordyn Jerain came with a dozen watchful guards, the bulkiest and most uncompromising of the hirelings he paid from his own pocket. No great warriors these, but street fighters and brutes whose loyalty was solely to the man who paid them the most; and the Shadowhand could pay better than anyone save the High Thane himself.

The party went openly through Ash Pit's noisome roadways, with little of the discretion that had characterised Mordyn's previous forays into this part of the city. Every onlooker – and there were some, even in this cold dusk, for Ash Pit never entirely slept – was driven off or turned away with snarled warnings and brandished cudgels. The Chancellor and his fierce entourage swept along like a savagely cleansing wind, leaving quiet and empty streets behind them.

When they came to the door they sought, Mordyn's ruffians dispersed, taking up stations at each nearby corner, disappearing down gloomy, tight alleys. Mordyn himself rapped on the weighty portal with his knuckles.

Magrayn swung the door open and regarded him with suspicious distaste.

'You are not expected,' she said, as distinctly as the King's Rot that had ravaged her face would permit.

'Nevertheless, I imagine your master will find the time to speak with me.'

Magrayn eyed the Chancellor, and glanced over his shoulder, noting the menacing figures lurking along the street.

'Won't he?' Mordyn persisted.

The doorkeeper grudgingly admitted him, and the Shadowhand was taken down into the cellars where the object of his journey was laired.

'Have I offended you in some way, Chancellor?' Torquentine asked, with a trace of hurt in his voice.

'What do you mean?' Mordyn asked.

'You seem a little . . . cold.'

'Would you have me pay you some pretty compliments? Or embrace you, perhaps?'

'Hardly. Your reach is famously long, but not, I think, long enough for the task of encompassing my prodigious girth.' Torquentine rested his hands on his immense belly with a satisfied smile.

Mordyn grunted. 'I am not in the mood for merry banter. I want to buy your services. Will you hear my offer or not?'

'Very well, Chancellor,' sighed Torquentine. It troubled him to find the Shadowhand so altered in manner, but by all rumour the man had suffered considerable misfortune during his adventures in Kilkry lands. Some allowance might be made for that, perhaps. 'You know I am always only too pleased to entertain your proposals. If this one is as interesting as—'

'Rest your tongue a while and listen. Igryn oc Dargannan-Haig will shortly be leaving Vaymouth. He will be sent to In'Vay, bound for the Lake Tower.'

'The final – and fatal – abode of the last King. Seems not inappropriate, if rather ill-omened for poor Igryn. Dare I guess that the former Thane is shortly to depart for the Sleeping Dark, then?'

'Be quiet. I want you to seize him before he reaches the Lake Tower, and transport him back to Hoke. To his own lands.'

'Ah . . . Chancellor, I am . . . For once, I find myself short of words.' Torquentine shifted heavily upon his huge cushions, rare consternation troubling his features. He blinked his one good eye. 'You want me to free Igryn? From chains the High Thane himself put upon him? That seems . . . Well, it's beyond even my not inconsiderable resources.'

'Nonsense. It's the High Thane's own desire you'll be serving. I will ensure that the escort is depleted at the appropriate time. I'll send you word of where and when the opportunity will present itself. Once you have him, it's well within your power to move a single man from one place to another undetected. You've spent your life making much bulkier cargoes disappear and reappear where they are least expected. It's not your resources that fall short, but your courage.'

'Indeed, indeed. Call me coward, then. I'll raise no protest. Craven, I am, when it comes to the matter of preserving my . . . lack of visibility, shall we say? What you ask runs counter to my most dearly held principles, not the least of which is to refrain from trampling the toes of those whose feet are larger than mine. Not, in other words, to swim in rivers where all the other fish have sharper teeth than I do.'

'What are you talking about?'

'I know my limitations, Chancellor,' Torquentine said. The first hint of alarm was stirring in his considerable gut. It was not just the faint flicker of contempt he heard in Mordyn's tone; the Shadowhand's entire demeanour was so brisk, so hasty, it smacked of carelessness. Or convoluted deceit. 'Killing Igryn's cousin exhausted my willingness to cavort amongst contending Bloods and Thanes. That wine's too rich for me.'

'You got what you wanted in exchange for that service. Ochan the Cook is dead.'

'Of course, of course. Most grateful to you for that, sincerely. But Igryn's a rebel, a prize of war. His lands are still unsettled, to say the least – growing more so, from what I hear. Blinded he may be, but if he's returned to his people a free man, an enemy of the Thane of Thanes . . . my wit is unequal to the task of discerning the benefit – to Gryvan, or you, or any of us – in such a development.'

'You are not required to discern such things.' Again that dismissive, curt edge to the words. The Chancellor had never, in Torquentine's experience, been quite so verbally rough.

'But how could renewed unrest – war, even – on our southern borders be in anybody's interest, when the Black Road is—'

'None of that is your concern.'

'Well, with regret, I must differ on that.' Torquentine recognised dangerous ground when he felt it beneath his feet, but he found himself unable to meekly submit. This vaunted Chancellor owed him a good deal; owed him at least an acknowledgement that the two of them were masters in their own, very different, arenas. 'War presents its opportunities, certainly, but they diminish precipitately if that war becomes too extensive, too disruptive. I, like everyone else, was under the impression all of this trouble with the Black Road would be tidied up rather more quickly – rather more *victoriously*, in fact – than is proving the case. Now you seem to be tempting yet more unpleasantness from an entirely different direction.'

'You will be very adequately rewarded for your assistance. And there's more. I want fires set in every warehouse and storehouse of the Goldsmiths you can reach. And the Gemsmiths, and the Furriers. I need it done urgently.'

Torquentine could barely believe what he was hearing.

'Oh, this is madness. You mean to make a fool of me. This is some strange jest, isn't it?'

'No.'

'You want the whole city given over to riot and mayhem?'

'I want you to do as I bid, and to enjoy the fruits of your efforts. I will give you fifty times the payment you've received for any other service you've done me.'

'Now I know you are jesting.'

'Not at all. And not in this, either: if you refuse me, you corpulent slug, I'll have you dug out of this burrow and burned alive on one of Ash Pit's famous fires. The world is changing, Torquentine. Those who don't change with it will pay a heavy price for their intransigence.'

After Mordyn Jerain had departed, Torquentine lay in such deep thoughtfulness, for so long, that the candles guttered around him. They failed, one by one, and his chamber eased its way into

gloom. At length he stirred and summoned his doorkeeper. She
came, Rot-faced, and knelt at his side.

'Magrayn, we are in an unenviable position,' he said distract-
edly, with none of the humour or affection that usually coloured
his dealings with his disfigured attendant. 'I am required by the
Shadowhand to court disaster, and to wage war upon enemies I
do not want. He offers me absurd riches if I agree, and threatens,
if I refuse, to instead wage war upon me.'

'You could kill him,' Magrayn suggested promptly. Her ten-
dency towards a practical way of thinking was one of the things
he treasured about her.

'Perhaps, though that would be an undertaking no more
palatable. To kill a Chancellor? Insanely ambitious.'

'Then we must find a way to satisfy him with the least risk
possible.'

'There might be ways. Might.' Torquentine shook his heavy
head, wishing the tangle of his thoughts might be so easily
unwound. 'But there's a foul taste to all this, Magrayn. We're
already in the midst of war, and he seems intent on starting
another one inside our own house. He invites chaos in
Dargannan-Haig, vengeful fury amongst the Crafts. I don't see
the sense in any of it. There's nothing to be gained by it.'

'The Shadowhand can unearth gain where others see only
dirt,' Magrayn said, brushing a flake of forgotten food from
Torquentine's fat cheek.

'Indeed. What if his gain wears the same cloak as our loss,
though?' He sighed. 'We've little choice but to play the
Shadowhand's game for now. Make such arrangements as would
be needed to move a man, in total secrecy, from here to Hoke. A
blind man. Put some eyes on every warehouse used by the
Goldsmiths, the Gemsmiths and the Furriers. We need to know
every nook and cranny of whatever nocturnal routine the guards
keep. And find someone in the Palace of Red Stone who can tell
us what's happening in there.'

'We've tried that before, without success. The Chancellor's household is . . . tightly controlled.'

'Try again, harder. We shied away from too much risk in our previous attempts; now, we may bear a little more of it, I think. Desperate times, my dear. Also, examine all our plans for making a hasty departure from this burrow, as the Shadowhand saw fit to call it. Make sure they remain both sound and secret. And bring the best killers we know to Vaymouth – those who can be here within, say, three or four days. I want them close at hand. When troubles gather, it's best to have troublesome friends within reach.'

'I will see to it all.'

'Excellent. Perhaps you could send me down some of those little apple tarts too? All this worry is terribly unsettling for my stomach. It needs some comforting, I think.'

*

Joy and despair contended for mastery of Tara Jerain's heart. Her beloved husband was restored to her, and she longed to rejoice in that simple fact. So fearful had she been during those long days when no one could tell her where he was, or even whether he still lived, that she had felt like some fragile vessel of the thinnest glass: a single clumsy word, a single barb of spite, might have broken her. The nights had been the worst, contorted by the agony of ignorance, haunted by the fear of the coming dawn and the possibility that it might bring with it some ashen-faced messenger bearing the worst possible news.

And now that terrible shadow was lifted. But another had fallen, for the husband returned to her was not the one who had left her. Their lovemaking on the night of his return, which during his absence had been an imagined island of hope amidst despair, had instead been perfunctory: a thing of habit or necessity rather than love. Nothing in the days since had shown that to be an aberration. Something in him had changed. Something had gone, and with the recognition of its departure Tara found joy losing its ever more tenuous grip upon her spirits.

Mordyn was bent over a table, his shoulders lit by the candles that burned all around. The swan feather of his quill shivered as it scraped across parchment. There was no other sound. He was utterly engrossed in his work.

Tara watched from the doorway. This was a familiar sight. Many times she had seen her husband at work in just this way, in just this warm light. Yet all was not as it had once, so comfortingly, been. The hunch of his shoulders was narrower, tenser, than it used to be. His hand darted to and from the inkwell with angry impatience. Even the sound was different: harsher, cruder, as if quill and parchment warred. He had always had the lightest and most precise of hands. She felt an aching sense of bereavement as she noted each one of these tiny differences. Yet how could she be bereaved, when the object of all her affections was here before her, alive?

She walked forward, her slippers soundless on the floor. Mordyn was too absorbed in his labours to notice her approach. When she set her hands gently on his shoulders, in the way she had done countless times before, he started and gave a half-strangled grunt of alarm. He glanced up at her even as he covered over what he had been writing with blank sheets of parchment. Perhaps he thought Tara would not notice this petty act of concealment, but she did. He had never done such a thing before, never shown the slightest sign of distrust or secrecy. What pained her still more, though, was the way he shrugged off her hands with an irritated shake of his shoulders. With that single loveless gesture, he wounded her to the quick. Tara was startled to find her eyes moistening, a premonition of tears. This man bore the face and form of her husband, but she no longer recognised what lay beneath that surface.

'What happened?' she asked, standing limp and empty behind him.

He must have heard the hurt in her voice, for he twisted about in the chair to look up at her, and though his gaze was at first unsympathetic, it softened.

'What do you mean?' he asked.

'You cannot have told me everything that happened to you. There must be more, to have changed you so much. If you won't tell me, how am I to understand? How am I to ease whatever troubles you if you shut me out?'

'No, no.' The affection in his voice rang hollow to Tara. She did not believe it, and did not know what to do with the horror, the crippling fear, that disbelief engendered. She loved this man with all her heart, and had never doubted his equal love for her. Yet now . . . now, she felt terribly alone.

'It's nothing,' Mordyn went on. 'I am troubled only by the amount that must be done, now that I have returned. There are so many demands upon my time, my thought. I'm sorry. I do not mean to cause you alarm, or concern.'

'You're so thin, so pale. You must be sick.' She could hope for that, in this horribly changed world; she could hope that her precious husband was sick, for it might explain, more gently and comprehensibly than any other explanation, why he had become a stranger to her. But he shook his head.

'I am well. Any pallor is only the mark of my travels, my tribulations. You will see: soon enough, I will have some fat back on these bones, some colour back in my cheeks. Do not worry.'

And he turned away from her again, bent back towards his writing table. That dismissal allowed anger to rise briefly through Tara's confusion and sorrow.

'What are you writing?' she asked sharply.

'Tedious matters. Nothing of consequence.'

'May I see it?' She reached over his shoulder and lifted a corner of the covering sheet. He slapped it down again.

'Please. I am in haste. Let me finish this in peace.'

Tara left without another word, forcing herself not to look

back as she went. She yearned to do so, to indulge the faint hope that she might find him gazing after her with all the old, profound love in his eyes, but she could hear that hateful quill scratching out its black path. He had forgotten her already, she knew; she, and all her concerns, had been expunged from his awareness in an instant. For years she had dwelled in the light of the warmest, most elevating sun imaginable. Now it was being extinguished, and the darkness descending upon her was all the deeper for the glory that had preceded it.

And, she reflected as she walked along a corridor of white marble, it had not even been his own hand in which her husband wrote. She knew his spidery, flowing script as well as she knew her own. Even that momentary glimpse of his work had been enough for her to know it was in another style altogether. He meant to conceal authorship of the text. Or his hand had changed along with his manner, his mood. His heart.

She paused at a narrow window that looked out over the rooftops towards the heart of Vaymouth. Gryvan's Moon Palace loomed like a pale mountain over the city. Snow was falling, drifting down in a slow, tumbling dance. Where once Tara might have seen a certain austere beauty, now she saw only bleakness.

IV

The Lannis warrior writhed on Malloc's spear like a great, impaled fish. Flopping around, he thought contemptuously. They die like animals. It was fitting.

The last of the Lannis men had fallen back to a bare knoll outside Kilvale. Only some thirty of them left now. The killing had begun before dawn, and carried on, in fits and starts, all through the grey morning. Most of them had died in the first hour, killed in their tents, beneath their blankets. Since then it had been more hunt than battle, the stragglers cornered in barns and orchards and ditches as they scattered. There had been, Malloc thought, perhaps two hundred of them when the cleansing began; now just these thirty, squatting atop the hillock, behind their wall of shields, their hedge of spears.

He ducked instinctively as arrows thrummed over his head. He freed his spear and trotted back to the Haig line. There was a great eagerness in him, so powerful it had him trembling, and it would be easy to give in to it, to go howling up the hill and throw himself at these traitors, these craven orphans of a shattered Blood. But he had spent half his life fighting in Gryvan oc Haig's service, and that long experience still spoke loudly enough – just – to restrain him. The final reckoning would not be long delayed. He could wait.

More than a hundred Haig warriors were massed at the base of the knoll, and more were constantly arriving, gradually spreading themselves out to encircle this last refuge of the Lannis survivors. Malloc pushed clumsily through the line of archers, ignoring the curses directed at him. He found his companions already resting on a grassy bank, sharing bread and water. One of them threw a cloth to him as he drew near.

'You've Lannis blood on your face.'

Malloc grunted and wiped his brow and cheeks.

'And you've none, I see,' he said to Garrent, his oldest friend, in the business of war at least. 'You been shirking?'

'They run too fast for me to catch them up,' Garrent said with a grin, shaking his left leg in Malloc's direction. He had twisted his ankle during the retreat from Kolkyre, and claimed it still hampered him.

Malloc slumped down beside him and grabbed the bread from his hand.

'Not running now,' he observed.

'More fool them. They'll last no longer than a maiden's virtue in Tal Dyre once there's a few more of us.'

Malloc looked around. A company of Taral-Haig horsemen was thundering up, their hide-armoured horses as menacing as the men who rode them. And behind them another fifty or more Haig spearmen came running, every eye fixed on their cowering quarry above. The archers had a rhythm now, flighting a steady shower of arrows up onto the hilltop. A few would surely find flesh.

'There's enough of us now,' Malloc muttered, tearing at the dry, hard bread.

'Oh, wait for the order, man. It'll come soon enough.'

'We're getting orders now?' Malloc said through a full mouth.

He had encountered no one who could say where the command for this had come from, whose the decision had been to settle with the Lannis men. Some murmured that Aewult nan Haig himself had issued the order, some that one or other of his Captains had taken it upon themselves. Malloc doubted such explanations. The killing had simply begun, in the night, like a rainstorm breaking of its own volition. Sometimes these things just happened because they had to.

The need for it had been building ever since word reached the army that the Bloodheir's messengers had been massacred in Ive. Lannis and Kilkry were already being blamed, around the campfires, for the mystifying defeats inflicted upon the Haig forces by the Black Road at Glasbridge and Kolkyre. Ever since then, it seemed to Malloc, the few Lannis warriors entangled in the Bloodheir's army had been marked men. The added weight of dead messengers had been too much for what little trust remained.

The army of the Black Road was not far away, though whether it still merited the title of army was uncertain. Those scouts Malloc had talked to reported thousands of the northerners spread across huge swathes of countryside in loose bands and companies, some of them in good order, some appearing to be leaderless mobs. Whatever their state, they could have attacked at any time in the last few days, but had not. Haig and Gyre thus faced one another in unresolved opposition, neither advancing, neither retreating. Malloc had not realised how agonising the tension had become until this bloody morning had offered itself up as release.

A single arrow skittered off the helm of a Haig swordsman further forward and spun into the long grass a few arms' lengths from Malloc.

'Toothless as old dogs, they are,' Garrent said.

It was true enough. It had all been too sudden, too fierce for much in the way of resistance. Malloc's one vague regret was that he had spent all morning struggling through wet fields and marshes in pursuit of fleeing Lannis men while – if the reports he had heard were true – others had found easier prey. Kilvale was full of Kilkry families exiled from their lands and homes by the Black Road's advance. Some of those who had been forced to take shelter in camps or farms outside the town itself, beyond the protection of Kilvale's Guard, had felt the force of Haig wrath today as well. Malloc would have liked to be a part of that. Lannis had never been much more than lackey to the arrogant inhabitants of Kolkyre's Tower of Thrones; if any Blood truly deserved chastisement, humbling, it was Kilkry.

But he had no complaint. He had killed, and would kill again before the day was out. And once it was all done, the army would be the stronger for it. Cleaner. Unreliable allies – traitorous ones – were worse than no allies at all. There was a healing to be had in this, a making right of so much that had been wrong. It took the edge off Malloc's shame at his flight – and that of so many other good Haig men – from the battle outside Kolkyre. A great deal had been inexplicably lost that day amidst the terrible, causeless panic that took hold of Aewult's army. Some of it, some respect, was recovered by this cutting out of the canker from their ranks.

If anything did trouble him, it was the unfamiliar joy this

carnage engendered in him. He had often found excitement in fighting, in ending a life and keeping his own, but this was different. This killing felt as if it somehow completed him, answered a fervent desire he had never before known. That seemed strange to him, but it was too sweet-tasting to concern him overly much. He wanted to drink still more deeply from this well.

There was a cry from up above. One of the Lannis spearmen fell forward from the shield wall, an arrow in the notch of his shoulder. He slid on his stomach a short way down the grassy slope as the shields closed up behind him. An arm stretched out, scrabbling at his ankle, trying to get a grip to haul him back. He was too heavy, and a further flurry of shafts quickly deterred the man who sought to help him.

'All be over soon,' Malloc murmured. It was odd that such a thought should stir regret, but it did.

'The Bloodheir,' said Garrent, suddenly leaping to his feet.

Malloc rose too. Everyone was stirring, making themselves appear ready and willing. Malloc craned his neck to get a glimpse of Aewult nan Haig.

The Bloodheir came with a dozen of his mighty Palace Shield, great men clad in metal, bearing pennanted lances, astride massive horses. Malloc smiled. Aewult himself was magnificent, cloak flowing from his shoulders, eyes fixed upon the miserable little crowd of warriors atop the hillock.

He drew his horse to a halt and bent to talk to someone in the throng that closed about him. Malloc had never been so close to any of his ruling house. To be able to see every line upon the Bloodheir's brow, the stitching in his great leather gauntlets, renewed his fervour. The urge to loose some wildly adulatory cry, perhaps draw a fragment of that noble attention to himself, was almost irresistible.

The Bloodheir straightened. He was nodding at something said to him.

'It's too late to do anything but finish it now,' Malloc heard him say. 'And if it's to be done, do it well. Make sure none escape.'

Those words were all it took. They spread through the Haig ranks, repeated by every eager mouth, and men began to move without waiting for any further command. One began to run, then another, then tens, then scores. Archers threw aside their bows, drew knives and rushed forward. All swarming up the slippery turf incline, all desperate to be in at the end of this, all filled with unreasoning, consuming hatred.

And Malloc was at the front of it, feeling as strong, as potent, as ever he had in his life. His legs pounded, his heart soared; they both carried him on and up to meet the waiting spears of a dying Blood.

V

Taim Narran could feel sweat slick on his back and shoulders beneath his shirt. Exertion made his face burn against the bitter air. Fatigue was building in his thighs. Yet still Orisian came at him. His Thane, less than half his age, battled on and on.

Taim retreated, a few quick steps back across the training ground, blocking sword blows with his shield as he went. Orisian came after him, on the very borders of control. It was often this way when the two of them fought. The longer the training bouts went on – and Orisian always insisted on extending them, pushing himself to his limits and beyond – the more aggressive the young Thane became, the more violent and unrestrained grew his attacks.

Taim let Orisian bear down on him, and twisted aside. Orisian went stumbling through and Taim gave him a smack on the side of his head with the flat of his blade as he went. To his credit, Orisian managed to keep his feet, staggering down almost to his knees before whirling about and surging up again.

The two of them battled back and forth. Servants had swept the training square free of snow, but the ground was still frozen, almost rock-like. Orisian's knuckles, even his cheek, were grazed from earlier falls. Nothing dimmed his willingness to come forward again and again, but exhaustion was at last blunting the ferocity of his attacks. His shield was drifting low, his feet becoming a touch sluggish.

Enough, Taim thought. He dropped his own guard just enough to offer temptation. Orisian lunged. Taim sidestepped, and brought his own shield up in a slicing arc. He opened Orisian's forehead with its rim. Orisian reeled, blood streaking down his face. Taim hooked a foot around the back of his knee, and sent him sprawling.

'We're done for today,' Taim said, kicking his Thane's sword away. 'You're not learning now, only exhausting yourself.'

Orisian struggled to his feet, wiping blood from his brow.

'I can carry on,' he said breathlessly. He looked around for his sword.

'Your mind's not clear enough,' Taim said. He sheathed his own sword.

'You told me once I had to fight by instinct, not by thinking.'

'True enough, but that only works with the right instincts. Anger fouls them up. Fight angry, and you won't fight long.'

Orisian looked downcast. 'I know. I try.'

'You do. And for as long as you concentrate and keep calm, you fight well. But something happens. You start fighting something more than just me.'

Orisian stooped to retrieve his blade. He made a clumsy effort to return it to its scabbard, missing at the first attempt.

'You must get that wound cleaned and bound,' Taim said.

'Yes,' murmured Orisian. He grimaced at his Captain. 'Did you have to hit me so hard?'

'Thought it might clear your head. It's not much more than a touch. It'll clean up fine.'

Orisian grunted, and walked slowly off towards the barracks. As Taim watched him go, he felt sorrow for the young man. He could not call it pity, for that was a sentiment Orisian would utterly refuse. Sorrow fitted better, in any case.

Taim was not certain what it was that came over Orisian when they trained. Some formless fury woke in him. Perhaps he became lost in the punishing rhythm of strike and counter-strike, parry and sidestep, and found himself battling against memories, or fears, or death itself. Perhaps each blow he aimed at Taim's shield was, for him, aimed rather at the whole array of enemies, and of misfortunes, that had taken his father from him, and Inurian. And Rothe.

That last death had been the one that finally and fatally weakened the child in Orisian, Taim reflected as he stamped smooth a few of the deeper marks they had gouged into the hard surface of the training ground during their bout. The second shieldman to die in Orisian's defence, and someone he had been wholly unready to lose. Nothing had been quite the same since then.

Taim shook the shield free from his left arm and took it towards the armoury. He walked slowly, for he was weary. And now that there were none to see, he allowed himself to limp. His thigh ached. Beneath his leggings, tight bandages covered the puncture marks and the prodigious bruise inflicted by that bone-encrusted Tarbain club. His weariness was not, though, so much of the body as of the mind and spirit.

Though he hid it meticulously from those around him, Orisian most of all, the days were taking a heavy toll. The fighting, the almost sleepless nights, the pervasive and insidious mood of despairing aggression. It all sapped his strength. And there was the sickening worry for his wife and his daughter, left behind in besieged Kolkyre. He had promised Jaen he would be there at her side when their grandchild was born. It would break his heart, and shame him, to fail in that promise.

Ranks of shields greeted him as he entered the armoury. They hung from the wall in overlapping rows. To call the place an armoury was overgenerous, in truth. It was little more than a storeroom, and a poorly ordered one at that. The shields might be neatly displayed, but spears were piled lazily and loosely against one wall. There were quivers of arrows in one corner, their flights frayed and broken. Taim hung his shield with the others. He closed the door behind him and made for the barracks.

What he wanted, with all his heart, was to be with his family, in front of a warming fire, talking of idle and foolish matters. But no matter how fervent that desire, Taim could contain it – much of the time, at least – within a sealed and silent chamber deep within himself. There were other promises that bound him, and even at the cost of a broken heart, he could not turn aside from them. He had pledged his life to the Blood, to the service of its Thane. For Taim that remained the greater part of what gave his life meaning.

There was a blinding white sun in the sky, unfettered by clouds for the first time in days. But its light seemed more to expose the world than to illuminate it. It sharpened every edge, bared everything beneath its cold wash.

As Taim walked along Ive's main street his nostrils were filled with the smell of wet ash. He passed by a long stretch of houses gutted and tumbled by the recent fires. Every detail, every seam and stain of the charred timbers, every smoke scar smearing across the stonework, was clear, precisely delineated by this acute winter light. He could hear an argument somewhere, a man and woman raging at one another. He could hear a baby crying too, off in another direction. In the raw, despairing need of that wail he sensed the expression of something deep. Something of the tune to which the world now danced.

He found Torcaill at the town's edge, standing with a dozen of his men. They were watching a band of townsfolk struggling eastwards across a field, leading a pair of mules that bore huge packs.

'There are scores of them leaving now,' Torcaill muttered. 'They think Ive's finished.'

'They're right,' Taim said. 'Where are they going?'

'I don't think they know that themselves. Most head east, hoping to lose themselves in the mountains or the woods.'

'They'll have a hard time of it out there. Bad weather, not enough food.'

'They will. Worse than hard, a lot of them. But it's their choice. If they lack the spirit to fight for their town, their Blood, they must bear the consequences.'

Taim glanced sideways at the younger man. Torcaill's vehemence was striking, and his eyes as he watched the departing townsfolk gleamed with a cold contempt. That anger that lurked beneath so many surfaces now was there, unforgiving, judging.

'They want to live,' Taim murmured. 'Keep their families, their children, alive. There's no shame in that. They've already seen indisputable proof that we can't keep the Black Road out of their town. If I wore their clothes, I'd do the same.'

A flock of birds shot up from a copse beyond the field. They sprayed out in all directions from the treetops, then veered back together and went arrowing together out of sight into the east.

'How's your leg?' Torcaill asked.

Taim shrugged. 'Wound's not gone bad so far. Any word from the scouts?'

'Half of them have disappeared,' sighed Torcaill. 'Killed somewhere out there, or fled perhaps. As for the rest . . . there're Tarbains burning farms half a day west of here. The army you fought on the south road is still there, camped at some village. There's another, bigger, in the hills to the west. My men saw their fires last night. They could be on us tomorrow, if they choose.'

Taim nodded. 'We're finished, then. Here, at least. If we stay, we're done.'

'Perhaps.' Torcaill's assent was grudging. He wanted to fight. 'Have you talked to Orisian about it?'

'He knows it as well as we do. He wants to meet with us, all of us, this afternoon. After the oath-taking. I think he'll tell us then what he means to do.'

Torcaill pushed forefinger and thumb into his eyes, grinding away the tiredness Taim knew must be lodged there. Nobody was sleeping well.

'They're to go ahead with that, then?' the younger man asked heavily. 'The oath-taking, I mean?'

'Why not?' Taim said.

Torcaill shrugged, but made no reply.

'Orisian is Thane of our Blood.' Taim turned away, heading back into the town's heart. 'Those who wish to take the oath in his name have the right. The duty.'

'But we've no Oathmen, have we?' Torcaill called after him. 'They're all dead. Or lost.'

'I'm to do it,' Taim said as he walked, perhaps too softly for the other man to hear. 'I'm to wield the knife.'

The boy was eight years old. Small and nervous. Perhaps more than nervous, for he paled as his gaze settled upon the knife held in his mother's open palm.

'In the name of Sirian and Powll, Anvar and Gahan and Tavan and Croesan, the Thanes who have been; of Orisian oc Lannis-Haig, the Thane who is now; and of the Thanes yet to come, I command you all to hear the bloodoath taken,' Taim intoned. The words sat strangely in his mouth. They were ancient, weighty words that only Oathmen should speak. 'I am Thane and Blood, past and future, and this life will be bound to mine. I command you all to mark it.'

The boy was looking up at him now, eyes wide. Taim tried to

smile at him, but found the expression difficult, as if it knew it did not truly belong in this moment. He turned instead to the mother, and held out his hand.

'The blade is fresh-forged?' he asked her. 'Unbloodied? Unmarked?'

'Never used,' she murmured, and passed the short simple knife to him.

Behind him, Taim could hear feet scraping on the floor as someone shifted position. Not Orisian, he suspected. The Thane had worn a solemn demeanour from the moment this woman first came to him asking that her son should take the bloodoath. The first time his name would be at the centre of this, the ritual heart of his Blood, and it was happening in exile from their rightful lands, in a hall borrowed for the occasion, with a mere warrior playing the makeshift role of Oathman. In the shadow of uncounted deaths. Not how any of them would have wished it to be, yet there was a weight to it, an importance. Taim felt it as much anyone, perhaps more than most. He tightened his grip upon the blade, and moistened his lips. He took hold of the boy's wrist and gently twisted it to expose the white skin of his underarm.

'You will give of your blood to seal this oath?' he asked the child.

A moment's silence, and then the boy whispered, 'I will.'

'Speak up, boy,' Taim said softly. 'Let them hear you.'

'I will.' Louder this time, but still tremulous. Good enough, Taim thought.

'By this oath your life is bound to mine,' he said. 'The word of the Thane of Lannis is your law and rule . . .' His tongue stumbled to a halt. Something had gone awry, and after a moment he realised what it was. Lannis-Haig, of course. It should have been Lannis-Haig. But something hardened in him, and he went on. 'Your law and rule, as the word of a father is to a child. Your life is the life of the Lannis Blood.'

He heard the softest of murmurs amongst the onlookers. Some, at least, had noticed his omission. None raised any protest. Such was the nature of the times.

Taim drew the blade across the boy's arm. He felt the briefest, instinctive tensing of the muscles, the slight tug against his firm grip. The child looked away. It was a shallow cut, and clean. A neat line of blood swelled out, but did not run.

'You pledge your life to the Lannis Blood?' Taim asked.

The boy nodded once, still averting his eyes.

'You must say it,' Taim murmured.

'Yes.'

'You bend the knee to the Thane, who is the Blood?' Taim released the boy's arm. He set his thumb against the flat of the knife, smearing a trace of the child's blood across it.

'I do.'

'Then none may come between you and this oath.' Taim stared at the thick fluid smudged across the dull metal. Such small things, this deed, these words, yet containing so much. Containing within their narrow bounds as much of his own life, as much of his history and meaning, as anything could. The mother must have thought the same, to seek out this moment for her son. Fleeing from horrors, she had found herself in an unknown town, destitute, amidst chaos; yet there too she happened to find her Thane, and from that turn of fortune she sought to give her child this boon. Perhaps the boy would not recognise it for the gift it was. Perhaps that would only come later; perhaps never.

'None may come between you and this oath,' Taim said. 'By it you set aside all other allegiances. The Blood shall sustain you and bear you up. You shall sustain the Blood. Speak your oath.'

The boy looked up from his wound. And Taim found he could smile at him now, an honest smile of reassurance and encouragement.

'I am Tollen Lanan dar Lannis-Haig . . . dar Lannis . . . son of

Cammenech and Inossa. By my blood I pledge my life to Lannis. The word of the Thane is my law and rule; it is the root and . . . and staff of my life. The enemy of the Blood is my enemy. My enemy is the enemy of the Blood. Unto death.'

'Unto death,' Taim said. He pressed the hilt of the oathknife into the boy's hand, and watched those thin fingers close about it. 'Unto death.'

'I didn't know there were so many of our people in Ive,' Torcaill said, after they had retired to a table in one corner of the barracks' main hall. Many of those who had gathered to witness the taking of the oath had dispersed. A few remained, scattered around nearby tables, taking grateful advantage of the food provided by the town's Guard.

'So many?' Orisian said. 'Less than a hundred, if you leave out our warriors. A handful, no more.'

'True enough,' Torcaill persisted, through a mouthful of dry bread, 'but they've come a long way to reach here. There could have been fewer. Far fewer.'

'I suppose so,' Orisian murmured.

Taim watched him as Orisian absently scratched at the scar across his cheek. He looked tired, but there was a certain stillness to him now, a settled quality that seemed new. Perhaps the boy – Tollen – had not been the only one offered an anchor by the taking of his oath.

'Those who've come so far already will have to move on again now,' Orisian said quietly. 'We should spread the word that their flight's not finished yet. It's not safe for any of us to remain here.'

'No,' Taim agreed. He kept his voice low too, recognising Orisian's instinct to keep such conversation from uninvited ears. Yvane and Eshenna, he noticed, were maintaining a studious, and somewhat contrived, inattention. The two *na'kyrim*, though they sat at Orisian's side, paid no heed to his words.

It might well be that these *na'kyrim* already knew more of his Thane's thoughts than Taim did himself. He had the sense that Orisian had deliberately excluded him, and Torcaill, and all the other warriors, from much of what passed between the three of them. He neither regretted nor resented that fact. A Thane could take such counsel as he saw fit, and Taim was in any case all but certain that their discussions concerned matters he understood – and desired to understand – nothing of.

'Ive is lost – and so are all who remain here – as soon as the Black Road chooses to make it so,' Orisian said.

'It is,' Taim confirmed. 'Tomorrow or the day after. Soon, in any case. Erval tells me the fighting men are already slipping away; fleeing with their families. The only thing that's delayed the end so far is that the Black Road seem to be losing discipline just as we are. But with or without leadership, they'll overrun us.'

Orisian nodded. 'I mean to take K'rina north.'

A horrified expression instantly appeared on Torcaill's face.

'North?' the younger warrior gasped. Taim hissed at him, and extended a monitory finger. Out of the corner of his eye, he could already see heads turning at some of the other tables.

Torcaill spoke more softly when he went on, but he did not disguise the disbelief, the disapproval, in his voice. 'We'd be stepping from storm into fire if we go north. What safety could we possibly find there?'

'How much can we find anywhere?' Orisian quietly countered. 'There're Black Road armies to the south and the west; too many for us to cut our way through. Nothing to the east but mountains, hunger and cold. Miserable as it is, that's the best chance for most of these people, but it's not for us. You want your Thane wandering off to starve in the wilderness? Chased off by the Black Road?'

'But what's to the north?' Torcaill muttered.

'There's Highfast,' Orisian said quietly.

'We don't even know if it's still standing,' Torcaill said. 'It could have a thousand Black Road swords inside it.'

'No,' Orisian replied. He remained entirely calm in the face of Torcaill's hostile tone. 'There were some captives taken in the fighting. Most were killed by the townsfolk, but Erval's men got one or two into their cellars. I had him . . . I had him find out what they knew of Highfast.' Orisian failed to suppress the grimace of discomfort – or guilt, perhaps – the words cost him. He looked not at Torcaill but at Taim. 'I thought I . . . I thought *we* needed to know.'

'Such things must be done sometimes,' Taim said in response to the anguish he saw in those young eyes. It seemed the kindest service he could offer his Thane at that moment. But he wondered where within him Orisian was finding the will to issue such commands. The youth he had once known would never have done so, he thought.

'And you trust their word?' Torcaill muttered.

'If they lied, they took the truth with them to the Sleeping Dark. But those who questioned them didn't think they were lying.'

'So Highfast has not fallen?' Taim asked.

Orisian shook his head. 'They all say not. And whatever rumours have been brought by the Kilkry folk who've sought refuge here say the same thing. It makes sense. Why would the Black Road spend any effort on it? It has no great garrison; it guards no road, or harbour, or farms. They know – everybody knows – it's all but impossible to take by siege, no matter how feebly defended.'

'I thought . . .' Taim murmured, glancing towards the two *na'kyrim*, 'I thought its defences had already been breached.'

'It was breached by something no walls could keep out,' said Yvane flatly without looking up. 'And by something that would leave those walls intact once it departed.'

'What if it didn't depart?' Torcaill demanded, that provocative edge still sharpening his voice.

Yvane turned slowly, twisting not just her neck but her shoulders round to fix the warrior with a hard, cold stare.

'There were . . . we felt deaths – *na'kyrim* dying – on that one day, but not since. We don't think everyone died. Not every light was snuffed out. Whatever disaster befell Highfast, it was not done to capture a fortress, or win a battle. It may not even have had anything to do with your bitter little war. There are other kinds of struggle. Hard to believe, I'm sure, but true nonetheless.'

Torcaill narrowed his eyes, but lapsed into angry silence.

'Still,' Taim said to Orisian, 'Highfast . . . Once there, we might find there's no way out.'

And he saw, in Orisian's eyes, a moment of distraction, of concealment. Of shutters being closed, locking away words that might have been spoken. Anything he says is only part of what's in his mind, Taim thought. There is more to this, perhaps, than Highfast.

'I see no safety whatever way we turn,' was what Orisian did say. 'We've already almost lost Yvane and Eshenna and K'rina. Can we keep them safe, or the Kyrinin, even amongst those who are supposed to be our friends? I don't think so.'

'But your people need their Thane, sire,' Torcaill said. 'They need to know that he's—'

'I have no people!' Orisian snapped. The sudden anger was transitory, but it startled Torcaill. He winced.

'A few dozen homeless wanderers?' Orisian went on, his composure reasserting itself. 'That's no Blood. And our handful of swords can make no difference when Gyre and Haig are throwing thousands against one another. *I* can make no difference. I'm no warlord, no hero. Croesan, or Naradin, or Fariel even; any one of them might have been fit to lead armies in the field, and fight great battles alongside their men. Not me.'

He did not sound apologetic or ashamed; he merely spoke a truth he believed.

'You have Captains to do that for you,' Taim said quietly.

'Yes, I do. Great ones. But I don't have the armies for them to lead. Our Blood is broken, Taim. Our people are dead, enslaved or scattered; our castles are overthrown. We are exiled from our lands.'

'Sooner or later, Haig's strength will tell.'

'Will it? I don't know. The war against the armies of the Black Road: perhaps it's not the one that really matters. Or not the only one, at least.'

'Aeglyss, you mean?'

'The world's changing around us. You feel it, don't you?' Orisian looked questioningly at Taim, and at Torcaill. 'Can't you feel the twisting of things in your heart, your mind? I don't sleep, so dark are my dreams. If I walk in Ive's streets, in every eye I see tinder, waiting only for some spark to turn it into a raging fire. I killed — and you did, Torcaill,— Kilkry men who had no thought save to shed blood. They're supposed to be our allies. It's all slipping away into chaos.'

He had been leaning forward in his chair, tightened by an urgency, a fierce desire to convey what he saw and felt. Now he slumped back.

'It may be that when we seized K'rina, we broke a thread in a pattern that was being woven. It may have been a mistake. I need to see if it can be undone. Anyway, Torcaill, I'll only ask you to come as far as Ive Bridge. Once we're sure the way to Highfast is clear, there's something else I'll want of you.'

'You need *ask* nothing of me, sire,' the warrior said sharply. 'Only command. Your will governs us in all of this.'

He clearly meant what he said, despite his earlier truculence. Orisian only nodded, and Taim thought he saw a hint of sadness in the set of the Thane's mouth. There were burdens there still, in the making of choices on behalf of others and the exercise of authority. However hard he tries, Taim thought, whatever cruelty he might permit in his name, this one will never have quite the cold instinct for it. He will never sit easy on a throne. But then perhaps Orisian did not, after all, truly believe there was any throne left for him to sit upon.

They each went their own way from that table: Orisian to speak with Ess'yr and Varryn, Taim to see what supplies he might buy or otherwise acquire without arousing alarm or suspicion amongst their Kilkry hosts, Torcaill to ready the warriors. Taim got no further than the outer yard of the barracks before he became aware of soft footsteps trailing him. He turned to find Yvane drawing near, stern-faced.

'Your Thane folds in on himself,' she said. 'Withdraws. He feels himself alone and adrift, and in response makes himself so. There are shadows, calling him into themselves.'

'He has been roughly treated by the world of late.'

'For many years, I think. I don't condemn him. All I say is, these are dangerous times for those with flaws in their armour. The houses with cracked foundations are the first to fall in a storm.'

'I didn't know you were a master builder,' Taim muttered. 'Or an armourer, for that matter.' The *na'kyrim*'s manner irritated him, though he recognised her intent. She did, he believed, feel a certain sincere concern for Orisian. As far as Taim could tell, the young Thane was uniquely honoured in that regard, since no one else save other *na'kyrim* seemed to merit it.

'He needs friends,' said Yvane, 'and may need them still more before long. Your hothead of a swordsman was part right: we *are* stepping from storm into fire, but this storm isn't one we can leave behind. It goes with us. Inside us.'

'Have you advised Orisian against it, then? If you think this leads us into . . .'

'Ha. You can be certain there's none less eager than me to revisit whatever's left of Highfast. But Orisian follows his instincts. And he may be right. Perhaps the only way to calm this storm, quench this fire, is from the inside.'

'Well, then. I'll walk at his side, wherever he goes.'

'I know. You seem to have the calmest head around here, the least open to the poison that's leaking into so many others. That's good. I don't know what it is that anchors you, but whatever it is, I hope it's stubborn enough to last. Stay close by Orisian, if you care for him, and watch him. If his sight becomes clouded, he'll need those whose eyes remain clear.'

'There's nothing wrong with his sight,' Taim said, bristling at the implied lack of faith in Orisian's resilience, or his judgement. 'Anyway, you've never seemed shy of making your opinion known. Don't you plan on being there, to polish his eyes for him?'

And the sudden sadness in her pale face – harbinger, it seemed to him, of a desolate despair that the *na'kyrim* barely held at bay – startled him into shame at his bitter tone.

'As I said,' Yvane sighed, 'these are dangerous times for those with flaws in their armour. But we *na'kyrim*, we have no armour at all against this. We're all flaw, our heads wide open to it. Believe me, I fear for your beloved Thane, but I like my own chances a good deal less than his. There may come a time when the very last people he should be listening to will be those who've woken to the Shared.'

She hung her head, as if momentarily defeated by the darkness of possible futures. Taim had never seen her give such an unguarded impression of vulnerability. He felt an urge to reach out and put a comforting hand on her arm, but he did not. He suspected there was enough prickly pride left in there to make any such gesture inadvisable.

'Just watch him,' she murmured. 'Help him if he needs it, and if you can. That's all I'm saying.'

'It doesn't need saying,' Taim said gently. 'I'd never do otherwise.'

Yvane nodded once and turned away, disappearing into the barracks. Taim looked after her, filled for a moment or two with an impotent sense of foreboding, not just for Yvane or Orisian, but all of them. Everyone caught in this churning maelstrom.

VI

Anyara woke in a sweat, with a soft cry and a racing heart. In her dreams she had been pursued by a twisted, bestial form of herself, driven wild by fear and anger and grief. The roiling darkness that had been all about her had thickened and churned to prevent her escape, holding her for her own clawed fingers to rend.

She wiped her brow, pulled her cloyingly damp nightgown away from her skin. These cruel dreams had ebbed a little in the first few days of her enforced sojourn in Vaymouth. Now they had returned with renewed and hungry vigour. Each night she spent in the Palace of Red Stone, they came more fiercely than the last. A few tears ran down her face, the echo of the unconstrained, fevered emotions of her sleep. She brushed them away and rose, feeling heavy, from the bed.

In the night, the palace was perfectly silent. Faint moonlight fell through the windows. The air was cool and still. Anyara settled a heavy robe about her shoulders and pulled its fur collar tight about her throat. She slipped her feet into soft hide sandals and went out into the passageway.

'All you all right?'

The voice startled her. Coinach stepped forward into the soft pool of silver shed by a little skylight.

'I forgot you were here.' Anyara smiled.

'Always. I thought I heard you but was not sure. I should have come in to check.'

'No, no.' Anyara waved her shieldman's self-doubt away. 'I'm fine. Can't sleep, that's all.'

She glanced at the simple wooden chair let into an alcove where Coinach spent each night.

'You can't get much sleep either, I imagine,' she said.

'I am not here to sleep, my lady. But I've had much worse beds in my time, in any case.' They both spoke in whispers. The heavy silence of the palace felt insistent, as if it would resent any attempt to disturb it.

'Will you walk with me a little?' Anyara asked. 'My head needs clearing.'

They went together along the corridor, the sound of their careful footsteps sighing along the stone walls ahead of them. From each narrow window high in those walls a diffuse beam of moonlight descended to illuminate them as they passed beneath it. There was the faintest lingering scent on the air, like a memory of warmer days.

'What is that smell?' Anyara murmured. 'It never seems to quite go away.'

'The Shadowhand's wife roasts spices on her braziers,' Coinach whispered.

'Oh. I never thought to ask her.'

Anyara led the way into a long, thin room that ran along the side of the palace. Facing them were tall, barred doors inlaid with patterns of pearl and dark wood. Anyara went to one and lifted the thin beam that held it closed.

'I'd like to see the moon,' she said.

But Coinach gently interposed himself.

'They sometimes have guards out on the terraces. Best to let me go first.'

He pulled open the great shutter, and the cold night air swept in. Anyara closed her eyes for a moment, savouring its cleansing flow over her face, through her hair.

'Come,' Coinach said. 'There's no one here.'

They stepped out onto the narrow terrace. Before them Vaymouth was a dark ocean, speckled with just a few faint points of light, bounded by the smooth, dark curve of its walls as they swept away into the distance. The Moon Palace rose, a lambent mass, above the city's heart, as if some wan, sickly giant had hunched his shoulders up out of dark earth. Anyara turned about, searching instead for the true moon. It stood just above the city wall, bright and large. She gazed up at it, letting its light fill her eyes and her mind for a moment. Then she dropped her head, and looked back to the sleeping city.

'Vaymouth's bigger than I ever imagined,' she said. 'I knew but didn't know. That sounds stupid, doesn't it?'

'No, my lady.'

'I'm afraid,' Anyara said abruptly, surprising herself. She had not meant to say that, yet the sound of the words seemed right. Fitting. 'I thought I could bear everything, anything, if I had to. I thought I'd mastered it, but now it's growing heavy again, all the fear and the sorrow. I don't want to be frightened. I hate it.'

Coinach was looking at her, but his face was in shadow and she could not be sure what expression he wore. She did not know quite what she wanted from him. Still, she felt an unexpected easing within her, now that she had permitted this small fraction of her fragility to show itself.

Out in Vaymouth's great darkness: a blooming orange glow, much stronger and larger than any of the other tiny lights shining there. Anyara frowned at it, puzzled. Coinach followed her gaze. The glow spread, and splayed itself outwards and upwards, a fiery fist swelling and then unfurling thick fingers of flame that reached for the star-strewn sky.

'That'll be an unpleasant waking for someone,' Coinach said softly.

There was another, further off, in an entirely different quarter of the city: another seed of fire that flickered into being and then built and built. The nocturnal silence that had seemed so natural before now felt out of place. The flames clambered ferociously higher and higher, their hearts turning white, but no sound reached the Palace of Red Stone. There was scent, though, the first bitter trace of smoke in the air.

'Look, there's a third,' Coinach said, pointing out into the night.

'And there,' said Anyara.

It seemed that every part of Vaymouth had its own eruption of consuming flame. The Moon Palace was growing dimmer, obscured by drifting smoke, its reflected moonlight outshone by a wilder, more sinister light. And the first sounds reached Anyara's ears: a murmur of calamity, anguished cries blunted and flattened by distance, the roaring of delirious firestorms made into a whisper.

'What's happening?' she wondered.

'I don't know.'

Anyara shifted uneasily. There was too much of the quality of her dreams about this. Too much of the madness she felt running beneath the skin of the world, like a black river under a carapace of ice.

'We should never have come,' she said, staring out at the beacons of destruction that marked out the whole territory of the city. 'I thought we could serve best by letting Aewult have his way. I thought there might be opportunity . . . but none of it's turning out as I hoped. We should have fought our way out of Aewult's camp rather than let him make us prisoners.'

'I would gladly have made the attempt, my lady, had you asked it of me. He had some ten thousand warriors, so I fear it might have proved difficult. Still, I would have made the attempt.'

*

'I will see it!' Gryvan oc Haig snapped at Kale.

That flare of anger was enough to make the shieldman nod curtly and avert his eyes.

'As you wish, sire,' the lean warrior said, nudging his horse on ahead.

'I will see what's done to my city!' Gryvan shouted after his guardian. 'It is my right, my duty!'

His own vehemence shocked him, and made him a little ashamed. He glanced uncomfortably around. Many in the mass of riders were looking at him. All, at least, had the grace to turn away when his own gaze fell upon them. It was unwise, Gryvan knew, to flaunt his anger – his confusion, if he was honest – so brazenly, before so many eyes, but his grip on his emotions grew daily less sure. They tore their way up through him, every setback bringing them closer to boiling over. He imagined them as some pack of beasts clawing at his innards, consuming him from within.

A hundred of his warriors, led by Kale and the rest of his Shield, surrounded him. He was within the walls of his own impregnable, wondrous city. Yet despite all of this, Gryvan felt exposed. Assailed. The faces of his people, who thronged the streets this morning and watched his passing from every window and doorway, seemed inimical to him. But he could no longer tell whether that was their true character, or whether he only painted them with his own bitter bewilderment at the course of events.

'The Captain of your Shield is quite right, sire,' Mordyn Jerain said, settling his own horse into step with Gryvan's. 'The city's mood is fragile. Caution would be wise.'

'They set a dozen fires,' Gryvan hissed, wrestling his voice into submission. 'Ten people dead, I hear. Someone thinks they can torch my city with impunity. Well, I'll see their handiwork. And then I'll see them, whoever they are, broken on wheels, and spitted on stakes and have their heads rolled in the dirt at my feet.'

'Quite so. I wish we could have spoken before riding out, though. There is much I wanted to discuss with you today. Had you not been already mounted when I reached the palace . . .'

'Now, suddenly, you want to talk? Well, it can wait an hour or two yet. Gods, does this not sicken you with fury? How can you be so unmoved? We made this city what it is together, you and I. It's your child as much as mine.'

'Children heal quickly, sire.'

Gryvan heard – or imagined, he could not be sure which – dismissive insolence in that reply and twisted in his saddle to snarl at his Chancellor. But Mordyn was looking away, angling his head up towards the rooftops.

'What's that?' Mordyn muttered.

Gryvan's anger faltered. He crushed the reins in his frustrated hands. But there *was* a sound, clattering in over the tiled roofs. Gryvan listened for a moment or two, teasing it out from amongst the rattle of hoofs on cobbles. He did not know what to make of it at first. Its nature was elusive, as if it both belonged and did not belong in the city. Then he had it. Riot. Mob.

'Swords,' he cried at once. He bared his own blade.

Kale was riding towards him, shouting at the lines of warriors as he came.

'You should turn back, sire,' the shieldman said to his Thane, quite calm. 'There is disorder up ahead.'

'No,' said Gryvan flatly. In this, suddenly, he found an answer to all the tumultuous ire that had been building in him for so long. His body knew what kind of release it required, and already his heart was pounding in anticipation. He dug his heels into his horse's flanks and the great beast sprang forward.

A crowd was surging through a little marketplace. It tore at shuttered windows, rendered barrels, stalls, even an old abandoned wagon, down to fragments of wood, and then sent that debris flying up in a cloud of useless missiles. It surged around the well at the centre of the square, and crushed its human bodies against the stone parapet. It overturned a massive watering trough and broke in the door of a long-empty hovel.

Down upon this ravening beast, the High Thane's hundred warriors fell like thunder. Gryvan himself was in the midst of the storm, seized by a bloodthirsty rage. He and his father, and his grandfather before that, had made this city and its people all that they now were. That there should be arson, that mobs should rampage through the streets – these things were an affront to the Haig line. They wounded him as surely as any blow to his own flesh. He would wet the streets of his wondrous city with the blood of those who offered such grievous offence.

Gryvan's sword rose and fell. He felt the shiver of its impact upon bone tingling up his arm. He felt the breaking of bodies that went down beneath his huge horse. A thousand voices, crying out in anguish, or anger, or pain, or terror, washed over him and he revelled in the fierce noise. He cut and slashed and barged his way to the heart of the square. A youth was standing on the rim of the well, lashing out with a length of wood. Gryvan cut his legs from under him, sent him tumbling back and down into the dark, stone-clad gullet.

The crowd fell away beneath the onslaught. What the city's Guard had been unable to quell, the hundred trained warriors on their warhorses snuffed out quickly and brutally. The passions that had burned in the breasts of the rioters twisted into terror. They scattered, and the riders went after them and cut them down in side streets and doorways. Gryvan sat astride his mount, sword still naked in his hand, surrounded by gore and corpses.

Kale dismounted and tore something from the neck of one of the bodies. He held it up to the High Thane.

'Most of them are Craftsmen, sire. Apprentices, at least.'

He dropped the clasp into Gryvan's outstretched palm. It bore the impressed image of a tiny hammer and scales.

'Goldsmith,' Gryvan murmured. He was weary now. Drained.

'Yes.' Kale nodded. 'Many bear the same badge, or that of other Crafts. A number of their buildings were amongst those burned last night. They seek those responsible, perhaps.'

'And they think that gives them leave to run rampant through my city?' Gryvan growled.

'There are too many who think they need no longer ask our leave to do anything,' Mordyn Jerain said, coming – now that the slaughter was done – to his master's side. 'The world ever seeks to test the will of great men. Now is the time of your testing.'

'And you've a thought on how I should meet it. Is that it?'

Mordyn Jerain dipped his head in knowing assent.

'Very well,' Gryvan said, casting a last, simmering eye over the bodies littering the market square. 'All of this must be answered. I'll hear you.'

'No.' Gryvan shook his head. It was part denial, part disbelief, part astonishment at the thought that what his Shadowhand was saying might be true.

'Yes,' insisted Mordyn quietly. 'Have I ever failed you, sire?'

'Not in anything of consequence,' Gryvan muttered.

'Indeed. Then trust me in this: a corruption has entered the heart of your domains. That which threatens to consume us comes not from without, but within.'

Gryvan paced up and down over the thick mottled rug. The beaker of wine in his hand was forgotten.

'Why did you not tell me all of this at once, immediately on your return?' he cried.

'I doubted it, sire. How could I not? Such things strain the sinews of belief. I thought it prudent to conduct certain investigations of my own. Now I have the sad proofs.' The Chancellor unfurled a roll of parchments from a tube at his belt. 'Copies of letters I was shown in Anduran, during my captivity. Messages the Black Road discovered there. Others I have found for myself since my return. And all sing the same foul melody, sire.'

Gryvan slammed his cup down on an ornate little table. He ignored the manuscripts that Mordyn held out to him.

'I'll not trust a single word that comes from the mouth of the Black Road,' he snarled.

'A wise precaution.' Mordyn nodded placidly. The tumultuous emotions that raged within Gryvan found no reflection in
his Chancellor. There was a calmness about the man that would
better suit reports of the weather. 'They no doubt take delight in
pointing out the rot within our own house. Yet whether or not
you choose to trust their intent in sharing their discoveries with
me, there is a truth to be discerned. A pattern.'

Gryvan threw himself down into a chair so violently that it
rocked back on its legs.

'Conspiracy against me? Against Haig?'

The Shadowhand rolled the parchments up once more and
slipped them back into their tube. He set it down beside the
High Thane's discarded wine cup.

'I will leave these for you to examine at your leisure, if you see
fit. But yes: conspiracy. The Crafts conspired with the Dornach
Kingship, promising to deliver up the Dargannan Blood even as
they were trying to buy its future Thane. They urged Lheanor oc
Kilkry-Haig to throw off his duties to you, and he in his turn
promised them free rein if they could foster war between us and
Dornach, and raise him up to be High Thane in your stead.'

'This is insanity,' breathed Gryvan.

'Of a kind,' the Chancellor nodded. 'Madness born of hatred
and ambition and greed. We have been slowly, quietly betrayed,
sire. For many years. Until the Black Road entered the fray, the
treacheries were discreet and careful. Now . . . now, our enemies
have been intoxicated by the chaos, mistaking it for our weakness. They become incautious. Aewult's every effort against the
Black Road was hindered – blatantly, fragrantly – by Lannis and
Kilkry.'

'I thought his accusations absurd,' Gryvan growled. 'Flailings
born of humiliation.'

'As might I, sire, had I not witnessed some of it for myself.
You know I would not absolve the Bloodheir of blame had he
earned it. He did not. I saw the contempt, the defiance, with

which he was treated. How else but by treachery can we explain his defeat, when he had ten thousand of your finest warriors at his back? And you've heard the same tale I have, of what happened to Aewult's messengers when they sought out the Lannis boy?'

'In Ive. Yes. Murdered.' Gryvan rubbed his brow. He felt overwhelmed. And his head ached.

'Indeed. Neither Lannis nor Kilkry Bloods has ever acceded, in their hearts, to your family's rule. And the Crafts . . . well, your rule has swelled their coffers, yet they have learned not gratitude, but ambition. Arrogance. The Goldsmiths stir up discontent; they send their mobs raging through the streets of your city like wild animals. My people have already heard it whispered in taverns and workshops that the Crafts set those fires themselves, as pretext. But a man whose enemies assemble to assail him is as much benefited as beset, for they reveal themselves.'

Gryvan frowned at his Chancellor.

'You begin to see, do you not?' murmured Mordyn, stepping closer. There was an eager edge to him suddenly. His eyes burned with a passion Gryvan had not seen there since his return from the north.

'See what?' the High Thane asked.

'A thousand years of history have taught us that it takes great men, strong men, to impose order upon this world. It takes men with the will to seize whatever opportunities chaos offers up; the will to bend events to the shape of their own desires. Grey Kulkain did it, forging the Bloods from the horrors of the Storm Years. Your own family has done it, rising from the disasters of the Black Road's very birth to overthrow Kilkry's dominion. Such momentous times are come again, sire. Your time.'

Gryvan rose once more to his feet. He clasped his hands behind his back and went to the nearest of the tall windows, through which a bleak light fell. There was his city, his precious city, arrayed before him in all its expansive wonder. His gaze fell upon the gaudy tower the Gemsmiths had recently chosen to adorn their Crafthouse with. A prideful statement, that. Perhaps one of intent also. He chewed his lip.

'The opportunity is here,' he heard Mordyn saying behind him. 'If we but have the courage to imagine it.'

'You doubt my mettle?' Gryvan asked darkly without turning round.

'No, sire. Never.'

Gryvan stared down at his black boots. His sons were flawed – he knew that – yet still they were his sons, and entitled to receive from him the same legacy he had inherited from his father: the ascendancy of the Haig Blood; order and security, imposed upon the turbulent peoples of these lands through strength, and through force of will. He could feel his cheeks colouring, a hot flush of rage at the thought that those who dwelled beneath the protective aegis of Haig power would dare to conspire against it.

'I was released by Ragnor oc Gyre's Captains as a token of their benign intent,' Mordyn said. 'The influence of the most bellicose factions within the Black Road is dwindling. They had slipped from Ragnor's control for a time, it's true, but that has changed. They understand that they cannot prevail against our martial strength, whatever minor victories they might have won thus far.'

Gryvan closed his eyes against the pounding ache that was building in his skull. His hands, still clasped behind his back, tightened, the fingers bars of steel locked around one another.

'They will retire from all the lands they have occupied,' Mordyn continued. 'They will withdraw across the Stone Vale, and make over to you all the territory they have seized. To you personally, sire, not to Kilkry or Lannis. They pledge a permanent peace, on condition that you rule those lands directly and unmake the Bloods that formerly held them. Ragnor knows that without Kilkry and Lannis to stir up these ancient, dry troubles, there can be peace between our peoples. In pursuit of the same quarry, he pledges in his turn to wipe away the Horin Blood.'

'Peace . . .' rasped Gryvan.

'The better to deal with those enemies that lie more nearly at hand. The Crafts. Dornach. The time is ripe. Everything you have long dreamed of lies before you now, sire. It is all possible, now that they have revealed themselves. We have only to reach out and grasp the future, to make it real.'

'I need . . .' Gryvan's tongue stumbled over his own words. There was some part of him that feared the fell anger, the grasping hunger, roiling in his breast. Yet the larger part rejoiced in the scent of crisis, the anticipation of long-held ambitions upon the brink of realisation. Kilkry, Dargannan, Lannis, all swept away. The Crafts humbled. Dornach bloodied, perhaps even subjugated. And King, perhaps? Perhaps even that?

'I need more certainty,' the stubbornly cautious fraction of him said as he turned back to face his Chancellor. 'I need to *know*.'

'We have a day or two,' Mordyn said with a flat smile. He seemed entirely unsurprised by Gryvan's hesitancy. 'No more, I would suggest. And no time at all, perhaps, for one or two matters.'

'Such as?' Gryvan asked. He wanted this to end now. His mind seethed, his temples throbbed. Why was it so difficult to think clearly? He wanted only to retire to his chambers.

'I hear rumours of a plot – fostered by the Goldsmiths, perhaps – to seize Igryn and return him to his lands, in the hope of stirring up yet more enfeebling trouble for us. Allow me to have him removed to In'Vay. Once he is there, out of sight and mind, he can be quietly killed. None will mourn his passing. None who are true friends to the Haig Blood, at least.'

'Very well. My wife no longer finds him amusing, in any case.'

'And recall the Bloodheir from Kilvale, sire. Send word at

once. Have him bring a few thousand of his men back here. The greater threat now is from Dornach, perhaps Dargannan; perhaps still closer to home, if the Crafts and those they have suborned think us weak. The people of the city grow more restive with every passing day. We may need Aewult's swords to cure them of that ill.

'The forces of the Black Road lack both the vigour and the inclination to test him again, and I can set them on the path back to their own lands with a single message. Better yet, if we but halt all movement of ships in and out of Kolkyre, they might yet wipe away the last vestiges of the Kilkry Blood on our behalf, even as they retire. Roaric will quickly fail, if we close the sea to him.'

'I need to know,' the High Thane repeated.

'I believe we can clear away whatever doubts you harbour, sire,' Mordyn said, nodding sympathetically. 'There is one here in Vaymouth who surely knows the truth of it, and might be compelled to share it. The Dornachman. Alem T'anarch.'

'The Ambassador?' Gryvan murmured, faintly incredulous.

'You must have the truth. You said as much yourself. Such truths cannot be won easily, or without daring. T'anarch . . . he has no supporters here, sire, no mobs to rise up in his name. And his masters have never concealed their contempt for us, their envy of our strength.'

'Would you have open war with the Kingship?'

'If this comes to nothing, whatever wounds we open may be healed. But there is war already, I think, open or otherwise. A great many will be rendered carrion by the end of it: those who shy away from the demands of the moment or yield the initiative to their opponents.'

Carrion, thought Gryvan, his weariness briefly pierced by lances of bitter anger. Yes, if there are those who think to test my resolve, that is their destiny. I shall not meekly surrender all that I hold, all that I have won. Let those who imagine otherwise learn the harsh lessons of their error. The weak, the foolhardy, the traitorous, become carrion. Such is the world.

VII

The scout came back into the copse on a lame horse. There was a bloody welt across its hamstring.

'Crossbow,' the rider said by way of explanation as he swung out of the saddle.

In the gathering darkness it was difficult to see much, but the man's voice sounded strained to Orisian.

'And you?' he asked. 'Are you hurt?'

'Nothing serious, sire. The woman with the crossbow: my knee met her helmet when I rode her down.'

'Were you followed?' Taim demanded. He was holding the horse's reins, stroking its neck while another warrior examined its wound.

'No.' The scout shook his head emphatically. 'It was just the two of them stumbled across me. Both dead. They were careless, wandering around looking for a deer or hare for the pot, I think, not someone to fight.'

'And Ive Bridge?' Orisian asked.

'Not more than three score spears to hold it, sire, as far as I could see. And only half of those look to be trained warriors.'

'No Inkallim?' asked Taim.

'None that I could see. Couldn't go too close, but no, I don't think so.'

'Good enough,' Taim grunted. 'We've likely got them over-matched, then.'

'We should wait until the night's got a firm hold,' said Orisian quietly. 'Let them get bleary with sleep. K'rina and Eshenna and Yvane can stay hidden here, with a dozen men.'

He half-expected Taim to demur, to try to persuade him to

remain behind with the *na'kyrim*, but the warrior said nothing. Orisian glanced up through the leafless branches towards the bruised sky. The cloud was thin; the moon, risen long ago, a diffuse disc.

'There should be enough light to see by. And if there isn't, we'll have Kyrinin with us. They won't.'

They had not made camp in the little patch of woodland. No tents were set up, no fires were lit, despite the searing cold. They merely sheltered there, from the desultory snow and from the revelatory daylight. Men and horses were crowded into the heart of the copse, all made listless and irritable by the enervating tension. Some sat on the damp ground, dicing or muttering softly to one another, or chewing on cured meats and oatcakes. Most stood by their horses, keeping them quiet.

Sentries were scattered through the fringes of the thicket, watching the snow-dusted fields and rough slopes all around. Low hills rolled their way westwards, sinking into the huge coastal plain. There were scattered farms and villages, fading in the distance into a flat haze of grey. Snow showers had come and gone all day, by turns revealing and obscuring grim signs of unrest and ruin. For a time a dark smear of smoke marked the site of some burning barn or farmhouse; later a dozen twisting, frail columns rose elsewhere, betraying the campfires of some roving band of reavers; once a great company of riders could be seen, sweeping across the very lowest slopes.

All within that concealing stand of trees felt the calm and quiet that currently embraced them to be a treacherously fragile, even deceptive, thing. A lie, told by a world that had turned into a savage and cruel mockery of itself, and could betray at any moment those who forgot how much had changed.

Orisian squatted down beside Ess'yr, holding his water pouch out to her. She blinked the offer away.

'We'll be moving soon,' he said quietly. 'Once it's as dark as it's going to get.'

The Kyrinin rolled her head, stretching her long neck.

'When you choose,' she said.

'I'm grateful for your aid in this,' Orisian murmured. Grateful for many things, in truth, few of which he could easily put into words.

'This opens the way north, yes?' Ess'yr said. 'We move closer now, to the place we belong. To the war we must fight.'

She meant the White Owls, he knew. She and her brother believed they were travelling towards their own personal renewal of the brutal contest between Fox and White Owl; towards the discharge of a lethal duty that had been upon them ever since the fighting at Koldihrve. Vengeance, Yvane would no doubt dismissively call it, as Orisian himself might once have called it. He thought – he felt – a little differently now, though those feelings were imprecise, as hard to grasp and examine as vapours.

'Where did it come from?' he asked. 'The hatred between Fox and White Owl, I mean.'

'From the beginning,' Ess'yr said softly, without inflection. 'From the shape of things. From the pattern the Walking God made. He spoke with many animals, not one, as he walked. Without difference, there is no pattern at all.'

It was an answer that gave him nothing, but he had not really expected otherwise. To his surprise, though, Ess'yr had a little more to offer.

'It is not thought amongst my people,' she murmured, 'that strife, and pain, and hate came to us only with the leaving of the Gods. These things have always been in the world, in its differences. They are part of what was made. When the Gods left, it was balance that was lost; not suffering that was found.'

Orisian nodded, though Ess'yr was not looking at him, and though her words gave rise to an inchoate sorrow in him.

'But there was no balance, even before the Gods departed, was there?' he said. 'We killed the wolfenkind. Every one of them.'

'Still, it was balance the Gods sought,' Ess'yr said. She sat there cross-legged, straight-backed, with her hands upon her knees and now she did fix him with a steady gaze. 'They chose to make us many, not one. They chose to put unlikeness into the world, where before there had been none. It must be, I think, that they believed such difference could bring balance. If it brings strife also, it must be that they thought that a fair price.'

Her eyes held him. The richness of her voice held him. He felt himself drawing nearer to her, to her life and her people. It took him, for a moment, out of the chill, fearful present; took him somewhere safer, better.

'My dreams have lost their balance,' he said, as much to himself as to Ess'yr. 'When I manage to sleep at all. It's cruel to find sleep so hard when the nights are at their longest.'

'They become shorter.'

'The nights? Do they?' He fell silent for a moment. Grief came up in him, rising in his throat, through his cheeks, touching his eyes. 'Winter grows old, then. I missed its turning.'

Ess'yr said nothing. The last fading light that reached into the heart of the copse caught the tattoos that crossed her cheekbone, set the slightest glint in her soft grey eyes.

'We used to celebrate on the longest night,' Orisian said thickly. 'In Kolglas. It's the night when winter's strongest, but also when it begins to lose its grip. There was feasting and dancing. And my mother sang.'

The immediacy of the memories was frightening, their intricate weight – grief and comfort too inextricably entwined to tell one from the other – so great that he felt himself buckling. But her voice was there, in his mind, coming to him across an impassable chasm of loss. He heard it, and at once it was gone, melting away into the sounds of the cold dusk, the accumulating darkness. The losing of it robbed him of whatever comfort it had offered; left him only with the grief. The bitter anger.

'Time to go,' he said through trembling lips.

Ive Bridge huddled in stony silence on the south bank of the river. Orisian remembered passing it as he made his first journey to Highfast, and he had thought it an unappealing place then. Now, it appeared ominous in its bleak isolation: squat houses crowded in on what little flat ground the terrain offered, and the bridge itself, hooking over the river like a bent finger. All of it was indistinct and menacing in the darkness, with only the faintest of moonlight to pick out its inanimate forms. A few lamps or torches burned in windows, but most of the village was all greys and blacks and imagined danger. He could just catch the soft scent of woodsmoke on the breeze. That smell too spoke to him with a threatening cadence these days.

Orisian could hear the River Ive down there in the crevasse it had made for itself on the far side of the houses, grinding and foaming in its mountain bed under the bridge. Somewhere beyond that noise, out in the utterly impenetrable darkness, lay the road that led on and up into the Karkyre Peaks, to Highfast. If he thought of that too clearly or carefully, doubt came crowding in upon him. He did not know how much trust to put in his own thoughts and instincts now, and chose instead – as much as he could – to hold his attention upon the present, the immediate.

Figures were moving down the rugged slope towards Ive Bridge: Ess'yr and Varryn, and a dozen warriors led by Torcaill. They did not follow the main trail that snaked its way into the village, but descended instead over steep, boulder-strewn ground, creeping from moonshadow to moonshadow. It would not be long before they reached the first outlying cottage.

Orisian rolled away and scuttled like a beetle – bent almost double, with his shield strapped across his back – to join Taim and the others. They waited in a cutting through which the trail passed before it began its descent into Ive Bridge. A fell sight: dark forms with a dusting of moonlight upon them, gouts of steaming breath rising from the horses, bared blades. Orisian hauled himself up astride his mount.

'They're almost there,' he said quietly to Taim Narran.

The warrior nodded, and eased his way to the front of the column.

'Go carefully,' Taim said as he rode on. 'Keep your reins tight until you're told otherwise.'

The horses were wary at first, distrusting the dark road. It made them careful and quiet, at least, but still Orisian felt the tension of possible discovery. The slightest rattle of harness or slip of hoof on a loose pebble sounded loud, punctuating the background rumble of the river. No new lights were lit in Ive Bridge, though. No alarm went up. He could see no sign of movement down there. Even Ess'yr and the others had disappeared from sight, as if they had been swallowed by the rock or the shadows.

They covered perhaps half the way down to the village before a sudden strangulated cry broke the night's skin. Even as its last anguished echo trailed away, Taim Narran was kicking his horse on. The long blade of his sword flashed once, a shaft of captured moonlight, as he flourished it, and then he was pounding off down the road. Orisian and the others followed. After that, it was a chaos of thudding hoofs, a jolting, jarring charge in which Orisian saw almost nothing but his horse's neck pumping up and down before him.

They burst into the heart of Ive Bridge before anticipation or fear had any chance to take root in him. The darkness made everything sudden and bewildering. Figures – men and horses – jostled all about him. Shouts and the clatter of hoofs and ringing of blades echoed from every stone surface, shivering back and forth on the cold still air until they lost all form and became a single raucous accompaniment to the slaughter. And slaughter it was, rather than battle.

Orisian glimpsed Torcaill's little band of warriors spilling from the door and windows of one of the cottages, rushing on without pause, breaking into another house to slay those asleep –

or coming blearily awake – within. Spearmen came stumbling out from a long, low building into the roadway, half-dressed, bare-headed, fumbling with weapons and shields as if still all but blinded by sleep. Someone rode straight into them, not even bothering to swing with his sword, using the weight and strength of his horse to batter them aside. Others, already dismounted, darted in behind and set to work with blades.

There was a fast and fierce efficiency to the bloody work of Taim's men. The killing went on all around Orisian, and he felt himself strangely divorced from it, like an uncomprehending spectator at some mad and cruel revels. Indistinct forms lurched this way and that all around him. His horse turned itself about in a tight circle, tossing its head in agitation. He let it carry him, and carry his gaze in a sweeping arc.

He saw Varryn and Ess'yr, improbably perched atop the slate roof of a hut. Their Kyrinin faces seemed bright in the moonlight, almost shining, the blue swirls of their tattoos almost luminous. The arrows that left their bows were so fast that they vanished into the darkness as if snapping out of existence in the very moment they were loosed. And as his horse swung Orisian about, cloud must have taken the moon, for the darkness deepened. He saw a knot of figures running for the bridge: Torcaill, he hoped, going as intended to block any escape. He saw an unmounted horse staggering, something trailing from beneath it, and only after a moment did he realise that it had been disembowelled. He saw two men rolling across the cobblestones, punching or stabbing one another in a frenzy.

Then the moon was unveiled once more, and in its sudden, muted light he saw the point of a spear lancing up towards his face. He instinctively knocked it aside with his sword, turning it across his horse's shoulders, then jerked his arm back to cut his assailant across the side of the head. It was a woman, he realised as she fell silently and limply away. Another figure veered towards him, another spear coming in at hip height, but then there was a wet thud and the spear was falling aside, the Black Roader pawing at an arrow in his neck. Orisian knocked him down with a single blow. He looked up. Ess'yr was there on the roof, already reaching to her quiver for another arrow. She turned away as soon as their eyes met.

Orisian kicked his horse towards the largest of the buildings. It must, he thought, be a tavern of some sort. His warriors were rushing in as he drew up before it. He heard screams and feet pounding on wooden stairs. There was a crash of splintering wood and a figure tumbled from one of the upper, shuttered windows, blurring down and hitting the ground a few paces from Orisian. He heard the crack of leg bones break in the impact. The man howled, but began to crawl at once, seeking shadows. Orisian dismounted and walked over to him. The man rolled onto his back. His face was contorted by pain, but he had strength and sense enough to curse Orisian in a northern accent so thick the words were almost unintelligible. There was venom in the voice, hatred and bile. Orisian hefted his sword, began to raise it. The man did not shrink away. He bared his teeth through his short dark beard and spat out vitriolic contempt.

Orisian hesitated, suddenly thinking of Ive. There had been an abandoned, almost accusatory, air about Erval as the Guard Captain had watched them ride out. The town had been a shell by then, all but empty. Only a few dozen left behind, likely to soon follow all the others who had already scattered into the east, into the frigid wilds. If they had been too slow to flee, this same terrible thing might be happening in Ive even now, Orisian thought. Killings in the street, the abrupt, unthinking ending of lives.

Someone came in from the side and planted a spear firmly into the chest of the Black Roader, who growled and cursed and coughed as he died.

It did not last long. Those who had held Ive Bridge were not, it turned out, the ferocious, faith-inspired warriors Orisian had expected. They were instead the drunk, the sick and the hungry; gaunt and frail many of them, others injured. All dead, soon enough.

'I'll take Ess'yr and Varryn, Torcaill and three men back to fetch Yvane and the others,' Orisian said, watching with Taim as his men dragged the corpses to the river's edge and heaved them into the torrent.

'Be quick,' Taim said. 'These were just deserters or looters, but it doesn't mean there's nothing worse around.'

'I doubt it,' Orisian murmured. 'There's nothing here for anyone. The lowlands, the towns; that's what they'll want. But yes. I'll be quick. Don't let anyone get too settled. We should press on as soon as I'm back.'

'Nothing to settle with,' Taim grunted. 'There's hardly enough food here for a quarter our number.'

They went more slowly back up the trail, Ess'yr and Varryn running ahead, disappearing into the darkness. Orisian watched them go with a twinge of regret. He had wanted to thank Ess'yr for her arrow, but there was a strange lassitude in him now. He felt faintly dizzy, and when he blinked saw inside his eyes the spittle-flecked lips of that hate-filled, broken-legged man working over crooked teeth.

He rode beside Torcaill. The warrior's head dipped lower, bit by bit. His hands rested loosely on his horse's neck. The animal began to slow.

'There's something I want to ask of you,' Orisian said quietly.

Torcaill jerked upright and blew out his cheeks.

'Forgive me, sire,' he said.

'It's all right. We're all tired. Listen, there's something I'd like you to do for me.'

'Whatever you command, of course.'

'No,' Orisian shook his head. 'I'll not command you in this.

Only ask. It's . . . it will be difficult. I'd like you to try to reach Vaymouth. Just you and a couple of men: whoever you'd want to choose. If you stay away from the main roads until you get into Ayth-Haig lands . . .'

The words trailed away as he became guiltily aware of how inadequate they were; how blandly unequal they were to the magnitude of what he was asking.

'Of course, sire,' Torcaill said levelly. 'If it's what you wish.'

'I want . . . I'd like you to try to find my sister, if you can. I'm not sure what's going to happen here, to me, but I think . . . I think Anyara might need help. Protect her. Get her out of Vaymouth, if you can. And give her a message from me.'

'I'll do everything—'

'Rider!' someone shouted, and a moment later Orisian could hear it too: the hammering of hoofs coming wildly, dangerously up the road towards them.

'Spread out,' Torcaill hissed, drawing his sword.

'It's all right,' Orisian said. 'Whoever it is, I doubt they would have got past Ess'yr and Varryn if they were a threat.'

It was one of the warriors who had remained hidden in the copse. He was fraught and dishevelled. There were wounds on his face, the blood black in the gloom. Orisian felt a dull dread in his gut.

'We were attacked, sire,' the man gasped as he hauled his mount to an ungainly halt in the middle of the road. 'Tarbains, just a handful.'

Orisian hung his head. 'Who's dead?' he asked quietly.

'Four men, sire. We killed all of the savages, though.'

'And the *na'kyrim*?'

'There was much confusion. We . . . Some of the horses ran wild. We were scattered, for a time, all of us. In the darkness . . .'

'The *na'kyrim*?' Orisian asked again, that dread now a hard, cold fist rising in his chest, making it difficult to breathe.

'Two of them are safe, sire. We found them. But the mute one, the mad one: she's gone. Not killed, but gone. In the confusion, she slipped away.'

Beyond the man, the two Kyrinin were drifting back out of the night, pale shapes slowly coalescing amongst the silent boulders on either side of the road. Orisian slumped in his saddle, abruptly and profoundly exhausted.

VIII

In the Vare Waste, amongst the mule-stubborn masterless men who scraped a living from its labyrinthine canyons and gorges, feuds long-forgotten or forgiven were reborn. Along the goat trails, through the scrublands, raiding parties ran. Men sent their wives and children to hide in caves while they waged petty wars over the boulder-fields. And still they found time to prey, as well, upon the Kilkry folk who came stumbling into that wind-blasted wasteland, fleeing the slaughter wrought by the Black Road.

In Dun Aygll there was no war, but minds still foundered: the people seized Rot-scarred beggars from the streets and burned them alive on pyres built amidst the ruins of ancient royal residences; a Tal Dyreen merchant, accused by rumour of using shaved weights, was dragged from his house and carried to the Old Market, and killed there, more than a hundred hands sharing in the deed.

On distant Tal Dyre itself, the households of two merchant princes elevated quarrel to murder. They hunted one another with knives through the lanes of the island's palace-encrusted slopes, until the nights grew deadly and the people fearful.

A Huanin trader, arriving as he had many times before at a Snake *vo'an* to exchange knives for furs, offered insult with an ill-judged remark implying them to be subservient to the Taral-Haig Marchlords. Some of the older women, even the *vo'an'tyr* herself, counselled tolerance; it was not the first, and would not be the last, time that the ignorance and stupidity of a slow-minded Huanin had led them to abuse the clan's hospitality. But younger, hotter hearts demurred. There was debate and then argument, and then threat and accusation. It might have gone further had the elders not stepped aside, the better to preserve the clan's peace. The young warriors broke the trader's wrists and ankles with stones, and set their hunting dogs on him.

On the Nar Vay shore, west of Vaymouth, two brothers – long of dark inclination, guilty of innumerable small cruelties in their childhoods – went one night, without cause, from house to house in their fishing village and took blades to their friends, and their family and their lovers. They killed six, injured more, before the menfolk gathered and pursued them to the gravel beach. One died beneath the cudgels and harpoons and scaling knives of the villagers; the other waded into the sea, going on and out with the moon-limned waves breaking across his shoulders, laughing madly until he was taken under.

And in Vaymouth – huge, jostling, choking, loud Vaymouth – the sickness rose, day by day, closer to the surface. The city so long accustomed to singing itself songs woven from chinking coins, hammers in workshops, the seductive cries of hawkers and pedlars, the gossip of washerwomen, found another more corrosive strand entering its harmonies. It found another voice with which to whisper its tales of itself. Anger murmured in its alleys and inns, bitter distrust and doubt sighing coldly through its marketplaces and potteries. In sleep and in waking, a dark imagination took hold of its inhabitants, and many succumbed to it.

The Craft apprentices rioted, each death of one of their number inciting the survivors to greater outrage. The Captain of the Guard in the Tannery Ward was killed by his wife's lover. His men took their vengeance upon the man, his parents, his sister, but found that bloodletting insufficient to sate their hunger and went on to the next house, and the next, and the next, looting and killing and feasting until they fell exhausted or drunk. Three women were killed in as many nights, their dismembered bodies found in dank dawns within sight of the Moon Palace's walls. Fear stalked the city, and bred the violence that it fed upon.

*

Anyara found the terrace from which she and Coinach had watched the fires burgeoning across Vaymouth a convenient and quiet refuge whenever the increasingly oppressive atmosphere in the Palace of Red Stone grew intolerable, and she needed the touch of cold, cleansing air on her face or a glimpse of the sky. The denizens of the palace never seemed to use it — not in this season, at least — and though there were sometimes guards upon it at night, during the day it was empty and silent.

On this particular day it was cold too.

'Could you bring me a cloak from my chambers?' she asked Coinach quietly.

He nodded and disappeared into the body of the palace. As soon as he was out of sight, Anyara felt guilty. It was hardly respectful, of either his standing or his capabilities, to treat a shieldman as if he were a maidservant. Yet Coinach had raised no protest. He never would, she suspected, almost irrespective of what she asked of him. She was aware that the two of them were acting less and less like a Thane's sister and her loyal bodyguard; more and more like companions — exiles — who found in one another the only friendship and support they could rely upon.

Still, there was a sharp chill on the air and she did need the cloak. And Eleth, the maid assigned to her, had been mysteriously absent for the last two days. Sick, the others had told Anyara when she asked after her, but their curt replies had an evasive impatience about them that did not inspire belief.

Perhaps, she told herself, they were just unsettled by the general confusion and nervous mood that had taken hold of all Vaymouth. There had been other fires since those first bright beacons of destruction blooming in the night. More riots. Anyara had heard the crowds roaring along the streets of the city even through the thick walls of the palace. Now she could see a distant pillar of smoke climbing into the sky. Some ruin, still smouldering.

She folded her arms, tucking her hands into her sleeves. She blew a long, slow breath upwards and watched the mist of it drifting and fading away. Voices reached her from somewhere below the terrace. She knew there was a long narrow walled garden down there, where nothing but a few harshly pruned and trained fruit trees grew.

The voices were instantly recognisable: Tara and Mordyn. Yet both had a strident edge she had never heard in them before.

'You took her riding, I hear,' the Chancellor was saying. 'Well, no more. She is to be confined within these walls, on Gryvan's command.'

'As you wish, of course, but tell me why, at least. I find no harm in the girl.'

'That's not for you to judge.'

'Not for me to judge? Don't speak to me as if I were one of your lackeys. I'm your wife, or have you truly forgotten that as thoroughly as it seems?'

Anyara, shrinking back from the terrace's balustrade, winced at the anguish in Tara's voice. There was much pain there, though it was so intimately entangled with anger that the two were hardly distinguishable.

'I forget nothing,' Mordyn said, suddenly gentle. 'I'm sorry. I'm sorry.'

'Then tell me why. I've never pried into any of your dealings needlessly, but now you set such briars about yourself I cannot even draw near. Tell me what this child's done. I've seen nothing in her save sorrow and strength, and loyalty to her family.'

'Have a care you don't align yourself with treacherous friends.'

A sound behind her had Anyara spinning about, raising her hands to fend off some assault. It was only Coinach, though, stepping out onto the terrace, carrying her cloak. He wore a questioning expression, but she held a palm out to him and pressed a finger to her lips. He came carefully closer.

'Treacherous friends?' Tara was crying out below. Her distress must be profound – all-consuming – to permit this kind of indiscretion, Anyara knew. There would surely be servants and guards who could hear all of this just as clearly as she could herself.

'You know,' Tara went on, her tone moderating a touch, veering back towards grief and confusion, 'you used to know, at least, that I would not allow so much as a feather's width of distance to separate us, but this talk of Lannis and Kilkry treachery is absurd. Whatever their failings, they would never do anything to weaken our resistance to the Black Road. Lannis owes its very existence to the struggle against them. They're obsessed with it. You know all this far better than I. Why can't you explain to me what's changed?

'Please! Don't turn away from me. Listen to me. Explain to me. I need to understand.' She was begging him now. 'Surely it's Aewult's clumsiness, his ineptitude, that's caused this confusion. You said from the start he should not have been sent north. You said—'

'What I said does not matter.' The Shadowhand's voice was leaden. All Tara's desperate longing evidently moved him not at all. 'What *is*: that's our concern now. There is conspiracy against us, against the High Thane. That is all you need to know.'

'All I need to know? How can you say such things?'

'I have no time for this. There is conspiracy. I have shown Gryvan the proofs of it, and he acts upon them as he sees fit. The

girl, and her Blood, stand condemned in his eyes, along with
many others. Her brother killed Aewult's messengers. He is to
be outlawed.'

Coinach was pulling gently at Anyara's sleeve. She glanced at
him, and his concern was clear. With good reason, Anyara knew:
if they were known to have overheard this fraught exchange,
troubles could flock about them as thickly as crows on a carcass.
But then, as was abundantly clear, they were already beset by
plentiful troubles.

'Proofs?' Tara snapped. 'What proofs?'

'My own report of what I discovered while in the hands of the
Black Road. Letters. Messages I've uncovered since then.
Enough, woman!'

'Messages? Those you wrote yourself?'

Then, suddenly, the sharp sound of palm on flesh. A stinging
blow.

'Don't question me,' cried Mordyn Jerain. 'Never question
me. And never speak such an accusation again, to me or anyone
else.'

Too forcefully to be resisted, Coinach drew Anyara back and
led her into the shadows of the long room at the back of the terrace. As she retreated, she thought she could just hear, almost
too faint for her to catch, Tara's soft gasps of shock, and horror,
and betrayal. Perhaps they were the choked remnants of sobs.

'We should get back to your chambers,' Coinach whispered.
'They must find us safely there, and safely ignorant, should
anyone wonder where we are.'

Anyara nodded. They went quickly and quietly back through
the corridors.

*

Alem T'anarch liked to think of himself as a man of refined but
modest tastes. The thin cord with which he tied his long pale
hair had gold thread braided into it, but the strand was so delicate as to be almost invisible. His sword, which he wore only on

the most important of occasions, had small diamonds set into its scabbard. They were discreet, though. Certainly not as boorishly indulgent as so much of the wealth on display in Vaymouth had become.

Alem had been ambassador of the Dornach Kingship to the Haig Blood for long enough to acquire a grudging respect for the vigour of his hosts, but this was increasingly overlaid by much less charitable sentiments. The overbearing self-confidence of Gryvan oc Haig, his family and his entire Blood had become tedious; all the more so since it had started to express itself in the ever more ostentatious adornment of Vaymouth with palaces and grand Craft establishments and pointless ceremonial. And in recent times there had been growing hostility towards Alem's own Kingship. It had become absurdly acute since Gryvan's discovery of Dornachmen fighting in the service of the rebellious Dargannan-Haig Blood. Alem had found himself treated without even the faint respect his position had previously commanded. He had been denied any contact with Gryvan or any of his high officials.

He now strode through the echoing corridors of the Moon Palace with, therefore, a mix of anticipation and trepidation. That he should at last be granted the audience he had long sought was a relief, but the manner of his summoning to it – abrupt, discourteous – did not bode well. His attendants, hurrying in his wake, looked worried. No one wanted war with the Haig Bloods – not yet, at least – but the possibility hung in the air like the stench of an approaching corpse-ship.

It was regrettable, Alem recognised, that Jain T'erin had sold his warband to Igryn oc Dargannan-Haig, but the Dornach Kingship had always produced a supply of stubbornly independent adventurers: sons disinherited by the fall of their fathers in one of the regular reorderings that swept through the nobility; warriors cut loose when the excessive popularity or success of their commanders led to the disbanding of whole armies. It was the way of things, and it was absurd to hold the King responsible for the deeds of those spawned by such developments. In truth, Alem's own subsequent demand for compensatory payments to the families of those dead mercenaries had probably been misjudged, but the instruction had come from Evaness and his doubts had been overruled. The late Jain T'erin – or his family, at least – evidently still had influential friends at court.

Alem and his party drew to a halt before the massive double doors of Gryvan's Great Hall. The guards standing there regarded them with the disdain which Alem had come to expect. He ignored them. The doorkeeper, a slight and ageing man, raised the ancient staff that was his symbol and pounded its gnarled, polished head against the door. The arrival of anticipated visitors thus announced, there was nothing to do but wait, which everyone did in tense silence.

That wait was, unsurprisingly, longer than was dignified. Alem studied the intricate carvings on the panels of the door. It was supposedly a relic of the Aygll Kingship, removed from Dun Aygll by some warlord during the Storm Years. Whether that tale of its origin was true or not, it betrayed the instincts of the Haig family. They sought to accrue to themselves some of the glamour once attached to the extinct Kingship.

There were notches and scars here and there, but the quality of the craftsmanship remained evident. Alem's gaze traced the intertwining coils of ivy and the elegantly depicted warriors. There were figures high up on the door whose faces had been cut away, leaving ugly wounds that marred the otherwise balanced compositions. Those, Alem knew, had been images of Kyrinin, once allies of the Kingship, later its avowed enemies.

The doors swung belatedly open, ending Alem's bitter musings. He advanced into the Great Hall, holding his head up and wearing a carefully neutral expression. His footsteps rang in the cavernous vaulted and columned hall. It was unusually empty, and the journey from the door to the Throne Dais at the far end felt uncomfortably exposed. Gryvan oc Haig was waiting there, his crimson cloak drawn across his chest. That was seldom a good sign, Alem thought as he drew near. Whenever that cloak was upon the High Thane's shoulders, it swelled his sense of his own grandeur. It was no more pleasing to see Abeh, Gryvan's wife, sitting in her own throne at his side. Alem could barely recall a single well-judged word ever having passed her lips.

The Ambassador was more encouraged by the sight of Mordyn Jerain standing close by the Thane of Thanes. The Chancellor's head was bowed, so Alem was unable to make the eye contact he would have desired, but still he felt a hint of hope. For all the dubious games Jerain undoubtedly played, Alem had always found him to be, if nothing else, intelligent and considered. It had been a relief to hear that he was safely returned to the city, and to Gryvan's side, after his prolonged absence. If anyone in this increasingly turbulent city might be prevailed upon to see the wisdom of a return to civility, it would surely be Mordyn Jerain.

Alem came to a halt before the dais, and bowed to the Thane of Thanes. He put a little more depth into the gesture than was usually his wont, for though he served a true King, and this man merited none of the respect such a title conferred, a conciliatory demeanour seemed the wisest course.

'I am grateful for the opportunity to present myself, sire,' he said, head still bent.

'Perhaps you should await developments before deciding how grateful you are,' Gryvan oc Haig replied, and Alem noted with unease the chill that ran through the words. Slowly, the Ambassador lifted his head, attempting a faint, relaxed smile. He caught the eye of Kale, the Captain of the High Thane's Shield, as he did so, and wondered at the dead, reptilian quality of the man's gaze. No, not even reptilian; the lizards that basked amongst the sand dunes of his homeland's coast had more life in their regard.

'It is fortunate that you reached us here without coming to any harm,' Gryvan said. 'The streets are somewhat dangerous.'

Alem was uncertain how best to respond to that. It seemed an odd gambit for a ruler to draw such attention to his inability to keep order in his own city.

'The masses ever find ways to test the will of their masters, I find,' he said smoothly. 'I think they will remember soon enough how unwise it is to so taunt the mighty, no?'

'Three nights of trouble, we've had,' Gryvan mused, his hands clutching the edges of his lurid cloak ever more tightly. 'Fires. Riot. Murders.'

'They will keep to their houses once it snows, or rains,' Alem said. He found it difficult to maintain a buoyant strand of levity in his voice, particularly as he had the strong impression Gryvan did not care what he said. Was, in fact, barely even listening. And the Chancellor still had not raised his head. Mordyn looked thinner than Alem remembered, his shoulders a little narrower.

'There is such a fervour in the people,' Gryvan said, 'one cannot help but wonder about its source. We are no strangers to discontent and dispute here, yet never – not in my lifetime, nor my father's – has it found such . . . shameful expression. Why is that, do you suppose? What has changed, Ambassador?'

Alem's hopes of a successful audience had been slender from the start. Now they withered like a blighted vine. Gryvan's soft-spoken words were laced with threat, with malice. Alem wondered whether the Shadowhand's studied disengagement was a silent message: a warning that he could expect no succour from that quarter. He cleared his throat.

'A man would have to be rich in presumption, I think, to advise a High Thane upon the rule of his own city. No? The one who stands before you now, sire, is not such a man. Not at all. The matters I hoped to discuss are entirely—'

'See how he seeks to slither out from under your boot,' hissed Abeh venomously.

Alem blinked in surprise at her outburst.

'My lady, I intend no slithering. I mean only that it is not my place to make comment on these unfortunate disturbances. In knowing that, I show only respect.'

'Unfortunate?' Abeh sneered. 'Do you pretend you don't rejoice in this ruining of Vaymouth? Do you claim your spirits aren't lifted by the sight of everything we have built here being torn down?'

Alem smiled. A stupid gesture, he knew, as likely to antagonise as to assuage the High Thane's tempestuous wife. It was born of bemusement. He smothered it as quickly as he could beneath a bland mask of – hopefully – foolish puzzlement.

'This was the fairest of cities,' Abeh snarled at him. 'Now it's being fouled. All this discord, all this damage. Ugly!'

Alem began to wonder if the woman had finally lapsed into the frothing, idiot decline that had always seemed her most likely fate, but he was saved from having to find a coherent response to her rantings by Gryvan himself.

'Hush,' the Thane of Thanes said, with a glance at his wife. 'Hush. We'll have no answers from him like that.'

'Answers?' Alem echoed. 'I came in expectation of . . . not such questions, at least. I am too slow, perhaps. It might be so. Yet I admit, I do not understand.' It was cold in this cursed hall, he thought. They could not even keep the winter chill from their own palaces, these fools.

'Be quiet,' said Gryvan. 'Mordyn?'

The Chancellor now at last lifted his head and took a step forward. There was not even a glimmer of recognition in his eyes as he regarded Alem; not a hint at the years of careful sparring that lay between them, the grudging respect the Ambassador thought had grown. It was a stranger who now looked down upon him from the dais, and an unfriendly one at that.

'I have seen,' Mordyn intoned, 'in Kolkyre and Anduran, evidence of conspiracy between Lannis and Kilkry, the Crafts and this man's Kingship. I was given letters that the Gyre Bloods found. I have uncovered more since my return.'

'This is absurd,' Alem protested.

'Silence!' Kale came striding forward as he shouted, halting halfway down the steps at the front of the dais. The lean warrior glared at Alem with contempt.

'The High Thane has been shown proofs,' Mordyn Jerain was saying levelly. 'The patterns, the tracks left by those who seek to undermine the rule of Haig, have been revealed to him. He sees clearly now, and all your lies and your pretences will not serve to cloud his sight again.'

'I tell no lies,' said Alem. 'If you accuse me of this, you are much in error. And giving great offence to me and my master.' His unease was transforming itself incrementally into fear. This discourse might wear a cloak of eloquence and be housed in a grand hall, but its substance was that of the alleyway, the knife fight.

'Do you deny, Ambassador,' Mordyn said, 'that your Kingship has conspired with the Goldsmiths to foment disorder? That you covet the lands of the Free Coast, and of the Dargannan Blood, and even up to the gates of Vaymouth itself? Do you deny that even now your armies assemble along your northern borders, at your ports, imagining us weak? Do you pretend that Dornach coin is not lining the pockets of the mobs tormenting Vaymouth's slumber every night?'

'All that, I deny,' Alem said. 'And if you have more, that I deny too, but will not tarry to hear it. You invite these imagined dangers of yours into reality by your insults, and I will give no aid to you in that. Therefore, I remove myself from your presence, sires and lady.'

He bowed, feeling the weight of his pounding heart in his chest, and backed away. He turned and saw Gryvan's men spread across the distant doorway, blocking it; others advancing down the echoing length of the hall.

'I must have the truth in this, Ambassador,' Gryvan said, almost sorrowfully, behind him. 'You will understand that. You understand power. Its necessities. The requirement – absolute, unwavering – to defend it, and preserve it. I cannot stand idly by when all that I have inherited, all that I will pass on to my son, is threatened.'

Alem turned back to face the throne. The servants and scribes who had accompanied him into this trap were clustering tightly together, looking nervously about as the Haig warriors drew slowly closer.

'I must act,' said Gryvan. 'I must. If the dangers that crowd about me prove illusory, so be it. Whatever harm is done can be undone in time. I will regret it, and endure that regret. But if I fail to act, and those dangers prove real, I will have wilfully squandered the labour of generations. You can understand, surely, that when I see signs of sickness in my body, however faint, however uncertain, it is better to examine them, to excise them even, than to pay them no heed?'

'Gryvan, I implore you –' Alem reached out his hands, unashamed by the supplicatory gesture and by the pleading in his voice, knowing in his mounting despair that nothing mattered save somehow reaching the High Thane, making him understand '– give thought to the consequences of this. Where has your sense gone? Whatever lies have been dripped into your ear, you . . .'

Alem could hear jostling behind him, cries of outrage. The High Thane's shieldmen were seizing his attendants or pushing them aside. Kale, the rangy leader of this pack of hounds, was stepping down from the Throne Dais, coming towards him with an air of malicious, eager intent.

'Thane, there is no sense in this,' Alem shouted, his voice climbing a shrill ladder of alarm. 'You must see that! You cannot truly believe we would play such crude games against you. You invite disaster!'

Kale had hold of his shoulders. He could feel the warrior's iron-hard fingers grinding into his muscles through the cloth. Beyond, Alem saw that Gryvan was no longer looking at him. The High Thane gazed up into the vaulted roof of the hall, detached, as if his presence were merely accidental.

'Disaster,' Gryvan muttered, so softly that Alem barely heard it, 'as I have been recently reminded, comes to those who allow events to precede them. I, Ambassador –' he said this into the great cavern of the hall's roof '– I choose to walk ahead of events. I choose to shape them, not be shaped by them. I am Thane of Thanes, and I am fierce enough still to hold my throne.'

They took the Ambassador from the Great Hall and bore him into the bowels of the Moon Palace. They followed seldom-used passages, and bundled him down dark and tight spiralling stairways. There was no glory or elegance there. No marble, no carvings, no fine and graceful tapestries. Only bare rock and rough-hewn steps; torches giving out tarry smoke and walls streaked with grime.

They took him as deep as it was possible to go, to places few ever visited, and fewer wished to visit. There they showed him cruel instruments. They showed him branding irons and hammers; water-filled barrels big enough to hold a manacled man; iron-tipped whips and flaying knives. Though his mind cowered in disbelieving horror, he denied them the words – the confession – they desired.

They tore his clothes from him. They ripped his finery into pieces and cast it into braziers. They cut away his hair with knives, so roughly that some of it tore from his scalp, and he felt blood on his head.

Though he knew nothing would come of it, he begged them to think again, to turn aside from this terrible course their Thane had set them upon. There was only hatred in their eyes, only abuse on their lips.

They asked him again to confess his crimes, and those of his people, and those of his King. And he could see how they craved his refusal. They wanted it, above all else, so that they should have the chance to break him. There was something unnatural, excessive in their eager ferocity.

He gave them what they wanted, for he would not betray his people with falsehoods. He would not invite the consequences such lies would have. His captors turned gladly to the tools that hung on the walls about them, that rested against stands and waited in the seething braziers.

And in time, bloodily, they broke the Ambassador of the Dornach Kingship in that deep and dark place, and he assented to every accusation that was relentlessly put to him. He gave truth to every falsehood the Shadowhand had uttered. And once that truth was given, and his purpose served, the High Thane's men put a knife into Alem T'anarch's heart and sent his corpse to be burned on the pyres, in Ash Pit, reserved for the bodies of murderers and thieves and traitors.

IX

Anyara was afraid. She sought for all the old, stubborn determination with which she had learned to resist fear and doubt and grief. But that determination was frayed, almost eaten away like some moth-discovered robe. The fear and hopelessness leaked through it. Her only other defence was distraction, and that she turned to willingly and with all the vigour she could muster.

'Could we steal horses and slip out of the city?' she wondered.

Coinach looked dubious. The two of them were sequestered in her chambers, the door locked from the inside, the shutters closed across the great windows. They conspired by candlelight, though outside it was a bright if cold afternoon.

'Nothing's impossible,' the warrior said carefully. His doubt was ill concealed.

'There must be Lannis merchants in the city, aren't there?' she said. 'Visiting Craftsmen? Someone who could help us, perhaps smuggle us out.'

'I don't know. I could try to find out . . .' He sounded doubtful.

'Yes. I'm forbidden to leave this gilded gaol cell, but you . . . No one actually said you couldn't go out into the city, did they?'

'Not that I've heard, lady, no. Seems unlikely they'd—'

'It's no use anyway,' Anyara said. 'What good are we to anyone, running away, sneaking off into hiding like some masterless bandit with a price on his head?'

She clapped her hands together in irritation, and in doing so snapped out the flame of the closest candle. She growled at it, and lit a taper at one of the others to restore it.

'We should be trying to find a way to undo some of this madness,' she muttered, frowning at the wick while she waited for it to take the flame. 'Change things, not flee from them. I didn't come here just to be locked away. If we can't unpick the Shadowhand's lies, Orisian, our whole Blood, everything is at risk. We need help.'

'Yes, though Vaymouth is hardly the most fertile ground to search—'

A hesitant, almost furtive, knocking at the door interrupted them. It startled Anyara. She almost dropped the still-burning taper, but swiftly recovered herself and gently blew it out. Coinach was already moving towards the door.

'Who is it?' called Anyara.

'Eleth, my lady. I have . . . I have clean bedding.'

Anyara nodded to Coinach, and the shieldman opened the door. The maidservant entered, her arms piled with sheets. She looked curiously from Anyara to Coinach and back again, clearly wondering what kind of business they had been engaged in, locked away together in a darkened room. The suspicion might have amused Anyara once, perhaps embarrassed her, but now she spared it no more than a moment's thought.

She noticed the change in Eleth at once. Gone were the girl's open, friendly expression, her casual chatter. She seemed smaller, more withdrawn. That alone Anyara might simply have ascribed to the fraught and fractious atmosphere in the palace, and the change in her own status from tolerated guest to prisoner. But there was more, she sensed. Eleth's cheeks drooped, her mouth was set in limp misery. She looked as if she had been crying recently.

'Are you all right?' Anyara asked as the maid opened the great chest at the foot of the bed and began putting in the fine sheets, one after another in neat, luxurious layers.

'Yes, lady,' Eleth murmured, and the fluttering of her words betrayed the lie.

'I've not seen you for days. They told me you were sick.'

'Yes, lady.' There were tears there, so close to the surface: a loosely lidded pot simmering towards a cold and sorrowful boil. Anyara toyed absently with the sleeve of her dress, wondering whether to press the matter. She felt a glimmer of concern for the girl, but it was overlaid by other, more urgent, preoccupations.

'Do you know where the Chancellor's wife is, Eleth?' she asked as the maid softly closed the chest.

'She is in the bath chamber, lady. Ensuring it has been cleaned as it should, I think.'

'I need to talk to her, Eleth. It's very important. Would you take me to her, please.'

'I am not sure we are supposed to . . .'

'I only want to talk to her. No harm can come of it. Please, Eleth.'

The door to the bathing chamber was open. As they drew near, a metallic crash and a skittering clatter rang out. The sudden noise, so obtrusively violent amidst the marmoreal quiet of the palace, halted Eleth in her tracks, and had her shrinking away. Whatever troubled the girl, it was pervasive, rendering her delicate.

'Wait here,' Anyara whispered to Eleth and Coinach, and she went alone, cautiously, to the doorway of the chamber.

The bath was set into the floor, its polished stone darkly gleaming. There was a soft, persistent scent of perfume on the air, perhaps in the tiles themselves. Heat washed over Anyara's face, for there were braziers burning in each corner of the room. One of them lay on its side, its glowing contents fanned out across the floor, a sprawl of fiercely luminous coals. Tara Jerain stood beside it, staring down at her hands.

'My lady?' Anyara said.

Tara did not respond. She seemed fixated, to the exclusion of all else, upon her hands and the angry red welts that were already appearing there.

'My lady?' Anyara repeated. 'Is everything all right?'

Slowly, Tara looked up. Her exquisite features had none of their usual lustre. She looked almost plain, as if her beauty had been washed out of her. At first, she gave no sign that she even recognised Anyara. She stared at her blankly.

'What do you want?' she asked at length, blinking like someone waking from sleep.

'I had hoped to talk to you about—'

'No, no. Not now. I'm sorry.' Tara waved a limp hand as she spoke. Desolate sadness; weeping, blistering burns laid across her fingers and palm.

Anyara stepped back, reluctantly dipping her head, disappointed to find her intentions thwarted. But Tara spoke again after a moment.

'Wait. Wait. I have . . . I seem to have burned my hands.'

'Eleth's here,' Anyara said. 'I'll send her for a healer. For bandages and salves.'

'Yes. Thank you.'

Anyara glanced at Eleth, who nodded and rushed away with evident relief. Turning back into the moist, scented heat of the bathing room, Anyara carefully advanced. Tara's arms hung loose at her sides now. The spilled charcoal murmured in fiery whispers on the floor. The orange light of those braziers that still stood danced across the innumerable tiles, the smooth stone.

'We have nothing like this where I come from,' Anyara observed.

'No? No, well I suppose we are privileged to enjoy such indulgences here.'

'Perhaps we should find some water, to cool . . .'

'No,' Tara said. She wiped sweat from her brow with the back of one of her marred hands. 'The healer will bring some, no doubt. The pain is . . . the pain is only pain.'

Anyara nodded. There was a depth of sorrow in this woman she recognised. Remembered. Loss was the only thing she knew that could at once so fill and so empty someone.

'You saw him in Kolkyre, did you not?' Tara asked. 'Before he was captured?'

'Your husband. Yes, I did.'

'Was he then as he is now?'

'I am not sure I know what you mean, lady.'

'Has he changed? Is he as you remember him?'

Anyara had no idea what it would be best to say. She should be calculating how to win Tara's favour. That had been her intent, after all, in seeking her out. There was no one else she could think of – no one with any influence – in whose ear she might find even a trace of sympathy. Yet calculation felt tawdry and futile in the face of such aching, familiar distress. 'He seems . . . distracted. Graceless, if you will forgive me, in a way he was not before. He frightened me even then, my lady, if I am honest, but now . . . now he frightens me still, but in different ways.'

Tara stared at her in silence. Anyara feared she had forfeited whatever connection might have been possible between the two of them. But then the Chancellor's wife nodded and hung her head.

'It is not true, what is being said – what he has said – about my Blood,' Anyara ventured. 'About my brother.'

'Truth is a rare currency these days,' Tara said dully. 'If you find it in short supply, you are far from the only one. What was it you wanted? My help?'

'I thought . . .' Anyara hesitated. She felt sweat upon her forehead, at her temples. A drop of it traced a crooked path down over her cheekbone. 'You know it's not true, I think. You understand that there is something wrong in all of this.'

'It is not my concern,' said Tara. A sad, reflective smile tugged at one corner of her mouth, bunched her cheek for a moment. She stared at the blank wall, and the smile faded.

Anyara could hear rapidly approaching footsteps: soft-slippered feet padding along the corridor. In a moment, she would no longer be alone with the Chancellor's wife.

'Something has gone wrong,' she said again. 'And whatever's happening, it can't be just about my Blood, or Kilkry. These lies must have a greater purpose. I don't know what your husband saw . . . I don't know what happened to him when he was captured by the Black Road—'

'Enough,' said Tara sharply.

'Don't you feel that everything's going wrong? Doesn't this all feel as if everything's getting twisted out of shape?' Anyara persisted, beyond fear or caution now, hearing Coinach saying something to those arriving outside the chamber; delaying them, on her behalf. 'Your husband . . . he said something strange to me, the other day. He said I had been in the forest, in Anduran, as if he was there with me, though I never met him until Kolkyre. He hasn't . . . he hasn't mentioned a *na'kyrim* to you, has he? A man called Aeglyss?'

The Shadowhand's wife shook her head slowly. She kept watching Anyara, intelligent eyes unblinking, as Eleth came hurrying in, half a dozen others with her: maids and healers. One carried a slopping bucket of water, another great rolls of bandages, a third armfuls of vials and stoppered bottles. The eldest of the men bustled over to Tara Jerain, casting a puzzled glance at the overturned brazier, carefully skirting its scattered contents.

'What happened, my lady?'

'I pushed it over,' said Tara faintly, holding her hands out for examination. 'It was very stupid of me. I felt in need of . . . noise.'

Anyara backed away, step by step, towards the doorway. Tara's thoughtful gaze never left her, even as the healers muttered over her wounds, and began to spread salves over them.

*

The carriage had an escort of thirty men when it left Vaymouth. It rattled through the city streets in a cacophony of clattering wheels and hoofs. Half the lancers raced ahead, ruthlessly sweeping the streets clear of bystanders. There was urgency, for they had been late leaving the barracks beside the Moon Palace. The Captain in charge of the escort had been unexpectedly summoned to attend upon the Chancellor himself, and then kept waiting, frustrated and listless, while the morning sank into a grey and muted afternoon. The audience, when it came, had been mysteriously pointless: a fierce repetition of previous orders, an insistent emphasis on the need for haste. The Captain left the meeting feeling both somewhat battered and thoroughly puzzled that he had lost so much time for no discernible purpose beyond being forcefully reminded of the urgency of his mission.

The column burst from Vaymouth's northern gate like a hound loosed in pursuit of a stag. The horses pounded up the road, shadowing the winding course of the Vay River upstream. The carriage shook, rocking from side to side. The great expanse of the Vaywater lay at least two days' journey to the north-east.

There, on the lake's only island, was the village of In'Vay, and its ancient, crenellated tower. It was a place with a bloody history, a place of execution and slaughter. More than three centuries ago, the warlords of the Taral plains had taken Lerr, the Boy King, there when they betrayed his trust to seize him at parley. It was there he had died, last of his line, strangled in the Lake Tower, his body weighted with stones and sunk into the Vaywater's embrace. It was there the Aygll Kingship had been finally, irretrievably extinguished and the Storm Years birthed.

Now another fallen lord was being carried to the Lake Tower. Those who rode in escort whipped their horses to a lather in hope of making up the time that had been lost in Vaymouth. The winter days were brief, though. In the shadows cast by its last light of the sun, they had parted from the great road that drove north to Drandar; their path was less travelled, taking an easterly curve.

There was only one great inn to offer shelter on this stretch. They stopped there to feed and water their horses, and get what rest they could before the next dawn. The carriage stood, square and silent, in the yard to one side of the inn all through the night. Eight men guarded it and the prisoner it contained, some sitting atop its flat roof, others leaning against its wheels, others walking in long, careful circuits of the yard, the inn and the whole hamlet.

Those who did not keep watch ate well beside roaring ash-wood fires, and drank well. Yet their spirits were not greatly lightened by such comforts. They felt the burden of their grave duty, and knew they would have need of punishing haste if they were not to come late to In'Vay. Many of them slept poorly, and some worse than that. By the morning, eighteen of them were crippled by twisting cramps in their guts. They could not sit straight astride their horses, let alone attempt the pace required that day. Acutely mindful of the Chancellor's wrath, the Captain barely hesitated: he beat the inn's master into unconsciousness, then left the sick behind and went with his eleven remaining men on up the road.

In the low hills that marked the northern limits of Haig lands, they came to a ford. The eyeless man within the carriage heard the wheels splashing through the water, grinding over pebbles. He was shaken roughly back and forth, clinging to his chains to keep himself from being thrown from his hard seat. His thighs and arms were already bruised from the violence of his journey. There were no gentle surfaces within this cold box, and he had no blankets or cushions to soften the blows.

There was a pause once the wagon came out from the river. He savoured the moments of comparative quiet. His ears still rang from the clamour that had filled his moving prison, every harsh sound that had been trapped in there with him, but now at least he could hear too the soft chuckling of the river, the distant call of some bird circling overhead.

Then, too soon, they were moving again, the carriage rumbling slowly up an incline. The noise gathered strength, shaping itself slowly into the formless sense-numbing roar he had come to know. This time, though, it was interrupted. Other sounds – sounds that did not fit – intruded and broke the rhythm of wheels and hoofs. Shouts. A horse's scream. Something falling, something thudding against the side of the carriage. Something cracking and breaking under a wheel. He was thrown onto his side as the carriage veered suddenly. He felt it tipping, one set of wheels lifting from the road, then it crashed back and went unsteadily on. More cries. More confusion. Then silence.

The prisoner pushed himself upright, angled his head to try to catch some revealing sound. The horses hauling the wagon had stopped moving, or they were gone. He heard footsteps and the bar on the door being lifted, the creak of hinges. There would be light, he supposed, flooding in, but he could not see it. He felt a chill breeze.

'You'd be the very blind man I'm seeking, then,' someone said, in a voice straight from the backstreets or the harbour taverns.

Igryn oc Dargannan-Haig lifted his head towards the words, empty eye sockets hidden behind a linen band. His manacles clanked as he tried to stand.

'Out with you,' the rough voice said. Igryn felt his chains suddenly tighten, hauling him towards the bitterly cold, fresh air. 'You've some travelling yet to do. What use you'd be to anyone, I can't imagine, but it's back to the city for you.'

3

The Broken Man

Break a man's bones, and he will heal, and cultivate hatred of you.
Break a man's spirit, and he is unmendable.
From *To My Sons and His Sons Thereafter* by Kulkain oc Kilkry

I

For more than a century, Kan Avor had rotted in the watery
chains of the Glas Water. They had fallen away with the breaking of Sirian's Dyke, but the city had entered another kind of
bondage: ice encrusted it. Every pool in its pitted and silt-
layered streets was frozen. Icicles fringed each protrusion of its
gnarled and knotted ruins. Whatever feeble thaw might begin
during the day was undone and reversed in the succeeding night.
Snow fell, and persisted in every shadow. Winter possessed the
city.

And there were other masters sharing dominion of the court-
yards and squares and broken towers. A febrile vigour that threw
out on occasion eruptive gouts of madness and brutality, and by
communal consent made sudden savagery the most natural, the
most basic, expression of the state of being. And the *na'kyrim*,
who resided at the heart of this great ruin, and about whom

everything turned, and by whose will all things were deemed to happen.

They came in their scores and their hundreds, drawn by rumour or by other, silent, far deeper instincts: men and women, those who were warriors and those who were not. Gyre, Gaven, Wyn, Fane. Even Horin. They came, many, without knowing precisely what drew them there, to the shattered city squatting amidst marsh and mud in the centre of the Glas Valley. Some died, in fights or of sickness or hunger. Others found a ruin for shelter, a fire for warmth, and slowly came to an understanding: that they had reached the axis about which the world now turned, the spring from which a terrible, cleansing flood was flowing out across the world. The lever that was overturning every now-outdated law and rule. And some sought to set eyes upon the lord of this cruelly transformative domain. Some sought out the *na'kyrim* himself.

In a dank, columned chamber where, in the very infancy of the Black Road, Avann oc Gyre had once held court, Aeglyss sat slumped upon a massive stone bench. He wore a plain linen robe. Bandages about his wrists concealed wounds that never quite healed. Meltwater dripped from holes up amongst the half-rotten roof beams. It spread dark stains across the great oaken floorboards of the hall.

Hothyn and three other White Owls stood behind Aeglyss. A dozen Battle Inkallim, silent and still and dark, were scattered down the length of the chamber, leaning against the crumbling pillars, staring out from the windows whose shutters had long since been torn away. Shraeve herself met the small groups of the *na'kyrim*'s adherents emerging from the winding stairway that coiled its way up from the street below. If she found no threat in their manner or possessions, they were permitted to approach him, to bathe in the flows of certainty, of conviction, that emanated from him.

'I am tired,' Aeglyss croaked to Shraeve as she escorted a pair of awed votaries up to his crude throne.

'These are the last two,' she told him. 'Afterwards, I have messengers to instruct before they depart for our armies, so you will be left in peace.'

'Peace,' Aeglyss said, with a crooked laugh. Then: 'Messengers. Kilvale?'

'Yes. In four days, as you instruct.'

'Good. Good. The ground will be prepared by then. You're sure, though? They must be ready. I will exert myself at dawn, but it will test me. The Shadowhand is a turbulent slave; I already pay a heavy price for his continued obedience. To reach so far . . . so many . . . it will not last long. They must move quickly, if my strength is to be added to their own.'

'It will be made clear,' Shraeve nodded. 'Dawn, four days from now. Our messengers will kill as many horses as it takes to get the word there in time.'

'Good. And once I give them Kilvale . . . I'll be safe, then. I'll have them. All of them. None would betray the man who offers such gifts.'

His skin hung slack from his face, as if slowly coming unfixed from the bones beneath. His hair was thin. Bare, blotched scalp showed through here and there. Blood veined the slate of his eyes; the rims of his eyelids were red and moist. Yet the man and the woman now crouching before him regarded him with wonder. They felt, rather than saw, his potency.

'What do they want?' Aeglyss asked. He would not look at them. He angled his gaze away, towards the pale square of one of the windows.

'Only this,' Shraeve said. 'To draw near. To know for themselves that their hopes have been answered in you.'

'And do they?' Aeglyss asked, still averting his gaze. 'Do they feel the truth of it, if I say to them that I can give them what them want?'

'Yes,' breathed the man at once, and smiled an exultant smile.

*

Orisian's horse baulked at the steep, rocky slope plunging down into the huge gully. He did not blame it. The hillside fell away, swooping down into a wide band of trees that curved west like a broad, dark river. Looking on it from above, it was impossible to see the stream that had cut this valley, only the tangled, leafless canopy of the countless trees that clustered about its course.

Orisian leapt to the ground and led his horse over to Ess'yr. The Kyrinin was crouched down, running a hand over the short, snow-speckled turf.

'You're certain?' he asked her.

She nodded towards the wooded ravine.

'She descended.'

'And the others?'

'Still follow, or pursue. Perhaps by sight, more likely by track. Six or seven. We are very close behind.'

Orisian hissed in frustration and beckoned the nearest warrior. He pushed his reins into the man's hands.

'Two of you watch over the horses here. The rest of us'll go down on foot.'

He saw the briefest flicker of reluctance on one or two faces, but none of the nine men hesitated. Torcaill was gone, bearing Orisian's hopes and fears for Anyara into the south. It left Orisian reliant upon the instinctive loyalty of these men and whatever leadership or authority he could muster himself. So far, those bonds had held firm. They dismounted and clustered about him. Eshenna and Yvane were slower, struggling stiffly down from the back of the horse they shared. Yvane glowered ominously at the animal as she walked away from it.

'You'd best call your brother back,' Orisian said to Ess'yr.

Varryn was some way along the lip of the gully. As they looked towards him, he stretched out his spear, pointing down towards the woodland. Ess'yr narrowed her eyes, and then closed them for a moment or two.

'They are there,' she murmured as she rose. 'Not far. They move quickly, make much noise.'

'They might have seen us already,' said Orisian, imagining how starkly silhouetted his company must be against the dull white clouds.

Ess'yr sniffed. 'Perhaps. Most likely not. They hunt; look ahead, not behind.'

'Let's go, then,' Orisian said.

They scrambled down, slipping and stumbling as they went, and the woods embraced them. The floor of the vale was flat, but the vegetation was so dense and tangled that it was impossible for any save Ess'yr and Varryn to move either quietly or easily. The two Kyrinin rushed ahead, one on either flank. Orisian led the rest through the thickets, trusting Ess'yr to give warning of any ambush. Had those pursuing K'rina been White Owls, he might have felt more caution, but both Ess'yr and Varryn were certain that the booted feet they tracked in the *na'kyrim*'s wake belonged to mere Huanin.

Yvane was labouring along close by.

'They might not harm her,' Orisian said to her as they ran. 'They might only want to find her, as the White Owls did before.'

'Maybe,' she gasped. 'If they know her. But she's empty – gone – so Aeglyss cannot sense her, cannot guide anyone to her. Chances are, they have no idea who she is. Just crossed her trail by accident. If they reach her first, it won't go well.'

The effort of speaking was too much for her, and she fell behind him. Orisian surged onwards, battering his way through trailing ivy and snagging, thorned stems. Panic clamoured within him, but he denied it. To lose K'rina now would be unthinkable. It would leave him – all of them – utterly lost. He would not surrender to that outcome yet.

There was no snow down here beneath the woodland's roof, but the ground was wet and studded with exposed rocks. A warrior coming up alongside Orisian, then moving ahead of him, went down with a gasp as his leading foot skidded away.

A shrill scream came from up ahead, piercing through the rumble of running feet and panted breaths. Orisian stumbled at the sound of it, slowed and unbalanced by a crippling fear for Ess'yr. But even as the grating cry was cut off, he recognised that it had not been born of a Kyrinin throat.

The ground shook. No, not the ground. The thin grass, the mat of dead leaves strewn through it, the low bare shrubs: they stirred. A spreading web of disturbance went across the woodland floor like the waves fleeing a stone dropped into water. The thinnest twigs in the canopy trembled, a palsy running through the outermost extremity of every tree. Orisian discovered the flavour of loam and leaf and wood in his mouth and nostrils, cloying, almost overpowering. He staggered from a run into a walk, looking this way and that.

'What is it?' he shouted over his shoulder to Yvane, already guessing the answer.

'Anain,' she rasped from some way behind him.

There was a roaring in the branches overhead, as if storm winds blew through them, but the air was still, the clouds glimpsed beyond, flat and unmoving. Orisian looked to his left. His warriors were rushing on past him.

As one darted by, and then another, Orisian glimpsed beyond them a subtler movement. Out in the dim depths of the woodland, there was change: a blunt, misshapen form that drew itself together for a moment out of trailing creepers and twisting briars, like a half-formed idea in clay beneath the hands of a potter. A knot of stems turned as he watched, and he had the potent, brief sense of being observed. Then a flashing, green blushing of fresh leaf burst forth, and the stems and branches fell apart, and with a rattle of wood something went racing away ahead of them, leaving a trail of impossible greenery breaking out from every bough in its wake.

*

'Wait.' Aeglyss lifted a single hooked finger. His cracked tongue flicked over his lips. 'I . . . hear. Movement. Movement. I catch the scent of . . .'

His head tipped back. A long sibilant hiss escaped him. 'Ah. See? The great beasts come out to play. They don't fear me enough yet, then. Not yet.'

His eyes went glassy, their bloodshot grey overlaid with a wet film. A string of saliva ran from the corner of his mouth.

There was the faintest whisper from his lips before they went slack: 'We'll see, then. We'll see what I've become.'

'What's happening to him?' whispered the man crouching down beside Shraeve.

Aeglyss swayed, and for a moment might have overbalanced and tumbled from the bench. He steadied, and sat there, sunken down onto his bones. His eyes closed.

'He reaches out,' the Inkallim said flatly.

*

There was a clearing of sorts, and at its furthest edge lay K'rina, curled into a little hollow between the roots of a great tree. One hand was clasped to her shoulder; blood spread across the skin. The spear that had wounded her lay by her side. There were bodies scattered across the grass: warriors of the Black Road. Some had Kyrinin arrows in them. One of Orisian's own men was going from one to another, ensuring that they were dead. To one side, Ess'yr and Varryn stood motionless, staring at the scene before them. For once, their blue-lined faces betrayed powerful emotion: awestruck fear.

All of this Orisian saw as soon as he stepped into the pool of cold light falling through the gap in the canopy. None of it held his attention, for he saw the same wonders as the Kyrinin, and was similarly awed by them. Beneath his feet, and spreading out in every direction, lush green grass covered the ground, and he could smell its newness and the earth it had broken in bursting forth. Every tree wore a verdant cloak of leaves, every fern had

unfurled bright new, fragile fronds. The scattered clumps of
moss all but glowed with the vigour of fresh spring growth. Life,
in delirious, impossible abundance, had come to this place.

And death, too. One of the men lying in the centre of the
clearing was all but obscured by the mat of long, binding grass
that had overgrown him, and by the coil of briars that had
engulfed his head, tearing the skin away from his face, pushing
down into his mouth, his throat, so violently that his jaw was
forced unnaturally wide, his lips shredded. Looming over
K'rina's huddled form was a Black Road warrior, a woman, who
stood erect not by the strength of her own legs but by the two
lances of wood that impaled her, one through her stomach,
another through her neck. Her dead eyes were wide with shock,
her mouth gaping. The tree beneath which K'rina now lay had
reached out those unnatural, spiralling spars from the mass of
its trunk and punched them through the Black Roader. As it
had done to another, a man, who lay on the other side of the
na'kyrim. A spear of a branch − too smooth and *formed* to be a
true branch − had come out from the tree's bole, and arced
down and punched into the notch between shoulder and neck,
transfixing the man, collapsing him down into a broken heap,
erupting from his groin and pinning him into the soft, damp
soil.

Orisian took a couple of stunned paces forward, fearing to
tread upon the luxuriant growth that should not exist yet did. A
similar unease afflicted his warriors, for they moved cautiously
and hesitantly, afraid to disturb whatever fell power had worked
this transformation.

Orisian felt Yvane at his shoulder. She was breathing heavily.

'Can you still feel it?' he asked her. 'The Anain?'

'Yes,' she said.

'It came to save K'rina?' Orisian whispered, half-questioning,
half-marvelling.

'He's here,' wailed Eshenna behind them.

Yvane slumped against Orisian, one hand pressed to her temple, the other clawing at his shoulder for support. He dropped his sword and struggled to hold her up.

The trees shook. They creaked and groaned. A painful beat throbbed in Orisian's skull, each pulse tugging at the corner of his eye, sending a hot tingle through his scalp.

'He'll see us,' Eshenna moaned. 'He'll see us.'

'Yvane . . .' Orisian murmured. Her legs had gone loose beneath her. She slipped down his flank onto her knees.

'Aeglyss is here,' she whispered. 'He's here. Gods, he's . . .'

A spasm seized her, and she vomited across Orisian's feet. He made to kneel down beside her, to put a protective arm about her hunched shoulders, but sudden sound distracted him. A harsh, fast rattle like breaking ice. A thousand splintering cracks rushed through the boughs; deeper ruptures rang in the bellies of the great trees; a mist of wood dust and fragments of bark filled the air. Rustling filled the undergrowth, as if an invisible army of mice was suddenly on the move. Before Orisian's eyes, a wave of death swept through the woods.

He watched the grass that had so recently flushed green now die and wither into countless brittle, brown curls. Leaves that had burst out, bright and fresh, only moments ago abruptly rusted and fell. Branches broke. Splits ran noisily up tree trunks. Saplings bowed and shrank. Out, out into the undergrowth ran tendrils of destruction, cutting grey pathways through the woodland. Every bush or tree they touched, every blade of grass or clump of fern, died in the blinking of an eye.

Eshenna was groaning. Orisian turned to her, and saw her fall to her hands and knees, then roll onto her back. He breathed, and felt the dry grit of dead vegetation in his throat. It filled the air, like the frailest veil of smoke. He coughed, and spat to clear his mouth. Silence descended. A stillness, like the space between two heartbeats.

Ess'yr was kneeling. She reached for the sear, dead grass before her, and it fell apart in her hand. Her brother stood beside her, his face now unreadable. But his chest, Orisian saw, rose and fell. Rapid, alarmed breaths fluttered in and out of the Kyrinin warrior. He stared, unblinking, at the great tree, now dead, beneath which K'rina lay.

'He killed it,' Yvane said. 'Impossible. Impossible. He's killed one of the Anain.'

'Is he gone?' Orisian bent and shook Yvane, made rough by his fear. 'Is he still here, in you or Eshenna? Did he see you?'

She was limp and unresisting in his grasp.

'No, no. He's gone. It wasn't us . . . He didn't . . . He came for the Anain. It . . . it rose too close to the surface. He felt its presence, and he hunted it. He wasn't looking for anything else.'

'He didn't find K'rina?'

Yvane shook her head. 'Nothing to find. There's nothing left of her. He cannot feel her any more than I can.'

Orisian released her and straightened. Eshenna lay unconscious on the pale carpet of dead moss and grass. The blight stretched out in all directions. Beyond its bounds, Orisian could just see stands of trees that still lived. Closer to hand, there was only the skeleton of a forest: greys and sickly browns, everything withered, everything bare and angular and bleak. Where the bark had fallen away from tree trunks, it revealed dry, flaking wood that held not the faintest memory of life.

Orisian walked towards K'rina. His feet crunched across dead stalks and fallen twigs. As he drew near, the two limbs that had impaled the Black Road woman cracked and crumbled, falling away into brittle fragments of dead wood. The corpse thumped to the ground.

*

They waited in silence in the musty hall in Kan Avor. Not a word, hardly a breath, escaped Kyrinin or human. Every one of them watched the *na'kyrim* trembling upon the stone bench. They watched great dark stains spread across the bandages around his wrists. So suffused were they with blood that it oozed out onto the backs of his hands.

All felt the surging of his power. They felt it in their skin: a shivering born of no cold. They felt it in the place behind their eyes where their self resided, in the blurring there, the sensation of their own minds melting into some vast, accumulative flow that cared nothing for them, did not even recognise them, yet was so immensely potent that it nevertheless gathered them into it. And they exulted in it. It filled them with the liberation of surrender to something far greater than themselves.

This awful, wonderful torrent overwhelmed them, and they grew thinner and thinner beneath its onslaught, until at any moment it felt as though they might be carried off, and parted entirely from the world and from their crude bodies.

And then Aeglyss sucked in a huge wet breath and coughed. He bent forward, almost touching his forehead to his knees. Strands of bloody mucus ran from his nostrils down across his mouth. He licked it away as he staggered to his feet. He brushed past the dazed man and the woman, who still abased themselves before him. Droplets of blood fell from his wrists as he moved. He wheezed, and out of the wheezing came laughter: an attenuated, cold mirth.

'So,' he gasped. 'So. They tried to kill me before, but now they learn . . . now they see what I am. I am too much for them, even for them. Now we know whose land this is. Whose world.'

As he spoke, the movement of his jaw freed flakes of dead skin from his cheeks. They drifted down like tiny withered leaves. He fell to his knees with a bony crack. Shraeve and Hothyn both came quickly to his side. They eased him up. So frail had he become that the Inkallim could almost completely enclose his arm with her hand.

'The flesh is too weak,' he murmured. 'Send them away. I don't want them to see me like this.'

II

Kanin led a company of four hundred into Glasbridge: every man and woman of his Blood he had been able to assert any kind of control over. Many he had wrested away from other roving bands, cowing their rebelliousness through displays of anger and violence. Most wanted nothing more than to wander on south in search of slaughter. He gave them slaughter of a different kind – the execution of those most vocally resistant to his command – and with it exerted a measure of fragile control, over some of them at least. He did not expect to maintain his authority for long. So turbulent had every heart and mind become that he could not imagine any sentiment, or rule, or order, lasting. But he did not need much time. In his dark calculation, he could see no further than a few days, weeks perhaps, ahead. Beyond that, nothing.

Glasbridge was half ruin, half armed camp. All squalor. Even in the short time since Kanin had last ridden its streets, much of the town had slumped still further into decrepitude. It lay now beneath a covering of snow, yet still there was a soft, warm hint of rot on the air. Under the white shroud, decay and corpses lurked. Those houses that had been damaged by fire when Glasbridge was taken by the Black Road, or abandoned since, were miserable sights, crumbling and sodden.

There were, amidst the wreckage, pockets of life and habitation. They found a sprawling stable yard near the centre of the town, with a travellers' inn and workshops – blacksmith, wheelwright – attached to it. A dozen or more sullen-looking horses were shut up in stalls, but it was the people that caught Kanin's attention: a hundred at least, milling about in incomprehensible activity. It all struck him as formless, chaotic. There were warriors amongst the crowds. Kanin saw badges and standards from Gyre, Gaven and Wyn, all mixing, keeping to no settled companies. Most of those who had occupied the yard were not fighters at all, though. They were ordinary villagers and townsfolk and farmers, fragments of the host of commoners that had come surging down through the Stone Vale in answer to the call of victory, the promise of restored lands and triumphant faith.

Kanin dismounted, and seized the closest man roughly by the arm.

'Who commands here?' he demanded.

'Commands?' the man repeated vacantly.

Kanin felt dizzy and disoriented. He found himself wondering, absurdly, whether he had changed so much, whether his isolation had become so complete, that he could no longer be understood.

'Whose camp is this?' he shouted in the man's face.

'Mine. Yours. It belongs to the Road.'

Kanin growled in contempt and thrust him away. Others were coming close now, drawn by curiosity or suspicion. He recognised no one. The faces came to him indistinctly, as if softened and disguised by the veil of his anger. He surged forward and seized the collar of another man's jerkin in both hands.

'Who claims Glasbridge?' he cried.

The man made no show of resistance. There was an odd, confused expression on his face.

'Fate claims us all, in these times. The Kall is upon us . . .'

Kanin threw the man to the ground, trampled over him to reach others. The thickening crowd made him feel enclosed, beset, and his rage flared in response. He pushed a woman aside.

'Has the halfbreed sent you?' she asked as she stumbled, and the hope in her words broke the last shreds of Kanin's restraint. He spun, and brought his sword out from its scabbard and round in a rising arc that caught the woman on the shoulder.

Someone rushed at him, lunging at his upper chest with a blunt pole. He dipped his shoulders enough to send the stave glancing away off his mail, straightened and brought his sword hacking up into the armpit of his assailant. And then horses were all about, clattering and barging; his own warriors pouring in on all sides and pushing the throng back, cutting into it and splaying it apart like a ship's prow punching into the surf.

Kanin ran to his own horse and sprang into the saddle. A great fury, and a great excitement, had hold of him.

'I am Kanin oc Horin-Gyre,' he cried as his horse turned around and around, as his warriors surged across the stable yard, scattering men and women, overturning cooking cauldrons and stalls and racks of weapons. 'My Blood sprang from this town, before our exile, and I claim it. I will hold it, in my own name, and that of the High Thane. No one else. No one else!'

In time, Kanin's anger abated. It left behind it that familiar raw bitterness that was always there now, that sense of solitary anguish. He gave no orders, made no plans. He merely watched in silence from the back of his horse while Igris and the rest of his Shield took charge, silencing with their blades any show of dissent amongst those gathered in the yard, then sending out bands of thirty or forty riders at a time to impose Horin authority upon the rest of the town. It was all necessary, Kanin knew, but it was only a prelude. Without rage to buoy him up, the present could not hold his interest; it was the future that constantly called upon his impatient attention. Only the future could offer him any release.

Once a sullen peace had descended, he went with his Shield towards the harbour. There had been barns and storehouses there, still holding unspoiled food, when last he had been in this town. He needed them, for if he could not feed his little army, it would turn to bones and dust in his hands. And without it, that future he dreamed of would never come, and he might never escape the horrors of the present.

'We are followed,' Igris muttered, riding at his side.

Kanin did not look round.

'I know,' he said. 'Hunt Inkallim?'

'Three of them. A few dozen paces back.'

'They've been watching us since yesterday,' Kanin said. He drew his horse to a halt and hauled it around.

The three Inkallim — two men, one woman — were standing in the middle of the street, flanked by three great dogs that had settled onto their haunches and sat there, their breath steaming out from their massive jaws.

'Wait here,' Kanin said to Igris, and rode back the way they had come. The Inkallim watched his approach impassively. Kanin's horse mistrusted the hounds, and he had to wrestle its head up with the reins to hold it steady before them. He stared down at the Inkallim.

'What do you want?' he asked. 'By whose command do you follow so obviously in my footsteps?'

'Cannek's,' said the woman, taking a pace forward. She wore simple leather and hide clothes, carried a crossbow slung across her back and leaned her weight on a spear with a subtly barbed point. Her face was plain, her manner casual. She regarded Kanin with all the presumed equality he had come to expect of the Inkallim.

'The dead make poor captains,' Kanin said.

'Yet we often find ourselves serving them. Do we not, Thane?'

He glared at her and curled his lip. She was unmoved, her placid gaze unwavering.

'What's your name?' he asked her.

'Eska. We were instructed, in the event of Cannek's death, to preserve your life, if possible. To give you what aid we could.'

Kanin smiled at that.

'The Road I mean to follow will make that a thankless task.'

Eska gave a laconic shrug.

'Follow, then, if that's your wish,' Kanin said, and turned his horse away from them. 'I may find a use for your talents in the days to come.'

'What is it you intend to do, Thane?' she asked him as he rode back towards his Shield.

'What Cannek couldn't.'

*

The Corpseway that ran from Kan Dredar's market square, past the great trading hall and on up the long ramp to the gates of Ragnor oc Gyre's castle was living up to its name. Evenly spaced along its length were forty gibbets, a score on either side. Each bore a naked corpse. Crows and ravens lifted casually into the air as Theor's party approached, then settled back to their stubborn, patient work upon the frozen bodies.

Theor glanced out from his litter. His bearers were tiring and their pace had slowed. The snow was thinner on the road than elsewhere, but churned into ruts and ridges by the constant passage of wheel and hoof, it made for hard work. The sight of the exemplary dead along the road did not greatly interest him. A great many were coming to their end this winter. Such times, periods when death gorged itself, came now and again, in the form of war or disease or famine. As if this failing world strove vainly to cleanse itself.

He grunted and sank back against his chair. His difficulty was that what was happening now felt entirely unlike cleansing to him. Quite the reverse, in fact.

He felt the ground rising. He could hear the bearers gasping for breath as they laboured up the incline towards Ragnor's stronghold. A horn blew somewhere within the outer palisade. It irritated him, if only because he could imagine Ragnor, alerted by that signal, already rehearsing his false friendship, his offhand threats. Theor leaned out once more, and shouted towards the troop of Battle Inkallim riding ahead.

'Quicker! I grow cold.'

There were forty of them up there, and another sixty riding

two abreast behind. All were dressed for war, in cuirasses of rigid black leather, carrying raven pennants and lances. Their horses were the finest left in Nyve's capacious stables. An impressive sight, but in truth Theor and Nyve alike had hoped for a still more assertive display of the Battle's strength. Nothing, it seemed, was fated to follow the course mere mortals might hope for in these times. Wild Tarbains, unyoked to the creed, had been raiding out of the Tan Dihrin; two hundred Inkallim had been sent to quell this resurgence of the tribesmen's long-quiescent martial ardour. In the disputed pine forests between Gaven-Gyre and Wyn-Gyre lands, woodsfolk had started bloody feuds; another hundred of Nyve's swords had departed to impose a peace the rival Thanes seemed reluctant, or unable, to enforce. It all left Theor with a lesser escort than he had anticipated, but that disappointment he could easily accommodate. What he found troubling was the pattern of it all, the constant sense of incipient, aimless chaos.

He was shaken uncomfortably from side to side as his litter-bearers struggled to keep up with the riders ahead. Another of the roadside corpses swung across his rocking field of vision. These grim ornaments that Ragnor had hung along his road were another token of insidious decay. Three riots there had now been in Kan Dredar. None of them difficult for the High Thane's warriors to put down; all of them surprising. Such rebellious, rampant demonstrations were unusual amongst the Bloods of the Black Road. Internecine violence was far from unknown, but these random eruptions of mindless strife were something new.

Could this be what the Kall felt like? Did the fated, promised destruction of this world begin in petty violence and murder? Mobs in the street, a *na'kyrim* raising himself up out of the chaos in the south?

The wooden gate in the palisade stood open. Behind it was a great ditch. Nyve's ravens clattered across the bridge that led to the inner, stone gatehouse. Theor closed his eyes briefly, willing his mind to clear itself of doubt and distraction. He did not know quite what to expect from this audience, but recognised that he would be ill prepared to meet it if he could not shed his gnawing uncertainty. He heard the next huge iron gate clank open, and breathed out. He was, he forcefully reminded himself, no child, no callow youth or novice of the creed. He was the First of the Lore. There could be, should be, no one more capable of meeting such turbulent times with resolution. It was difficult, though, when lack of sleep blunted every thought.

The gigantic pitched roof of Ragnor's Great Hall held no snow. Water dripped from its every eave. It would be hot inside, Theor knew as he clambered a little stiffly out from his litter. Ragnor kept his fires burning day and night. The First of the Lore stood before the mighty doors of the hall and stretched, digging his fingers into the muscles at the small of his back. The Battle Inkallim arrayed themselves across the hard earthen courtyard. He glanced at them, and adjudged them suitably stern and ordered. They made tidy ranks, and maintained a meticulous silence. A valuable demonstration for the dozens of Ragnor's warriors who had gathered to watch that there were some, amidst the chaos, who still understood and practised discipline.

Ragnor's silver-haired Master of the Hall came down the steps from the doorway to greet Theor, his fluid movements belying his advanced age. Theor suppressed a momentary twinge of jealousy. His own bones seemed to carry the clear memory, and weight, of every year he had lived. He made a point of ascending the steps slowly, with dignity, as he was ushered within.

Three great open hearths lay down the centre of the Great Hall. Fires roared in them, sending smoke billowing up into the roofspace, coiling its way around the multitudinous interwoven rafters. The fumes and the heat stung Theor's eyes at first. He blinked and wrinkled his nose as he advanced towards the platform at the far end of the hall. All the benches and couches and rugs he passed by were unoccupied. This was unusual. More often than not, a good proportion of the High Thane's household could be found in here, whether or not their presence was needful or useful.

Theor glanced up at the antlers and bearskins that adorned the walls. Ragnor oc Gyre was a man who liked to hunt, and many of these trophies were his own. The greatest of them, though – a vast splayed set of many-tined antlers that put Theor in mind of a pair of gigantic needle-clawed hands – were a legacy of the High Thane's grandfather, who had won them after a hunt that famously had lasted a full day. The huge stag that once bore them had been a beast of some superstitious import to the Tarbains whose territories it roamed, and its death had done as much to subdue them as any number of burned villages and executed chieftains. A good day's work in the service of the creed, that had been. Better than any Theor could remember Ragnor performing.

He cleared his throat, trying to cough away the dry taste of smoke, as he drew near the group assembled around the High Thane's empty throne. It was a vainglorious confection, that great seat, draped in wolfskins. The sight of it always jarred with Theor's instinct for austerity. But then there was much associated with Ragnor oc Gyre that jarred with Theor's instincts.

The High Thane himself was absent. Theor was only slightly surprised to see with whom he would be awaiting Ragnor's appearance: Vana oc Horin-Gyre stood there, with her arms folded, surrounded by a small group of attendants and maids.

'I heard a rumour that you might be in attendance today, my lady,' Theor said, inclining his head respectfully.

'The Hunt keeps you well informed, no doubt,' she replied with distant formality. The Horin Blood – and Vana's late husband Angain in particular – had long been a most resolute and valued ally to the Inkallim, and to the creed. Indeed Vana herself had secretly delivered one of the High Thane's own messengers into the hands of the Hunt, and thereby confirmed Ragnor's connivance with the enemies of the Black Road. Theor wondered if his troubled mood led him to imagine the antipathy he now, unexpectedly, detected in Vana's manner. He favoured her with a black-lipped smile, giving it a curl of apology.

'Avenn has many eyes, indeed. Their attention is often benign. They watch friends as closely as any.'

'If you say so.'

Vana had always been a fiercely independent woman, Theor knew. This, though, was more than that. There was hostility there, he was sure.

His ruminations were interrupted by the loud and expansive entrance of Ragnor oc Gyre. The High Thane came from a small door behind the throne, in mid-laugh as he burst into his Great Hall, the massive warriors of his Shield sharing in whatever jest so amused him. He wore a cloak of thick fur, a breastplate of polished nut-brown leather, a belt with a bright silver buckle the size of a man's palm. And an expression that shed all its mirth in an instant as his eyes fell upon Theor and Vana standing there awaiting him.

He said nothing as he removed his sheathed sword from his belt and settled heavily onto the throne. He rested the metal-shod tip of the scabbard on the planking of the dais and leaned forward a little, both hands clasped about the hilt of the great weapon.

'I have had enough,' he said. 'I have had enough of my people rioting in the streets of Kan Dredar. Of my farmers and smiths and miners and fishermen abandoning their labours and marching off into the south to fight your precious sacred war. Of bickering Thanes suddenly plaguing me with demands they be granted this piece of the Glas Valley, this town, that village, while they cannot even maintain order in their own lands.'

Theor looked from side to side.

'I would be grateful for a chair or bench,' he said placidly. 'My old bones—'

'This will not take long, First,' snapped Ragnor. Theor had expected the High Thane to at least wear a skin of respect. Apparently it was not to be, and that was unsettling.

'I am going to tell you what I want,' Ragnor said. He was rocking his sword back and forth very slightly on its tip, his glinting eyes fixed first upon Theor and then Vana oc Horin-Gyre.

'You, lady, are going to send word to your son beseeching him to return at once. Beseech, or implore, or command, or entreat. Whatever is required. I want him back here, with every man or woman of your Blood he can shepherd along with him.'

Vana drew breath to reply, but Ragnor flashed a warning hand towards her, palm outward.

'I am not done. Your husband started this madness. From what I hear, your son has become the least of the horses still running the race, but I want him out of it altogether. Perhaps if the people see those who set all of this in motion retiring from the fray, a flame of sense might be lit in their heads.

'And you, First,' Ragnor turned to Theor. He had the grace to moderate his tone a little, but still it was menacing. 'You, I want to see exercising some of your vaunted authority in the service of the Bloods rather than the narrow interest of the Children of the Hundred.'

'The faith,' said Theor quickly. He could not keep a trace of resentment from his voice. 'We serve the faith. Nothing else. The Bloods created us for that purpose, and we adhere to it.'

'Well, I say the faith is stumbling towards disaster. The people talk of the Kall; they churn themselves up into a frenzy. Why does the Lore remain silent? I want you to speak, First. Shed this unaccustomed shyness, and speak loud and clear to the people. Tell them that this is not the Kall. Tell them that the world is not about to be unmade. Tell them we are not fated to fritter away everything we have built here in this doomed war against an enemy we cannot yet defeat.'

Theor pursed his black lips. There was, he suspected, no response he could make save unequivocal submission that would satisfy the Thane of Thanes, and submission had played no part in the century-and-a-half history of the Lore. Whatever doubts, whatever unease he wrestled with, he had no intention of absolving Ragnor of his responsibility to advance the creed, whatever the odds, whatever the cost.

'And have Nyve rein in this she-raven of his who seems to be set upon causing as much trouble as possible,' Ragnor muttered. 'I should never have permitted Shraeve to go south with Kanin in the first place.'

'Permitted?' said Theor softly. Ragnor glowered at him.

'Am I the only one who sees the ruin we rush towards?' cried the High Thane in exasperation. 'Grain rots in barns because there aren't enough hands to mend the roofs. Cattle fall sick because half the herdsmen who should be watching over them have gone off in some mad trance believing they can storm Kolkyre single-handedly. We run short of furs. Furs! Because the Tarbains who should be hunting for them have rushed off in search of loot, and those who remain are suddenly possessed of an urge to relearn the banditry of their forefathers.'

He sprang to his feet and stamped towards the door behind his throne.

'There are brawls in the quietest of villages. The slightest of arguments erupts into murder. The orders I send south go unanswered or unheard. My messengers fall silent or disappear. Why? What madness has taken root?'

He threw open the portal and gestured, beckoning some unseen attendants beyond it. Theor glanced sideways at Vana, but the woman maintained a stern and dignified stillness, gazing ahead impassively. If she was troubled or distressed, she concealed it well.

In answer to the High Thane's summons, three prisoners were hauled out onto the dais by guards: two men and a woman. They were forced to kneel in a line, facing Theor and Vana. Theor frowned, and then raised his eyebrows in startled anticipation of might follow.

'This man,' said Ragnor, jabbing a finger at the first of the dishevelled captives, 'was passing through Kan Dredar on his way to the Stone Vale. He's one of yours, lady. He took it upon himself to knife two men in a tavern brawl, and then to attempt the same upon the Guards sent to arrest him.

'This –' he advanced down the line, and indicated the second kneeling prisoner '– is the ringleader of a mob from Ramarok on the coast. They were hungry because the seal hunters have gone south. They thought a family was hoarding food, so they burned them out of their house and slaughtered them – husband, wife, children – in the street. Clubbed them to death. Then they set upon one another. Killed another dozen.'

The High Thane stood behind the last of them: a long-haired young woman who was calmly watching Theor. The First returned her gaze, sensing that there was some meaning or intent in it, but unable to tease it out. Ragnor looked down at the woman, curling his lip in contempt. He grabbed a handful of her hair and shook her head roughly.

'This,' he snarled, 'this one I am not sure of. She might be a mere tool, a mere agent. Or perhaps she is the thing itself: one of Avenn's shadow-haunters. I don't know, and I don't care.' He shot a meaningful glance at Theor. 'If she's of the Hunt itself, I don't care. She was rousing the villagers in the lands around Effen, preaching the coming of the Kall, filling them with the fire they needed to send them off across the Vale of Stones. All but emptied three villages, she did, and when she was commanded to cease, she disappeared, only to be found repeating her game two days later.'

Ragnor released the woman, slapping her hard across the back of the head as he stepped away. Guards moved into place behind each of the prisoners. They held cords in their hands.

'Ragnor, wait,' Theor said, taking a pace forward. He did not know if the woman was one of the Hunt, but if she was . . .

'No,' Ragnor said flatly. 'I have no patience left, First. I will not wait any longer, for anything or anyone.' He nodded to the guards.

Theor stepped back. Vana, he realised, was not watching; she was staring up at a ram's skull mounted high on the wall, pouring her attention into the polished bone, the curled horn. The cords slipped around necks. They were twisted tight at once. They dug into skin. Mouths stretched open, tongues fluttered. Eyes gaped. The woman struggled to rise, but the guard behind her kicked the back of her knee and pushed her down again. On each of the three throats a red blush spread; muscles and sinews stood despairingly taut. Something collapsed with a soft crunch.

A distorted rattle escaped the woman's throat. Her executioner redoubled his efforts, tightening, crushing. One of the men − the one from Ramarok − died first. Then the woman, then the Horin man. They fell, or were pushed, forward, and lay crumpled on the dais.

Ragnor oc Gyre scuffed the woman's long hair away from her face, exposing her protruding tongue and the string of saliva loosed from her mouth.

'Do you see?' the Thane of Thanes murmured. 'Do you understand? I have gibbets and stakes and pyres aplenty. If I have to fill them all, use every one of them, I will have an end to this. However many have to die, I mean to cure us of this madness. This disease. I have had enough.'

Theor's litter-bearers hurried to take up their positions, and watched him expectantly as he emerged onto the steps outside the Great Hall. It was snowing once more. The hundred Battle Inkallim were still spread across the yard in a great arc. Theor stood just outside the doors, rubbing his hands together. They tingled uncomfortably at the sudden transition from the warmth of the hall into the day's bitter chill.

Vana oc Horin-Gyre appeared at his side. She paused, pulling up the seal-trimmed hood of her cloak. Her attendants hurried to fetch their horses from wherever they had been stabled.

'I saw a bear slain on the day of your husband's interment,' Theor said quietly. 'Ragnor's own Shield quilled its breast with crossbow bolts. You saw it too. The High Thane himself laughed that it might be an omen, of the fall of a great lord or a sudden change in the order of things.'

Angain's widow looked sharply at him, then returned her attention to the task of pulling on sleek calf-hide gloves.

'The Road does not grant us omens, of course,' said Theor. 'But still. There is change in the air, I think. I fear.'

'Spare me any further involvement in your noble enterprises, First,' said Vana, and now the bitterness in her voice was unmistakable. 'I thought I had the mettle to succeed my husband, to match his fervour, his strength. I find I do not. I am weary, and I have no remaining interest in the creed, or omens, or the wars you choose to fight. My family has already paid a high enough price.'

'It was never our intent, or desire, to do anything other than nurture the fire that your husband, alone amongst all the Thanes, kept alight. Many of the Inkallim who crossed the Vale were specifically tasked with keeping your children safe if—'

'Then they failed,' Vana snapped. She flexed her fingers inside the gloves irritably. 'You failed. Wain is dead. Kanin, by all accounts, is shunned by those now guiding the war. That vile halfbreed who first whispered thought of war in my husband's ear rules in Kan Avor, I hear, with this Shraeve of yours serving as his Shieldmaiden. That is not what my husband hoped for.'

'There is much, I agree, that is unexpected in all of this –' Theor nodded sympathetically '– but it is not given to any of us to predict fate's course.'

'No?' Vana said. She glared at him, but he saw more pain than anger in her eyes. He felt a sudden sympathy for this woman who found her strength unequal to the challenges the world presented. 'I'll make a prediction for you: I will never have my son back, just as I will never see my daughter again. Ragnor wants me to summon him, as if anything I could say would change anything. I know my son, First. Wain is dead. Kanin would return only if there were none left to punish for that, deservingly or not. He will require a surfeit of blood, and still it will not heal him. In search of that healing he can never find, he will go on and on until he drowns in the blood of the dead.'

'As will we all, eventually,' Theor murmured as Vana walked away from him, descending the steps to where her grooms now waited with the horses. 'It's the fate of this world to drown in blood, sooner or later.'

III

'You've never heard of it before?' Orisian asked.

Yvane shook her head. 'I'd never have believed it possible. I hardly believe it *is* possible, even now.'

She was walking alongside Orisian's horse, trudging up the long, bleak track to Highfast. Her tolerance for riding had been thoroughly exhausted, and no one made any protest at her refusal, for she did not slow their progress. All of them, horses included, were bleary and sluggish. It had been two nights now since any of them had had any meaningful rest. Above, clouds spun and churned about the Karkyre Peaks. Gusts of eye-watering wind came tumbling down from the heights to sting their faces. Slabs of snow were scattered all across the mountains, clinging to whatever seams in the rocks gave them purchase and shelter. Most of the snow had been scoured from the track, but sometimes, when they were in the lee of some huge ridge or cliff, there were drifts deep enough to make progress painfully slow.

'We saw it, though,' Orisian said.

'We did. We saw something done for the first time, as far as I know, in all the world, in all its history. Myself, I was happier when I thought such a thing impossible. He is stronger than the Anain. He – one man, one *na'kyrim* – has killed . . .'

She splayed her hands, as if pushing away words, or thoughts, that she could not accommodate.

'It doesn't change anything,' Orisian said.

'No?' Yvane grunted. 'Tell your Fox friends that. They may disagree.'

Orisian glanced ahead towards Ess'yr and Varryn. They were thirty or forty paces further up the track, pushing on, heads down, with more stubborn resilience than anyone else could manage. Neither of them had spoken of what they had seen in those woods, when the Anain had appeared before them, and died. They alone had seen it killing the Black Roaders, and Orisian could barely imagine what that must have meant for them, to witness first the waking of the forest, and then its destruction; to see one of the beings they considered tutelary spirits of their lands, their lives, snuffed out like the feeblest of candle flames. Who, Orisian wondered, did the Kyrinin imagine would protect them from their restless dead, if the Anain could no longer safely venture near the surface of the world?

'But still,' Orisian said quietly, 'it doesn't change anything.'

Yvane looked at him. He met her gaze without flinching, and saw nothing in her of the fire, the challenge and argument that had so often been there. She was instead thoughtful and grave. After a time, she pursed her lips and looked away.

'The Anain know now that they can't oppose him. If they thought to use K'rina against him . . . Now they cannot even protect her, or guide her, for if they rise up, Aeglyss has proved he can kill them. Ha.' Her curt laugh was sad, mournful. 'They raised a forest once, to still a war. Now this one man is too much for them. And no; I suppose it doesn't really change anything. We merely go from dark to darker.'

The doors of Highfast were closed. They stood tall and narrow, ancient but firm. Thick snow was falling as Orisian led his company across the arching stone bridge that tenuously wedded the mountain to the pinnacle from which Highfast clambered in mounting buttresses and walls and towers into the sky. Orisian had his collar high and tight about his neck, but still meltwater trickled down from his numb face and spread its chill beneath his jerkin. Snow layered every flat surface of the fortress, a succession of white ramparts stepping towards cloud.

The guards – disembodied voices crying out from hidden windows or battlements – refused to open the great doors. That angered Orisian.

'Bring your Captain here,' he shouted into the blizzard, standing in his stirrups as if that would strengthen his voice. 'Herraic still lives, doesn't he?'

They had to wait then, hunched down in their saddles, heads turned away from the wind-blown snowflakes. No one spoke. The ride up from Ive Bridge had been a miserable, punishing journey. To be denied shelter now that they stood at the very gate of their destination was unbearably, unacceptably bitter.

'I'd not thought to see you here again, sire,' came Herraic's familiar voice from above, stretched and buffeted by the wind.

'Open the gates, Herraic. You know me well enough. I've forty men here needing shelter, half a dozen of them wounded or sick.'

'But it's not just men, is it, sire? Forgive me, forgive me, but I see woodwights and *na'kyrim* there in your ranks. It's ill fortune, ill-timed, that you bring them to our door.'

Orisian looked round. His warriors lined the bridge, stretching back in double file, the last few all but obscured by sheets of snows. He could see Yvane and Eshenna, uncomfortably sheltering between horses in the midst of the column, and K'rina, tiny, tied tight to Taim's back. Ess'yr and Varryn were almost hidden, standing at the rear. It must have taken a keen eye to find them. Or a suspicious one.

'They ride with me, Herraic,' Orisian shouted angrily up at the invisible Captain of Highfast. 'You've seen them all before, save one. You know they're no threat.'

'Things change.' There was regret in his words, though he still shouted them into the storm. 'I like it no better than you, sire, but things change for the worse. Trust's too rare, the dangers too great, for any chances to be taken now. Since you left . . . there's been too much blood shed since you last came to my gate, sire.'

Orisian slapped his thigh in exasperation.

'Herraic!' he shouted, his ire swelling his voice and bearing it up against the walls of the fortress. 'Do you truly mean to bar your doors against the Thane of a Blood that's fought and suffered alongside your own for more than a hundred years?'

'There'd be few more welcome than you, sire. But Kyrinin and *na'kyrim* . . . no, I cannot. Not now, not after all that's happened. If you'd been here, if you'd seen . . .'

Orisian stopped listening, let the wind bellow over the Captain's words. He dismounted and trudged through ankle-deep snow to stand at the head of Taim's horse. Holding the animal's bridle, he glanced at K'rina. The *na'kyrim* seemed to be sleeping, her cheek pressing into the warrior's broad back, though it was difficult to tell with her what was sleep and what daze, what simple absence.

'You can untie her now. Send five men back up the track with Ess'yr and Varryn and the *na'kyrim*. Tell them to get well out of sight but go no further than they need to. We'll send for them soon.'

'We'll have a roof over our head tonight after all, then?' Taim grunted.

'Without doubt.'

Taim stood at Orisian's side as he hammered on Highfast's great doors with the hilt of his sword.

'You've got what you want, Herraic,' Orisian cried. 'Let us in.'

The doors groaned and rasped as they swung slowly open, protesting at such disturbance of their cold-stiffened bones of wood and iron. Herraic and four of his warriors waited within, a few paces along the stone tunnel that lay beyond the entrance. The Captain of Highfast was a short and stout man who had struck Orisian as somewhat nervous and fragile of spirit even on their first meeting. He had shed some weight since then, and the shadows beneath his eyes and the hesitancy of his movement gave him the air of a beaten man. Orisian strode up to him and stood face to face.

'I'd expected a warmer welcome.'

Herraic looked anguished. 'I offer all I can, sire. There's little warmth for any of us within these walls.'

'How many swords have you got left?' Orisian asked, waving his own warriors forward. They advanced on foot, leading their horses noisily up the long passageway. Swarms of snowflakes came billowing in around them.

'Less than twenty,' Herraic stammered. 'And a few willing men amongst the foresters and villagers who've found refuge here.'

'Good,' said Orisian curtly. He looked beyond Herraic, saw that the first of his warriors was entering the deep, high-walled yard beyond the passageway. He nodded to Taim. The warrior moved more quickly than even Orisian had expected, driving Herraic back against the wall in a single lunge; grasping the Captain's throat with one wide hand, with the other freeing his sword and touching its point to Herraic's belly.

'Yield your castle, Captain,' Taim said quite softly and calmly.

One of Herraic's men started forward, but Orisian interposed himself, sword and shield readied. He felt no hesitation, no uncertainty. Exhaustion had emptied him of everything save a sickening kind of desperation. He had no talking, no reasoning, left in him; neither the patience nor the strength for anything other than a swift resolution. The advancing warrior must have seen something in his face or his eyes, for the man hesitated. The wind surged down the passageway. Orisian could hear and dimly see his men dispersing to confront and disarm Highfast's garrison. His eyes were failing, though, crippled by weariness. Snowflakes boiled in the air between him and the warrior he faced, streaking white blurs across his vision.

'Herraic . . .' he said.

And behind him, choked out through Taim's crushing grasp: 'Yes . . . yes, sire. I yield Highfast to you. Please.' It was the voice of a broken man, and as Orisian carefully lowered his sword and shield, he could hear Herraic begin to weep.

There was no fighting. None of Highfast's defenders had the appetite for resistance. At Herraic's command they laid down their arms with apparent relief, and though they were sullen and resentful, all permitted themselves to be herded into the largest of the dining halls. A dozen families were assembled there too. They huddled in the corner, watching Orisian and Taim and the rest. The parents hugged their children close, as if guarding them against some fearful sight. As if some avatar of the terrible outside world had breached the walls of their sanctuary and now stood before them clothed in threat.

Standing there, surveying this miserable gathering, Orisian was for a moment struck breathless by overpowering shame that he could instil such fear in mothers and fathers and children. He closed his eyes, bit his lower lip and turned away. He was not to blame. He did only what was necessary.

'Give them food and drink, if you can find some,' he murmured to one of his men.

He drew in a deep breath and blew it out again. It trembled in his throat and chest. He did not know how much longer he could bear this. He needed sleep, craved it as a starving man might crave food.

Herraic was sitting, elbows on knees, head in hands, on a bench. Taim stood over him. Orisian saw sympathy in Taim's face as he regarded the fallen Captain, and somehow the sight of that gave him a fragment of strength. There remained some little space, some capacity, for something other than anger, or fear, or exhaustion, even now.

'What happened, to so poison this place?' Orisian asked Herraic.

Highfast's Captain slowly lifted his head, blinking

'The Dreamer woke, and . . . and I don't know. The *na'kyrim* fell to slaughtering one another. Woodwights came; there was madness. A madness in the air, in the heart. It was a horror, sire. If you could have seen . . .'

'Where are the *na'kyrim*?' Orisian demanded. 'They can't all be dead, can they?'

Herraic winced, as if struck.

'Where are they?' Orisian asked again, taking a step closer to the portly Captain.

'There's an old cellar, once for wine and ale. We keep them there.'

'Show us,' Orisian said quietly

The stench was startling: ordure and sweat and mould and misery, all hot in Orisian's face as the cellar exhaled a gout of its vile breath. He stood only for a moment on the threshold; saw in the sickly candlelight the hunched forms of men and women crowded into corners, lying asleep or unconscious or dead along the walls, two or three coming unsteadily towards the faint light admitted by the opening of the door. A moment was enough to see all this, and to feel the unreasoning anger boiling up in him, to feel tears burning in his eyes, not knowing whether they were born of the acrid stink, or despair, or pure, perfect rage.

He spun about and lunged for Herraic. The Captain gave a yelp of surprise and raised his hands in defence, but Orisian rode a ferocious wave and would not be denied. He slapped Herraic's hands aside, seized a bunch of his jerkin and punched the man back against the wall. Herraic stumbled at the impact, and Orisian bore him down to the floor of the passageway.

'Orisian!' he heard someone shouting. The cry was distant, coming from far outside the narrow, choking ambit of his attention. He pressed a knee onto Herraic's chest. The Captain of Highfast struggled, but was pinned into the angle between floor and wall. Orisian tugged at the hilt of his sword. The wall hindered him: his knuckles jarred against the stonework. He felt no pain, but the delay saved Herraic.

'Orisian!' someone shouted again. Taim Narran, he knew, though the knowledge had no purchase upon him, no meaning that could penetrate his inundating fury. He twisted to free his sword. Herraic was pushing at him, the Captain's eyes stretched in alarm.

Then an arm was about Orisian's chest, drawing him calmly but irresistibly up and away. Herraic rolled out from beneath him and scrambled to his feet. Orisian bucked for a moment against Taim's restraining grasp, then ceased his struggles.

'We've foes enough already, sire,' Taim murmured as he withdrew his arms.

Orisian said nothing. He stared bitterly at Herraic, who had backed himself up against the opposite side of the passage, quivering like a hunted and cornered fawn.

'It had to be done,' Herraic gasped. 'It had to be done. You don't know what it was like. The safety of my men . . . We couldn't be sure of anything.'

'Where are the rest of them?' Orisian asked.

'Dead,' said Herraic, then hurriedly: 'Killed by the Dreamer, or the wights that came. You don't know what it was like. Please . . .'

Orisian ground his right hand into a fist, clenching his fingernails into the palm of his hand. Only thus could he master the desire to reach again for his sword. The dancing shadows thrown by the torchlight surged and pulsed at the edge of his vision, a mocking chorus that seemed to urge him on and demand violence of him. The floor rocked beneath his feet. Herraic clearly saw something of the battle raging between instinct and restraint.

'They're safe here,' the Captain of Highfast cried, imploring. 'Tempers are running hot and hard, too much for me to control. If I'd let them wander about, I couldn't be certain of keeping them alive. I couldn't be sure of their safety.'

'Feared for your own, more likely,' Taim Narran said levelly. He had a hand on Orisian's arm again, gently drawing him back round towards the cellar doorway.

'Are you all right, sire?' he asked.

Orisian puffed out his cheeks and nodded. He turned his back on Herraic. Standing in the doorway, short and pale and blinking, with his hands clasped up by his chin, was Hammarn of Koldihrve. The old *na'kyrim* looked with faint curiosity at Orisian.

'I know you, I think.' He smiled, pleased by the acuity of his own memory. 'Yes, yes. Rode a ship with you, and walked a road. Though you were prettier then.'

Orisian brushed a reflexive fingertip along the line the scar on his cheek. Hammarn looked from side to side, his face twitching into anticipation, both alarmed and excited. 'Is the lady with you? The one with the nettlesome tongue?'

Orisian gave a sad, gentle grunt. 'Yvane? Yes, she'll be here, Hammarn. Come, I'll take you to her.'

IV

'What else would you expect?' asked Yvane. 'The oldest of hatreds, the oldest of fears. And they could hardly have a better excuse to surrender to it. Aeglyss reminded them of where those fears come from. And with his corruption of the Shared feeding their every doubt, every suspicion, every buried resentment . . . no, it's no surprise.'

'You'd forgive them?' asked Orisian, disbelieving. 'You, of all people?'

They were descending a long sloping corridor, just the two of them, walking slowly down into Highfast's foundations. The passageway was dark, save for the torch Orisian carried. The flame flapped now and again, sending their shadows careening over the square-cut stone facing of the walls. Even here, close to the stronghold's roots, the air moved. The breath of the Karkyre Peaks found its way in through the porous skin of Highfast to these deep places.

'I didn't say anything about forgiveness,' Yvane told him.

'But you accept it.'

'And nothing about acceptance, either,' the *na'kyrim* said. 'You're too young.'

Orisian came to a sudden halt and turned to her, angry.

'Or I'm too old, too bruised,' she said quickly. 'Either way, horrors that seem fresh and new to you are stale to me. What happened here, what Herraic and his men did, that's the stuff of every tale I heard in my childhood. It's the commonest of currencies between Huanin and *na'kyrim*, at least since the War of the Tainted. I despise it. Loathe it. I'm just not surprised by it.'

He glared at her, then shook his head and continued down the sinking passage.

'Perhaps I've lived too long,' Yvane muttered as she followed him. 'But it's not just that. I fear anger, as you should. Let it in, give it nourishment and it'll overrun you.'

Orisian said nothing, marching sullenly on. His fist about the burning torch was painfully tight, he realised. It took a moment of concentration to soften the muscles and take some of the iron out of his fingers. He knew she was right, and he did fear what might happen inside him – what might already be happening – if he yielded to the torrent of emotions he could sense running there. But anger was not the strongest, the most dangerous current; the shadow he felt at his heels, its ever more familiar breath across the nape of his neck, was a desolate hopelessness. It was despair not rage that would claim him if his defences faltered.

They spiralled down a rough staircase, a columnar vein bearing them ever further from the distant, forgotten sky. Of all the surviving *na'kyrim*, only Hammarn had remained up in the portions of Highfast that had been built atop the pinnacle rather than carved out of it. He had passed the first night of his recovered freedom in a small, high sleeping chamber with Yvane and K'rina. All the rest, with barely a word, hardly a moment spared to gather food and water, had disappeared into these ancient, chthonic depths. As if to turn their backs upon the world and separate themselves from it. As if compelled by fear, or shame, or bitterness to bury themselves.

An errant shadow angling across the stonework of the stairway caught Orisian's eye. He paused, touched fingertip to rock. He traced the carved symbols, their edges blunted and bevelled by time.

'Look at that,' he muttered. 'A stonemason's mark, I think. That must be . . . how old?'

Yvane leaned against the wall, a couple of steps above him. She was a little out of breath. 'Seven hundred years or more. One of Marain's masons, perhaps.'

'So many lifetimes, and it's lain here in the stone all that time.

Kings, and wars, and Thanes, all come and gone, half-forgotten.'
He let his hand fall. He felt the weight of the unknown past
here. A thousand and more years, with all their suffering, all
their deaths, lost to memory. None of it of consequence now, yet
all of it real and heavy.

'Do you want to rest?' he asked Yvane quietly.

'Don't be silly,' she muttered, a reassuring touch of the old
brashness there in her voice. 'It's hardly any distance now.'

Orisian nodded and resumed his descent.

'Plenty of places they could have chosen to sulk in, though,'
he heard Yvane saying irritably behind him. 'Seems a bit overex-
cited of them to burrow quite so deep.'

The *na'kyrim* had gathered in a chamber where Highfast's hollow
roots brushed the precipitous surface of the mountain. The shutters at the windows were propped narrowly open, giving a
glimpse of the immense open spaces, the plummeting drop, that
lay outside; admitting a dull light and cold threads of unceasing
wind.

Simple beds filled much of the room, and many were occupied
by the sleeping or the sick or the weak.

'Look at this, look at this,' Yvane murmured in distress as
they walked the length of the chamber.

In even the plainest, most human of *na'kyrim* faces Orisian had
until now always seen some trace of their Kyrinin parentage: a
composed serenity, an elegant balance in their features or those
calm grey eyes. Now he saw only wounds, of body and spirit
alike. Eyes had the nervous restlessness of the hunted and
hounded. Skin was marred by sores or cuts or burns. Cheeks had
sunk into hollow bowls, sucked in by hunger or misery. One
woman lay unmoving save for the constant, silent working of her
thin lips, a smear of burned and raw flesh disfiguring one side of
her face and crusting up across part of her scalp. The wound was
coated in a slick white salve, but it looked inflamed. Orisian was

glad that she had her eyes closed, for he feared what he might see there had he met her gaze.

He felt his anger as a pain in his chest. It knotted itself there, and because he fought to keep it locked away, it raged all the more brightly and bitterly. It clamoured for release, demanding that there must be punishment, that only the suffering of the guilty could answer this suffering of the innocent. But he refused it. He had never known its like, never known this hot, sharp conviction, like a howl inside him, that the only healing he could ever hope for was with a sword in his hand and blood upon its blade. But still he refused it.

Eshenna was seated on one of the beds closest to the windows. Little gusts of wind stirred her hair. Her hands were folded in her lap like white fallen leaves.

She looked up as Yvane sat beside her on the thin mattress. Orisian saw the same thing in her eyes he had seen in so many others: a defeated, drained emptiness.

'This is where I belonged,' Eshenna murmured as she looked down once more to her hands. She held some tiny fragment of cloth there, twisting it around her long fingers. 'These are the people I belong to. I should never have left. I should have been here.'

'No,' murmured Yvane.

'We couldn't have made any difference,' Orisian said. 'None of us. Not here.'

'I know,' Eshenna whispered. 'That's not why I should have been here.'

And Orisian understood her. He felt the same longing rising up in him: not to have been here in Highfast when Aeglyss came, but to have slipped Rothe's grasp when his shieldman dragged him out of Castle Kolglas on the night of Winterbirth. To have plunged back into the fire and the fury and been at his father's side. Try to save his father, try to save Inurian. And, in failing, to be released from the burden of all that had flowed from that one night.

He closed his eyes. All his anger easily folded itself into a shaming despair, a profound sense that nothing was as it was meant to be. He should have paid the same price that had been demanded of Kylane and Kennet, Rothe and Inurian. And he could have wept then, thinking of his mother and brother, bound in linen winding sheets, riding the corpse-ship out to The Grave. For the first time he understood, not with his head but with his heart, what had been inside his father all those years since the Heart Fever stole away Lairis and Fariel. It was not grief; it was the desire to have gone with them. It was guilt at having let them go alone.

He blinked at Eshenna.

'Where's Amonyn?' he managed to ask.

'The Scribing Hall,' she told him.

'I know the way,' Orisian said.

The cavernous space of the Scribing Hall felt cold and dead. Wet ash was piled thickly against some of the walls and smeared across the floor. In one corner was a great, precarious heap of half-burned timbers, fragments of shelves and tables and chairs. Thick black soot streaked the walls and darkened the ceiling. Everything, everywhere, lay beneath the finest grey dust of destruction. A few meagre stacks of books and manuscripts had been assembled on some of the surviving desks. Many were scorched, their edges charred and curled. It was a pitiful remnant of the innumerable writings Orisian had seen when last he entered this library.

'That's what remains to us of all the labours since Lorryn first came here,' Amonyn murmured. 'More than two and a half centuries.'

Orisian remembered seeing him on his first visit to Highfast; one of their Council, he thought, though they had never spoken as far as he could recall. There seemed to be a consensus amongst the *na'kyrim* that this man, as much as any, was now their leader.

He was tall and handsome, still possessed of a certain grace and air of physical power despite recent hardships. He was subdued, though. Sorrowful and weary.

Orisian stirred a strandline of ash with the toe of his boot.

'Cerys . . . the Elect . . . died here,' said Amonyn. He sighed. 'It would have broken her heart to see it thus. It breaks all our hearts.'

'Asking too much to start again,' Orisian said. It was half-statement, half-question.

Amonyn pressed long, milk-nailed fingers into his eyes. There was a strength about him, but it was not an unopposed strength. It was there, and evident, because it was required. Because the man it fortified was beleaguered.

'There are those who wish to leave this place and never return. Too much grief here. Too much horror.'

Orisian nodded silently. Amonyn lifted his gaze towards the small windows high on the far wall. They admitted only a watery light.

'This was meant to be a sanctuary for us,' the *na'kyrim* said. 'And in the end it was one of our own kind who breached it. It was the Shared, ours alone, that undid us. But then, sanctuaries can only ever come to one of two ends: they cease to be required or they fail. It was never likely that Highfast's end would be of the first kind, I suppose. That would have been asking for deeper changes in the world than are common.'

'Where would you go if you left?'

'Dyrkyrnon, for most.'

'I imagine there's no place there for a Scribing Hall, or a library.'

'It seems unlikely,' said Amonyn quietly.

'You should stay. All of you.'

Amonyn glanced sideways at him. A shrewd, thoughtful look.

'It would be, for many, the harder choice to stay. Something was lost here, and it could never be recovered. Safety, for a people who find the world ill-provided with that quality. They – we – trusted this place.'

The *na'kyrim* studied Orisian as intently as a gemsmith examining a stone.

'There was less sadness in you when last you were here,' he said. 'Less darkness. Eshenna has told me a little of what you have seen since then. She expressed some concern about you.'

'She need not worry.'

'No?' Amonyn sighed. 'Such wounds as you bear are difficult to conceal from *na'kyrim*. From some of us, at least. Doors that were once open in you are now barred. Windows have been shuttered. It is not unusual for any of us, when we are bruised, to retreat in the hope of avoiding further injury.'

Orisian crossed to one of the smoke-blackened desks and rested back against its edge. The solitude and disconnection he had for so long now felt growing within him were softened for a moment by a vivid sense of Inurian's presence. He could recall his lost friend's face with fresh clarity, envisaging it graced with a sympathetic smile. There was much about Amonyn that reminded him of Inurian.

'I've not chosen to bar any doors,' he said, 'but . . . things have changed. All those I most valued are dead, or have been parted from me. And I am Thane now. I imagine Thanes must always be somewhat alone.'

Amonyn raised his faint eyebrows and gave a slight shrug.

'I have little experience of Thanes,' he admitted. 'I think any man, though, whatever his station, will break if he takes all the weight of decisions, all the assaults of the world, upon himself alone.'

'You've seen K'rina?' Orisian asked.

Amonyn hesitated for a moment, as if debating whether to concede such a shift in the conversation. The decision was made, and he nodded.

'Do you understand what has happened to her?' asked Orisian. 'Eshenna claims she is some kind of . . . weapon. Or trap.'

'It may be so,' Amonyn said. He was grave, his voice tinged

with sadness. 'Her essence is either gone, or so deeply buried as to be beyond giving any sign even in the Shared. When she is near, I feel . . .' He curled the fingers of one hand in the air, reaching for precision. Defeated, he let his hand fall back to his side. 'There is a hunger there. A mindless hunger. And the spoor of the Anain are upon her, like the tracks of deer in the earth. Whatever has been made of her, they did the making.'

Orisian pursed his lips. His hands closed upon the lip of the desk. The wood felt brittle and dry beneath his grip. He looked at his palm and saw a bar of ash across it.

'There is something of her that reminds me of Tyn, the Dreamer,' Amonyn said, wincing at the memory. 'Of what Aeglyss did to him. How he . . . emptied him, and then wore the empty shell himself. K'rina is a shell, but what is now within? Perhaps nothing.' He sighed. 'But in truth no one here can tell you any more than Eshenna or Yvane have already done. To learn more about K'rina, we would need to go much deeper into the Shared than any of us would dare. What Eshenna has already discovered . . . It was an act of great bravery, or desperation, for her to search it out.'

Orisian nodded. 'Too much for her, I think,' he said. 'I regret that. It was at my insistence that she did it.'

'You won't find anyone here eager to repeat the venture. The beast found his way inside our defences once already. We would not invite him in again.'

'It must be very difficult for you, to be frightened of the Shared,' Orisian said.

There was that instant of acute, appraising attention once more, as if Amonyn was surprised to hear such sentiments from a Huanin.

'It is,' the *na'kyrim* said quietly. 'We have lost more than one home.'

'And until Aeglyss is gone, you can none of you return to the one that's inside your heads.'

'We must exile ourselves from the Shared. K'rina's wound was not serious. She has needed no more than the most mundane of ministrations. But there are those within these walls who are dying from their wounds, their ailments. I might save some of them, if I had the courage, or the strength, to allow the Shared to flow through me. But I do not. None of us do.'

Orisian looked up at the huge roof of the hall, dropped his gaze to the few surviving books collected on nearby desks. 'You should stay, all of you. That's what I came to tell you. You'd be no safer – probably less – out there on the roads, perhaps even in Dyrkyrnon. I will leave men here to guard you, and to keep Herraic and the others in order.'

Amonyn stooped elegantly to pull a fragment of parchment from a drift of ash. He frowned at it briefly then let it fall. It fluttered down, black and illegible.

'Not everything that is broken can be mended, however much we – you – might wish otherwise. Some things . . . do not mend.'

'I know that,' Orisian said. 'Believe me, I understand that. I know that the past cannot be changed, cannot be undone. But the future . . . I still believe, still hope, that can be changed, can be shaped by what we choose to do. And enough has already been lost. We shouldn't give up any more without a fight. Anything that's worth preserving, it needs to be fought for now, don't you think? Or there will be nothing left at all of any worth, any brightness.'

'Everyone has to choose their own battles to fight,' Amonyn said quietly. 'We will see, though. Give us your warriors to guard us, and perhaps. Perhaps. There might be some of us willing to remain. You don't mean to stay here yourself, though.'

Orisian shook his head. 'I can't see any other choice. If I hid away here . . .' The words faded, losing themselves.

The *na'kyrim* angled his head, smiling now with the very smile Orisian's memory had put upon Inurian's face.

'There's always choice. We seldom understand our every reason for doing what we do, but somewhere, hidden or not, made or unmade, there's always choice. We each choose our own battles, as I said.'

There was, high in the great keep of the ancient fortress, a wide chamber from which the Wardens of the Aygll Kings once exercised the power of those distant monarchs. They judged those who disturbed the peace of the long road Highfast guarded; they levied the tithes that paid for Dun Aygll's palaces and for the many royal pleasures of their inhabitants; they marshalled the warriors who enforced peace upon the Karkyre Peaks, and all the land from Ive to Hent to Stone. As the road fell into ruin, as the Storm Years sent the mountain folk down onto the plains in search of easier, safer lives, as Highfast itself declined into its long slumber, so that chamber had grown quiet. Each dwindling of Highfast's garrison had seen its inhabitants retreat into ever more restricted portions of the vast stronghold, withdrawing from many of its innumerable passages and halls and turrets. So this lofty chamber had emptied of voices, and populated itself instead with dust and silences and the webs of hopeful spiders.

Orisian called all his warriors there because he wanted privacy from Herraic and his sullen, subjugated men. Because he wanted light, and the sight of the sky, to be attendant upon this moment. From the windows here, where Highfast reached almost to its utmost height above its vast, precipitous pedestal, he could see an ocean of scudding clouds brushing over serried ranks of peaks.

'I will take K'rina into the north,' he said. 'To the Glas Valley. As close as I can get to Kan Avor, and to Aeglyss.'

He looked not at the faces of those assembled before him, but at the old, indistinct carving of a crown set into the stonework above the door. He felt strangely unfamiliar to himself, as if some part of him had stepped aside from his tempestuous core, where fear and confusion and agonies of doubt boiled. He was unexpectedly calm.

'It is a journey she was meant to make, I think, until we – I – stole her away from it. Now she cannot make it alone, so I will take her. Past Hent, and through Anlane. Most of you are to stay here, and I'll want your pledge to keep safe all who are within these walls, human and *na'kyrim* alike. Guard them against whatever may come from outside, or from within. It's the only service your Blood, and your Thane, requires of you now.

'If there are ten of you who are willing to come with me, and with K'rina, I would welcome your aid. No more than ten, for there'll be no battles if I can help it. At this time of year, this season, most of the White Owls should be quartered in their winter camps. With care, we might go entirely unnoticed. But I will take no one who does not come by their own free choice.'

Taim Narran stepped forward, of course, even before Orisian had drawn breath: a single, determined pace closer to his Thane. Others followed him, one by one, the only sound their soft feet on the flagstoned floor. And for Orisian there was both relief and guilt in the sight of them coming out from amongst their fellows. Offering themselves, and their lives, to him.

Afterwards, as the warriors departed, descending the long stairways, Taim Narran came to him.

'Are you sure?' was all the warrior asked him, gently.

'Not sure. I've seen and heard enough to make me think it needs doing. And I'm here; there's no one else to do it. But you don't have to come, Taim. Highfast will need a strong hand to hold it, and there's no one I'd trust more than you. You've a wife and a daughter waiting for you who'll need you after all this is done. I'd be glad to see you stay, truly.'

Taim Narran only shook his head sadly at that, and went after his men. Orisian and Yvane were left alone in the broad chamber, the *na'kyrim* watching him with hard eyes.

'Stay,' Orisian said to her. 'You've done enough. More than enough.'

'I'll come for K'rina. She deserves that much of us, at least. There should be someone of her own kind there to care for her, to watch over her. Someone who understands something of what she was, what her life was, before she became only a tool of those with wars to fight.'

'I care for her,' Orisian said. The fires in him were damped down, for now. He wanted only quiet. He would not argue with Yvane. And there was, in any case, a truth he could entirely understand in her subdued anger.

'Perhaps you do,' she said. 'Perhaps you think you do. But still she is used. By the Anain. By us. *Na'kyrim* have learned – hundreds of years have taught us – to find caring and trust and safety only in one another. In our own. If there is anything of K'rina left, lost in the Shared or sealed away inside her body, she deserves to look out and see a face like her own. And I played my part in helping you to find her. Whether that was wise or not, I don't know, but I'll not walk away from her now.'

She left him there, and he stood for a time breathing the damp air, tasting its age and its abandonment. Listening to the timeless, unending wind tumbling over the skin of the fortress. Watching as flurries of snow began to swirl once more past the windows.

When he at last stirred himself, he went to find Ess'yr and Varryn. He said not a word to them, nor they to him. He merely settled himself onto a bench and watched them. They rolled spare bowstrings about their fingers and packed them away in pouches. They sewed new seams into their hide boots where they had started to split. They sighted along the shafts of their arrows in search of imperfections, smoothed the feathered flights. They inspected their water bags for wear and for leaks.

All of this they did unhurriedly, silently. That concentration, that graceful intensity of attention and purpose, was soothing to

Orisian. It spoke to him of acceptance, of calm accommodation to the future the world offered up. For so long, as a child searching for solace in the wake of the Heart Fever, he had imagined that there might be other kinds of lives than his, ones that rode the tempests of the world with greater ease. He had seized upon every hint that Inurian let slip about the ways of the Kyrinin, taking them to be tokens of just such lives; fragmentary promises that other possibilities existed beyond the walls of bereaved Castle Kolglas.

He could still summon up some trace of those childhood hopes, but it was the memory of them that offered comfort now, not their substance. He knew more; was no longer that child.

Varryn stood tall, and held his long spear straight at his side. For the first time in many days, he looked directly into Orisian's eyes and spoke to him.

'We go now into the lands of the enemy?'

Orisian nodded wordlessly, feeling that faint, still peace drift away. And he watched as the thinnest of smiles tightened on the Kyrinin warrior's face. As the tattoos that told the tales of the deaths he had wrought flexed on his skin.

'Then I will wet my spear with their blood. And they will learn the Fox still live.'

V

Eska of the Hunt left her dogs behind in Glasbridge and walked alone into the Glas Valley, towards Kan Avor. There was deep snow across the fields, but still she shunned the roads, the better to avoid any inconvenient attention. It found her in any case.

Before she was out of sight of Glasbridge's dark outline hunched down on the western horizon, she saw three figures coming towards her across a pristine expanse of snow. They laboured, though whether that was due to the depth of snow, or because like many others in this ravaged valley they were sick or starving, she could not tell at this distance. It hardly mattered. They did not have the look of warriors, certainly not Inkallim, and thus, even hale and hearty, were unlikely to be any threat to her. She strode on along the line of a snow-buried ditch, ignoring them.

One of the men called out to her as they drew near, angling across the great white field to intercept her course. His accent marked him as Gyre, from the Bloodstone Hills; most likely, she thought, the Frein Valley. She had been there once, tracking the killer of one of the Lore. She had always had a talent for voices, for reading them and remembering their cadences. It had been useful, on occasion, in her service of the Inkall.

She read disorder and desperation in this man's voice. She marched on, head down. The snow crunched crisply beneath her booted feet.

'Wait, there,' the man shouted again.

Eska still did not look round, but she could hear that they were close now, too close to ignore. She must either run – she could easily outpace them, no doubt – or face them. There might be something to be gained, she supposed, in talking to them. Some fragment of information, perhaps. That was, after all, the currency she dealt in, and the substance of the task Kanin oc Horin-Gyre had bestowed upon her.

She stood still, and turned to face the three men. They were grimy and gaunt. Hungry, she judged, but not yet quite enfeebled by it. One at least had a feverish look that suggested illness. She quickly made the necessary assessment: a staff one leaned upon, a hammer hanging from a belt, a tiny knife, a scabbarded sword that must have been stolen or looted from the dead. They were much like scores, perhaps hundreds, of others scattered all across the Glas Valley: ordinary folk who had marched in the wake of the Battle, fired by faith or greed or hope, only to find the business of fighting an ill-supplied war in the midst of winter more brutal and breaking than they had imagined. Debris left behind as the stronger, more vigorous flood had swept on into the south.

'Any food?' the nearest of the men asked without preamble.

Eska shook her head silently.

His eyes tracked her lean lines, tracing the form of her muscles beneath her hides. His gaze lingered for a moment upon her spear, darted down to her leather boots.

'No food,' he mumbled. 'Where are you going?'

'Kan Avor,' she said. 'Have you been there?'

The man shrugged. She saw a flicker of unease, perhaps remembered horror, in the eyes of one of his companions, though.

'I would be interested to know how things stand there,' she said. 'Who you saw there. What is happening.'

'Nothing good,' the first man rasped. The others clearly deferred to him. 'Too much . . .' He wrinkled his nose, as if at a foul stench.

'Too much of what?' Eska enquired, and as soon as she did so, saw that her efforts would be fruitless. The man grimaced. He was angered.

'Too much of everything,' he muttered, then: 'You're not like us, not like everyone else. Who are you?' His tone, the way he stared avariciously at Eska's boots, made clear that his curiosity was not born of any desire for friendship.

'I am of the Hunt Inkall,' she said levelly. That was as much as she would share.

'One of Tegric's Children? Ha, ha.'

He sounded enthused at the thought of such reputed prey. It was absurd. In normal times, such men should be cowed by her presence, her implied abilities. Such calculation was clearly beyond them now. They, like so many, had abandoned their judgement in favour of baser, more feral urges. Eska saw it all around her in recent days. Some seemed barely affected by the strange, ubiquitous sickness of the mind; many — most, she thought — were slowly, incrementally slipping into madness. She had even found herself becoming increasingly ill-tempered, murderous rage sometimes held at bay only by a lifetime of habitual self-discipline.

Now, though, regarding these wretched men, she thought in dispassionate, practical terms. They were clearly disinclined to provide her with any useful knowledge. So be it. They could not prevent her escape, but if by some bizarre chance word of her approach preceded her to Kan Avor and there fell into an unfriendly ear, matters might become unnecessarily complicated.

She felt faint regret as she came to her decision. These lives would end without having greatly aided in the advancement of the creed. But then, each and every life could only be as it was written, nothing more and nothing less. Fate had brought these men to her; she was but its tool in this.

The ringleader advanced, leering as he did so. She staggered him with a blow from the butt of her spear into his ribcage. The same movement, rebounding in a smooth arc, satisfying in its precision, brought the barbed spear-point back to lay open the second man's face. She glimpsed the blood-flecked bone of his cheek as she spun on one foot and crouched, punching the base of her spear into the snow for support, straightening a leg to crack her heel into the third's knee. He howled and hobbled sideways. The snow tripped him.

Eska rose. The first of her assailants had recovered his balance, and was clumsily drawing that purloined sword with all the facility of one who had never held such a weapon in his life. She drove her spear into his belly with enough force to lift him off his feet, and left it there. She kicked the man who had fallen in the side of his head as he began to rise. He slumped back. She took a handful of his hair and hammered the heel of her free hand once into the bridge of his nose. There was a splintering crunch and he went limp.

The one whose cheek she had cut was staggering away, vainly trying to press back a flap of skin to his face, his hands fumbling in the blood that she had freed. She followed him, tearing her barbed spear free from the dying, howling ringleader's stomach as she went. She put it into the small of the fleeing man's back. She twisted it and pulled. He came staggering back towards her, caught on the barbs. She threw a foot up against his spine and kicked him free. He fell forwards.

Eska walked on towards Kan Avor.

She came to the city across ground that remembered its recent inundation. It had been the Glas Water, before the breaking of the Dyke, and that sodden past remained close. Beneath the snow, a thin crust of ice and frozen mud lay like skin over soft silt. Her feet sometimes broke through into cloying, part-liquid earth that was thick with dead reed stems and half-decayed water weed. Clumps of straggly, leafless willows stood here and there, their pliable branches bent by snow and icicles. Once, ice crackled under her foot and dropped her into an ankle-deep pool of black, almost glutinous, water. She at once unlaced her boots and dried both them and her feet as best she could. In the north she had seen toes, even legs and lives, lost for want of such simple precautions.

Sitting there, rubbing at her skin to warm it, she noticed the end of a leg bone jutting out from the mud close by, the ball joint like a smooth fist. It was not the first bone she had seen: there had been half a jaw, four ribs protruding from the snow like the fringe of a broken-toothed comb. All human. The dead lay thickly here. It might be, she supposed, the result of the Heart Fever that had raged through the Lannis Blood a few years ago, but the remains looked to have more age to them than that. She preferred to think them the dead of Kan Avor Field, the great battle fought here a century and a half ago, when the Black

Road was driven from these lands. She found that a pleasing thought.

'We came back,' she whispered foolishly to the leg bone as she rose and continued on her way.

Kan Avor lay beneath a fetid fog. Eska felt its moisture on her hair, her skin. And she felt its stench close like an invisible hand over her mouth and nose. She smelled mud and rot and death and smoke and waste, so potent, all of them, that even through the muffling snow and ice they fouled the air. The frozen ruins were teeming with people, far more than she had anticipated. And there were bodies, which was just as she had anticipated.

A woman lay stiff and taut in the doorway of a house that had long ago lost its roof. Her dead eyes watched Eska pass through lashes beaded with frost. One arm was bent at the elbow, lifting her splayed grey hand towards the street. Dogs had chewed off the fingers. In a little square, a corpse hung from a protruding stone high up on a wall. They – someone – had suspended him by his arms and killed him, possibly slowly, with a multitude of blows. Eska's cursory glance was enough to pick out perhaps twenty separate wounds. His clothes, soaked with blood, had frozen rigid and black. From the toe of one naked foot hung a tiny icicle of blood, a single fat drop arrested in the act of readying itself to fall.

The smell of roasting flesh drew Eska to a ruined house. It must once have been a noble residence, for there was a stable block, and in its yard a crowd had gathered to watch the hind leg of a horse being turned on a spit above a crackling fire. It was a twisted echo of the place's former purpose, but that did not interest Eska; she thought instead how wasteful it was to consume an animal that might have carried a warrior south or hauled firewood or supplies.

She noted, as she progressed through the hallucinatory dream that Kan Avor had become, each accent, each ragged banner,

each subtly distinctive variation in raiment. She found people of
every ilk. Warriors from every Blood; countryfolk and townsfolk;
Tarbains; Battle Inkallim. Even some of the defeated Lannis
Blood, from whose manner it was impossible to tell whether
they were prisoners or slaves, or equal and welcomed followers of
the halfbreed. All save the Inkallim mingled with little regard
to status or origin, as if all previous associations and bonds had
been overlaid or broken all together. Only Nyve's ravens – or
better perhaps to name them Shraeve's now – held themselves
aloof.

And there were Kyrinin. Eska saw just a few of them, lingering silently at the fringes of human gatherings, moving through
the shattered streets on obscure errands. She despised them for
their presence here. Such as they had no rightful place in the city
that, however ruined, embodied the history of the Black Road.
She averted her gaze from their tattooed faces, their rangy forms.
But she counted them, as she counted everyone.

She came to a crowded street, one that stank of mud and
humanity. The people gathered there milled about without evident purpose. They snarled at one another when they were
jostled, but otherwise were all but silent. Some were barefoot.
Some, too poorly dressed for the harsh weather, sat shivering in
doorways or at the foot of walls. Eska moved amongst them,
noting with contempt how far these fellow northerners of hers
had fallen; how destitute and weak many of them appeared. She
felt no pity for those amongst them who so clearly suffered from
the cold or from hunger or from sickness. Their own stupidity
was the cause, as far as she was concerned, and it earned for them
every miserable moment.

Many of the men and women often looked towards a door in
a crumbling edifice along one side of the street. Others glanced
constantly up towards empty windows above. Those blank, dark
apertures were framed with moss and ferns sprouting from the
seams of the stonework. There was nothing to see, but Eska felt

the simmering collective excitement. All attention, conscious or otherwise, was upon some invisible focus behind those walls, beyond those windows.

Eska drifted through the throng, counting, always counting, always studying. She strove to avoid notice, but she could hardly conceal her health, her weapons, her clean leathers and hides. People stared at her. She kept her eyes empty, unresponsive.

Then the door was opening, and a stillness fell across the street as if a wind had suddenly fallen away. Into the eerie calm came Shraeve of the Battle and other Inkallim, and Kyrinin, and last of all Aeglyss the *na'kyrim*.

He was stooped, as if so old that his very bones were bent by the burden of years. He walked unsteadily, each pace a short and sliding shuffle. His hair was thinning, and where it remained the strands looked fragile as spider's web, almost translucent. Every bone in his face was visible beneath the bleached, cracked skin. His hand, when he extended it towards some adoring spectator, bore fingers like crooked twigs. Where his fingernails should have been were raw sores. So reduced and brittle and damaged did he appear that it was difficult to tell that he was *na'kyrim* rather than human; the dwindling of his body masked the differences, drawing all his features down into indistinct decrepitude. Had Eska seen him on the street of some city, not knowing who he was, she might have veered away from him, thinking him the bearer of some wasting plague.

And yet. There was in him something that held the eye. Something that caught her breath in her throat, and filled her with the deep certainty that this frail, eroded figure was far more than mere man. All around her, people were kneeling. Smiling. Eska knelt too, the better to merge with the crowd. But in doing so she sensed, if only distantly, the rightness of the gesture. She felt, between her thoughts, in the gaps left in her skull by her own mind, the movement of this broken man's thoughts, the ferocity of his desires and his remorseless capacity to fulfil them.

She felt these things, and could have been transported by them as one consumed by hunger might be on catching the faint scent of the richest imaginable food. But she did not succumb.

Eska had come to the Hunt as a child too young to speak or walk. An orphan probably, though there was no way of being certain since the records were imperfect. She had no memory of what preceded the discipline and the apparatus of the Hunt, and her every desire – even her faith in the creed – had been subsumed by her devotion to the Inkall. She had no sense of needs or imperatives beyond service to the Hunt. As the vast unspoken, promissory temptations of the halfbreed's presence washed about and through her, she clung to that clear and narrow allegiance, and found it sturdy. She remained observer, not participant.

Aeglyss raised his arms. He was perhaps too weak to straighten them, for his hands came little higher than his head, the elbows remained crooked.

'Friends,' he murmured, and the word came to Eska from both within and without. It embraced her and soothed her. She smiled despite herself.

'Faithful friends. We move towards the light of a new sun, you and I. Great changes are upon us, and I am their herald, their helmsman.'

Whispers in the crowd, like the rustling of leaves: affirmations and adorations. Eska could feel the edges of her attention contracting. This halfbreed drew everything in towards himself.

'I have promised many things,' Aeglyss said. 'And the time comes when I shall make good those promises. This world has ever been found wanting. From my first breath, I have gone, step by step, into its dark heart, and over all those years it has shown me how it revels in cruelty, how it feeds upon deceit, takes pleasure in the suffering and the death of those who least deserve it.'

The truth of all he said was like a light burning inside Eska's eyes. It was bright, and she could imagine the warmth and the comfort it could offer, yet she was not blinded by it. Narrowly, determinedly, she thought of the crossbow on her back. Its weight grounded her. Had she been prepared, with crossbow in hand and a bolt ready for its string, she might have killed this halfbreed here and now, before Shraeve or the watchful Kyrinin could intervene. She concentrated upon that thought, and turned it over and over in her mind, as if practising some protective ritual of the sort the Tarbains once favoured. She girded her mind with imagined visions of the lethal act, clinging to them.

'All of this I have seen,' Aeglyss called out, 'and I have learned it well. And now I am granted the strength to cure the world of its ills.'

Kanin had told her not to throw her life away in any attempt upon Aeglyss. Eska doubted the Thane's insistence that no single dart or blade was likely to prove fatal to the *na'kyrim* – she had yet to find a neck that would not yield to a sharp-edged caress – but she was prepared to wait a while longer before testing it.

Aeglyss was smiling now, in a wolfish way. Eska thought she saw contempt there, as he surveyed the kneeling, bowing host filling the street, but she doubted anyone else would share her impression.

'A world must be broken before it can be made whole again,' Aeglyss intoned. 'There must be a purging with fire and with blood. We must strip everything back to bare soil before we can plant new seeds. Is it not so?'

'Yes,' Eska heard a woman at her side murmur, and others all through the crowd. A hundred whispers of assent.

'And thus is the purpose of all my suffering revealed. Though I did not seek it, the strength is in me to subjugate all the world to a single will. I – we – shall lay bare the earth. Start afresh. I shall remove all dispute, sweep away all pride. There will be no more envy, no more traitors. Only the faithful.'

Eska repeated that word to herself within the chamber of her head: faithful. She could feel the ardour trying to shake its way free of her stern self-restraint; she could feel that eager, ambitious portion of her spirit struggling to carry the rest of her into surrender and submission to the halfbreed's certainty. But it was not, she thought, the creed to which he truly demanded faith. It was to him. Though he spoke in the language of the Black Road – the unmaking of the world, its purging by bloodshed – it was not the return of the Gods he hoped to usher in, but his own dominion. Cannek had told Eska as much, before his illfated endeavours at Hommen. He had told her that Aeglyss was, at heart, a mad child. Nothing more. She had always thought Cannek a perceptive, perhaps even wise, man.

'Tomorrow, at dawn, there will be wonders,' Aeglyss proclaimed, nodding as if compelled to do so by the irresistible truth of what he said. 'Tomorrow I will descend upon our enemies, and undo them. I will deliver to you, and to us all, the greatest of victories. I will give to you the place of the Fisherwoman's birth.'

The roar of delight shivered back and forth along the street, echoing from the stonework. Some woman, overcome, leapt to her feet and ran towards Aeglyss, arms outstretched, wild ecstasy in her face. She was blind to all save him, sending those who obstructed her path sprawling away. She wept and laughed as she ran.

One of the Kyrinin standing beside Aeglyss, tall and powerful, his face thick with tattooed swirls and curves, rapped the heel of his spear once upon the cobbles, let it spring up free. He caught it again, stretched out a foot and planted it firmly, then snapped the spear forward. It went flat and true into the woman's chest and lodged there. Her frenzied, delirious wail was cut short as she plunged back and down.

'Tomorrow, you may witness the wonder,' Aeglyss said as if

nothing had happened. The woman was groaning, but no one paid her any heed. Eska could not see her any more, but the spear stood erect and it trembled with the woman's faltering breaths.

'Those who are here at dawn, you will find me there, in the hall above.' Aeglyss gestured towards the windows. Every head was tipped up to follow his hand. 'I shall exceed Orlane, and Dorthyn, and all who went before. In your name, in your service, I shall make dust of the past, for these are new times we live in, and a new world we are making. Attend, and see what wonders I work on your behalf.'

*

Glasbridge's harbour was empty of boats. The deserted quayside stood silent, its moorings idle, its taverns and shops burned or deserted. Wet slush covered its stones. Offshore, amidst the turbulent waves driving in from the vast estuary, the short mast of some half-sunken fishing boat rocked like a swamped sapling. Kanin stared at it for a time, narrowing his eyes against the sleet sweeping in on the wind. He imagined for a moment that its movement, the regular, solitary beat of its instability, might convey some message to him. There was nothing there, though.

He turned to the crowd standing there on the quay, a miserable, bedraggled assemblage. Some of the last dregs of Glasbridge's Lannis inhabitants. There were only a few men of fighting age. Women and a few children, old men, frail men, regarded him with various kinds of contempt and resentment. Sixty of them, nearly one in six, as best he could guess, of those who had not died during their town's destruction and capture, or not escaped it. They had been dragged and driven here like recalcitrant sheep, full of hate but too battered and defeated to offer any resistance.

Kanin's warriors ringed the Lannis folk, enclosing them in a silent cordon of spears and swords. He doubted such precautions were really necessary. These were broken people. And that was something he meant to change, even if only a little.

A Gyre man was kneeling before him, his hands tied behind his back. Kanin spat meltwater from his lips.

'You know me,' he shouted across the wind at the townsfolk. 'You know I've made this town mine. I've opened the food stores to you, fed you as well as we eat ourselves. Those of you who'd been made slaves or servants, I've freed you from that.'

He grimaced at a sudden flurry of sleet.

'This man killed a Lannis girl yesterday.'

He kicked the Gyre captive in the back, sending him sprawling into the slush. Igris hauled the man back onto his knees. The shieldman had great coiled chains looped over his shoulder, found in the storeroom of a half-wrecked smithy.

'Now you see how things go in my town,' Kanin shouted, and nodded to Igris. The shieldman hesitated. He winced.

'Do it,' Kanin hissed.

Others of his Shield came forward. They helped Igris to entwine the chains about the Gyre man, securing them with cords. One took his ankles, another his shoulders, and they carried him to the edge of the quay. The man stared at Kanin all the way. There was no hatred in his dark eyes, only accusation.

'I go without fear,' the man said, quite distinctly, quite calmly.

'I don't doubt it,' muttered Kanin. 'But still you go.'

His warriors swung their cargo once, then heaved him out. The sea swallowed him with a deep, hollow smack and he was gone, leaving not the slightest trace in the relentless waves slapping up against the stonework. Some of the Lannis townsfolk crowded to the edge, pushing past the guards, craning their necks to try and follow the man's descent. One kicked slush after him. Another whispered curses Kanin could not hear above the wind and water.

'I don't expect love or loyalty from you,' Kanin said. They turned back to him, and he saw new patterns in their faces now:

puzzlement in some, suspicion in others. 'I do expect the sense to see that things can change. Have changed. I will shield you from the basest cruelties of your conquerors. I will permit no more of your children to die, or be stolen away by the ravens. I will feed you, and clothe you, as well as I feed and clothe the most devoted of my own followers. I will even seek boats and, if I find them, give them to you, and not hinder your departure.'

He could see out of the corner of his eye Igris watching him with poorly disguised horror. He had not told his Shield or any of his warriors his full intent today. There had been no need or point in doing so. He was Thane, and more than that he was a man alone, engaged in an undertaking none of them could see clearly enough to grasp. Only he understood what extremities the times demanded.

'But not all of you,' Kanin said, concentrating upon the attentive, bewildered townsfolk. 'I want you to go amongst your fellows, and tell them what you have seen and what I have said here today. And tomorrow I will have all of you who can hold a weapon, and have the strength to walk for a day, assembled here at dawn. I don't care who – men or women, it doesn't matter – but you will come here, and I will arm you and train you and give you an enemy to oppose.

'Because I am not your worst enemy, and you are not mine. I will show you the greatest enemy your Blood has ever had, the one responsible for all your suffering and shame, and you will fight him at my side. I will give you back the honour of your Blood. Those you leave behind here will be protected and preserved for as long as you keep this bargain with me. If you fail in what I require of you, you will all suffer the consequences.'

They stared at him, a mass of disbelief and confusion, and he stared back. Resolute. Unwavering. In the silence, gulls came drifting in off the sea, their cries sharp.

'That is all,' Kanin said, and turned. He walked away, ignoring his own warriors and their questioning glances. He could hold them for a time yet, he was sure. For long enough.

Only Igris came hurrying after him, sword tapping at his legs, mail shirt clinking.

'It doesn't seem right, sire, to be fighting the faithful when the war is so far . . .'

Kanin spun and leaned towards the shieldman, pointing a single finger at his eye.

'The war is where I say it is. By the oath you took to my father, you made the Blood's battles your own. The Thane is the Blood, and I am Thane yet. I choose our battles. Never forget it. I know what must be done, for the good of the faith, for the good of us all.'

Igris quailed before his lord's wrath, and Kanin stalked away. He was right in this. He was certain of it. If he was the last and only man in all the world who could see what had to be done, so be it. He had strength enough for that, whatever it cost him, wherever it led him.

Two figures awaited him a short distance down the harbour-side. They were leaning against the side of a broken cart, watching with wry amusement: two of the three Hunt Inkallim who had made themselves his shadows.

'Have you found what I need?' Kanin asked them.

'You have a rare talent for spreading havoc and confusion, it seems, Thane,' one of the men murmured.

'I asked if you have found what I need,' barked Kanin.

The man inclined his head, deflecting – or dismissing – the Thane's anger.

'Seventy of them. Every corpse-in-waiting this town has to offer. Most should live long enough to serve your purposes. A fine concoction they are: fevers and sores and suppuration. We've got them safely sequestered beyond the reach of any healers. Not that there are many of those to be found hereabouts.'

'Good. I want them in Kan Avor tomorrow. I'll have Igris arrange an escort, and drivers for the wagons. No word from Eska yet?'

The man shook his head, and Kanin grunted. He strode away.

'You'll make our task of keeping you alive difficult, Thane, if
you turn your own people against you,' one of the Inkallim said
behind him.

Kanin stopped and hung his head for a moment. Then he
turned and stared at the man.

'I didn't give you the task. I don't care how easy or otherwise
you find it. What happens will happen, since none of us chooses
the course of the Road. Do we?' He asked it dully at first, but
then again, more pointedly, more openly: 'Do we?'

VI

The heat of bodies and of breath warmed and moistened the air
in the hall. Three hundred people, perhaps, crammed in, standing in expectant, reverent silence. Eska stood at the rear of the
crush with her back to one of the gaping windows. She could feel
the bitter wind that came up the Glas Valley on her neck, even
as the warmth of the hall brushed her face. There was snow on
that wind, and an occasional errant flake came tumbling over her
shoulder to alight, and vanish into water, upon the hair or jacket
of those in front of her.

The hall was gloomy, barely recovered from the deepest dark of
night. Out to the east, Eska knew, the sky would have caught the
first grimy smear of the new day's approaching light, but here in
Kan Avor it would be some time yet before true dawn would
break. No lights burned, and in the near-darkness, with such a
close-packed crowd, it was difficult to see the halfbreed seated on
his stone slab of a throne at the far end of the chamber. When he
spoke, his voice was all but disembodied, grating out from the
columns, from the wooden floorboards.

'I killed one of the ghosts in the green. You could not understand what that means. You who hear nothing of the true thunder rolling beneath the world cannot know what it is to ride its storm winds, to master them thus. No matter. There's none left, now . . . none left . . . who could describe even the outline of what I have become.'

The hush was profound. No one breathed, none stirred. Hundreds stood there in the dark, held by that strained voice stealing across the stonework, threading its way in amongst them, running its icy touch across their skin. It seemed, even to Eska, a thing not born of a living, limited throat, but rising from the matter and nature of the world itself: as innate, as inevitable as the breaking of waves on a wild shore, or the rushing of a stream through its mountain bed.

'I will give you more easily measurable wonders,' Aeglyss said.

Such a slight figure, Eska thought, so small and frail alone there on the bench. Yet so utterly dominant of every eye, every mind. There was, in these extended, rapt moments, nothing else of consequence in the hall.

'Because I know the course of your desires, because I know that what I demand of you must be earned by gifts, because it falls to me to shape all things now; because of all this, I will give you what no other could. You and your creed ascend now, on my wings.'

The halfbreed fell silent, and his silence took something out of the world, leaving all who had been listening bereaved and diminished. There was nothing that could fill the void his presence left as he drew it back into himself, bowed his head still more deeply into his chest and let out a long, dwindling breath. But light began to come, seeping in hesitantly, eroding the lingering darkness, putting grey accents on every form. And amidst that meagre brightening, they waited and watched.

*

The Bloodheir was gone. Summoned back to Vaymouth by the Thane of Thanes, it was said. Malloc cared nothing for the two thousand men who had marched with him; it was the departure of Aewult nan Haig himself that weighed upon him. Some, Malloc knew, would welcome the Bloodheir's departure. There were those – all but traitors to his way of thinking – who thought Aewult's leadership a factor in their recent defeats. In the night just ended, by the glare of their campfire's flames, Malloc and his companions had killed one such, a man who slighted the Bloodheir's courage, his merit. The others had held him down and covered his mouth, and Malloc himself slipped a blade twice, thrice, between his ribs. They had dragged the body to a ditch and hidden it amongst reeds there. None could reasonably punish them for their deed, but it would be for the best if the question never arose.

There had been a certain comfort in the killing, a small confirmation that the world retained some semblance of sense and balance. Strangely sweeter to him than the taking of any of the other lives he had claimed in his long service of his Blood, it gave Malloc a memory to set in the scales against his disappointment at the Bloodheir's departure. He stood now, with Garrent and the others at his side, by the banks of a wide, shallow stream, and remembered the feel of that disloyal, foul-mouthed fool dying beneath his knife. The man had been a Taral-Haig archer, somehow separated from his company in the darkness.

In the new day's half-light, the waters of this stream looked darker and more turbid than they had any right to be. There were many such brown waterways scurrying down towards the sea from the northern fringes of the Ayth-Haig moors. It galled Malloc to find himself in such a peripheral posting, when any battle – if there was even to be such a thing – would be decided nearer the coast, beside the road that pointed the way south. That was where most of the remaining Haig forces were gathered. None defended Kilvale itself. The town would stand or fall by the strength of its own inhabitants and the warriors of its own Blood. There had been killings traded between Kilkry and

Haig. Only word of the Black Road's approach and the with-drawal of every Haig sword from the town had stilled them.

In truth, Malloc doubted the rumours of impending combat that had drifted through the army, with the smoke of its hundreds of campfires, in the evening and night just passed. He had long ago learned to distrust the misshapen guesses that infested any assemblage of fighting men like madly breeding cockroaches. The whispered reports of Black Road companies massing half a day to the north of Kilvale seemed to him no more reliable than any of the hundred other tales he had heard in recent weeks. Some clearly gave them more credence, though, so he found himself here in the misty morning, staring across the chattering waters at rough, undulating ground studded with countless clumps of low trees and shrubs.

For all his conviction that this would come to nothing, Malloc clung to a faint hope that he might have the chance to draw his sword today. The waiting, the indolence, had become insupportable. He had never known any body of men so in need of bloodshed. He revelled in the tightening of his own chest at the thought that he might, at last, have the chance to make amends for the defeats inflicted by the Black Road. This was supposedly the only fordable stretch of the river above Kilvale that the Black Road might reach in a single day. Malloc had no idea whether that was true, but it offered at least the possibility that there would be fighting to be done, so he chose to believe it. He chose to hope.

What breeze there was on this sluggish morning was out of the west, and it suddenly carried upon it the faintest, most tantalising hint of battle. The damp air brought a murmur out of the furthest mists: the muted song of war. Malloc's heart thumped, as if fed by the distant sound. He firmed his grip upon the shaft of his spear, shifted his weight from foot to foot. Nobody spoke, in all the ranks of men. Their mood was expressed not in words, but in the creaking of leather, the rasp of swords being drawn, the soft settling of helms onto heads.

Malloc saw figures far out beyond the river, imprecise movements at the limit of his mist-curbed vision. The Black Road came in loose array, slowly, spread out amongst the scattered trees, and they came armoured in mounting noise. Voices merged into a rising clamour, forming a fierce, disembodied chorus of intent that seemed almost to come from the hidden sky, descending upon Malloc and his companions from above.

There was hunger in that sound, an impersonal pledge of savagery. And as it drew nearer, and as the figures came closer and solidified, Malloc felt sudden fear stealing through his mind. It rose up from within him and ran cold needles over his scalp, sent a tremor running through his arm so that his spear shook. It changed him in a moment, as if he had stepped across a threshold, entering a chilling shadow, becoming someone else. His every thought was smothered by a mounting, absolute dread, a crippling fear of what might – what *would* – happen with his next heartbeat, or the next.

In the last vestigial corner of his former mind, he remembered this. He had felt it before, on the day of this army's humiliation beyond Kolkyre. Then, as now, all strength had leached from his arms and legs, all reason and courage fled from him. But this was deeper, this was reaching for the core of him, crushing what lay behind his eyes beneath an overwhelming despair.

Malloc gasped, feeling his breath clog in his throat. He looked sideways, and saw Garrent, close by, anguish tugging at his face, mouth opening, lips trembling. Malloc's hand shook once more, and his spear toppled from his numb grip.

'Stand firm!' he heard someone shout behind him, but the voice was wild, desperate, fully aware of its own futility.

Malloc could see the men and women coming towards him clearly now. He could see their lips moving, and the noise buffeted him, the baying of hounds, the cry of a thousand crows, promising to pick the flesh from his bones. Another few moments, another few agonising beats of his tumbling heart, and they would be at the river, setting their feet into its waters. There were riders here and there amongst the throng, towering in Malloc's sight, their mounts great beasts with blood falling from their fanged mouths. He moaned, felt his legs quiver.

Those on either side of him were backing away. Garrent was turning, letting fall his own spear just as Malloc had done. The first of them was in the river: a woman, leaning forward in anticipation, the water breaking around her ankles, a feral grin upon her face, fire in her eyes. She was staring, it seemed to Malloc, right at him, into him. He saw her sword and knew, with utter precision, what it would feel like when that blade pierced his bowels and twisted there, tearing his guts, opening him.

Then the whole host of the Black Road was running at him, howling, the horses pounding in curtains of spray across the ford, and Malloc wailed and fled. They all did. There was nothing but flight, a great jostling crowd pounding away over the rough grass. Malloc knew he was already doomed, already dead; he knew it with a certainty he had never felt before in his life. Still he fled, for his body would permit nothing else.

Crossbow bolts came whipping past him. Someone fell across his path and he trampled them. A horse came thundering up beside him, and another man went down, speared. He felt a blow on his back, and pain, but ran on. He pushed others from his path. He stumbled and went down onto hands and knees. His own terror pulled him to his feet and drove him on. Black Roaders were flowing around him, ahead of him, in amongst the fleeing warriors. Malloc heard their wild joy, saw an axe come down in a great arc onto a skull, saw a mounted swordsman laughing as he hacked again and again.

Malloc ran as if in a fell dream. He was weeping, he knew. He could hear his own voice, though he did not know what he was saying. Blood spattered his face and he tasted it. There were bodies all over the ground, like boulders, like logs. He clawed at the air before him, wanting to tear his way out of this place, this world, to whatever lay beyond, for he could not endure another moment of this.

Someone battered against his shoulder and spun him. He staggered back, facing the enemy now and seeing them pouring towards him in limitless numbers, a vast, mindless dark flood engulfing the land. A man hit Malloc across the throat with his sword, not pausing but running on in search of further prey. Malloc slumped to his knees. Blood bubbled in his mouth. He could see a woman running at him, spear levelled. He lifted his hands, but they were heavy and limp, parting as they rose as if in welcome.

The spear hit him high on the chest and knocked him onto his back. He glimpsed grey mist above. He did not remember who he was or what he was doing here. His form contained nothing but fear. It was all of him. Then that mist was blotted out by figures clustering about and above him, and they were stabbing him and kicking him. The blows rained down, and he felt them as a stooping flock of birds plunging into his body. Something was coming towards his face, towards his eyes. His heart stopped, and the descending shape made itself the blade of a sword, falling slowly like a piece of the sky come loose. It grew until he could see nothing else. And then it gathered him into its darkness and took him away.

*

Light had come into the hall in Kan Avor as fully as it ever would on this grey day. Eska could feel stiffness and ache spreading in her legs. Others, their muscles less honed than hers, had long ago sunk to the floor, sitting cross-legged on the wet boards or leaning against walls or pillars. Eska glanced out of the window. Snow was billowing through the quiet streets outside, spilling over and through the shattered ruins of this once-great city.

The cold air set her face burning, chilling the beads of sweat that still studded her brow. Her heart had slowed now, returning to its normal leisurely pace, but the memory of the hammer beat it had raced to was there in the cage of her chest. They had been moments out of time, those, a waking dream that felt endless from within its embrace. A dream of exultant, elevatory violence and joy. It had come without any warning, plucking her away from this hall, this city, and bearing her up out of the dull confines of her own head. She had been blind and deaf, riding the fury of others, feeling the wind of countless lives howling away into nothingness, knowing what it was to be at once herself and thousands, an overpowering sense of omnipotence and inevitable triumph. In that timeless span, she had been part of something vast, glorious, and unstoppable.

Plunging back into the hall, looking out from behind her own eyes and becoming aware once more of the hundreds of separate, silent figures crowded in there with her, had been disorientating. She had felt a cavernous loss in the pit of her stomach. Some of those present were undone by their parting from such glories, and fell wailing to the floor. One began to claw frantically at the rough stone of one of the columns, as if trying to climb back to the heights from which he, and all of them, had been so abruptly torn. He tore his fingertips to bloody shreds before he calmed, and slipped down, unconscious.

Eska knew only one thing: a great victory had been won for the creed. The enemies of the faith had been consumed by a fearful storm. And she had been there, within that storm. Beyond that, nothing was clear to her. Was she in error to resist this delicious madness? Could this halfbreed, now slumped and shrunken and still, insensate upon his bench, truly be the incarnation of the Kall, come to destroy the world and release it from its long suffering? Kanin oc Horin-Gyre meant to bring Aeglyss down, but she doubted now whether that was anything more than a lone sailor proposing war upon the storm, the sky itself.

A pair of Battle Inkallim were approaching her through the

crowd, one coming from the doors, the other from behind the stone bench where Aeglyss was still slumped, insensible and dormant. They came slowly, drifting almost casually between the close-pressed bodies. She should have sensed their movement long before. In her distraction she had missed what the rawest of trainees would have seen at once.

It seemed unlikely that the ravens meant to kill her here and now, but if they did it would be futile to fight them. Spear and crossbow had been left secreted amongst the ruins outside, for none save Battle Inkallim or White Owls were permitted to bring weapons into the halfbreed's presence. She visualised the drop from the window behind her to the empty street below. The leap would almost certainly break her ankles or legs, but she readied herself for it. Cautious habit had placed her here, within reach of that last, desperate recourse, when she first entered the hall. It would be her only chance if blades were bared.

Her eyes and those of the closest Inkallim met as he edged to within a long arm's reach of her. Neither blinked, neither betrayed any sign of emotion or concern.

'Shraeve would speak with you when this is done,' the man said. Quite without nuance or threat. 'She requests that you remain behind when all the rest leave here.'

Eska thought for a moment, maintaining her steady gaze.

'I am required elsewhere,' she said, matching the man's relaxed manner with her own.

'It will not take long,' he said, and turned his back on her as the second of the ravens settled in on the other side of her. The conversation was, she concluded, at an end.

Aeglyss grunted then, and every head turned towards him. An expectant murmur suffused the hall. Those who had been sitting or lying on the floor rose to their feet.

'It's done, it's done,' the *na'kyrim* breathed, pushing himself up from the bench with one hand. His voice still set the hairs on

Eska's arms and neck on end, but it was a hollow sound now, and rough-edged. She narrowed her eyes and saw, as he came, bent-kneed, to his feet, how his supporting arm trembled, how his head stayed low as if his neck no longer had the strength to lift it. How a single drop of dark red blood fell from his nose.

'Now you see . . .' he stammered, and then his whole form was shaking. More blood was flicked from his nose and mouth. His shoulders quivered, their bones visible through his thin gown. He took a single tortured step forward and his legs suddenly twisted. He fell and thrashed about, beating arms and legs against the floor.

Waves of nausea pulsed through Eska; beats of pain throbbed in her temples. She winced and felt her breath congeal in her chest. Groans and moans escaped a hundred throats. Many swayed on their feet, grabbing at those next to them to keep themselves upright.

'Clear the hall!' Shraeve cried as she knelt beside Aeglyss, trying ineffectually to restrain his flailing limbs.

The doors were thrown open and Inkallim and Kyrinin drove the throng out with fists and spears and threats. The people wept as they left, and wailed. Some fell to their hands and knees, vomiting, and were beaten and kicked until they roused themselves to struggle out. Eska made to follow the flow, but one of the Inkallim at her side held out an arm to bar her way.

'Wait,' he said. 'You may still be required.'

She disliked his tone. Though she might grudgingly accede to the right of the Lore to issue instructions to the Hunt, there was no tradition of submission to the will of the Battle. More than that, her head was spinning, her vision blurring at the edges beneath the onslaught of whatever strange sickness of the mind was pouring from the *na'kyrim*. She longed to escape from this choking, stinking chamber. But she was unarmed and hardly capable of forcing the issue, so she remained.

As the last of the onlookers were herded out, Shraeve finally

mastered Aeglyss' convulsion. She held the *na'kyrim* down, pinning his arms. Aeglyss was panting, shallow breaths rushing in
and out of him. His eyes were closed.

Goedellin came shuffling out of the shadows at the rear of the
hall, the end of his twisted stick rapping on the wooden floor.
He had been hidden until now from Eska's sight. She was surprised, and troubled, to find him here.

'What ails him?' the old Lore Inkallim asked Shraeve.

'I do not know,' she said as she stood up.

The two of them stared down at the halfbreed. He was
entirely unmoving now save for the fluttering of his chest. He
looked like a strangely animated corpse. The White Owls edged
nearer to him. Shraeve's ravens drifted closer from all parts of the
hall. The gaunt, senseless *na'kyrim* exerted a grim fascination
upon them. Blood was flowing, Eska saw, from his wrists. The
sleeves of his gown were soaked with it.

'I don't understand,' said hook-backed Goedellin, almost
plaintive to Eska's ear. She curled her lip in momentary contempt at the man's feebleness. What use was the Lore if it could
offer no guidance in times such as these? It was no wonder the
Battle had made itself master when the eldest Inkall so meekly
lapsed into confusion and uncertainty.

'No,' muttered Shraeve. 'That does not surprise me.' She was
staring at Eska even as she curtly dismissed Goedellin from her
attention.

Eska nodded slowly and slightly in acknowledgement of
Shraeve's gaze, and the Banner-captain of the Battle advanced
towards her.

'You came here from Glasbridge, we think,' Shraeve said. The
hilts of the two swords sheathed across her back rocked as she
gave her shoulders a loosening shrug. Eska took comfort in the
thought that even this formidable raven felt the tension, perhaps
even the pain, the halfbreed spilled out from himself. She made
no reply to Shraeve's question, though. She would offer nothing

willingly to Cannek's killer.

'And presumably you mean to return there,' Shraeve continued, 'since if killing Aeglyss was your plan, you would likely have made the attempt before now.'

'He would be dead,' Eska confirmed.

'Perhaps not.'

'It is difficult to defeat an assassin who places no value upon their own life.'

'Difficult,' said Shraeve with the thinnest of smiles, 'but not impossible.'

Eska could see in her cold eyes that she meant Cannek, and despised that faint flicker of satisfaction she detected in the other woman. Cannek had willingly submitted himself to the judgement of fate. It ill became anyone to permit themselves more than transitory pleasure or regret at his death. Shraeve, it seemed, was less mindful than she should be of the creed's warnings against the corrosive effects of pride.

'The Inner Servant —' Shraeve gestured towards black-lipped Goedellin without taking her eyes from Eska '— wishes to travel to Glasbridge. I invite you to escort him. It would be for the best. Your presence here causes unwelcome disquiet.'

'Can I not come, as so many do, merely to witness for myself this man you claim as such a boon to the creed?' Eska could not help but play out in her imagination a deadly dance with Shraeve. She could picture those swords sweeping free of their scabbards, could see how her own spear — if she had it — might dart beneath or between them to pierce Shraeve's carapace of black leather. There could be no certainty of how such a dance would end. Eska was sure of only one thing: it would be brief. The first faltering, however slight, would resolve it.

'There are many who fear the Hunt's vision has become clouded,' Shraeve said. 'That you have lost sight of what is important.'

'And that is?'

'That we – all of us – are rising to our final glory. That we have mastered two Bloods already, and today – even now – our armies hunt the fleeing host of a third. This is what Tegric and his hundred died for.' Shraeve's voice rose as she spoke, acquiring a joyous vigour. 'It is what the Fisherwoman herself died for, and all the thousands since then. This is the time that all those deaths have made possible. If you deny it, you deny them. Make them meaningless.'

'It sounds like a matter the Lore is better placed to judge than the Battle,' Eska said placidly. Her head was clearing now. Her nausea had subsided, leaving only a sour twist in her stomach.

Goedellin looked up at the mention of the Lore. His stained lips were pressed tight in a miserable pinch.

'There is time yet for . . .' Shraeve began, but then Aeglyss was rolling onto his stomach with a thick gurgling splutter. The White Owls and Inkallim who had gathered around him started back.

Aeglyss crawled on all fours. His hands flexed against the planking of the floor like frail white spiders. The open sores where his fingernails had once been split and leaked noisome fluid. His scabrous head bobbed up and down. Blood dripped from his face, hair fell from his scalp.

'Help me, Shraeve,' he sobbed. 'Help me. Save me. I am lost.'

His gown hung limp from the bones of hip and shoulder and ribcage.

'Am I safe yet? Am I safe? I can't tell; can't tell anything any more. I don't know.'

Eska saw unguarded confusion and distaste flutter for a moment on the faces of a few: several of the woodwights, one or two of the Inkallim. There are flaws here still, she thought. There is room for doubt in some hearts, when the madness is not fully upon them.

'It's killing me,' Aeglyss groaned. 'Tearing me apart. It's too much, too much for my body, my bones. Oh, what have they done to me?'

He crawled, jerking, across the floor like some demented child made of sticks and string. Shraeve went to him and knelt at his side. She shot a wildly hostile glare in Eska's direction.

'Go,' she hissed. 'Take Goedellin with you. Take him to that pathetic Thane of yours.'

Goedellin hobbled towards the door without further urging. He glanced uneasily, again and again, at the twitching *na'kyrim* as he went. Eska followed him without looking back. She heard Aeglyss muttering as she went.

'It's not enough. This'll eat me away unless I can see into the heart of it, see all of it. I need to go deeper. I need to go further.'

Shraeve's whispered reply was too soft for Eska to hear. But Aeglyss shouted, and she could hear him still as she descended the stairway that carried her and Goedellin out into the derelict city.

'No,' the halfbreed cried. 'I need more. I need to be more. It's tearing me apart, unless I master it. I need to be made afresh. Again! Again!'

VII

In the night, those uncomfortable beneath Kanin's yoke had come for him, seething out of Glasbridge's alleys and ruins. It was not the Lannis folk who rose, but the motley bands of Black Road looters and idlers and thieves that had occupied the town before his arrival. Titles and past allegiances meant nothing, it seemed, in this newly savage world; scores had come, half of them armed with nothing more than staffs or kitchen knives, to test this Thane's determination. They had not found him wanting.

While the mob battered at the iron-stiffened door of the Guard House and smashed in the shutters on its windows,

Kanin himself had led his Shield and twenty other warriors out over the wall of the little yard in which Glasbridge's Guard had once drilled. They had fallen on the rear of the baying throng, so suddenly and unexpectedly that the slaughter had been trivially easy. The killing brought Kanin less relief, less respite from his tortured preoccupations, than such deeds once had. It was purposeless beyond the preservation of his own life, and he set little store by that measure of purpose.

In the wake of it, though, standing with the dead and the crippled strewn about him, with groans and whimpers populating the darkness, he had rediscovered some little of the cleansing cold fire. One of his own Shield, a tall man, black-bearded, had cornered some ragged Gyre villager in the doorway of one of the shacks opposite the Guard House. As Kanin watched impassively, the shieldman's shoulders shook, his sword sank to hang loosely at his side. The man he should have been killing was immobile for a moment, bewildered, and then fled into the night.

Kanin seized the shieldman's shoulder and spun him about. There were tears on the man's face, and the sight of them roused all of Kanin's ire.

'What are you doing?' he shouted.

'I cannot, sire.' The words were tremulous. The man's brow furrowed. The sword fell from his limp hand.

'Cannot?' Kanin snarled. All of the others were watching now. There was nothing else, in that silent, dark street, save Thane and shieldman.

'It's all wrong. We're fighting our own. I don't understand why . . .'

Kanin cut him down, and the man fell without a sound, his legs folding beneath him. Another blow, as he lay there staring blankly up, finished him. Kanin stalked back towards the Guard House, pushing through the ranks of his warriors. He glimpsed in Igris' face as he passed the subtle flinch of repressed doubt and distaste.

He turned on the threshold.

'Any who doubt me, who lack the courage to stand by their Thane, their Blood, come to me with a sword in your hand, and test your fate against mine. I don't fear it. I'll gladly face anyone. But if you've not the spine to do that, you'll fight and you'll die for me as your oaths demand. I will bring down those now ruling in Kan Avor or I will die in the trying. So will you.'

Now, watching oily black smoke boil its way into the morning sky from the corpse fires, Kanin still felt the echo of that anger shivering through him. There were none left he could rely on, or trust. Not even his Shield. None who saw what seemed so obvious to him. If he did not move soon, he would be betrayed, abandoned.

'We passed carts carrying the sick to Kan Avor, Thane,' Goedellin said behind him.

'Did you?' Kanin muttered without interest.

He turned reluctantly away from the window. He was wasting his time even talking to the Lore Inkallim, he suspected. Eska, who had brought the man hobbling into Glasbridge that morning, had implied as much in her curt report of what she had seen in Kan Avor.

'The men who guarded them told us you had sent them.'

'What of it? I do as I see fit. The creed has ever enjoined us to do so. Well, it seems fit to me to send sickness unto sickness. Fever breeds fever, my nursemaid always said. Let it fill Kan Avor, I say. Let the halfbreed find his streets filled with the stench of the dying.'

'Is it true that you have given arms to Lannis men? That you are training and drilling them to fight alongside your own warriors?'

Kanin ignored that. Once, his upbringing, his faith, might have required him to submit to the judgement of this learned man, so wise in the ways of the creed. Now he was entirely, coldly uninterested in the opinions of the Lore. He was a man without any allegiance, any duty, save to his own determined intent. He was entirely alone, and that very solitude rendered him impervious to all judgements save those of his own heart.

Goedellin shook his bowed head. 'But there must be unity, Thane. The faithful must be—'

'The faithful must be cured of the madness that has come upon them,' Kanin said flatly. 'I know corruption when I smell its stink, even if your nose is failing you. It's not glory that we're all rising towards, but chaos. Subjugation to the will of that mad halfbreed. We're becoming beasts, and he is the beating heart of our affliction. Our ruin.'

'Is it truly the curing of the faithful you seek, or merely vengeance for your sister's death?'

Kanin could easily have struck him then. It would cost him nothing to kill this revered man, nothing that he had not already sacrificed at least. Only the fact that he heard not accusation but weariness in Goedellin's voice stayed his hand.

'They thought in Kan Avor that you had sent the Hunt to kill him,' the Lore Inkallim said.

'Did they. And did you ask Eska? You had time enough, didn't you, to get to the truth of it, between there and here?'

Goedellin frowned.

'She was – is – unwilling to speak with me,' he muttered.

'Ha! Then you've come to dig out my secrets, old man? Are you running errands for the halfbreed now?'

He might have expected some indignation in response, but Goedellin seemed a man lost, too adrift on the currents of his own confusion to rise to such provocation. He merely shook his head, chewed his dark lips.

'I went to Kan Avor in the hope of fostering unity, Thane. There is much that needs mending.'

'I agree. And I know how to mend it.'

'No, no.' Goedellin was unsettled. He clasped his hands,

interlacing his fingers, then parted them again. 'The faith, the faith. It must be of a single mind in times such as this. We stand upon the brink of—'

'What, then?' Kanin interrupted. 'Would you have me make common cause with Shraeve and the halfbreed? Surrender myself to the same madness as everyone else? I won't do it.'

The Lore Inkallim shook his head despondently. Kanin narrowed his eyes. Understanding blossomed within him.

'You don't know, do you, old man? You doubt. You suspect I'm right . . .'

'I don't know,' Goedellin conceded. Softly, like a defeated, shamed child. 'I don't know. I had thought it might become clearer to me. But I see things, I feel things, so . . . unnatural. It is . . .'

'Foul,' Kanin encouraged him. 'Wrong. It is against all reason for one such as Aeglyss to be the answer to the creed's hopes.'

'Reason?' Goedellin murmured. 'Reason has never been a cornerstone of the creed, Thane. Fate does not submit itself to reason.'

Kanin groaned in exasperation.

'Seek guidance, then, from your First, if you're too fearful to make your own decisions.' he sneered. 'If you've not the courage for it, send messengers to Kan Dredar, telling them how things have gone awry. Hope that Theor and the rest will render the judgement you're incapable of.'

Still there was no reaction from Goedellin. No anger, no resentment, no bruised self-importance. Kanin had never seen one of the Lore so enfeebled by uncertainty.

'My messages go unanswered,' Goedellin said miserably. 'I do not even know if they have reached the Sanctuary.'

Kanin did not conceal his contempt. 'I'll waste no more time on you. Look at yourself, Inkallim. Where's all the strength, the discipline of the Lore now? You're supposed to be the ones who guard the people against error. What use are you, when one half-breed can steal everything away from under your very nose? The Battle, the people, the creed itself.'

The Thane pulled open the door.

'Try your visionary dreams for answers, Goedellin. If your reason isn't enough, or your masters in Kan Dredar, try your secret roots and herbs. I'll find you a bed, if you want one, and you can reside here as long as you wish, but spare me any more of your fumblings, your flailings.'

Goedellin grunted. 'Perhaps. Seerstem's brought no clarity yet; quite the opposite. But perhaps. I hope for understanding.'

'You hope in vain,' said Kanin scornfully. 'Your dreams won't bring you anything, because you don't even know the right questions to ask. This stopped being about the creed, about fate, a long time ago, but still you think there's some truth to be teased out of it. There isn't. This is about blood now, Inkallim, and who is willing to spend and spill the most of it. This is about who is fierce enough, determined enough, to come out of the fighting pit alive.'

He left Goedellin sitting there alone, a sad and shrunken figure hunched down in a chair. A man left puzzled and bereft by a world that had twisted itself into a shape he could no longer comprehend.

*

Outside the ruins of Kan Avor, on the fringes of the sodden plain that had once been the Glas Water, a huge willow tree stood. It carried snow in the joints of its soaring branches. Its immense trunk burst from the ground and sprayed up into the air like the antler-crown of some titanic buried stag. When it was young, spindling its way up out of the wet earth amidst a host of its eager fellows, Avann oc Gyre ruled in Kan Avor, and the streets of that place bustled with the life of a thriving Blood. Later, there had been slaughter within sight of it, and the blood of thousands had sunk into the loam, to its youthful roots. As it rose to its full stature, so the Lannis Blood had risen around it, and a great dyke had been constructed, and the proud city so near at hand was drowned. The long seasonal pulse of the Glas Water ruled its life thereafter: in the winters, the waters came to lap around the base of its slowly swelling trunk; in summers, they retreated. And in those dry times, the people of the valley came and cut away its peers one by one. It had been alone for many years, standing in solitude amidst pool and marsh, spared the axe by chance which the years turned to habit.

Upon this solitary giant a multitude converged. They came from Grive, and from Anduran, and from Targlas beyond it, trampling new pathways into the expanse of blank snow that lay across the valley. It was not only the people of the Black Road who assembled there on the frigid flatlands. The subjugated folk of the Lannis Blood gathered too, some by choice, some driven like cattle by their new rulers. The promise of momentous events was abroad and compelling. They came from vast Anlane itself: White Owls emerging in bands of ten and twenty from beneath its vast bare canopy.

Most of all, they came from Kan Avor, the dead city reborn yet still dead. They swarmed out from that rubble in their hundreds, disgorged from its every crevice. And in the midst of them came the *na'kyrim* himself, riding a wagon pulled by gigantic Lannis horses that had once hauled timber from the forests. He sat in it alone, braced against straw bales wrapped in cloth, armoured against the cold by a heavy cloak that he enfolded about himself so deeply his shape was lost beneath its weight. Ice crackled under the wheels as they crunched through the frozen puddles along the track.

Forty Battle Inkallim rode in escort. Hothyn and his Kyrinin walked after the cart in a great dispersed crowd. On either side, as far as any eye might see, the *na'kyrim*'s people were strewn across the white plain, all of them moving through the winter

towards that single huge willow tree: a convocation of the mad
and the wild and the desperate and the fierce.

The wagoner snapped his switch at the rumps of the horses
with one hand, hauled sideways at the reins with the other. The
wagon creaked round in a tight circle and groaned to a halt
beneath the spreading tree. The westering sun glowed coldly
behind cloud. The multitude gathered. A thousand plumes of
exhaled breath misted over their heads.

Shraeve the Inkallim drew her horse to a halt beside the
wagon and leaned towards its lone passenger.

'This still seems ill advised,' she said quietly.

Aeglyss looked out with filmy eyes from within his ragged,
enveloping cloak. Twin runnels of mucus had dried – or frozen,
for he had a bloodless, heatless glaze to his skin – under his nose
and across his lips. What little more of his face was visible was
cracked and flaked. He shivered.

'Are you dying?' Shraeve asked.

'Dying?' rasped the *na'kyrim*. 'Perhaps. Becoming, more
likely. Becoming something new.'

His voice was thin. Gone was its rich, seductive lustre and its
smooth caress. Now it was the crumbling away to dust of dead
bark, the rustling of crisp, fallen leaves beneath a foot.

'You fear my death?' he asked her. 'Or is it your own loss of
influence you fear? The loss of the fire at which you warm your
hands? Without me, how long would you last?'

'I do not see the necessity. That is all. You have more than
enough—'

'What would you know of necessity?' snarled Aeglyss, his sharp
anger fouling his throat and almost choking him. 'You know
nothing about me. About what I was before, what I am now. I
hear a thousand voices, countless voices, in my head. I hear the
dead and the living. I suck in hatred and fear and sickness with
every breath. My body burns and breaks around me, consumed by
this . . . this flood pouring through me. And I can't mend it. I

can't still the voices.'

Shraeve scowled at the wagoner, who had twisted on his seat and was looking back at Aeglyss with an expression of fearful awe. Seeing her displeasure, he turned away once more, and made himself small.

'I have to give them more. They'll cease to love me if I don't give them more,' Aeglyss hissed. 'I know. I know. They'll turn on me if I don't give them more. Show them more. They always do, eventually. Always.'

His eyes were closed now. His head tipped back. The hood of his cloak fell away, revealing his almost naked head. The skin was so frail and thin, the bones of his skull seemed to show through it, giving it the sheen of ivory.

'The Shadowhand strains against the bonds I've set on him. His is a fierce will. I must be stronger, if I'm not to lose him. And the Anain. I hear them still, thinking their great, hateful thoughts. Distant . . . distant, but I hear them. They'll come again for me one day, when their hate is greater than their fear. I need to be the flood itself, not just the channel the flood flows through. You wouldn't understand. How could you?'

Shraeve's horse had dropped its head to nuzzle the snow in search of grass. She tugged irritably at the reins.

'It will all have been for nothing, if you die now,' she said.

Aeglyss' head sank down until his chin rested on his chest. He coughed and wheezed.

'Nothing? Maybe. But let your precious fate decide.' He spat the words contemptuously. 'If it's a new world you want out of this, this is how it happens. This is the only way it can happen, because without it I will come apart. I don't fear death. I can master it. I just need to go deeper, further; to the root of the world. So do it. Do it, raven.'

There was no more talking after that. Only the brutal business of hoisting the fragile *na'kyrim* up on the tree's creased trunk, the driving of nails through the old, unhealed wounds in his wrists.

A hush cloaked all the hundreds, the thousands, gathered to bear witness. They stood in a vast arc, all silent, all watching the hammers, feeling their beat like that of war drums. They were exposed, in that great flat land, to the twilight's raw wind and to the sleet that gave it teeth, but no fires were lit, no shelters erected.

Darkness descended, and the mighty tree buried its uppermost branches in the night. The crucified *na'kyrim* was lost against the dark trunk, save for his pale face, his white hands. Those scraps of him shone amidst the murk. The attendant host was unnaturally still, held fast by reverent expectancy. The sleet turned to rain. The snow in the tree's intricate web of boughs was eroded. That spread across the ground slumped into slush and turned the earth beneath those innumerable feet into mud. And still they waited. Still they anticipated . . . something.

There was not a single voice to be heard, save that of some distant owl and that of the night itself: raindrops pattering through twigs and into puddles. And then the soft, soft moaning of the *na'kyrim* came drifting out from the tree. It went through the crowd like a breeze, yet was stronger by far than the wind that drove the rain. With it, slowly, came his suffering, and that seeped through the skin of them all. His pain took root in every bone, and it was a wondrous pain that bound them together in the sensation of rising, ascending through its layers towards some endless presence that waited to embrace and unite them.

As his limbs shook and strained, so convulsions spun their way through the throng. People fell to the ground and thrashed in the mud. He rasped out a score of hollow, panting breaths, and others wailed and clawed at their scalps, tore at their hair, suddenly succumbing to horrors that danced inside their heads. Some rode the crashing waves of emotion and experience that pulsed out from the *na'kyrim*; others were undone by them, and tumbled and broken by them.

Some wept quiet tears of joy in the darkness; some fell to

their knees; some lost themselves entirely in uncomprehending terror and fled screaming. The assault on every mind did not diminish, but grew stronger, more remorseless. People saw places that lay half a world away; they lived entire lifetimes, in moments, that belonged to others; they heard the voices of the dead. They knew for an instant what it was to be Anain or Saolin, or to be a *na'kyrim* crucified upon a tree with the Shared become indistinguishable from his own mind. And madness came in the wake of that knowledge, and claimed one, then another, then dozens.

Killing began. Stranglings and beatings and knifings and suffocations in the sucking mud; flurries of lethal movement in amongst the great trembling mass. Kyrinin ran, lithe and agile, hissing as they lashed about them with their spears. The deaths drew no attention. Those standing next to a man who was dragged down did not notice, so enraptured or possessed were they by the transcendent power surging all about and through them.

It lasted for a long time. The rain died away. Fragments of moonlight fell through passing gaps in the cloud. They lit the *na'kyrim*. Made his blood black. All across the great assemblage scattered outbursts of anguish, or weeping, or laughter cavorted like eddies in a wild current. And slowly the horrors and the visions and the power receded. Those driven to savagery by them halted, stood looking in confusion down at those they had slain. Minds clumsily recovered themselves from madness, remembering, bit by bit, their former shapes.

There came a time when the *na'kyrim* opened crusted eyes and whispered, 'Take me down.'

The Inkallim did as he commanded. He wept at the agony of it, and sank into limp unconsciousness. They carried him – there was no weight to him at all – towards the wagon. People came stumbling forward out of the crowd, reaching out, longing to touch him, longing to draw near to the fount of such frightful, vast outpourings. The ravens pushed them away.

They laid his bloody, broken form in the bed of the wagon and it groaned its way back towards the invisible ruined city that waited out in the night. Shraeve alone rode with him, seated at his side, watching the shivering of his eyes beneath their cracked and bleeding lids. As the wagon progressed through the great, now silent, assemblage, those it passed fell in behind it; those ahead of it pressed closer and closer, hoping to see for themselves its incomprehensible and awe-inspiring cargo.

But Shraeve alone heard him when he murmured, 'Not enough. Not enough. Still it's too deep, too wide. Infinite.'

*

Kanin heard Goedellin's cry through the stone walls of the Guard House. It roused him from the bleary stupor that passed for sleep these days. At first he was not certain whether it had been a figment of the nightmares that so often tortured his brief slumbers, but then it was repeated, and the agonies of fear it expressed washed away any last fogs from Kanin's mind. It was the cry of someone exploring depths of anguish most could never imagine, and it grated upon the ear and upon the heart.

Kanin pulled his boots on, cursing the stiff, tight leather. He could hear footsteps and worried voices in the corridor outside. He threw a cloak about his shoulders and hastened from his bare sleeping chamber.

Igris and three or four others of his Shield were already gathered outside the door to Goedellin's room, all wearing the tired, limp pallor of those abruptly roused from sleep. From within another rasping, sickening wail.

'The door's barred,' Igris said with a vague and helpless spreading of his hands.

'Then break it!' shouted Kanin.

One of the shieldmen kicked at the door. It did not yield.

'Idiot,' growled Kanin, pushing them all aside.

Once, twice, he pounded at the door with his heel. At the

second blow, there was a cracking of wood, but still it resisted. Kanin could hear a loud whimpering in there now, like some great dog bemoaning a grievous wound. He roared and stamped against the door. It sprang open in a burst of splinters.

Goedellin lay on the low bed, fully clothed. A tiny box was spilled on the floor beside him: a miniature wooden chest, engraved and inlaid like a child's toy. Wizened fragments of seer-stem lay around it. The Lore Inkallim was twisting and writhing, splaying his hands in defence against some invisible threat. He moaned and thrashed, dark spittle foaming on his black lips.

Kanin bent over the Lore Inkallim, averting his face from those clawing hands. He grasped Goedellin's shoulders and pressed him back onto the mattress.

'Wake, old man!' he shouted.

Goedellin bucked beneath his grasp, impossibly strong for one so frail and contorted by age. Kanin feared that he would break bones if he exerted his full strength, and backed away. Goedellin howled, a ravaged sound.

'Fetch water,' Kanin snapped at Igris, who was staring in wide-eyed alarm at the frenzied form upon the bed. 'And a healer!'

The shieldman went, but even as Kanin turned back to the Lore Inkallim, he could see that it was too late. Goedellin's hands clenched; his eyes opened; his stained tongue fluttered between his lips. His back, his hooked back, arced against its curve as his head and shoulder thrust down against the pillow. His breath rattled out of him.

And then he was still. Fists still raised, eyes still staring up at the blank ceiling above, mouth still agape, tongue lying there limp in a pool of brown spit. Kanin extended a hand, holding the back of it still just above Goedellin's lips. He did not really need to check. He could see the truth in those blank eyes.

'He's dead,' Kanin muttered.

He stooped and picked up the little box from the floor. He turned it over in his hands then dropped its carved lid shut with the touch of a finger.

'It's seems even the dreams of the Lore have turned against them,' he murmured.

VIII

The track from Highfast to Hent was wind-lashed, snow-blasted. It rode the high bare slopes of jagged ridges, rising and falling across the spine of the Karkyre Peaks. Sharp-sided valleys lay below, gorges clawed out of the body of the mountains by immense talons. Clouds surged in from the west, engulfing the track and the summits around it, veiling them in mist and snow, then sweeping on and away to leave them bathed in sunlight, roofed by a curving expanse of pale blue sky. Sometimes, in those clear moments, Orisian could look down into the valley beneath them and see nothing but great slabs of cloud and fog, the peaks and ridges bare islands protruding from a sea frozen in the instant of its boiling.

Even when the sky was naked above, and there was no snow or sleet, the wind never ceased. It buffeted and bit them. Orisian, like most of the others, wore a woollen scarf across his nose and mouth, and kept the fur-lined hood of his jacket pulled as far up and over his head as it would go. They had taken the best clothing they could find from Highfast's stores. Still the cold found its way in. Had he not suffered its savage attentions before, and more acutely, in the Car Criagar, it might have been intolerable. Now, he merely shrunk himself inside his cocoon of wool and cloth, and endured.

The horses suffered the most, becoming sluggish and sullen. They held their heads low. Soon, they might become more hindrance than aid. Whether or not the weather gentled, or the track became less snow-clogged and treacherous, there would come a time – perhaps two days, perhaps three – when they reached the edge of Anlane. And that, Orisian suspected, would be no place for riding.

Often, his mind retreated from the harsh reality of the journey, drifting and stumbling its way through corridors of memory and distraction. But they were seldom clean. Untainted. He remembered the day before the Winterbirth feast at Castle Kolglas. So much of that memory was warm, coloured impossibly joyful by the darkness of what had followed it: walking beside Anyara through the market, hearing the light, bubbling chatter of the festive throng, smelling the sticky richness of honey cakes. Yet as he relived it in his head, Orisian found shadows bleeding in at the edges of the scenes his mind recreated. Faces in the crowd that blurred and leered and grimaced, until he turned his imagined attention full upon them, and then they were gone. Not there at all.

And then he was walking with Inurian over the rocks beneath the castle's wall. Looking for . . . something. Even the pain of that memory was sweet, for there, before his mind's eye, was that lost face in all its precise simplicity and affection. So close he could have touched it. So alive. Yet he could hear that the waves slapping at the rocks were heavy, thick with something more than water. Inurian's lips moved, but Orisian could not hear him, only the seagulls screeching overhead. And their cries became the anguished wails and laughter of mad children.

He was looking down at a corpse. A woman, frozen into a stiff huddle. Snow on her head, in her ear, in the pit of her eye. He was looking down on her from what seemed a great height, yet for all that distance he could see the ends of her eyelashes protruding through the snow. He could see the strands of loose cotton that had frayed from the collar of her coat.

'Couldn't say whether she's Kilkry or Black Road.'

'What?' Orisian said, blinking.

Taim Narran twisted in his saddle, looking back.

'Couldn't say whether she's Kilkry or Black Road,' he repeated.

Ess'yr and Varryn were standing over the corpse, staring down at it. It lay off to the side of the rough track, beneath the shelter of an overhanging boulder.

'Died of cold, not of blade,' Varryn said.

'Herraic said we might reach Hent in a day, if we didn't pause,' Orisian said, still dislocated, half of him caught up in that place where the dreams and memories lurked. 'How long till nightfall, do you think?'

Varryn flicked a glance towards the western sky, lifted his chin as if to scent the air.

'The third part of the day is yet to come,' the Kyrinin said.

'We should keep moving, then.'

Ess'yr and Varryn ran ahead of the horses, disappearing beyond the rugged writhings of the trail. In the moment when they dipped out of sight, Orisian felt that familiar tug of foreboding and fear. Every moment that he could not see Ess'yr, could not satisfy himself of her safety, was soured by worry. He did not doubt her capabilities but still he worried. Death, it seemed to him, was becoming ever less respectful of the capabilities of those it claimed.

He could hear two of the warriors talking behind him. Low voices, jumbled by the wind, the words separated, some snuffed out, some thrown together. He could not make out what they were saying.

His mind wandered once more, lulled by that sound, human yet incomprehensible, and by the slow and steady crunching of his horse's hoofs on loose stones and bare rock. He drifted. And this time he saw Ess'yr's face, just as he had first seen it when slipping in and out of a wounded fever. It was as clear to him now as it had been then. Clearer. The beauty of it, the soft and flawless near-white skin, the framing curtain of hair with an almost metallic yellow glint to it. The eyes, unguarded, grey as flint, looking into his own. He rode in the embrace of that memory.

Hent was stranger than Orisian had expected. It sprawled across the eastern flank of a long, descending ridge. The highest of its buildings lay almost at the crest of the ridge; the lowest, close by the seething river that ran north between fringes of scrubby willow and alder. The buildings themselves were like bulges in the skin of the mountain, as if its innards had burst forth in crumbling disarray and then been reassembled into habitations. The shape of each was governed by the natural form of the rock to which it clung. There was barely a straight line to be seen, save the slate tiles that clad each roof. Snow was piled in every wind-shadow.

The trail dipped down from its perch high on the slope to sweep through the centre of the tiny town, and re-emerged beyond it, scarring its way on towards the low hills and dark brown stain of forest that lay to the north.

A solitary figure was moving, down there amongst all the stone; staggering as if drunk between slope-sided houses. Just that one movement. All the rest was as imperturbably motion-less as the giant boulder field it resembled.

'We went to within a spear throw,' Ess'yr murmured at Orisian's side. 'No watch. No guard. Stink of . . .' She cocked her head. 'Stink of Koldihrve. The Huanin there, and their drink.'

'We heard thick sleeping,' Varryn observed.

'What does that mean?' asked Orisian.

'The body sleeps,' said Ess'yr, 'but the nose does not.'

Orisian frowned, then: 'Snoring?'

Ess'yr shrugged.

'And there is the smell of death,' Varryn said.

They fell back to where Taim Narran and the others waited. All were dismounted save K'rina, who was bound to the saddle of a placid horse by a thick weave of cords and rope. She was hunched forward and low, almost to the animal's neck, in that strange borderland between sleep and unconsciousness that she occupied most of the time.

'The western side of the ridge is steep,' Taim said as soon as they drew near. 'Not even a goat trail that we could see.'

'We could go that way, though?' Orisian asked.

Taim wrinkled the bridge of his nose.

'If necessary. It would be difficult. Dangerous and slow. We'd have to leave the horses.' He looked at K'rina. 'She's in no condition to be clambering around on a mountain slope. What of the town?'

'Seems almost empty,' Orisian muttered, glancing back towards Hent, now hidden by a hump of bare rock. 'The Black Road must have been there, maybe still are. But it's as near to dead as makes no difference.'

'Still, we couldn't pass through without being seen,' Taim said.

'No.' Orisian shook his head.

'Cloud coming,' Varryn said, looking up beyond the ridgeline towards the grey western sky. Banks of low cloud were indeed streaming in, their vanguard already wisping around the highest outcrops of rock and spilling frail tendrils down the slope.

Taim looked dubious.

'That could help,' he said, 'but even so . . .'

Orisian's mouth was dry. He swallowed. The world was disappearing before his eyes, lapsing into a blur of moist grey. He could hear his own heartbeat, as if the foggy sprawl of those clouds was deadening and silencing everything else so completely there was nothing else left to hear. Nothing to attend to save his own thoughts, and he barely recognised many of them. He wanted to be rid of them, these flickers of doubt, murmurs of fear. Stirrings of a hot and unfamiliar bloodthirst.

'We'll try. The place is half-abandoned, and whoever's left

there isn't expecting us. We'll try to go straight through.'

The slow, silent descent into the town proved a crossing from the fixed and steady world into the domain of madness.

The first of the stone houses loomed out of the mist. Orisian went, as soft-footed as he could, to crouch in the lee of its irregular wall. The moisture-laden air rolled thickly over his face. Up ahead, the mist took Ess'yr as he watched, fading her into its concealing mystery. Varryn went with her, and first one then two of Taim's men.

Orisian could hear nothing. He could see little more. Just the intricate patina of lichens and mosses that had colonised the rough stone blocks of the wall. Just the narrowing, undulating trail, now gathering water, harvested from the sinking cloud, into its crevices. He could feel tiny beads of water forming all across his skin, merging with one another into a cold sheen. He licked his upper lip, drinking the stuff of the sky.

Taim Narran eased past him, moving without haste in a low crouch. The warrior rounded the corner of the house. He went almost soundlessly, leaving no trace but the gentle turning of a pebble under his heel. Orisian edged forward. He had his shield on his arm. It was cumbersome, but its weight and breadth were comforting. This place, and these moments, felt unsafe, as if the skin of things was wearing thin. There were whispers of trepidation in his head, and he had the distracting sense that they came not from within but from out there, just beyond the fog-defined limit of his vision. As if there was something waiting for him. Beckoning him.

He looked around the corner. Taim Narran was there, hunched down with his back against a strange, conical structure of rocks – a storage chamber of some kind. He pointed silently to the opposite wall of the narrow alley. Orisian looked, and at first could not understand what his eyes told him. There were bulbous shapes hanging from the wall: bloated waterskins or rocks some river had smoothed into unnatural spheres. Orisian frowned. The mist thinned briefly, showed them to him more clearly, and then drew a dank veil once more. Skulls. Human, as far he could tell. Adorning the back wall of a house like mad decoration.

He stared at Taim. The warrior raised his eyebrows and shuffled back to join Orisian on the main track.

'Stay close,' Taim whispered.

He led the way forward, still cautious but moving more quickly now. Orisian followed. Those distant murmurs inside his mind came now from skulls, which he imagined to festoon every invisible building out beyond the wall of mist. Two more warriors were close behind him, and beyond them somewhere the rest were waiting with Yvane and K'rina and the horses. The animals had their hoofs muffled, in the hope that they might pass unnoticed once the way had been cleared or secured, but Orisian felt an inexplicable certainty that whatever was here in Hent had already noticed them all, had already begun to gather itself all around them, unseen.

A sound from up ahead, vanishingly faint: indecipherable but swiftly followed by a sibilant whimper. Then scraping, uneven footsteps and a shape was coalescing out of the grey nothingness. A man stumbled into sight down the centre of the track. He staggered against the bulging wall of a house, then came on. He wore an ill-fitting chain jerkin over a ragged hide jacket. One foot was booted, the other bare. There was an open wound in his throat, robbing him of the power of breath and speech even as it spilled his blood down onto his chest. As Orisian watched, the man's eyes rolled up into his head and he pitched forward. Taim darted up and caught him as he fell, then lowered him gently to the ground, one precautionary hand clamped over his mouth and nose. The man died without any further sound.

Orisian and Taim knelt by the corpse, both of them gazing ahead. There was no more movement in the shifting, rolling bank of mist. A sickly scent rose from the dead man: an alloy of ale and vomit.

'Is he Black Road?' Orisian whispered.

Taim put a finger to his lips.

They went on, deeper into the town's heart. A face startled Orisian, looking up at him from a shallow gutter cut along the side of the track. It was a girl's face, tiny and delicate, softened and blotched and a little deformed by incipient decay. She had been dead for some time. Orisian could not help but look into those smeared eyes. As he did so, he found himself looking not at this nameless girl but at the face of mute Bair, the stable hand who had died in Castle Kolglas; and the darkness of night rather than the gloom of fogs enveloped him, and he could smell smoke and straw and horses. The vision was more acute, more merciless, than memory. It mastered him and held him there, on the night of Winterbirth. He heard the clamour of battle, the crackle of flames, and experienced once again the dizzying mix of fear and anger that had been in him then. And he was turning, knowing already what he would see; knowing that his father was about to die, a knife in his chest. He did not want to witness that again, but still he turned towards it, caught by its irresistible pull.

There was a hand on his arm, and instead of his father, he saw Taim Narran, leaning close in, staring worriedly into his eyes. Orisian sucked in wet air and nodded. Taim looked unconvinced, but released his grip and moved on.

The track twisted and plunged down between two houses that angled out of the mountainside like flat ledges. Varryn was crouching on one of the slate roofs, at Orisian's eye level. The Kyrinin was holding out a hand in warning. Taim shrank back, extending his own arm to nudge Orisian half a pace back up the track.

Even as they retreated, a figure appeared in the doorway of the hut, directly beneath Varryn. A frowning, gaunt-faced man peering about him like someone roused from sleep by a puzzling but unthreatening sound in the night. He rubbed at his stubbled chin as he looked down the track and then up. His eyes met Orisian's and widened. His hand frozen in mid-movement, he said something: still puzzled, but with the first foretaste of alarm in his northern-accented voice.

Varryn flicked himself flat onto the roof and his two long arms darted down, one hand spreading across the man's mouth, the other clasping his throat in a cage of rigid fingers that dug into the skin, crushing. The man gave out a muffled, groaning yelp, only half-stifled. He twisted against Varryn's grip, and it seemed he might be free in a moment. Taim Narran rushed forward, heedless now of the noise his boots made on the rocky path. He punched the man once in the centre of the chest, with all his strength and with all the weight of his sword, its hilt firmly clenched in his fist. The man flew back into the dark interior, his breath gusting out from him, and Taim followed him without breaking stride.

Varryn gathered up his spear and bow and vaulted lightly down from the roof. He glanced once in through the doorway and then, evidently satisfied by whatever he saw there, looked up at Orisian.

'There are few,' he said quietly. 'They die easily.'

'Are any of the townsfolk left?' Orisian asked. His own voice sounded distant and hollow to him. 'Have you found any of them?'

Varryn said nothing but dipped the point of his spear down the slope of the path. Orisian's gazed followed, and he saw there lying in the mist another corpse. The hands were tied behind its back. The head was gone, leaving an open, rotting stump of neck. Orisian blinked at it, then looked down at his feet. When he lifted his eyes again, Varryn had disappeared and Taim was emerging from the house. His sword was dark with blood. He held up a short length of cord.

'Woven from human hair,' he muttered. 'He was wearing it like a necklace.'

'What happened here?' Orisian wondered.

'Madness,' Taim said. His expression was troubled. For the first time he could remember, Orisian saw a fleeting distress there, an unease that bordered upon fear.

'Can you feel it?' Orisian asked, not knowing what answer he hoped for. He did not want to be the only one who sensed the sickness boiling in Hent's gut, and congealing out of the air. But then, if he was not the only one, it meant that the sickness was real. It was here, closing on them.

Taim shook his head, not in disagreement but confusion.

'Something,' he said. 'I feel something.'

There was an anguished cry from somewhere ahead. Another death amidst the vapours.

'Go and bring the others on through, as fast as you safely can,' Taim said to one of the warriors coming hesitantly up behind them.

As the man trotted back the way they had come, Taim grimaced at Orisian.

'The sooner we're clear of this place the better, I think,' he said.

Orisian opened his mouth to agree but was struck dumb by the insubstantial figure that he suddenly saw a little way up the slope, in the entrance to one of the tight, twisting paths that ran between Hent's high-walled yards and squat houses. The form was at first too faint to be sure whether it was made of flesh or from tendrils of heavy cloud. Its features were obscured or absent. Yet he knew who it was.

He took a step up the track.

'Fariel,' he murmured.

And the mist-shape of his dead brother turned its vague head towards him. Had there been eyes there, they would have been upon him. Orisian lost all awareness of where he was, or even when. For the space of three heartbeats – and he felt them, each one, loud and sharp in his breast – there was only him and this memory of Fariel.

'I'm sorry,' Orisian said. 'I tried.' He did not know what he was saying, or why. It was the need in him, the despair, that spoke.

'Orisian!'

The shout snapped him out of his dark reverie. Taim Narran was pushing past him. Just in time to block a spear thrust delivering by a laughing, leering woman. She wore a mail shirt, a dented metal skullcap of a helm, heavy boots that rose to the knees of her thick hide leggings. It was the garb of a warrior, yet she fought without skill, without guile. Spittle flew from her lips; her eyes rolled this way and that in their sockets.

Orisian fell back onto his heels. Taim flattened his shield, driving the point of the woman's spear into the ground. His sword came down and smashed through the spear's shaft; would have taken the woman's hands too, had she not released it an instant before. She came at Taim again, reaching for him with bare hands, not hesitating. Grinning, muttering. He snapped his sword up, and the backhanded sweep hit her on her cheekbone, gouged its way up into the side of her face. Sent that little helmet soaring away, down the hillside, clattering off a wall before the hungry mists swallowed it. Orisian stared after it. He heard it bouncing once, twice: metal on stone. Ringing like some ailing, cracked bell. And then there was silence.

'I saw the dead,' Orisian said.

He was sitting on a cloak spread over wet grass. Hent was some way behind them. They had travelled deep into the night, driven on by a common, unspoken desire to put as much ground as possible between them and that awful place.

There had been not just skulls, but finger bones threaded onto sinews and hung from the eaves of houses. A corpse spreadeagled on a flat roof, hands and feet tied. The tiles beneath it stained by blood, for the woman had been alive when she was stretched out there, and when the carrion birds had come spiralling out of the sky. A tiny compound, the workspace of a stonecarver, now filled with bodies. They lay three deep, with snow draped over them.

Of the Black Road company that had wrought such havoc upon that remote town, only a handful had remained for Ess'yr and Varryn and Taim and the rest to kill. Some had died of disease, some had apparently been killed by their companions. None of the dead had been interred or burned. They lay amongst the townsfolk, discarded and forgotten. It was as if, once Hent's inhabitants had been slain, the mad rage that fuelled their slaughter had demanded yet more tribute of those it possessed. And they had mindlessly done what it required of them.

'Not the dead,' Yvane said beside Orisian. 'Memory. The Shared. The dead – the echo of them – persist in the Shared as long as there are those still living who remember them. Much longer than that, if stories are told of them, if their names are not forgotten.'

She shifted uncomfortably upon the cloak, searching for an accommodating undulation in the hard ground beneath.

'It is Aeglyss, spreading. The walls between our minds and the Shared are breaking down. For you, today, it came as the dead, as death itself. It will come to each of us as our own minds and inclinations permit it. As they invite it. For those who know only struggle, only anger and killing . . . well, we saw back there what it does to them.'

'What about you?'

'I hold it at bay. So far.' There was a subtle strain in her voice. 'I felt something last night. A . . . I don't know. Something. He grows stronger, or at least sinks deeper into the Shared.'

Orisian looked into the east. He was not sure whether he imagined it, but there seemed to be a hint of dawn out there. A grainy lightening of the horizon.

'If the Shared can bring the dead to the surface like that, then is it the Sleeping Dark?' he asked, watching that possible, longed-for, distant daybreak.

'Oh, if you want answers to questions like that, you need to ask them of a wiser head than mine.'

'There must be those who have thought of such things.'

'There are. At length, and for many years, in Highfast. And elsewhere. Why do you suppose some of the Kyrinin imagine the Anain, the lords of the Shared, to be the shepherds of their unresting dead? Does it matter, though? The answer?'

'I don't know,' Orisian said at length. 'Is Inurian there, then? In the Shared?'

'Not him. The dead are dead. Gone. What remains in the Shared is only the memory of him. The sound of his voice, the sense of who he was. Something like him, but not truly him. He has ended.'

Orisian nodded, sad.

'It might be best if you tried to shut such things out,' Yvane said gently. 'It's only something inside you, wounding itself with the Shared.'

'But I remember them so clearly.'

'That's good, I imagine. It would be, anyway, in quieter times. Just don't let the memory of them crowd out the living for you.'

The dawn did come, and blearily illuminated a vast landscape. The ground sank away to the east of them in successive lines of grass-clad hills, interspersed with crags and snowfields and clusters of scrubby trees. Beyond that, sweeping off towards the faint and hesitant sun, lay Anlane. Endless, from this high vantage point. Rolling like a brown and grey sea into the indefinable distance, where it and the huge sky blurred into nothingness. All the world was silent forest, and Orisian feared it. He looked out over Anlane's illimitable wilds and imagined it to be alive, a gigantic sleeping power that waited only for his footsteps to disturb it. A place that, once entered, could not be left.

Taim Narran was checking over the horses nearby. Yvane was kneeling beside K'rina's prostrate form, changing the bandages on her shoulder wound. The warriors, one by one, were mounting their horses as Taim approved their condition. It was all done with hardly a word.

Ess'yr came across the grass to Orisian. She was holding something out to him. He looked down at what lay in her palm and at first did not recognise it.

'Too long since the last we made of these,' Ess'yr said.

Two cords, each of them with a dozen or more small, tight knots spread along their length. A dozen memories, Orisian knew. A dozen thoughts, embodied in those tiny tangles of cord, to go into the wet earth in place of a lost, irrecoverable body.

'You and Varryn?' he said quietly. He was afraid to reach out and accept these tokens, afraid of their implications and importance. But Ess'yr sank her hand a little closer to his own, tilting it to let the cords edge closer to her fingertips.

'It is not a good time for the dead to wander, to go unrooted in willow,' she said. 'When Anain can die, there are none to shepherd the restless dead.'

Orisian willed his hand to rise, and accepted the two cords into his grasp. They were light. Yet he felt every knot in them as a hard point pressing against his skin. He stared down at them: the beaded kernels of two lives.

'Which is yours?' he asked.

Ess'yr touched a finger to one of the strands.

'If you live and we do not, plant them beneath stakes of willow,' she said.

Orisian nodded numbly, for he could never have refused her this. That she should bring such a thing to him, and make him its guardian, filled him with a kind of awe. And a faint, intimate hope, perhaps, glimmering there deep inside him. But he feared it too, this responsibility that he knew with absolute certainty would bring unbearable pain should he ever be called upon to discharge it.

'If you are to die, I do not think you will do it alone,' he murmured. 'I may not be able to do as you ask.'

'Perhaps.' She sounded unconcerned. 'But the *ra'tyn* is done now. The promise I made to Inurian. It is spent. Where we go now, where you choose to go, Varryn and I have other battles to fight. We become a spear *a'an*, entering the lands of the enemy. I have done what I can for Inurian. For you. We will go as far as we can with you, but . . .'

The words trailed away. Orisian lifted his head and looked into her eyes. So imperturbably calm and knowing, those flinty windows, yet revealing nothing of what lay beyond them, within.

'I understand,' he said. 'I will keep them safe.'

The thought came to him suddenly, woken by the sorrow of potential partings, potential loss.

'Will you wait for a moment?' he asked her.

He found a cord of his own, sealing the mouth of a canvas bag that held only a few remnant scraps of food. Long enough, he thought.

He sat cross-legged on the cold, damp grass and began looping a chain of knots into the cord's length. He was clumsy, but stubbornly persisted. Each knot he moistened with the tip of his tongue, as he had seen Ess'yr and Varryn do, long ago in the *vo'an* where he had woken from wounded slumber to her face.

One for the time before the Heart Fever, a bright memory of family. Then one for his mother, one for his brother, one for his father. The memories came clearly, carrying equal parts of comfort and misery. One for Inurian, one for Anyara. That last hurt him more than he expected, for its texture of distance and parting. But he remembered her strength and her unruly vigour, and found a smile. One for Rothe, too raw and recent to linger upon, no matter how much he longed to recall only the man's gruff companionship and loyal affection. And the last of them, tightening into the strand, clenching itself into permanence, for Ess'yr. For what might have been, in a world, or a life, other than this one.

He wept a little, running his finger over what he had made, but nor for long. He took it to Ess'yr, who had been standing patiently some way down the slope.

'Will you bury it for me, if the time comes?' he asked her.

She took it from him, cupping it, coiled like a thin, sleeping snake, in her hand.

'Not in a *dyn hane*,' she said. 'Not with the true people.'

'No,' he said. 'I understand. But somewhere? Somewhere fitting for a Huanin?'

She regarded him silently for a few breaths. He felt like reaching out to her, touching her, trying to convey how deeply this request expressed his heart. But, soon enough, she nodded in assent and closed her hand about the cord of his life.

IX

Ever since riding out from Highfast, the conviction had been growing in Taim Narran that he was moving towards his death. That he would never again see Jaen or his daughter. That his grandchild would be born, and would grow, without him. He did not fear death. He had seen countless others fall to it, and learned its banal and crude flavour, over the years, but that had never taught him fear. The Sleeping Dark promised only an eternity of unbeing: no pain, no grief, no suffering. Nothing to fear but a great deal to regret: the sorrow his absence would inflict upon those he left behind, the sights, the people he would never see again. The immense incompleteness of everything he would leave behind, for there would always, inevitably, be uncounted things he should have said or done, messages he should have conveyed.

The trees came first in ones and twos, scattered across the long, shallow slope they were descending. Then clumps of them, more and more, until they merged into a single unbroken canopy. Anlane closed itself above and behind them.

Taim felt his tension mount in response to the deepening of the shadows. This place had been a battleground for his Blood from the moment Sirian first wore the title of Thane. It had been a meagre, intermittent kind of war, the struggle against the depredations of the White Owls, but a war nonetheless, and a savage one. Merciless. Anlane could never, to someone of Taim's upbringing and experiences, be anything other than a bad memory.

The trees crowded about them, a numberless host moving imperceptibly slowly to smother them. Perhaps even absorb them. Taim was aware of a change in the air. It was as if they had entered the body of some immense sleeping creature, and burrowed now ever deeper into its living flesh. It was not warm, but the wind was gone, the sharp edge of the cold dulled. New scents drifted up from the forest floor: wet bark, rotting leaves.

Soon, much sooner than he had hoped, Taim was ducking to avoid branches that reached out across the dwindling trail the Fox had found for them to follow. The path narrowed to something only deer or boar might pass along without difficulty. Twigs and outstretched tendrils of ivy brushed Taim's legs and the flanks of his horse, to the animal's increasing displeasure. Behind him, he could hear men cursing as boughs grazed face or scalp.

And then there was a huge tree lying across the trail, coated in slick moss, a thin crust of half-melted snow lining the length of its trunk. To one side its great root plate had been torn out of the earth and stood now like the flattened, upraised hand of a giant. To the other, its branches had, in their crashing descent, crumpled

a huge swathe of the woods into an impenetrable tangle of shattered timber, bent and bowed saplings. Its fall had torn a great
rent in the otherwise inviolate canopy, a wound in the skin of
Anlane. Taim felt the cooler breath of the sky drifting down onto
his face. There was a fine drizzle on it. Rain, not snow, he thought.
That at least was something to be thankful for.

He sighed and twisted in his saddle. Orisian was not far
behind, waiting expectantly for word.

'We're done with horses, I think,' Taim said.

They walked on in silence. The land folded itself in creases,
humps and hollows around which tiny brooks trickled. There
were outcrops of rock with trees growing from their crannies.
Again and again, the path disappeared altogether, to human eye
at least. Each time it did so, Ess'yr or Varryn would be waiting
some little way ahead, almost invisible amidst the undergrowth
and shadows until betrayed by movement, beckoning the lag-
gard Huanin onward.

Taim sent two men forward: four more eyes, inadequate as
they might be, to ward against surprises. Necessary as the abandonment of the horses had been, being on foot in such foreign
terrain had darkened the already fragile mood. There was an
almost palpable sense of vulnerability amongst the warriors.
They had the skittishness of sheep, starting at every sound – real
or imagined – and darting their eyes this way and that. Only
two of the party did not seem to share this nervous trepidation,
Taim saw when he glanced back over his shoulder. Yvane, who
led K'rina steadily along. And Orisian. Whose calm was almost
unnatural. Almost unsettling. He looked to Taim like a man
whose burdens, whose fears, were becoming less rather than
more. That Taim found troubling.

Ess'yr and Varryn and the two scouts Taim had sent out were
standing together up ahead. As he drew near, Taim was at first
unsure of what he was seeing. A spindly sapling had been cut off

at chest height. The break was clean and angled: the work of a
blade rather than of wind or heavy snow. It had left the thin,
shortened trunk with a sharp point. And onto that point, and
then down like thin cuts of meat impaled on a vertical spit, five
small squarish pieces of some strange material had been forced.
Like a child's pretence at flags, Taim thought vaguely as he
leaned closer, puzzled.

One of the crude pennants was torn and ragged where some
animal seemed to have been gnawing at it. Another had some
faded swirling blue insignia upon it. That shade, and those
shapes, had a familiarity to them that he could not at first
resolve.

Orisian, kneeling and lightly touching one of the scraps
between thumb and forefinger, spoke the conclusion Taim's own
mind belatedly approached.

'Skin.' Orisian withdrew his hand without haste.

'Huanin and Kyrinin,' Ess'yr confirmed. Her distaste, disgust
even, was evident.

Yvane brushed past Taim's shoulder and squinted at the grue-
some array of flayed squares.

'*Ettanaryn*,' the *na'kyrim* grunted. 'Not of the usual sort, though.'

'What are they?' Orisian asked.

'When the *a'an*s roam far in the warm season, they mark the
edge,' Ess'yr told him. 'The furthest reach.'

'It's an old way of marking the limits of hunting grounds,'
Yvane grunted. 'Clan territory, for those clans that still live by
the oldest traditions. Not like this, though. Not with skin.'

'Huanin and Kyrinin,' Ess'yr observed quietly. 'All fresh cut.
No more than two, three days.' She flicked a fingertip at the
palest fragment of skin, with its dull blue patterns. 'White Owl
kin'thyn. They cut the face from one of their own.'

Varryn was already moving away, drifting silently ahead,
deeper into the forest. Taim watched him go. It was a grim
border they were crossing now. Whatever lay beyond it could

only be horrific, if its limits were circumscribed by such tokens of mutilation. It was not, Taim expected, going to be a place welcoming of humankind.

'Eyes open,' he murmured to the men nervously gathered around. They were, all of them, staring fixedly at the limp squares of skin.

'Eyes open, hands ready,' Taim said more sharply, gesturing them onwards with a sweep of his arm.

They bedded down that night on a gentle slope amidst a stand of uniform, straight ash trees. There was to be no fire, of course. The only shelter from the persistent but thin mist of drizzle was the thick canopy of intermingled branches and a few holly trees clustered along one side of their campsite. It would be a hard, miserable night, Taim knew, but he doubted anyone had been expecting much sleep.

Taim unrolled the blanket that he would fold about himself to fend off the worst of the night's chill. The ground was at least softened a touch by a thick layer of dead leaves. A strange mumbling distracted Taim from this unappealing prospect. Coming out of the darkness like the muted babble of a tiny brook: a faint and frail voice.

Taim followed the sound. It took no more than half a dozen paces to reveal its source. Sitting there, arms folded, legs crossed, his head sunken, was one of the warriors. Eagan. A young man – barely twenty – born in Grive. Son of a beekeeper, Taim remembered. He had fought well at Ive Bridge. Now he was lost in some waking dream. His senseless whispering was relentless, and strained despite its quietness. His head dipped and rose in shallow nods, as if keeping time with some beat in his ramblings that no one else could detect.

'Eagan,' Taim said softly, standing over the warrior.

There was no response, only that wordless rambling, rushing on and on.

Taim bent and put a hand on the man's shoulder. Eagan looked up. His lips still moved, still danced, but there was suddenly no sound at all. In the deep gloom of the forest floor Taim could not see his eyes clearly but was almost certain he would have found no recognition there. He squeezed the shoulder more tightly.

'Eagan,' he said again.

And the man snorted. Shook his head once, sharply. Unfolded his arms.

'Sir?' Eagan asked.

'Stretch yourself out. Try to get some rest.'

Taim returned, thoughtful, to his own blanket. A little further down the slope, he could see the figures of Ess'yr and Orisian kneeling together in the leaf litter. The Kyrinin brushed dead leaves from the surface of a flat stone. She began to break apart one of the flat, round oatcakes they had brought as rations from Highfast, and spread the crumbs out on the stone. Orisian did the same, copying her every action with an eerie precision.

Taim knew what it was. He had seen the Kyrinin perform this same small ritual before, making offerings to ward off the attentions of the dead. It was a part of their strange beliefs, and the amounts of food thus wasted were of no consequence, so Taim had never raised any protest. But for a Thane of a True Blood to share in the act? Watching them now, with their careful, measured movements and almost reverential manner, half lost in the shadow and darkness, it would have been possible to mistake them for two Kyrinin.

Taim lay down, flat on his back. He was glad that he was – he hoped – the only one to have seen Orisian in such close communion with the Kyrinin woman. It was unsettling enough for some of the men to note how clearly comforting and easy their Thane found Ess'yr's presence, how attentively he sometimes watched her. For all the disarray and riot the world had fallen into, there remained boundaries that many would not willingly see crossed.

Taim closed his eyes, not in hope of sleep but in search of distracting, warming memories that might take him away, however briefly, from this cold forest. The wound in his leg, taken at Ive, ached dully. The muscle was stiff and sore. He reached for the image of Jaen's face, the texture of her skin beneath his fingers, the knowing affection of her smile. And he reached too, with hand rather than mind, for his sheathed sword. He held it to his chest, and clasped it tight.

*

There was a corpse in the street outside Jaen Narran's house in Kolkyre. She stared down at it from one of the upper windows. Some youth – sixteen or seventeen, she judged – who had been killed in the night. Dogs came nosing about. The few people who ventured out from their homes disregarded both the dogs and the human carrion that attracted them. They seemed wilfully blind, as if a surfeit of horrors and troubles had left them incapable of acknowledging another.

Jain leaned out and shouted at the dogs. They looked up at her, still stretching out towards the dead flesh of the youth. She beat the open shutter with the palm of her hand, but the dogs did not fear her. They turned back to the corpse, sniffing at it. Jaen took the bowl of water from beside her bed and slapped its contents out towards the beasts. They loped away then, without panic. They would be back, she knew.

An old man walking stiffly down the street had stopped to watch. He stared up at her now, puzzlement on his face. Jaen glared at him, then withdrew, pulling the shutters closed behind her.

The killings and the fighting and the fires and the cries came mostly at night but, like some rot slowly expanding beyond the darkness that had formed it, they colonised each passing day more aggressively than the one before. All of Kolkyre had taken up arms, and though the greatest hatred was reserved for the Black Road army encamped outside its landward walls, there was too much of it to be entirely absorbed by that single, inaccessible foe. The anger found other outlets for its immense unspent reserves, and turned the city in upon itself.

Jaen heard all the tales from the servants in the Tower of Thrones, or from the homeless Lannis folk she supplied with food and blankets and firewood: murder and thievery, feud and suspicion. Those who hailed from lands beyond the Kilkry or Lannis Bloods were dead by now, or hiding behind barred doors and closed windows, too fearful to dare the unruly, hostile city streets. Those who were wealthy had turned their homes into fortresses, protected by hired clubmen. The Guard fought brief wars against gangs of the hungry and the desperate and the mad. Order was never more than a transient presence, liable at any moment to be rent by some new upwelling of chaos.

Jaen thumped down the rickety stairs, letting her feet convey her frustrations to the boards. Her daughter Maira was there, leaning back in a cushioned chair. Though the child in her was yet too small to swell her belly, she rested a hand there nevertheless, gently protective. Her husband Achlinn was hanging a pot of water to boil over the fire, hissing at the heat of the glowing embers.

'You rise earlier every day,' Jaen said to her daughter.

Maira smiled. It was an exhausted smile, but contented too.

'I don't sleep, and I'd sooner be up than lying there awake. Not that Achlinn thanks me for it.'

Her husband grimaced in mock demonstration of his suffering. He was a gentle man, Jaen had always thought. Good enough, just, for her precious daughter. This placid scene was enough to blunt Jaen's ill humour.

'Are our guardians awake?' she asked.

Maira nodded towards the door in the rear wall.

'They went to get a little rest. I told them it would be all right. I feel bad, each of them having to stand watch over us for half the night like this.'

Jaen grunted. 'Too bad for them I need to go to the Tower this morning, then. One at least'll have to do escort duty.'

The two gruff Guardsmen had been assigned their protective responsibilities by Roaric oc Kilkry-Haig himself. At first Jaen had thought it unnecessary and faintly embarrassing. Now she valued their taciturn presence. Part of her regretted her refusal of the Thane's offer to take up residence in the Tower of Thrones itself. She found its austere isolation, looming over the rest of the city like an intrusion from some other, entirely unconnected place, unsettling, and had preferred this comfortable billet in a house much closer to the quarter where the displaced people of her own Blood had settled. But each day – and more particularly night – here amidst the city's gradual disintegration made her doubt that decision more. On Maira's behalf, if not her own. Perhaps the time had come to seek the security of the Tower's impregnable stone.

The corpse had gone by the time she ventured out onto the street, following cautiously behind her scowling guard. Someone must have dragged it away. She was glad. There was a dog sniffing the ground where it had lain. The animal looked up at her with a disappointed expression as she passed.

A crowd had gathered at the gate in the low wall encircling the mound from which the Tower of Thrones needled its way up into the sky. The guards were beset by showers of shouted demands, interspersed with aimless and vitriolic abuse. Following her doggedly determined escort, Jaen could hear people crying out for access to the Tower's food stores, accusing some family or other of riot, clamouring for an immediate sally against the besieging forces of the Black Road. She hunched her shoulders and ducked as she was jostled this way and that. Jagged words teemed about her head like an army of angry wasps.

Entering into the gardens beyond the gate was a relief. Jaen sighed and shook her shoulders. Matters were definitely taking a turn for the worse. She resolved, as she ascended the path towards the Tower, to bring Maira and Achlinn here that very afternoon. The city outside this mute and ancient fastness felt entirely too volatile.

Ilessa oc Kilkry-Haig was waiting, as expected, in her chambers. Jaen was surprised to find Ilessa's son, the Thane Roaric, already there, and in full and heated flow.

'They betray us,' the Thane was saying. 'There's no other description . . . no other word does justice to their treachery.'

He saw that Ilessa's attention had been drawn elsewhere, and looked over his shoulder. Jaen, standing in the doorway, dipped her head.

'Forgive me, lady,' she said. 'The maid did not tell me you had company. I will wait outside.'

'No, no,' said Ilessa, beckoning Jaen. 'I told them to admit you as soon as you arrived. We are almost done here. It will do no harm for you to hear this, anyway.'

She returned her gaze to her son, challenging him to dispute her invitation to Jaen. The Thane seemed unconcerned. Barely interested, in fact. He was entirely focused upon his own furious thoughts.

'Not a single supply ship's berthed in two days. And the Captain of the last to reach us was quite clear: Gryvan's forbidden any vessel to dock here, and he's got his own and Tal Dyreen hulls on the water to make sure his ban is observed.'

'We've stores enough to last a while longer,' Ilessa said. Her tone was measured, in contrast to Roaric's bluster.

'But only a while,' the Thane growled. 'And only if we keep them tightly controlled. People will get hungry. They're already in a foul temper. In every kind of unreasoning, foul temper. I'd have Gryvan by the neck if he was here, High Thane or not.'

He made a fist of his hand, his knuckles whitening as he crushed the life out of an imagined throat.

'Fortunate that he's not,' Ilessa murmured.

'The day will come. This will all be over eventually, and then I'll have—'

'I? I?' snapped Ilessa, her composure cracking a little. 'It's not just you, Roaric. You're the Blood, all of it, now. Think of it. If you want anything to be left of it when this is all over, you need to see clearly what must be done now, not give yourself over to fancies of future vengeance.'

Roaric frowned but held his tongue.

'If food supplies need to be rationed, so be it,' Ilessa said. 'We need to plan for that. And we can still run small boats – smugglers' boats – along the coast and maybe out to Il Anaron. They might slip through Haig's fingers.'

'It won't be enough,' Roaric said darkly. 'But you see to it, if you think it worth your time. I'd sooner fight for our freedom than creep about like cowed outlaws. We're alone now. Black Road on one side, Haig on the other. Both wanting to tear us down, break us down. Well, I won't permit it! Yes, I'm Thane, if that's what you want to hear. And I'll be a Thane, a Thane with a sword in his hand and fire in his belly.'

He brushed past Jaen without acknowledging her presence. Ilessa stared after him. She looked to Jaen like a woman grown accustomed to desperate sadness; still burdened by it, but used to it.

'He turns all his grief into anger,' Ilessa said quietly.

'He has a lot to grieve over. A lot to be angry about.'

'He does.' Ilessa gestured towards a bench in the bay window. It was overlaid with a beautifully woven carpet. 'Sit with me.'

Jaen did as she was bid. She had come here, as she did almost every day now, to talk with Ilessa about the needs of the hundreds of Lannis folk caged within Kolkyre's walls alongside its natives. But that seemed a matter for another time.

'I didn't know about the ships,' she said. 'I can hardly believe Haig would abandon us. Not even abandon us; worse, turn against us. Offer us up to the Black Road.'

Ilessa shook her head in sorrowful astonishment.

'Nor I. Yet here we are. The world's forgotten whatever sense it once possessed. It's all like a bad dream from which we can't wake. Every hand against us. Our own hands against us.' She cocked her head towards the window. 'Sometimes, when the wind's right, you can hear screaming, shouting, even from up here. Our own people, losing their minds, down in the city.'

'It's not good. I was thinking . . . perhaps it is time – past time – my daughter and I came into the Tower. If there's still room for us.'

'Of course.' Ilessa smiled. 'I should have insisted upon it before now.'

She pushed back her hair with a slow hand. It smoothed the creases from her brow, just for a moment.

'You must be worried about your husband,' she said.

Worried, thought Jaen. No, that is not the word. There is no word for what I feel. To be at once terrified, stalked by impotent panic, and at the same time calmed by that very impotence. There is nothing I can do for Taim. Wherever he is, he will live or die by his own strength, his own capabilities. And I will be either made whole again, or broken for ever.

'My husband has a habit of surviving,' she murmured. 'Of coming back to me.'

'I hope you are right.'

'Hope is all we have, my lady. It fades a little every day, but I cling to whatever shreds of it remain.'

'I wish my men had learned the same habits your husband did,' Ilessa said. The sadness in her words was distant, thoughtful. Cavernous loss and sorrow were there, though, an echoing chamber in the background. Jaen could not bring herself to feel fortunate, but she could recognise her own suffering as that of someone who feared what might happen; Ilessa's was that of someone assailed by what had already happened, and could never be changed. Which was worse, she could not say.

'Roaric is being consumed, slowly,' Ilessa continued. Still quiet. Still treading a precarious path over a chasm. 'Death seems to rule the world now. It walks among us, feeding off the madness. It's too much for my son. I fear for him. And for all of us. Though I love him with all my heart, I fear where he might lead us.'

Jaen saw then which was worse, for no matter how much had already been lost, how much darkness had already come, there was always more to fear. And once the texture of loss had been learned, it was much easier to imagine its return.

4

He Who Waits

In the twilight of the First Age, when the One Race was drifting towards its final, fatal war against the Gods, they sent an envoy into the high Tan Dihrin. His name was Martanan, and he climbed through storm and snow to the peak of peaks, where the turning sky struck fire from the utmost pinnacle.

There he found, cut into the rock of that summit, the great stone throne he sought, and he knelt before it and called out to the God whose place it was to appear before him. The God came, and filled the throne with his dark form. And his raven companions came, and settled upon his shoulders. Martanan bowed his head at first, for he was afraid to look upon the fell countenance he had called forth. But he was the emissary of his people, and he owed them courage, so he lifted his eyes and spoke.

'We call you He Who Waits, great one, and live in fear of your attention. We call you Death, and your shadow is long, falling across us even in the midst of life. I am sent to ask you this question: why must it be so? Why have you, the immortal Gods, made us so frail and fragile? Why do you keep the boon of life unending only for yourselves?'

When Death replied, his voice was deep and terrible, and it sprang from the mouths of his ravens.

'Because without endings there can be no beginnings. To live for ever is a burden, though you know it not. We choose not to inflict its weight upon you.'

'If burden it is, still my people desire it. The burdens we bear now are no less. Those we love die, and we are beset by grief. We ourselves die, and are forgotten. We die, and all that we have built and laboured for is undone after us.'

'Even so,' the God said. 'Even so. There must be death in this world, lest all meaning be lost.'

'Yet still we would choose otherwise,' Martanan said, and at that the ravens rose into the air and their black wings assailed him.

'You may choose how you live,' the God cried through his birds. 'You may choose how you shape meaning out of my shadow. We grant you that freedom. But choice is empty in the absence of consequence. Without it, you and everything you did would mean nothing more than does the aimless motion of a cloud in the sky. There must be consequence, and I am its final measure and its shape and its weight. Every one of you, sooner or later, will come into my embrace.'

From *First Tales* transcribed by Quenquane the Simple

I

The main gates of the Battle Inkall's sprawling compound were closed and barred. Theor of the Lore leaned out from his rocking litter as the bearers stumbled through the snow towards the imposing and entirely unwelcoming facade. The low wall stretching away on either side of the gate was lined with Inkallim: statues of black leather, each with a tall spear held perfectly erect.

And, outside the gates, a still more numerous host. Seventy or more of Ragnor oc Gyre's warriors. His Shield, in polished chain mail that borrowed a dull gleam from the grey sky; mounted spearmen, whose horses bore metal plates across their brows and cheeks. And the High Thane himself, massive and magnificent in a huge cloak of sable fur that spread back over the haunches of his own great mount.

Theor's litter-bearers struggled along the front of this martial array, and came to a panting, trembling halt before Ragnor. The High Thane stared down silently as Theor clambered stiffly out. The First's feet crunched into the snow, and he felt its cold pressure even through the down-lined hide of his boots. He straightened, and ground his fingers into the small of his back where the muscles had tightened.

'What are you doing here, First?' the High Thane asked. Blunt. Confrontational, unless Theor misread him entirely.

'I heard there was some difficulty,' Theor said. 'I thought I might be of assistance in resolving any misunderstanding that may have arisen.'

'No misunderstanding.'

A breeze ruffled the High Thane's hair and spun his horse's steaming breath away. Theor winced up at him, narrowing his eyes. It was not easy to see details of his expression, silhouetted as he was against the sun-lightened afternoon clouds. His voice was giving little away now, only a steely determination.

'Ah.' Theor nodded. He glanced towards the Inkallim studding the top of the wall, and then back to Ragnor. 'I will confer with those within, High Thane.'

Ragnor said nothing. Theor turned and trudged towards the gates, beckoning his exhausted bearers to follow him with their burden. It was not far from the Lore's Sanctuary, further along the slopes above Kan Dredar, but they had covered the distance quickly. Theor had understood the need for haste as soon as word of what was happening reached him. He had not wanted to come. The Sanctuary he had left behind him was in a ferment of dismay and alarm. Two Lore Inkallim had inexplicably died, on successive nights, while dreaming their seerstem dreams. And they had died not peacefully, but screaming, convulsing.

'I told you what I wanted,' he heard Ragnor saying behind him, in measured tones. 'And that my patience was at an end.'

Theor paused. He angled his head a fraction towards his

shoulder but did not look round. One of the gates creaked open, just wide enough to admit him and his attendants, and he entered the domain of the Battle.

'I did not know you were here,' Theor said to Avenn, First of the Hunt.

He strove to disguise his unease but could not hide from himself the bitter twist of suspicion, distrust even, he felt. It was rare for the Firsts to meet; rarer still for the Hunt and Battle to consort without the presence of the Lore. In such febrile, fragile times, it lit an unreasoning flame of resentment in Theor to find Nyve and Avenn together. He should be too old, too secure in his authority, to succumb to such sentiments, yet both security and the wisdom of age were states he felt ever more thoroughly exiled from.

Avenn smiled thinly. Her long black hair had a lifeless, leaden quality to it. The pinprick scars of a childhood pox that marred her cheeks gave her a faintly aged, damaged look. But there was vigour, almost delight, in her eyes.

'Interesting times,' she said.

She would, of course, think so, Theor reflected. She had been born for moments such as this: tumult and contest. Opportunity, as she would see it. For whatever reason, the Hunt had always chosen such as she for its leader. A passing thought, like a beam of light glimpsed through scudding cloud: Shraeve should have been of the Hunt not the Battle. Her ferocity, her passion, would have found a better home there. Theor grunted, and let the insight go.

'*Narqan?*' Nyve asked.

The First of the Battle was seated by a roaring fire, a pitcher and cup of the vile liquor on a table by his side.

'No,' muttered Theor. He moistened his stained lips. The dry heat of Nyve's chambers had rendered them brittle.

'He wants all the children,' Nyve said, pouring himself

another draught of the fermented milk. 'Two hundred or so have reached us, this last day or two. Spoils from the Glas Valley.'

'Has he said what he wants them for?' Theor asked wearily as he sank into a chair opposite Nyve.

'What does it matter what he says?' said Avenn, but he ignored her.

Nyve took a thoughtful sip from his cup, lifting it between the knuckles of his crippled hands, and bared his teeth as the liquid burned its way down his throat. Theor knew that feeling well enough, and gave a faint grimace of his own at the memory.

'He claims he wants them to tend his herds, mine his ores, carry his stones,' the First of the Battle said. 'All the tasks he says go undone because our war has called so many of the faithful into its embrace. Foolishness, of course. What help would a few score children be? They're the strong ones, true enough. Those who survived the winnowing of the march up through the Stone Vale. But children, still.'

Theor nodded. 'He wants them because if he leaves them here, they will become Inkallim one day. Those who live; those who can be brought into the faith. He wants them because in taking them he thinks to prove a point to us, to the people, to himself.'

'Because we will not abase ourselves before him and do as he bids us,' muttered Avenn.

'Indeed,' Theor agreed. Still he kept his attention upon Nyve rather than the mistress of the Hunt. His old friend was the crux of things here; he was certain.

A log slipped from the fire and shed sparking embers across the hearth. Nyve extended a foot and pushed it back into the heart of the flames.

'How long has he been waiting at your gate?' Theor asked.

Nyve lifted his eyes towards the ceiling as if in thought.

'Since midday or thereabouts. His pride, his stubbornness will not permit him to depart just yet, it appears.'

Dread was tightening its icy fingers about Theor's heart.

Here, amidst this warmth, in the company of those who should be his most comforting allies, ensconced in this soft and soothing chair, he felt the ground beneath his feet crumbling away, tipping him towards a dizzying chasm. Did neither of these two feel it? No, he knew. Other extremities had mastered their hearts.

'It serves no purpose to taunt him so,' he said. 'Give him this small victory.'

'No,' said Avenn at once. She pushed herself away from the window frame against which she had been leaning. 'He will not be satisfied. He has turned against us, against the creed. Three loyal servants of the Hunt have been executed, on his command, this last week. Now is not the moment to shirk our responsibilities, when the eyes of the Last God are upon us, when the Kall—'

'Do not dare!' cried Theor, snapping his head around and fixing the rangy woman with a ferocious glare. 'Do not claim the authority of the Lore as your own!'

Avenn inclined her head in submission. It was a thin sheen, though. Theor could see that quite clearly. She was not in the least cowed. How had it come to this? How had everything, every past certainty, become so unclear and unstable? How had fear, and the fury it engendered, become so deeply rooted in him?

'I do need the children,' Nyve said quietly. 'We have lost a great many of the Battle in the south. And here, for that matter. Ten killed in fighting on the border between Gaven and Wyn only two days ago. Time was, our mere presence was enough to quell the most recalcitrant of troublemakers. No longer. Now it requires our blood, our lives. And it has all left me with fewer of my ravens here than for many, many years. I am disinclined to concede our weakness by yielding to his demands.'

Everything about the old Inkallim was calm and composed. His clubbed hands rested on the arms of the chair. His head was cocked at a relaxed, friendly angle. A trace of a smile even passed across his lips. Yet Theor looked at him and almost despaired. He could see it behind those sparkling eyes, he could hear it in the silent corners of the flame-lit room: the beating of the raven's wing. His friend had crossed some inner threshold. And Theor, for reasons he did not entirely understand, could not follow him.

'Not yet,' Theor murmured, and then, more clearly, lifting his chin: 'The breach is not irretrievable yet.'

'No?' said Nyve. 'We are too far down this road to turn back. I will not recall the Battle from beyond the Vale. Perhaps I could not, even if I wished it. What is happening there is out of our hands. I cannot give Ragnor what he wants. Fate determines all now.'

'As always.' It was easy, instinctive, to utter those two words, but Theor wondered if they sounded as hollow to the others as they did to him. Almost certainly not. 'But give him this one, small thing, and we create the space for something to change. We allow for the possibility that fate may choose another course. Do not assume that we must part company with the Gyre Blood now. Today. That is all I ask.'

'We cannot ignore what is happening,' muttered Avenn. 'Better to reach for the inevitable future than turn our backs on it, and enter it blindly.'

But Nyve pursed his lips and thought, staring all the time into Theor's eyes.

'Very well,' he said at length. 'He can have his children today. But no more. The Inkalls are nothing if they submit to the will and whim of a Thane. What we serve is greater than Ragnor, than his line. We have always known that. All of us.'

He smiled sadly as he spoke, and in that smile Theor saw their parting. They both knew, in their different ways, that something was ending. And they both saw, he suspected, other, harder endings drawing near, closing upon them from the horizon of the coming days.

*

'You're drooling,' Torquentine said.

Igryn oc Dargannan-Haig sucked spittle back from his lips.

'Untie my hands, if it offends you,' the blind Thane growled. He sat hunched upon an upholstered bench. He straightened, pressing his back against the stone wall. It would not last, Torquentine knew. Twice already Igryn had gathered himself, put some dignity into his spine, and each time something in him – or some absence in him, perhaps – gradually bent his back down again, twisted his mouth into a leer, laced his words with venom and turned his measured breathing into panting, rasping gasps. It was as if there was a beast within him that could be resisted only for so long before it began to reshape him. It put Torquentine in mind of the long dead wolfenkind.

'I'll keep your hands bounds for the time being, if it's all the same to you,' he said. 'Or even if it's not, of course. Wipe the man's chin for him, would you, my dear?'

This last he spoke to Magrayn, and she went at once to gently swipe a cloth over the Thane's bearded chin. She was not the only one of Torquentine's attendants present. This was one of those rare occasions on which he had felt it wise to invite men of violence down into his buried lair. Two of them stood close by Igryn: muscular, their faces battered by a lifetime's rough usage. They were good, both of them, at performing the more brutal kinds of tasks. Between them, they had killed five men by Torquentine's command over the years. And more on their own initiative, no doubt. It was not only to keep a wary watch upon Igryn that Torquentine wanted them close, though. The streets of Ash Pit – and of all Vaymouth – were unpredictably tumultuous; the whole city was turbid with distrust, suspicion, accusation. Mayhem simmered, and burst erratically into the open. These burly clubmen offered some small reassurance that such disturbance would be resisted should it seek to reach down into Torquentine's abode.

Both of them had been amongst the band that had seized the

disgraced Dargannan Thane on the road to In'Vay. And never had Torquentine taken less pleasure from the successful outcome of one of his endeavours. The very presence of Igryn here in his secret sanctuary would have been enough to set him squirming in distress, had his great bulk not argued against such physical expression of his inner turmoil. He settled for tugging absently at loose threads in the seams of the great cushions upon which he reclined.

'I have but one eye myself, you know,' he told Igryn.

'No, I do not know. I know your appearance no more than I do your name, or your intent.'

'Oh, my appearance is magnificent, I assure you,' Torquentine grunted. 'But, since the Thane of Thanes saw fit to take your eyes, you will just have to imagine it for yourself. And let us leave my name similarly obscured. As for my intent . . . that, that is a good question.

'But tarry on the subject of eyes for a moment. You know how I lost the one that is, I assure you, absent? No, of course you don't. It was in fact laid open by the blade of a dockside ruffian. I too, in those days, was something of a dockside ruffian, so I describe him thus without malice or disapproval. This was before Gryvan was Thane, you understand. I'm sorry. Does his name offend you?'

Igryn was grimacing once more, his lips straining slowly back to reveal clenched teeth. At the mention of the High Thane, a snarl had begun to form at the corner of his mouth, and was poised there still, half-born.

'In any case,' Torquentine continued, carefully burying his unease beneath a casual tone, 'this man of whom I speak, he was, as it turned out, of unusual descent: father a Tal Dyreen, mother from the Free Coast. He'd been living a rat's life in and around Vaymouth for years, but it did not teach him much love or respect for the Haig Blood in whose house – whose lands – he was a guest. Indeed, he made that lack of affection for his hosts abundantly clear, at tedious length, one night in a tavern down by the dock-yards. I listened as long as I could, but in time I felt compelled to challenge his views. I did so with a knife, and he defended them similarly. In due course, the matter was resolved in my favour. It cost me an eye, but it cost him his life, so I have always been mindful that I paid much the lower price that night.'

Torquentine fluttered his bloated fingers in Magrayn's direction. She pulled a clean, fresh cloth free from her waistband and laid it across his palm. He carefully mopped sweat from his cheeks and brow. So many breathing bodies within this confined space had made it moist and warm.

'Are you still listening, Thane?' he asked.

Igryn was hunching forward once more. He had begun to work his jaw as if chewing some resistant matter. Strands of his hair were hanging down across the bandage that covered his eye sockets.

'Straighten him up, would you?' Torquentine muttered to his men, who were staring distastefully at the Thane. One of them planted a broad hand firmly on Igryn's shoulder and pushed him, a little more roughly than was necessary, erect. Igryn's head cracked against the stonework, but he did not seem to notice.

'I hear an idiot dribbling nonsense. Is that you talking?' Igryn ground his chin into the notch between neck and shoulder. 'My beard itches.'

'If you've brought fleas into my home, I'll be sorely disap-pointed,' Torquentine muttered. 'But to return to my point. I was a different man in those days, you understand. And not only in my possession of two eyes. I was somewhat . . . more modestly proportioned, shall we say? More germanely, I was somewhat hotter of temper and fiercer in my adherence to the Blood of my birth and upbringing. But – and this is the important part, Thane, so I hope you are listening – though the fires of my loyal ardour may have been damped down a little by the years, they are far from extinguished.

'I am a part of my Blood. A part many might wish to excise, I suppose, but a part nevertheless. I belong. And I believe, in my deeply buried heart, that the Bloods are a boon to this world. I believe that without them, and without my Blood in particular, we would sink back into the self-mutilation that has so often afflicted us as a people, as a race. As a godless world. You will therefore understand, Thane, that it troubles me greatly to see the Haig Blood convulsed, as it is now, by a multitude of difficulties.'

'You'll find no sympathy in me,' Igryn sneered. He turned his blind head towards Torquentine. The smile upon his bruised and misused face was ugly. Mad. 'I'd like nothing better than to eat your Thane's warm heart out of the bowl of his broken chest.'

'Unfortunately, I do not doubt the sincerity of your desire in that regard. And therein lies my dilemma, for I find myself at a loss to know what to do with you. Quite aside from my instinctive wish to do no more harm than is strictly necessary to the Blood of my birth, change is something I find distinctly undesirable at the best of times. I would go so far as to say, in fact, that I am thoroughly averse to it, for reasons both temperamental and professional. And there is altogether too much of it in the air at the moment. Wanton, egregious change for no better reason than that everyone seems to have forgotten the limits of appropriate behaviour. Do you know who commissioned me to bring about your removal from the custody of Gryvan's men, Thane?'

'No,' hissed Igryn through gritted teeth. 'And I don't care.'

'How ungrateful of you. What would you do if I were to return you to your own lands?'

'Make you rich. Raise an army. Avenge myself upon your Blood and render as many of your women sonless, brotherless and husbandless as I could.'

Torquentine emitted a curtailed, stifled laugh. He glanced over to Magrayn. She was as impassive, as quietly observant as ever.

'Surely he would have been dead long ago, were he as guile-lessly stupid as he appears?' he said to her.

Magrayn frowned. It was an expression that made the exposed, corrupted flesh of her rotted face stir in interesting ways.

'He is sick,' she suggested. 'Deranged.'

'Quite possibly,' Torquentine said. 'I have not left this chamber for some time, Thane, yet I have a thousand eyes, a thousand ears, spread all through this city, all through the lands of this Blood, and others. I see, and I hear, everything. All of that knowledge flows back to this chamber, and pools here in me. And what do I glean from it? What do I discern of the shape of the world?'

He waited for a response from Igryn, but the Thane was silent, his head turning very slowly, very slightly, from side to side.

'I see the Crafts and the Moon Palace edging towards outright war,' Torquentine continued. 'I see your own lands rent by unrest. Not mere banditry but utter lawlessness, and rumours of Dornach ships already scouting your shores with half a mind to land an army by all accounts. I see the Black Road seething across the borders of the Ayth Blood like a swarm of wolves, consuming and destroying. I see murderous mobs rampaging in the streets above us here, battling the Guard. Everywhere I see unreason and savagery and disintegration. It is as if every desire, every ambition now runs unbridled. The fetters of restraint have been cast off by all those upon whom they served a most valuable purpose.'

He sighed. Even as he spoke, he could feel the creeping anxiety that had nested, of late, in his chest. He was a man who craved, who needed, order and control and organisation. Everything, in fact, that the world now seemed determined to slough like some redundant skin.

'And all of it growing worse. Each part of it feeding off the rest, each brutality precipitating another, each stupidity exceeding the one that went before. I have even crept my eyes and my ears into the very house of the man who decided you should be free, Thane. I watch him, I eavesdrop upon him. And I mislike what I see and what I hear. Things have changed in strange and unreadable ways. In that house and everywhere. This puts me in a sorely testing position.'

Igryn laughed. A cackle, like a crow.

'I will eat his heart,' the Thane of the Dargannan Blood murmured.

Torquentine raised his eyebrows and scratched disconsolately at his folded throat.

'As you say, Magrayn: sick. He surrenders himself all too willingly, I think, to the malady that besets the whole world. Ah well. As I was about to explain, I find myself unwilling to comply with my instructions. Returning him to his homeland would only feed a fire that already rages beyond control. I have no wish to play the part of midwife at the birthing of a world given over to unreason and chaos. I just cannot bring myself to do it.'

'Shall I return him to the storeroom?' Magrayn asked.

'Indeed. And make sure there's nothing there he can hurt himself with. Until I decide what to do with him, it's rather important he stays alive.'

The two guards unceremoniously hooked their hands under Igryn's armpits and hoisted him up from the bench. He did not resist, but seemed unable to support his own weight. His legs buckled at the knee and he hung like an ancient, infirm greybeard propped up on a fence.

'Seems like nothing much, doesn't he?' Torquentine reflected sadly. 'Yet because of him, I invite the wrath of the Shadowhand. I all but betroth myself to catastrophe. Constantly surprising, the way things turn out, isn't it? And I never took much pleasure in surprises.'

II

Yvane was trembling, Orisian realised. They had paused beside a pool into which the waters of a stream plunged from a low cliff. Moss and ferns festooned the rock face, a miniature, verdant abundance still resplendent in the green that winter had stolen from the rest of the forest. These were no mighty falls. The column of water that churned down into the pool was slight by comparison with that Orisian had seen at Sarn's Leap, long ago. Still the sound, the cold mist that drifted over his face, was enough to make him think of Inurian. Enough to prickle his heart with needles of guilt and shame. They had left the *na'kyrim* there alone, and he had died. He had died on his own. What a fearful, awful thing that seemed to Orisian now: that a man so gentle and so deserving of better, had died alone, amongst enemies.

Focusing his attention upon Yvane gave him a handhold with which to resist the tug of those lacerating memories. She sat cross-legged beside K'rina, who was curled into a ball, arms folded about her knees. As Orisian watched, Yvane held out one of her hands before her, the fingers spread. She stared at it. Even from a few paces away, Orisian could see that it shook. Yvane frowned in concentration. She was trying to still her hand, Orisian realised. She failed, and let it fall, palsied, into her lap.

'Is it bad?' he asked quietly.

'I can smell wolfenkind,' she replied. Her voice was somehow different. It had an attenuated fragility to it that was new. 'The memory of them. I can hear them running through a forest far older than this one. It sounds like death.'

'It's not long now,' Orisian said. 'Another few days, that's all. Then we can—'

'What?' said Yvane sharply, glaring at him. 'You really think it will be that easy? What is it you think is going to happen?'

Orisian stared blankly at her. She was changing, he thought. Bit by bit, she was becoming someone he did not know. Perhaps they all were.

'It won't be easy for her,' Yvane muttered, looking down at K'rina. The other *na'kyrim* appeared entirely at peace, hugging herself into a safe, quiet ball.

Splashing behind him distracted Orisian. He twisted around. The warriors were along the edge of the pool into which the falls tumbled. Some were drinking its clear waters, others soaking tired and blistered feet. One had waded out, barefoot, into the middle of the pool. He stood there, unsteady on hidden rocks, arms outstretched as the spray from the waterfall threw shifting, tenuous veils across him. He was, Orisian saw to his alarm, weeping. He made no sound yet his face was contorted with grief, his cheeks bunched in anguish.

'Eagan, get out of there,' Taim Narran was saying.

The warrior gave no sign of having heard the command. He drew his arms slowly in, closed his hands over his face. He was shaken by silent sobs.

'You'll not be fit for walking if you don't come out of there,' Taim said, more sternly now. He was not angry yet, but there was urgency there.

Orisian rose to his feet. Eagan was entirely unresponsive to his Captain's voice. Orisian could feel fear settling itself over him like a cape, and he did not know why. A flicker of movement drew his eyes up to the top of the waterfall. Varryn was there, tall against the pale sky. He and Ess'yr had been – as they always were now – scouting ahead, roving like hunting dogs through the forest. Now he stared down with the piercing, attentive eyes of a hawk. Even as Orisian watched, the Kyrinin set down his spear and unslung his bow from his back.

'Wait . . .' Orisian said, but he said it softly, and the words were drowned out as Eagan took a few lurching, splashing steps back towards the edge of the pool.

The warrior's hands fell away from his face. With one, he began to tug helplessly at the thongs that bound the neck of his jerkin; with the other he reached out to Taim. No more tears fell, but still his expression was one of despairing horror.

'I can't . . .' he gasped out.

He sounded very young to Orisian. He sounded like a distraught, helpless child.

'Get out of there,' Taim said.

He held out a hand. Eagan locked his grasp about Taim's wrist and hauled violently, dragging him instantly face forward into the water. Taim vanished below the surface with a booming, hollow splash. Eagan surged up onto the bank and staggered back the way they had come. His sodden leggings spilled clouds of droplets. His naked feet, bleached by the cold of the stream, slithered on the wet grass.

'Wait,' Orisian shouted, moving to intercept Eagan.

Two of the other warriors took hold of their companion, grabbing handfuls of his collar and sleeves. He howled and threw one off. He struck the other on the cheekbone with the heel of his hand, and the man stumbled back.

'I can't,' Eagan cried. 'We can't!'

Orisian stepped in front of him and stretched out his arms to block Eagan's path.

'It's all right,' Orisian said, the stupidity, the inadequacy of the words ringing in his ears.

His eyes met Eagan's, and he knew in that instant that the man was lost. That something in him had given way. He saw something else there, in those wide and desperate eyes, and it set his hand moving towards the hilt of his sword before his mind recognised it. Beyond Eagan, Taim was rising, water pouring from him.

'No,' said Orisian as his sword began to slide from its scabbard.

Eagan's own blade was slipping free as he staggered towards his Thane, as heavy and inevitable as a falling tree. There was a thud, and a spasm of distraction twitched across Eagan's face. The feathers of an arrow trembled above his shoulder. The shaft had come in steeply, from the top of the waterfall, to lance down into his back. It was not enough to stop him, though it gave Orisian time to get his sword free and raise it to block Eagan's ragged swing.

Orisian staggered back.

'Eagan!' another of the men shouted as he came up behind. Confusion and anger and shock writhed together in that single word.

Eagan spun around, and his sword spun with him. It took his comrade high on the side of the face, and the man fell leadenly back, his eyes wide in surprise as the blade streaked his blood across the air. Another arrow darted down and found its target, but Eagan did not fall.

He turned back towards Orisian, raising his sword above his head as if to bring it bludgeoning down. He gave out a strained keening, a grief-stricken, doomed wail. Orisian drove the point of his sword up into his stomach, under his ribs. Eagan was struck abruptly dumb. He dropped his own weapon and slumped sideways.

Orisian stared down at him, listening to his shallow, faltering breaths. Eagan's eyes were open. They stared at the grass into which his head was pressed. The spaces between his breaths grew longer and longer.

Taim came striding up from the pool, hair pasted across his forehead, water still falling from his chin and the cuffs of his jerkin.

'Stand back, sire,' he said to Orisian.

Taim kicked Eagan's sword away and knelt to look into the man's face.

'He's finished,' Orisian said bleakly.

Taim only nodded as he rose to his feet once more. Eagan was not breathing any more. Nor was the man he had struck with his sword. The others were all standing motionless, with the waterfall splattering away behind them, staring either at the dead men or at Orisian. In every eye that was upon him Orisian detected – or thought he detected – accusation. He looked up to the head of the falls. Varryn was still there, silhouetted, unstringing his bow. Orisian nodded once towards the Kyrinin warrior. Varryn simply turned away and disappeared from sight.

'Not long now,' Orisian whispered to no one but himself. 'Please.'

The dead White Owls were strewn all along the eastern flank of a long, low, forested ridge. The trees were sparse along the crest of the ridge, and many of the corpses lay exposed to the sky. They were not alone. Ravens spiralled overhead, croaking in protest at this interruption to their feasting. As Orisian trod carefully between the bodies, a buzzard swept heavily up from a nearby tree and glided away over the canopy. The thin snow that persisted on this higher ground was patterned with innumerable tracks: the prints of the men and women and children who had died here intermingled with those of their killers, overlaid by the marks of the eaters of the dead. Several of the corpses had been opened or gnawed. Fox and crow and bear had been busy.

Orisian did not know what to think. He had never seen so many Kyrinin dead. Although these were notionally his enemies, and their clan had taken Rothe's life and made war upon Ess'yr's people, he could not help but lament the transformation of so much grace and power into sanguine ugliness. Without life to animate them, the bodies looked ungainly. Pathetic almost, with their disordered, frozen clothes, their scattered bundles of belongings. He could make no connection between these sad shells and the Kyrinin he had seen, and known, and fought in the weeks since Winterbirth.

Yvane and K'rina lingered further up the slope. The bulbous bare rocks almost hid them from sight. Taim and his men were moving amongst the bodies, each following a solitary, silent path from corpse to corpse. Looking for what? Orisian wondered. There was no life here, not even its faintest residue. Taking the measure of death, perhaps. Feeling its texture, learning afresh its look.

Ess'yr and Varryn were coming up towards him, emerging from the deeper shadows down there in the thick forest, where the dead and the tree trunks and the dark ground merged into uniform gloom. Varryn's expression filled Orisian with an imprecise, all-encompassing regret. The Kyrinin was not smiling, but his eyes gleamed with restrained excitement.

'It is good,' Varryn said as they drew near.

'No,' Orisian said. 'No, it's not.'

Ess'yr held out the bloodied stub of an arrow. It had been broken off halfway along the shaft.

'White Owl,' she said. Orisian was glad not to hear her brother's eagerness reflected in her. But nor did he hear any trace of sorrow, any hint of distress at this slaughter.

'The enemy kill each other. Like a snared beast, they tear at their own legs. Their own bodies. It will make our path easier.'

'Easier,' Orisian echoed. He stooped down to the dead White Owl girl who lay at his feet. Half-dusted with snow, she was face down. Her arms lay neatly in at her sides, one leg bent, the other quite straight. She was small. No more than ten years old, he guessed. He picked up a little bow from where it had spilled out of the bedding roll she had been carrying. Like a toy, he thought. And remembered that he had seen the same thing in the hands of a Fox child, long ago by the banks of the River Dihrve.

'Let's keep moving,' he said. There was a foulness about this place. He wanted only to leave it far behind.

As the two Kyrinin trotted down into the next broad vale in Anlane's endless undulations, Orisian noticed one of Taim's warriors staring after them. There was no warmth in the man's fixed gaze. No sentiment at all, in fact, save mistrust. Suspicion. We're all snared now, Orisian thought. Every one of us.

*

Across the moors north of Dun Aygll, the host of Black Road spread. It splintered and crumbled, like a vast flock of birds that had ridden fierce winds but found them, in the end, too potent and been scattered by them. It consumed everything it encountered: farms and villages and the fragile remnants of the Haig army. And it consumed itself. Tarbains hunted stragglers of any ilk, slaughtered and stripped them. Parties of Battle Inkallim rode back and forth across the bare and sodden land, seeking to reassert control over this vast beast, only to find it ungovernable. As often as not, they encountered nothing but madness and frenzy and feral bloodlust. Where they could not impose order, they imposed death instead, for there was a kind of madness upon many of them as well.

The masterless villages on the eastern shore of the Vaywater, where no Blood and no Thane held sway, turned on one another. The fishermen and goatherds and hunters and weavers laid down the tools of their crafts and took up knives and axes and spears instead. They fought over disputed fields and over stolen goats. They paid no heed to other concerns, and one settlement – Karlakan – was thus taken unawares when a wandering band of Heron Kyrinin, straying perversely far from their territories, descended upon it in the night. By dawn, blood was running down into the waters of the great lake and curling away in stained eddies.

In Koldihrve, at the mouth of the Vale of Tears, the men of the town hunted *na'kyrim* after nightfall.

The Heron and the Hawk, who had planted peace staffs along their boundaries only one season ago, disinterred all the grievances that had been so recently buried. The young men and the young women took up their spears once more. They raided, as they had done before, but this time they went not in their tens but in their scores, and wherever the spear *a'an*s went, they left not even the youngest of children or the frailest of elders alive.

And in Anlane the White Owl Kyrinin made war upon themselves. A few who had doubted all along the intoxicating promises of the *na'kyrim* Aeglyss, and found themselves dismayed by the fierce passions that now seemed to rule their fellows, spoke out. And were slain. The last of them was cut apart on the hard ground before the lodge of the Voice herself. But the killing, and the dissent, once begun did not stop. Though many of the warriors were long gone, venturing far beyond the clan's territory to assuage their lately rediscovered martial pride and hunger for the blood of their people's myriad enemies, enough remained to fight over every trifle, and even the least warlike, the youngest, the oldest, the most infirm, found enough passion burning in them to lift a spear or set arrow to string.

The dyke had been broken, and through the breach came flooding every resentment and division. Rumour and accusation spun all through Anlane like seeds upon the wind. *Vo'an*s began to break apart, families and warbands taking to paths that would normally remain untrodden until the summer, many neither knowing nor caring whether they were fleeing or pursuing, hunter or hunted. The wise chanted in their tents, questing after truth, but no answers came. Only fear and confusion. But still they chanted, and hoped for clarity, while outside and everywhere in the Thousand Tree-Clad Valleys the bloodshed continued.

III

The contours of the darkness within Ragnor oc Gyre's fortress in Kan Dredar were subtle. Slight gradations laid a patchwork cloak of blacks and greys and shadow over the foundry and the bakery, the barracks and the stables, the low keep where the High Thane dwelled; and the Great Hall loomed over all with its huge steepled roof and its giant doors, around the edges of which light and noise and heat bled into the winter's night. All else was quiet. Rats ran along the base of the storehouse wall, noses down. There was smoke coiling out from the armourer's workshop, but the fires from which it sprang had long since been left to dwindle. The smiths were in the Hall with everyone else.

Beyond the outer palisade, in the trees down by the river, an owl called. There were none to hear it, save the guards in the watchtowers and at the gates, and most of them were too busy bemoaning their drawing of such a cold duty while the rest of Ragnor's household had its revels. None to hear it, save those guards, and one other.

Shadow separated itself, a part of it coming free and slipping silently across the narrow stretch of ground between storehouse and Great Hall. Two rats, startled by this sudden intrusion into their nocturnal dominion, scampered for their tunnels in the hard earth.

The assassin who came to rest crouching at the foot of the hall's looming rear wall had ash thickly smeared over his face. Every garment he wore was black. His hands were sheathed in gloves thin enough to ensure their movement would not be hampered. He paused there, secure in lightless obscurity, and took a few steady breaths to regulate his heartbeat and clear his mind. Satisfied, he rose smoothly to his feet, still pressing himself against the stone wall. The whites of his eyes were the only imperfection in his sombre concealment. They darted this way and that now, like pale pebbles. And found nothing to concern him. No light in any overlooking window, no movement.

Turning, he extended one arm up and took hold of the rough stonework. He was lean but nonetheless powerful. Fingers like steel bars raised him up the wall. His boots were light, little more than black-dyed slippers of soft calf-hide. It was easy to find places for both hands and feet on the surface. He climbed without haste, for haste was the enemy of both precision and silence. If anything betrayed him now, it would be sound rather than sight. There was not even enough moonlight for him to see the details of the wall before his own face. He went by touch and feel, and by memory. He had studied the route he must follow from down below over the last two days.

The small crossbow on his back was tied tight to prevent any movement. The cords constrained him only very slightly, not enough to impede his ascent. That distant owl was calling again, and that pleased him. It gave the night a veneer of normalcy and calm, and would thus offer false comfort to those keeping watch. It allowed him to think that fate might favour his endeavour.

Up to the very eaves he climbed, and into the utter darkness of their overhang. Fingers locked into crevices, he drew up his knees, bracing his feet between the rough-cut blocks of stone. Now he was entirely hidden. Even someone wandering unexpectedly along directly beneath him would struggle to descry his lofty presence, should their gaze drift improbably upwards.

Another moment or two to moderate his breathing and his heart. Then exploratory fingers delicately extended along the very top of the wall, tracing the line where the stones met the protruding woodwork and beams of the huge roof. He could hear the voices of those within, dull and indistinct, a rumbling murmur punctuated by occasional laughter or shouts. He shut the distraction out. He dwelled only in this moment, thought only of his own body, his holds and what his reaching hand sought.

Soon enough he found it: a gap where uneven stones and prised-apart wood combined to yield less than two hands' span of space. Even through his gloves he could feel the heat of the air oozing out from that opening and he could smell the smoke and the scents of food and drink and bodies that the hall exhaled through this tiny flaw in its fabric. Two crab-like cramped movements across the stone were enough to take him there, and now, with his eyes directly before it, he could see the soft orange firelight reflected on dark woodwork within. One hand hooked in there gave him enough security to loosen the crossbow's bindings with the other. The weapon preceded him into the roofspace. He emptied his lungs to shrink his chest and followed it, forcing himself through this most narrow of entrances.

Others had preceded the assassin up this wall, just a handful of times. One had climbed to open the way, easing apart wooden struts just enough to admit a lean and determined body. He did not know how long ago that had been, for it was not his place to know such things. One or two, after that, had entered the High Thane's hall just as he now did, though they had brought only their ears and their eyes with them, seeking only information. He came with more fatal intent, and felt himself to be the first. The only one that mattered.

The roof of the Great Hall rode a massive and intricate fretwork of beams and timbers, a supportive weave of wood and nails. Like a marten making its sinuous way through the branches of a forest canopy, the assassin edged towards an angular perch, where he would be concealed from all but the most acute of eyes but able to lock his own gaze upon Ragnor oc Gyre, who feasted below.

The High Thane filled his wolfskin-clad throne. His lavish gestures and bellowing voice said he had already drunk more than his fill. As had most of the others who thronged the length of the great chamber. They sat on benches and rugs, crowded round the three huge fires blazing in their open hearths. They milled about – many unsteadily – brandishing cups and joints of meat. Some fought, and those around them paid no heed to their struggles, consumed by their own kinds of madness. One – an old, bearded man – was naked, and danced on the fringe of the flames, gabbling nonsensically, his body turning pink and raw as the heat raged at him. There was a dead man lying by one of the fires, his blood spread around his neck and shoulders. In one corner, close by Ragnor, a woman – one of his Shield – was hunched over the corpse of a hunting dog, pulling at it, flaying it.

Shadows swept and cavorted around the walls, flung there by the light of those exuberant fires: not just the soft-edged blurs of the churning host, but the starker, sharper darknesses cast by the huge antler trophies that hung everywhere. The assassin found the frenzied scene repellent. He had been brought up to another kind of life, one that could never condone such mad indulgence. And that upbringing came now to its purpose and goal. All his discipline could not wholly suppress the eagerness blossoming in his breast. This moment was what he was for; it was the sum of all his years. Though the bestial passions he saw expressed below him were not something he could share, there was passion of a sort within him. A yearning to be the deliverer of death, a long-ing – such as he had never felt before – to be the weapon by which fate delivered its judgement.

He rocked fractionally, testing the stability of his position. It was good enough. Still, he kept his movements slow and con-tained as he drew back the string of the crossbow. The smoke that pooled amidst the rafters of the hall was stinging his throat and eyes. His body wanted to sniff or cough, but he mastered the animal urges.

Below, Ragnor was shouting something at his Master of the Hall, who stood beside the throne, an island of morose solemnity amidst the sea of merriment. The old man did not appear to reply, but the High Thane laughed. The assassin eased one of his two bolts from the tiny flat quiver that he wore inside his black shirt, and nestled it into place on the bow. The weapon was not powerful, but Ragnor seldom wore chain at times such as this, so it need only punch the quarrel through cloth and hide and skin. It was more than capable of that. And once the bolt found its place in the High Thane's flesh, it too was capable of doing what was needful. It was finely, savagely barbed, and would fight all attempts to free it from a wound. And it would foul that wound too, for a crust of excrement and soil and spittle was dried upon its point. Whether quickly or slowly, Ragnor oc Gyre would die.

The assassin had to lean a little to one side to gain the clear straight line to the High Thane that he desired. He made the adjustment cautiously, his hips and thighs and back tensing to keep him from overbalancing. His muscles were trained for such exertion, and he barely noticed the effort required. Slowly, he dipped his head to sight along the waiting bolt. Smoke rasped at his eyes and he winced. His vision blurred for a moment and he had to clench his eyes shut, squeezing tears out. The smoke was worse than he had expected. He blinked again and again, still holding his head quite still and steady down over the crossbow's butt. His sight cleared.

He breathed out, whispering as he did so, 'My feet are on the road. I go without fear.'

And the string cracked forward, and the barbed bolt flashed free from its shallow gutter.

And Ragnor oc Gyre leaned across towards his Master of the Hall, crying some jovial abuse at him.

And the crossbow bolt thumped into the throne, pinning the collar of Ragnor's jerkin to the wolfskin and wood.

The assassin was already moving, turning back towards the hidden gap by which he had entered. He heard the howl of outrage, the roars of confusion and alarm, but did not look. He would not do so until he was poised on the brink of escape. If, in that moment, there seemed the time and opportunity for the second bolt, he would try again. If not, he would vanish out into the night and come again, elsewhere, tomorrow or the next day or the next, until the Gyre Blood was relieved of its Thane.

He reached through the smoke and the heat and the tears that filmed and dulled his eyes for a slanting beam to haul himself round. And almost missed the hold, his fingers slipping for a moment over flat wood. He swayed. His other arm came up to balance him, and the end of the crossbow it carried jarred against another timber. Jarred free. The crossbow fell, plunging down into the world of light and noise and anger below.

He could see the narrow black void that marked his escape route, and darted towards it. He could smell the cold, fresh night air beyond, could imagine the freedom of the open black sky above his head. And crossbow bolts were flying up, like a flurry of answers to the challenge he had dispatched downwards. They smacked splinters from the wooden lattice through which he moved. They would not find him, he was sure. Already he was consumed by the sour sense of failure, but still he did not doubt he would live to serve the creed another day.

Until one bolt out of the flock that swarmed up towards him impaled his trailing hand, nailing it to a beam. Through the very centre of the back of his hand it went, and buried itself deep in the wood. He gasped, not in pain but in surprise. And in frustration, for he needed that hand as he swung forward. He stared through bleary eyes at the very place he would be reaching for with it. He could see, indistinctly, the saw marks in the flat face of the timber. He blinked, and overbalanced, and fell.

His arm wrenched at his shoulder joint as his entire weight was abruptly hung from that single impaled hand. It held only for an instant, then the bolt tore out from his flesh, ripping itself free between two fingers. He tipped backwards as he fell, gazing up into the darkness of the roof. An outstretched antler of one the trophies on the wall stabbed into his thigh, and gouged down the back of his leg to his knee, tumbling him in the air. He plummeted head down, a host of snarling faces rushing up to greet him from below.

*

'What were you thinking?'

Theor had his hands half-raised, poised as if arrested in the midst of some violent movement. He could not tear his gaze away from them. His eyes took in the aged, slack hide that his skin had become, the terrible impotence of these limbs that once, surely, must have felt capable and powerful. The fury that was in him was in them too, seething and burning in the palms and the fingers. And it was such a pathetic thing, that fury. It was empty, powerless to change anything. Powerless even, he felt, to express itself honestly.

'What were you thinking?' he cried again at Avenn.

The First of the Hunt glared at him. He suddenly imagined himself seizing her by the throat, crushing and crushing the contemptuous, arrogant life out of her with these same trembling hands. He imagined her slumping to her knees, gasping for breath that would not come.

Slowly he lowered his hands. It would not happen like that, of course. He was a feeble old man, a boat drifting broken-ruddered amidst rocks and storms. She was of the Hunt. Fierce, strong. And certain of her purpose. Her faith.

'I did what the times, the circumstances, the creed, seemed to called for,' Avenn said.

Not even a semblance of deference in her any more. She would not deign to make the most passing pretence at submission to the Lore's authority. Theor could only shake his head.

'He was feasting,' Avenn snarled. 'Feasting? In times such as these? Celebrating what? The fact that we've made ourselves his subjects. The fact that he can steal a hundred orphans from the Battle merely by demanding it. The fact that he can kill Hunt Inkallim without fear of redress, without us raising a hand or a blade to prevent him. The fact that we lack the will to pursue this grand, this glorious enterprise that has been begun through to its utmost conclusion. The fact that we falter.'

Oh, the fire that burned in her was bright. Theor could remember when such sacred fervour raised him up just as it now did Avenn. It had not been so very long ago, yet it felt an age. It felt as if those righteous sentiments and certainties had dwelt in the heart of an entirely different person. Someone else. Someone who had not been prey to the doubts and the sickening fears that now ate away at him.

'This sudden caution that cripples you is unwarranted, First,' snarled Avenn. She was striding up and down on the reed matting that covered the floor. This was a chamber meant for peaceful contemplation. Theor had brought her here for the sake of privacy and discretion.

'But you goad the High Thane into striking out against us,' he muttered, that rage that had briefly so animated him leaching away. It was unsustainable. 'Ragnor's temper already runs hot as a fever. He's been walking upon the brink of unreason for days. Now . . .'

He hung his head.

'I regret nothing,' Avenn said. 'Fate will dispose things as it sees fit. I came to tell you of this only out of courtesy.'

'But you came too late. You come to me in the morning to tell me of something done the night before. That is not courtesy but contempt.'

'You know how things stand now,' Avenn muttered unapologetically. 'I have given fate the chance to make its choice. To move forward.'

Theor could have wept, and he did not know why, beyond the certainty that there was a terrible wrongness in all of this. And that the awful, crippling guilt he now felt was somehow deserved. He had come to mistrust so many of his feelings, his instincts, and to fear their turbulence, tossed about by gales that seemed to come from outside him, but that . . . that guilt felt true and clear, even if he did not understand whence it sprang.

'You've done nothing but give Ragnor the excuse to tear the Inkalls apart,' he said leadenly, recognising the futility of anything other than silence.

'It had to come, sooner or later,' Avenn shouted. 'This is the time when all matters will be resolved. This is the time when the world must come apart, when all hopes and intents shall fail, save that of fate itself. This is the end of this world, old man, and if your wits and your courage had not failed you, you would see that as clearly as the rest of us. You betray the Lore, and the faith, with your craven reticence.'

'No . . .' Theor could find no words, no armour against either her accusations or the world's collapse.

'The First of the Battle will stand by the Hunt in this, even if the Lore will not,' Avenn said.

'Did Nyve know?' Theor asked, dreading the answer.

'No. But he will not contest fate's course. He will welcome it.'

That was true, of course. The flood that seemed to be bearing all of them along in its destructive embrace had taken hold of Nyve. It was more than a lifetime's friendship could hope to resist.

'And Ragnor will leave him no choice now,' Avenn continued. She spoke almost casually, as to some servant or follower. 'He will surely come against us. Good. The people will rise up in our defence if he makes war upon the Inkalls.'

'You think that will deter him?' Theor said. 'You think he cares any more about what is wise or considered? He doesn't care. He is as blind as . . . as all of us.'

'Fate will show us the way. And if that way is to ruin and rue, so be it. How could the end of all things and the birthing of new be attended by anything but ruin?'

'You're mad,' murmured Theor, turning away, walking towards the door. 'As are we all now.'

He left her there, not even glancing back to see whether the First of the Hunt followed him out of the meditatory chamber. There was nothing more to be said. The world had become inimical to words, and to reason. The madness that had so many others in its grip would brook no resistance from those – like Theor – who found themselves beyond its grasp; and so he was to be forgotten, ignored. He could no longer find the strength within himself to resent or oppose that.

Outside, it was snowing, but it was a meagre, grainy kind of snow. The flakes were not the buoyant fat flowers of midwinter, but icy granules that came on desultory gusts of wind. Thick snow still lay over the Sanctuary, the relic of what had already been a long, hard season. There would be a thaw soon enough, Theor knew. The days were slowly lengthening. The mountain streams would fatten with meltwater and rush white and blue down into the valley. The lying snow would merge into the earth and bloat it, turn it to mud. There would, eventually, be a breaking of buds and a piercing of that mud by soft new shoots. If the world did not come to its end. If this was not, in fact, the Kall.

Theor was tired. No, more than tired. Utterly drained. Lifeless, lightless.

A young Inkallim came a little hesitantly across the snow towards him. A girl whose name he could not recall. So much seemed to be slipping away from him now.

'First, there is a messenger come from the Battle.'

Theor came to a shuffling halt. The hem of his robe settled over the snow.

'From Nyve?' he asked wearily.

'Yes, First. The messenger asks that you return with him to consult with the First of the Battle. There are . . . apparently, there are companies of Gyre warriors moving out from Kan Dredar. Moving up the slopes.'

'Of course there are,' sighed Theor. His bones felt heavy, as if they were encrusted with defeat and disappointment, so thickened and burdened by their own weight that he could hardly lift them. All he wanted to do, all he could conceive of doing, was sleep. Hide away behind a locked door, in darkness, and be nothing for a time.

'Send the messenger back where he came from,' he said. 'Tell him I will come later. Not now. Later, if I can.'

He trudged on, moving beneath the pine trees that filled so much of the compound. The young Inkallim had not moved.

'What is happening, First?' she called after him. It was not quite fear that coloured her voice. Not yet.

'Nothing, child,' Theor said without stopping or looking round. 'Nothing.'

IV

When Theor woke, it was from an intermittent slumber that had done nothing to renew him. He rose stiffly and dressed. His skin felt every scrape of his robe's rough material. He felt no hunger or thirst, no desire of any kind that might lead him out from this bare chamber. Yet there was nothing to hold him here either. Solitude brought no easing of his despair.

He went out, and found others clustered in the corridor, conferring in muted whispers. They looked up, startled, at his emergence.

'You should see . . .' one of them stammered.

He let them lead him to the walls of the Sanctuary. Let them guide him up the steps onto the narrow walkway cut into its inner face. He went numbly, without expectation.

What they wanted to show him was smoke. It was climbing up into a sky thick with white clouds, tracing its darker way against that bleached background in two twisting columns that merged as they rose, and then slowly bent and spread to drift in black sheets high above the snow-clad hills. Those who accompanied him talked and fretted, but Theor took none of it in. He gazed up at that dark pillar ascending from the earth towards the firmament above and felt nothing. No surprise, no confusion, no fear. He found himself beyond such things.

It was the compound of the Battle burning. There was nothing else out there on the wooded slopes that could give rise to such a conflagration. The wind was coming from his back, otherwise Theor did not doubt that he would have smelled the ash, the burning timbers. Perhaps burning flesh. Perhaps he would even have heard the cries of the dying, the commotion of sudden death.

As they stood there on the wall, a shape emerged from the trees, coming steadily towards them. Some cried out and pointed, tugging at Theor's arm to direct his attention. He did not respond. It was a grey horse, trotting along, following the hard-packed snow of the path between the deeper, pristine drifts that flanked it. It came at its own pace, following its own course, for the man who rode it was slumped forward, draped limply around its neck. Even from this distance, it was not hard to recognise him as a Battle Inkallim. The blackness of his hair, and of his leather armour, stood out against the pale hide of his mount and the luminously white snow.

The man's blood had stained the horse's shoulder, forming a dark red-brown blemish that flexed and pulsed as it moved along. There were crossbow bolts standing proud from the man's back. Two of them, Theor thought, though he could not be sure.

'We must intercede, First,' one of those gathered upon the wall cried, all panic and confusion. 'They will listen to the Lore, surely? The High Thane, the Battle, they must listen to the Lore. No one else perhaps, but us.'

Theor did not know what to say. Neither Ragnor nor Nyve would listen. They had boiled over and could hear nothing but the roaring of their own hearts, their own rages. The time when consideration, negotiation, moderation might gain any purchase upon anyone had passed. Fury bestrode the world and would not yield its dominion. That Theor himself could not partake of the heady brew rendered him isolated, at a loss. For whatever reason, he had been left becalmed and irrelevant in some backwater while the river flooded on without him. As if fate had no further need for him. If it even was fate that governed this torrent.

He turned away while the horse was still approaching with its grim cargo. He descended from the wall, ignoring the questions and pleas his fellow Inkallim belaboured him with. He went silently back to his own small bedchamber and closed the door behind him, and took a little box out from its hiding place.

Three of the Lore had now died within the walls of the Sanctuary while dreaming seerstem dreams. It was unprecedented. Theor himself had forbidden any others to venture into that once-so-soothing territory. But now . . . there was nowhere else to turn. He could find no truth or sense any longer on this side of the seerstem gate. There were no answers here. Nothing for him to hold on to. He felt entirely defeated by the vastness of the world and its confusion.

He took out one of the shrivelled fragments from the box and regarded it blankly. He did not truly imagine it could bring him any of the clarity he so craved, but that tiny hope persisted. Even before the deaths began, there had been little save troubling turmoil to be found in those strange dreams. But still he set the seerstem in his mouth and crushed it between his teeth. He lay back on the hard bed and closed his eyes.

Slowly, slowly, the seerstem took him. It dulled him and enfolded him and gently parted the threads holding him to the waking world. He sank, and the darkness bled across his eyes and silence leaked into his ears.

And he saw a thousand flickering shadows darting back and forth across a limitless gloomy expanse. He felt a thousand fluttering touches on the skin of his thoughts. A thousand sparks of anger, of fear, hate, anguish, awful grief, each one no more than an instant, like an ocean of tiny, transient stars flaring and dying across his mind. They dizzied him and dazzled him and he wailed soundlessly in his dreams at the deluge. This place to which seerstem gave entry had twisted so radically away from its once-familiar and restful form that it now felt like an exposed pinnacle surrounded by a churning storm. Standing there he was besieged and buffeted by clamorous delirium.

Whatever faint hope he had nurtured that there might yet be answers to be found here was shattered, and its fragments torn away on the howling winds that blew through him. Lights flashed before him, and he knew they were not lights but lives. It was a fearful lightning storm of being. It was too much. Panic boiled in him, and he longed above all else to escape this invasive maelstrom, but the seerstem had him, and he could not choose to wake from its clutches yet.

And then he was not alone. He saw nothing, heard nothing, but he felt a presence settling all about him, as if the black sky had descended and gathered itself into a single shell that enclosed him. It was a cold presence. One that pressed upon his consciousness, probed it with insistent fingers.

'Who are you?' Theor stammered. 'What are you?'

'No.' The voice was inside him, reverberating in the chamber of his mind. 'Here, the questions are mine to ask. Who are you? Another of those who stumble blindly about the fringes of this place. Another trespasser who does not belong.'

'I am . . .' The man did not know his name any more, for that part of his memory, and his self, was eclipsed by this immense all-encompassing presence. He fell silent.

'This is not for you. All of this, not for you. Your blood is too singular. Too clean, too pure.' The voice spat that last word with venom. It burned the man. 'Your kind does not belong here.'

'Who are you? Are you . . . are you the Hooded God?'

'Oh, your dreams of the Road. These pathetic comforts you preach to yourselves. Like children, afraid of the dark, afraid of being alone. To be alone; I could teach you about that. I could show you. No, I'm not your Last God.'

The man felt himself failing. He was crumbling beneath the weight of this vast attention.

'He Who Waits?' He mumbled it; he gasped it. 'He Who

Waits, then? Not gone at all, but always here? Always with us, all this time?'

The laughter was all around him, all through him, tearing at him.

'You'd make me Death?' And a heavy silence, a nothingness for a time. 'I don't know. I don't know. I want . . . I wanted everything to be different. Not death. That's not what I wanted. I only wanted . . . I only wanted . . .' Agonies seeped from the voice into the man, filling him with another's suffering. And it continued: 'None of this is as I thought it would be. But it cannot be changed.'

Swiftly as they had come, the doubt and sorrow that had suffused the voice receded. The darkness grew deeper. The shadows massed.

'But this place is not for you. This is my body, my flesh. My blood. You are within me, and that is not . . . So, yes. A God, if you like. I am sitting now, in a cold room, in a ruined city, talking to someone . . . talking . . . failing. My body decays. I cannot mend it. Nothing can be mended now. But I am here too. And greater here, beyond decay.'

Theor remembered who he was then. He was granted that, as the presence shrank away from him a little, and withdrew itself from the fabric of his thoughts. He fell, from nowhere towards nowhere, simply plummeting through a roaring void; and the awful presence was that through which he fell, and it was with him also, gathering and taking hold of his essence.

It whispered in his mind, 'If I am to be a God. Let it be Death.'

It tore Theor apart. He felt himself opened and splintered. Shards of his awareness were ripped away. This foul, omnipotent being that claimed the mantle of Death flayed his mind with claws of pure loathing and rage. It poured all its jealousies and hatreds and bitterness into him, and they dismembered him. In the last, flickering, dimming glimmer of Theor's own thoughts, beyond the agony and the terror, there was only a long, descending murmur of regret and a lingering bitter certainty of failure and error. That faded. And fluttered. And finally wisped away, dispersing into the unbounded, eternal Shared.

And in the Sanctuary of the Lore Inkallim struggled to hold the First's flailing limbs steady. He bucked and arched on the trestle bed and spat black-tainted foam at them as he screamed. Then he fell suddenly silent and still. The Inkallim backed away from him, alarmed. Tears streamed from his open, staring eyes. His heart pounded, and each mighty beat shook him, and drew a single gasping breath from him. Until there came one clenching of his heart that did not release itself; one breath that was cut short and lay unfinished in his throat. His hands twisted the bed sheet beneath him into knots. And Theor, First of the Lore, died.

Outside, in the snowbound grounds of the Sanctuary, the ancient pine trees stood as they had done for so many years. Tiny birds spiralled up their trunks, seeking insects wintering in the crevices of the bark. Above, midway between the sharp peaks of the trees and the thinning cloud, buzzards were circling. Tiny drops of rain – not snow but rain – were flickering down. The buzzards arced away, lazy wings bearing them towards Kan Dredar in the valley below, or towards the compound of the Battle Inkall. There would be food for them there.

*

'I see them,' Igris said from the window.

Kanin oc Horin-Gyre set down the bowl of cold broth he had been holding to his lips and twisted in his chair.

'You're sure?' he said to his shieldman.

Igris nodded. He was staring out over a street on the very south-eastern fringe of Glasbridge. This part of the town had been beset by both flood and fire when the town fell to the Black Road. The house in which they waited, and in which Kanin took a hasty meal, had no roof to it. The floorboards were charred; the

shutters at the window from which Igris looked out hung split
and smoke-blackened and broken. There was even now, long
since the floodwaters had receded, a damp stink of rot to the
place. Kanin had had to sweep a thin crust of snow from the
table when they first entered.

He wiped soup from his lips with the back of his hand.

'How many?' he asked without getting up.

'Can't tell yet, sire,' Igris replied.

'Eska said there were twenty, when she saw them on the road
this morning.'

'Might be twenty. Or they might have seen her. Perhaps they
split up.'

'They didn't see her,' said Kanin scornfully. 'She's of the Hunt,
man. You think they get themselves seen except by choice?'

Igris shrugged. There was weary defeat in that sluggish movement.

'We'd best go down to greet them, then,' Kanin said, pushing
back his chair and getting to his feet. He lifted his chain shirt
from where it lay on the table and shrugged it over his head.

'Are you sure?' Igris murmured. Such a small sound, so frail,
to come from such a man. It was resigned yet perhaps still carried the faintest thread of hope that his master might turn aside
from his chosen course. Kanin glared at his shieldman's back.

'You question me? Doubt me?'

Igris said nothing. Kanin took a heavy cloak down from a
hook on the wall.

'Just do what I require of you,' he said. 'Do as your Thane
requires. You've enough honour, enough memory of who you
are, to do that, I hope.'

His shieldman followed him out onto the street. The man
stank of reluctance, and Kanin despised him for that. The slush
outside was almost ankle deep. The night before had been the
first in a long time that had not frozen. As a result, Glasbridge's
white covering was softening, turning grey, melting into its

ruins and its mud. Kanin splashed out into the centre of the road and stood there, feet spaced enough to give him a firm stance, cloak flicked back clear of his sword. He waited.

The riders came around the corner in single file. The horses moved very slowly. One by one they came into sight: six, ten, twelve, then fifteen, twenty. All black-haired. All tall and upright. All clad in dark leather with iron studwork or buckles or hilts glinting softly here and there. Ravens, riding into Glasbridge. Kanin smiled to himself.

Then, still fifty or more paces distant, the lead rider halted her horse with the merest rolling of her wrist to tighten the reins. She stared down the street towards Kanin. Others of the riders came sedately forward and conferred with their leader. The muted exchange was curt. She nodded once, and two men peeled themselves away from the rest, easing their mounts round and heading, just as unhurriedly as they had come, back out towards the fields beyond the town.

Kanin's smile died on his lips. His disappointment was far more bitter than he would have expected. It did not, in truth, matter greatly. After today, everything would rush onwards. The end – whatever its form, whatever its nature – would come quickly, and nothing and no one could change that. But he had hoped that this beginning might at least be perfect, flawless. It would have felt good.

The Inkallim were coming on again, once more falling into a disciplined file. They had that arrogant, assured air that attended every member of the Battle. Kanin loathed it, now more than ever. Their forerunners had betrayed his Blood. They had abandoned it in the Vale of Stones thirty years ago, watching its finest warriors go down beneath the blades of a Lannis army.

And now he stood, Thane of his people, in a ruined street, as Battle Inkallim came pace by careful pace towards him, and everything was at once the same and entirely different. This time Lannis was gone, burned away to ashes. But again Horin was betrayed. The Battle had stolen away every victory Kanin's Blood had won for the faith; they had handed it all to the mad halfbreed. They had condemned the world to his vile rule. They had lifted the man responsible for Wain's death up on their shoulders and made thousands bend the knee to him.

Kanin made fists of his hands to stop them shaking. Today, today it would begin.

The lead rider came to a halt before him. Two more let their horses drift wide to flank her on each side. She stared down at Kanin impassively.

'Thane,' she said.

He nodded. 'You've come for me, I assume?'

'We have a message for you.'

'From Kan Avor. From the halfbreed.' He did not conceal his contempt. It washed over her. Her pride made her impervious, he thought. It made her careless too, perhaps.

'You have gathered many spears here, Thane. Gathered them where they are not required. The war, the struggle of the faithful against the faithless, is happening far to the south of here. At Kolkyre. Beyond Kilvale. That is where your spears are needed.'

'Because your strength falters?' Kanin smiled. 'Because everything comes apart in your hands? I see, raven. I hear. I know your armies melt away like the winter snow come the thaw. I was there. I saw it start. Madness sprouting everywhere. Disorder. By now I'm sure your many Captains cannot hold more than a handful of spears together, cannot muster anything but the smallest of companies that will actually follow an order.'

Her face was an impassive mask, but he could see the truth of it in her eyes.

'That's what you've achieved for the creed, raven,' he told her. 'Chaos.'

'Your strength is required,' she said flatly.

'You don't understand what you've helped to create, do you? Strength is not measured by the enumeration of spears and swords any more. It is not measured in armies. Strength is a matter of will now. It's about who can stand against the madness and keep a steady course through the storm. It's about who can keep sight of what they need to do.'

'Your swords are required, Thane. Do not fail the creed now.'

'You threaten me?' he said. 'A Thane?' And he laughed at her. He possessed his own kind of madness, he knew. A sort of joy at the setting aside of all pretence and delay. A storm of blood would be released, and he felt joy at the prospect of it, for he had wearied of everything else. Nothing else could offer him any meaning, or peace, or rest. Nothing else, he felt certain, offered any kind of salvation, to him or to anyone. So there would be blood, and he would rejoice in it.

'My strength is my own,' he said. 'I'll keep it to myself. Tell me, is there much sickness in Kan Avor? Are there fevers eating away at your halfbreed's slaves yet?'

Her eyes narrowed just enough to please him. 'You have warriors hidden in two houses behind us, Thane. You cannot imagine that is enough to prevent word of your betrayal reaching Kan Avor. You cannot imagine it is so easy to kill the Children of the Hundred.'

Again he laughed. That savage joy was pounding in him, coursing through his veins like invigorating fire. He imagined that with it inside him he might be capable of anything. He might be capable of shaking the whole world to its foundations.

'Oh,' he laughed, 'I do not imagine it to be easy. That is why I have warriors hidden in a great many more than two houses, raven.'

He raised his left hand. Before the movement was finished, there were crossbow bolts standing in the chests of the three Inkallim before him. They appeared there with dull thuds, as if snapping out through the ribcages from within. But they had come, Kanin knew, from Hunt bows. Eska and her two fellow Inkallim. He harvested another small, bitter joy from that: Inkallim killed Inkallim at the behest of a Horin Thane.

One of the ravens fell at once, sliding with blank eyes out of his saddle. The other two swayed but remained astride the horses.

Those first three bolts were the vanguard of a swarm that clattered in from every direction, lashing at the column of Inkallim. One quarrel darted so close by Kanin's face that he felt the brush of its fletching on his cheek. He did not flinch. He seized the slack reins out of the woman's limp hand. She was starting to slump forward, folding herself about the bolt buried in her chest, but she still breathed. Kanin twisted the horse's head out of the way and stabbed his sword up into her stomach. It did not penetrate her leathers, but it was enough to knock her to the ground. As she fell, Kanin heard crossbow bolts strike the horse's flank. The animal screamed in panic, and tore itself free of his grasp.

His people were pouring into the street, hurrying to close with those of the Inkallim that had not already fallen. His people, he called them. The truth was, he had brought more Lannis men than warriors of his own Blood to prepare this welcome. He trusted their visceral hatred of the ravens more than he trusted the loyalty of his own swords. His father would have been ashamed, enraged, had he lived to see such things. Kanin did not care. It no longer mattered.

The Children of the Hundred fought as he would have expected them to: ferociously, fanatically. Many of them were wounded, with bolts nestled in their flesh, but they fought nevertheless. When a horse fell or was dragged down, its rider rolled clear and rose and carved a path into the converging throng. When the ravens died – pierced, as often as not, by a forest of spears lunging in from every side – they did so silently. Still fighting.

Two of the Inkallim came riding through the crowd towards Kanin. Their swords flashed, slashing down first on one side, then the other, as they cut away every enemy that closed upon them. They had eyes only for Kanin. Those they killed and maimed did not even merit their attention.

Kanin grinned at them as they drew near, and hefted his

sword. Igris was at his side. One of the Inkallim was suddenly twisted by the impact of a bolt in her shoulder. That was enough to open the path for the spear that jabbed up from below and pierced her. The other burst free of the mob, his horse surging into a charge. Igris ran forward. To Kanin, it seemed a slow and dreamlike moment: the sound of the battle receded, his shield-man drifted into the path of the horse. The great beast moved with strange grace, forelegs rising and falling, lifting mud and slush in elegant plumes from the road.

Igris did not try for the Inkallim. He ducked low and veered sideways, and hit the horse's leg with his sword. The blow sent the blade spinning away out of his hand but broke the animal's leg too. Kanin watched with detached fascination as the horse buckled, ploughing down into the wet sludge, rolling, sending up a great curving curtain of spray. The Inkallim leaped from the horse's back and erupted through that curtain, reaching for Kanin. It all seemed so slow. Kanin's mind raced, but his body followed its commands with what felt like glacial lethargy. He leaned back and twisted as the Inkallim came towards him. As the raven's blade came up, levelling itself, arrowing itself in.

The impact was stunning. It smashed the breath out of Kanin's chest, sent him sprawling, punched off his feet. His cloak spread and flapped about him. Like wings, he thought foolishly as he hit the ground and slid on his back. The sword had torn across his breastbone, ripping open his chain shirt, lac-erating his chest. He could feel his own hot blood on his skin. But it was not a deep wound. By the smallest of margins, the blade's point had come at too sharp an angle to punch its way through the cage of his ribs. Not dead, was all Kanin thought as he struggled to get to his feet. Not dead yet.

The Inkallim was rising too. His sword was gone, twisted out of his hands. Kanin still had his. He scrambled forward, slith-ering through the slush, and lashed out at the Inkallim's ankles. The man leaped above the swing. Then Igris came roaring in and hit him about the waist, embracing him, bearing him down. The two of them rolled, and flailed, and clawed at one another.

Kanin stood over them. Every breath lit bands of fiery pain that encircled his chest. His legs felt loose, his sword terribly heavy in his hand. The Inkallim somehow got a heel into Igris' groin and half-kicked, half-pushed the shieldman away. Kanin took his chance. He hacked down at the raven's head, once, twice, until the skull broke and caved in. Again he struck, and again. It took him that long to master himself. Fighting off waves of dizziness, he extended a hand and hauled Igris to his feet. The shieldman was gasping, wild-eyed.

'Well done,' Kanin murmured.

He turned back to the battle, and found it to be over. Dead littered the street. One horse was limping in a trembling circle, another pounding away riderless. It had cost better than thirty lives to bring down those few Inkallim, but it had been done. Townsfolk were beating some of the corpses, pulping them with staffs and clubs. Stiffly, painfully, Kanin sheathed his sword and pressed a hand to his wound. It would need cleaning. There would be fragments of cloth or metal to be picked out of his opened flesh. But it would not kill him.

'Enough,' he shouted. The pain almost choked him, and he had to close his eyes for a moment. When he opened them he spoke more softly, more carefully.

'Enough. We're done here. Now it's Kan Avor.'

V

As she moved through the Palace of Red Stone, treading lightly along its polished passageways, Anyara became aware of a low, almost subliminal, sound. At first it seemed to be emanating from the marble, as if it resonated to the beat of some vast drum deep in the earth. But the sound grew slowly more distinct and constant as she reached the northern side of the palace. It took on its own character. There was some great crowd, she realised, out there on the streets beyond these quiet marmoreal precincts, and this was its single voice, built out of a thousand individual cries and shouts, the tramping of many feet, the jostling of bodies one against the other. Built out of the fury of the mob.

The realisation roused more curiosity than fear in her. When she chanced upon an open door, she drifted cautiously through it and into an empty room. Though she could not pretend to feel safe, moving alone through the palace's intricate passageways, she would have gone mad hiding away in her chambers all day and all night. She had crept out, carefully ensuring that she did not disturb Coinach, who had for once lapsed into an uncomfortable-looking sleep at his watch post in the corridor outside. She thus breached both the Chancellor's command for her to remain in gentle incarceration, and Coinach's trust that she would allow him to guard her as he thought necessary. The first breach she cared nothing for; the second she felt was justi-fied, for Coinach desperately needed sleep, and she knew herself how rare and precious were those brief spells of slumber undis-turbed by restless dreams.

It was a dining room, but one evidently not used during the winter, for the long table was entirely bare, the fireplace spot-lessly clean, the tapestries on the wall concealed behind sheets to protect them from any intrusive light. There were tall windows, but they were shuttered, and the shutters were secured with heavy, ornate copper hooks.

The noise was unmistakable now, even though Anyara had never heard quite its like. A great collective rage. It was an unsettling sound.

'What are you doing here?'

She turned towards that ice-laden voice, its chill daggers cut-ting through the tumultuous rumble outside. She fought the black fear it loosed in her but could not prevent its rise. She felt herself shrinking, retreating into a corner of her mind.

'I was looking for your wife, Chancellor,' she managed to say.

Mordyn Jerain smiled at her, but he did it with his teeth, not his eyes. He was between Anyara and the only doorway, and that frightened her. She squeezed her hands together in search of a steadying focus.

'You hear it?' the Chancellor said. He came a few paces closer to her. She edged back until she felt the edge of the table against her thighs.

'You hear the mob in full cry? That is the sound of an ending,' Mordyn said, cocking his head. 'That is the sound of change. Perhaps you hear it, and you think it a wild thing, beyond control.'

He had an air of contentment, as if he listened to the sweetest and most melodious of music.

'Not so,' he mused, his eyelids languidly drooping. 'I made it. It is as much a product of my craft as the crop a farmer harvests is the product of his. Such has ever been my gift. To shape that which others assume cannot be shaped.'

There were, now and again, even through the Palace of Red Stone's thick walls, and those heavy shutters, individual voices to be heard amidst the otherwise formless noise: jagged rocks briefly exposed and then drowned again by the churning waves. Other than that, the sound could as easily have been born of animal throats as human.

The Chancellor seemed lost in reverie, and Anyara moved to ease herself around him towards the doorway. His eyes at once sprang open and alert, and he reached out and laid a hand on the tabletop, blocking her path with his arm. He was oppressively close to her.

'In truth,' he breathed, 'the crop is not quite ready for the scythe. Another day or two. No more, I think. Then the harvest comes.'

'I do not understand such matters,' Anyara said, marshalling all the submissive, compliant girlishness that came no more naturally to her than flight would to a fish. 'I have no interest in them.'

'Indeed?' Mordyn said with arched, coldly amused eyebrows. 'You are something of a novice when it comes to dissemblance, I see. But do not worry. For now, my interest in you could not be less were you some dim-witted scullery maid. It is given to precious few to exert some influence upon the course of great events; to guide the current, rather than be merely carried along by it. You, my dear lady, are not one of those few. You are a gnat. No, of even less import. You are a common prisoner. Your Blood is extinguished.'

'My brother will—'

The blow, an open-handed slap that had every strand of the Chancellor's strength behind it, was so sudden and violent that she reeled. Lights danced across Anyara's vision. Pain blazed in her cheek with such ferocity that she wondered if he had split it open.

Mordyn came after her before she had a chance to compose herself. He seized her neck with one hand, her flailing arm with the other, and smashed her face down onto the table. He pinned her there and leaned over her, hissing into her ear.

'You are not listening. Your brother? Where is your brother, lady? Hiding somewhere. Cowering like some craven child in a hovel, or a cave. Or dead, perhaps. Do you think he's dead?'

'Orisian's not dead.'

'No? It doesn't matter. He is of no consequence. Less even than you. Do you understand? Entirely, utterly of no consequence. None of them are. The day of Thanes enters its twilight. They will pass. They will fall. Another power is coming, and it will rule in their stead.'

'Let go of me!'

'No. Listen. I have seen, and I understand, what is coming. I

am a part of it, and I will be one of those to rise, at his side, from
the wreckage when the new dawn comes. Your brother will not.
He and all his kind, Thanes and Kings and Bloodheirs and
Stewards, their time is ending.'

He bent still closer to her ear, so close she could feel his lips
brushing her skin.

'Your time is ending.'

'You're his, aren't you?' Anyara said. 'Bound, like Tarcene.
Somehow, he made you his tool. His toy.'

Those fingers on her tightened. She felt the nails digging into
her skin, pressing harder on the muscles and the veins beneath.
She could no longer tell what was the sound of the mob outside
and what the rushing of her own blood, its beating in her head.

'What is happening here?'

Anyara could not move, could not see the doorway, but that
voice – light, clear, graceful – was enough to abruptly calm her
fear.

Mordyn released his grip upon the side of her neck and
stepped away from her. She no longer felt the heat of his breath.
Stiffly, cautiously, Anyara levered herself up off the table. One
side of her face burned, and she could feel the print of his hand
there like a brand; the other ached from the impact with the
table. She refused to touch either. She would not give him that
pleasure.

Both she and the Chancellor looked towards the door, and
towards Tara Jerain standing there, in a gown of surpassing elegance, her hands neatly clasped across her stomach.

'What is happening here?' she asked again. Perfect composure. Not a hint of accusation or displeasure, only bland enquiry.

Anyara glared at Mordyn, but he had already dismissed her
from his thoughts. He was moving towards the door, adjusting
his sleeves, sweeping back his hair. He paid no more attention to
his wife than to Anyara. He brushed past Tara, jolting her shoulder out of the way.

'You will regret that,' Anyara said levelly but loudly to his back.

He paused, already almost lost in the shadows behind Tara.

'I don't think so,' he said without looking around. The Chancellor laughed, and disappeared into the corridor.

And with his departure, as the muted roar of the riot rose and fell like waves rubbing up against the walls of the palace, Tara's mask crumbled. Her hand covered her mouth, her brow tightened and creased into grief. Her eyes gleamed with unshed tears.

'My lady,' Anyara said at once, walking quickly towards her, one arm outstretched in a calculated gesture of both sympathy and appeal. 'I need your help. Something terrible is happening, to all of us. I know you see that. I know you do.'

Tara said nothing, her mouth, and whatever pain it might have expressed, still hidden behind that smooth hand. But her soft anguished eyes were firmly upon Anyara.

'Take me to the High Thane,' Anyara said. 'Please. It's all I can think of to do, and I can't do it without your help.'

The Moon Palace was in a ferment. Servants ran hither and thither, every one of them wearing much the same expression of alarm and weary unease. The guards, who seemed to be posted at virtually every door, every junction of passageways, stared with intense suspicion at all who came within sight. A number of them watched with particular narrow-eyed attention as Coinach passed them, but none made any move to intercept him. He was in the company of the Chancellor's wife, after all.

As she and Tara hastened into the palace's heart, Anyara noted several ladies of the High Thane's court rushing along, shepherding young children like a gaggle of geese. All of them were dressed for travel, in hooded cloaks and fur gloves and stout, if refined, boots.

'People are running away,' Anyara murmured.

'Do you blame them?' Tara asked her.

And Anyara could not, in truth. She had seen enough of the city's condition, during the brief but fraught journey from the Palace of Red Stone, to convince her of the absolute wisdom of leaving its confines. The earlier riot had died down but left its flotsam scattered through the streets. A few bodies. Many burned-out houses and workshops. Heaps of debris – broken pots, roof tiles, shards of wood – strewn everywhere. And fearful faces peering from windows.

Tara had been inclined to turn back when a company of the High Thane's warriors had ridden at the gallop through a crossroads ahead of them. Anyara had prevailed upon her to continue, though not without some unease of her own. It was all uncomfortably reminiscent of what she had seen at Koldihrve, albeit on a grander scale.

In the distance they had been able to hear fighting. Everywhere there had been the faint but persistent smell of smoke. Coinach's disquiet had become more and more pronounced, until he too had tried to insist on a return to the Chancellor's palace.

'We're no safer there,' Anyara had said sternly, angling her face to ensure he could see the livid bruise already blooming where Mordyn Jerain had struck her. The anguished expression on his face at the sight of it instantly made her feel profoundly guilty. Ashamed of her cruelty. It had been her choice alone to shed his protection.

Now, struggling through the nascent chaos within the Moon Palace, she doubted her insistence on coming here. Not out of any fear for their safety, but because she was beginning to wonder whether any place so self-evidently veering towards panic could exercise enough will and authority to actually control events.

They finally found their way to the chamber of some court official. Anyara was gratified by the fawning deference the man displayed towards Tara, though he was infuriatingly non-committal regarding the prospect of an immediate audience with the High Thane. Tara's demeanour changed markedly and instantly. She berated the man with stern authority, and he hurried off, suitably chastened, to make the necessary enquiries.

They waited, tense, in that chamber for what seemed a long time. Anyara could tell, from Coinach's distracted manner and the way he chewed absently at his lip, that he was struggling with himself over his failure to keep her safe from harm. She longed to offer him some comfort, but it was something she did not want to discuss in front of Tara, so she held her tongue and made a point of smiling warmly at her shieldman whenever she caught his eye.

The audience was granted. They were ushered, with all appropriate haste, along high, echoing corridors, to a side room adjoining one of the feasting halls. It was surprisingly sparsely furnished, though the wall hangings were exquisite and the rug one of the most obviously costly Anyara had ever seen.

Gryvan oc Haig sat in a broad dark chair with high arms. There was no other seating. Anyara, Tara and Coinach were forced to stand in a line, on the centre of that luxurious rug. Kale, chief amongst the High Thane's shieldmen, stood to one side, staring fixedly and pointedly at Coinach. He looked to Anyara like a miserable, surly man.

Tara executed a tidy curtsy for the Thane of Thanes. Anyara copied her, aware that she made the gesture appear entirely graceless by comparison.

'I would have received you in more pleasing surroundings, my lady,' Gryvan growled at Tara, 'had you not come in such disreputable company.'

To her credit, the Chancellor's wife betrayed no hint of discomfiture at such a gruff welcome. Her poise, given the extremity of the distress Anyara knew very well she was controlling, was remarkable.

'The times seem most disreputable, sire.' Tara smiled. 'One can't always choose one's company as freely as one would wish in such circumstances.'

Anyara ignored the subtle insult. Nothing mattered save inducing Gryvan to listen to what she had to say. Impatience was rampant in her, but that too she strove to ignore and silence.

'I like to think I may choose mine,' Gryvan said. He still had not looked at Anyara. 'What is wrong with your hands?' he asked Tara.

She glanced at the discreet bandages that protected the worst of her burns.

'It is nothing, truly. A slight accident, that is all. I can be unaccountably clumsy on occasion.'

Gryvan nodded. He had all too evidently lost interest in the subject as soon as he asked the question.

'We will be brief, sire,' Tara assured him. She kept that smile perfectly in place, and not for an instant did it look anything other than entirely natural and sincere.

Gryvan appeared far from satisfied, but he lapsed into a heavy silence. There were dark, sagging bags of skin under his eyes, Anyara noted. A tremor, perhaps a tic, in his cheek that she had never noticed before. A latent accusatory anger in his gaze. None of these struck her as promising signs. Tara glanced at Anyara and nodded.

'Sire,' Anyara began, then paused to gather herself, for she realised her voice had sounded a little too urgent and assertive. 'Sire, I know you will not be inclined to give credence to anything I say . . .'

Gryvan grunted a dry affirmation to that.

'. . . but I beg you just to hear me out. There's something wrong about everything that's happening, you must agree to that.'

'I must do nothing,' Gryvan interrupted her. 'High Thanes are permitted to make their own choices about what they do.'

'Of course, sire,' Anyara said hurriedly. 'Forgive me. I mean only that something seems amiss in the sudden rising to the surface of so many tensions, so much dissent. I believe I know the cause of some of it at least, perhaps all of it. That is all I came to tell you, sire, for though you doubt the loyalty of my Blood to yours, I can assure you—'

'What nonsense is she prattling about?' Gryvan asked Tara.

The Chancellor's wife inclined her head sympathetically, projecting complete understanding of Gryvan's irritation.

'Well,' Tara murmured, 'I have a suspicion there may be just a grain of truth in her ideas, sire. We may – we do – disagree, she and I, on the details, but I fear . . . I fear there is indeed an . . . an issue that may have to be resolved.'

'An issue?' Gryvan said, frowning.

'Your Chancellor, sire,' Anyara said. 'He is not himself. Entirely and completely not himself. I think he has . . . may have been bound by a *na'kyrim*. As Tarcene was, sire. Orlane Kingbinder. There is a man, Aeglyss, who marches with the Black Road . . .'

'Bound?' Gryvan cried incredulously. 'Have you come here to mock me?'

'Perhaps not bound, sire,' Tara said quickly. 'Perhaps not that. But . . . my husband is behaving strangely, sire. Ever since his return. Much that he has done and said is . . . confusing.'

'Are you accusing your own husband of treachery?' Gryvan demanded.

'No, sire.' Tara's edifice of control and good humour was at last crumbling. Anyara could see, and hear, the chinks in her armour widening. 'No, not that. But something ails him. It might be wise to place less weight upon his advice than you have been accustomed to do in times past.'

'Oh, believe me,' said Gryvan in dark and threatening tones, 'I already have ample reasons of my own to do just that. And doubts, lady. I have doubts. But binding. This . . . this prisoner is talking of binding. That would be . . . something else entirely.'

'You've no more cause to make a prisoner of me than you have to . . .' Anyara cursed herself for the sharp retort, but it was too late. Gryvan settled his full, glowering attention upon her.

'Your brother is outlawed.'

Anyara could clearly hear the danger in the High Thane's voice, yet she could not stop herself.

'The accusations against him are lies,' she said bluntly.

'Lies? Then where is your brother?' The High Thane's face was abruptly contorted by rage, stretched like a freshly scraped hide pegged out to dry. 'Where is your brother?' he howled, spittle flying, a red blush of anger spreading through his cheeks, his neck. 'I don't see him here, where he belongs. Now, in time of crisis, in time of crisis . . . where's the boy?' He stabbed a stiff finger in Anyara's direction. Like a weapon. 'We fight wars, we are beset by enemies, by traitors, and where is he?'

'I—' Anyara began, but there was to be no voice in this echoing chamber save one.

'Traitors!' Gryvan snarled. He looked like a dog, Anyara thought. A dog hauling at its leash, all teeth and fury and foam. 'This city . . . this city was founded by sailors and fishermen, before the Gods left this world. Long before the Kingships, there were markets here, and watchtowers, and granaries. The Aygll Kings kept a winter palace here for a time. The . . . the . . . Before the War of the Tainted, there were Kyrinin here, in these streets. They had huts down by the river. You see? Do you see how old this place is? How ancient?

'But it was my grandfather who built the wall. It was my father who raised the Moon Palace. It was us, our line, that made it great. I'll not yield it now, if that's what you think. I'll not let everything be taken away from us. Not as long as I've strength in my arm and a fire in my heart.'

'Sire,' Tara began in a placatory manner, but Gryvan shouted over her.

'Out! Get out!'

Tara bowed and began to back away immediately. Anyara could not surrender quite so readily.

'Sire . . .'

'Out,' hissed Kale, the shieldman. The unexpected sound startled Anyara, as did what she saw in his eyes. She allowed Coinach to gently pull her out into the corridor.

*

'Mad?' Torquentine grunted. 'Is she sure?'

'She seems so.' Magrayn nodded. She was watching with a somewhat sceptical, concerned expression as a dozen burly men attempted to ease her prodigious master sideways from his bed of thick cushions onto the massive trolley standing ready to receive his weight.

'And do we have any faith in her judgement in such matters?'

'Well, she is only a maid. But she has served in the Palace of Red Stone for some time. She should be capable of recognising . . . unusual, perverse behaviour on the Shadowhand's part.'

'The man engages in little else,' Torquentine observed. 'Move your hand, man. I've some . . . a rash, shall we say.'

The wheels on the trolley creaked ominously as the first of Torquentine's buttocks was allowed to rest upon it. Magrayn grimaced. Torquentine noted this and frowned.

'You assured me this has been tested,' he pointed out.

'Indeed. It has.'

Torquentine found her tone considerably less reassuring than he would have hoped. But he had committed himself into his doorkeeper's capable hands once he had made the decision to depart for pastures new. It was too late to lose faith in her competence.

'Do we trust her? This maid?' he asked. 'She is not some ploy of the Shadowhand's, turning our curiosity against us?'

'I think it unlikely. We have convinced her, I am sure, that her father's life is forfeit should she fail us.'

'Hmm. The mattress on this trolley is distressingly thin. How long must I remain perched upon it?'

'Not long.'

He recognised her imprecision as predictive of extended discomfort. If not suffering, indeed. He chose not to press the
matter, as the only alternative would be to remain here in his
Vaymouth cellar, and that prospect pleased him still less.

'No reason, I suppose, that the Chancellor should be excused
from falling prey to the malady of the mind claiming so many
others, merely by virtue of his wit and title. When an entire city
plunges into disorder and rapine and pillage, nothing should
surprise us.'

'Particularly if the Chancellor concerned helped the plunge
along himself,' Magrayn said. With Torquentine settled upon his
unconventional transport, she nodded to the men standing ready
by the far wall of his subterranean lair. Obedient to her command, they began to remove the false stones set in the wall,
slowly exposing a tunnel running off south-westwards.

'Indeed, indeed,' Torquentine mused as he watched the men
work. 'There's the most disquieting element in the whole affair.
Still, I suppose if we conclude the Chancellor is mad, it clarifies
a good deal. A madman may do anything. He may wantonly
arrange the torture and murder of a rival Kingship's
Ambassador, thereby all but inviting them to make war. He
may arrange for the escape of a rebellious minor Thane, thus
practically ensuring the renewal of the rebellion so recently
crushed.

'He may, if rumour is true, persuade the High Thane to withdraw a portion of his army from the field on the very eve of what
consequently proved to be our Blood's greatest defeat in battle.
Leaving those intolerable Black Road creatures considerably
closer to Vaymouth than to their own borders and with notably
little between them and us to distract them. He might even,
absurd as it sounds, find someone – some insufficiently cautious
and rightly regretful fool – willing to set a few fires, and use said
fires as a lever to break apart the bonds which held together our

city's evidently fragile arrangements of power and patronage and mutual restraint.'

The widening portal in the wall revealed a straight tunnel with walls of soft, muddy earth supported by an extensive framework of struts and beams and planking. It smelled bad down there, and Torquentine wrinkled his nose. It also looked unpleasantly wet. There was water trickling down the walls, and lying in slack pools as far as he could see.

'Not an attractive view,' he said. 'Still, I cannot bring myself to remain in a city become so distressingly unpredictable and violent. It's impossible to conduct any kind of useful business. Particularly when one is about to give quite possibly mortal offence to one – possibly more – of the most powerful men in the land.'

'You have decided, then?' Magrayn asked.

Torquentine nodded. 'One last task for you, my dear, before we fly from this sadly precarious nest. Take our inconvenient prisoner to the Moon Palace and leave an appropriate message. If Mordyn Jerain's the rot at the heart of all this trouble, we may as well give some assistance to those who might be able to cut it out. There'll never be another coin to be made out of this city, illicit or otherwise, unless someone does.'

'I will meet you at the docks,' Magrayn said.

A number of hands gently but firmly pressed against his back had Torquentine trundling indecorously forward. He felt like a morsel being wheeled into the waiting gullet of a giant snake.

'The boat is fully prepared?' he asked Magrayn as she moved towards the door.

'It is. The captain has all the specified supplies on board for the journey.'

'Good, good.' Torquentine tapped his chin with a single stout finger. A certain despondency was settling over him at the thought of what lay ahead. 'I must admit, I do not look forward with much glee to the process of boarding ship.'

'Don't worry,' Magrayn said lightly. Had he not known better, Torquentine might almost have thought he detected the contours of a smile struggling to emerge upon her lips. 'They have strong ropes and nets. I checked.'

'Ropes and nets,' Torquentine muttered glumly, shaking his head, as his doorkeeper disappeared to prepare Igryn oc Dargannan-Haig for one further, and likely final, journey. 'Ropes and nets.'

VI

On the best days, Jaen Narran could imagine, to look out from a high window of Kolkyre's Tower of Thrones would be to see views truly fit for a Thane, and once for High Thanes. Westward, the city sweeping down to the sprawling harbour teemed with life, and beyond it lay Anaron's Bay with its lines of gentle waves marching in one after another. Perhaps, she imagined, on a clear and sharp day, it might even be possible to glimpse Il Anaron itself, the great island out in the distance. Eastward, the long curve of the city wall and then the broad expanse of the plains – thick with rich green grass in high summer, those – mounted gradually in successive ranks of ridges and hills until finally they merged into the very foothills of the Karkyre Peaks.

But the best days had long been absent from Kolkyre. Now the view to the west showed a silent and moribund harbour. That to the east revealed not immense fields thick with grass but the huge black and brown stain of the besieging forces of the Black Road, arcing around the city like a scar.

A scene rather closer to hand held Jaen's attention now, though. She stood beside Ilessa oc Kilkry-Haig, staring down at the violence being done within the Tower's own encircling wall. The Steward's House, where Lagair Haldyn, Gryvan oc Haig's mouthpiece, resided, abutted that wall, down at the foot of the mound on which the Tower of Thrones stood. It was in fact built into the fabric of the wall.

Now, the Steward's House was under assault. Crowds of Kilkry warriors milled about, some battering at its door with a heavy wooden beam, others tearing at the wooden shutters closed over its windows. Marshalling these disorderly and frenzied forces was Roaric, the Thane himself. He sat astride his finest warhorse, his Shield arrayed about him, further up the mound. Now and again he would shout some command or encouragement. Jaen and Ilessa were too far above to hear what he said, but his words never seemed to have any significant effect, in any case. The warriors he thought to guide were in the grip of their own fury. Once he had given them a target for their simmering resentment and frustration, in the form of the Steward and his household, they had followed their own instincts and hungers, not their Thane's instructions.

Lagair Haldyn had been barricaded inside his official residence for several days, Jaen knew. He was far from alone in taking such measures. The city streets had become entirely unsafe for any except the most savage and determined. Still, he had even better reasons than most for keeping out of sight, given the deep-seated hatred with which the Haig Blood was now almost universally regarded in Kolkyre.

Ilessa and Jaen waited only long enough to see the Steward dragged out into the gardens before they turned away. They could not avoid his screams, though, which were piercing and easily loud enough to reach up to the heights of the Tower. They were abruptly curtailed.

'That's the end of any chance of reconciling with Haig,' muttered Ilessa as they descended hurriedly down the central spine of the Tower.

'Such chances might have been slim in any case,' Jaen ventured to suggest.

'Oh, I know. I can regret their abandonment, nevertheless. But my son was not to be swayed in this or in anything else. Not any more. The fever is upon him, and wholly his master.'

The resignation in Ilessa's voice was not flawless. Jaen could still catch the trace of desperate sadness that was there. The woman was seeing the last of her family surrender himself to the practices of the slaughterhouse. Whatever virtues Roaric might once have possessed, they were of the past now, for day by day he had become someone ruled by a single obsessive need: to lash out, to struggle against the chains he felt so heavily upon him. The Steward's misfortune was to be the most easily within reach, and thus the first to suffer.

They found Roaric at the foot of the stairs, issuing flurries of orders to his attending Captains. They were in the same eager, fierce mood as their Thane. As word of his intent had spread, so had that mood. So had the anticipation of blood, and the yearning for it. Whatever sickness it was that so beset Kolkyre, one of its clearest and commonest effects, Jaen had observed, was to convince those falling victim to it that they could be healed only by the shedding of other people's blood.

'Is there nothing I can say?' Ilessa asked her son, ignoring the warriors crowding around him. Roaric waved them away.

'No,' he said, pulling on his gauntlets once more.

'If you do not meet with success . . .'

'If a man feared defeat, he would never give battle,' Roaric snapped. There was contempt in his tone, and Jaen could see how it wounded Ilessa. Yet she must have known this would be her reception, and had chosen even so to make one final attempt.

'Every victory is inevitably succeeded by defeat,' Roaric went on dismissively, as if he addressed a child. 'It is the nature of our lives. A man might fight a thousand battles and emerge triumphant from every one; still, he will suffer defeat in the end, for we die and we are forgotten. If we cannot face defeat, we must live always, throughout our lives, in fear. For it awaits us all.'

'Very wise, I'm sure,' muttered Ilessa. 'In this instance, if you are defeated, your city is liable to fall with you.'

'What would you have me do?' cried Roaric furiously. His cheeks reddened. 'We starve because Vaymouth will send us no supplies. We kill one another. We lie awake at night, too terrified of our dreams to attempt sleep. We are withering. Your people, Mother, are dying. Every day. Every night. Well, if death wants us, let us at least force it to come for us as we fight.

'You've seen what's happening to them out there.' He lashed an arm out in a vaguely easterly direction. 'The Black Road fails just as we do. Hundreds of them have gone off into the north or the south. Those who remain fight amongst themselves, scatter further and further across the land. Every night you can hear the cries of the dying. Every day there are more bodies piled up outside their camps. They're rotting away.'

'Let them rot, then,' Ilessa said quietly. Her calm in the face of Roaric's violent emotions was extraordinary. 'Let them kill one another. Let them sicken and die. If we can but hold together for a while . . .'

'We cannot! We cannot. I cannot.' Jaen could see the anguish in the young man now, breaching for once the anger that so often disguised it. 'We are shamed. All our lands gone, save this one city. Every battle lost. Haig treating us like . . . like vermin. It must not stand. It must not stand. Not if I'm to be a Thane worthy of the title. Not if . . . Not if . . .'

'Would you have me watch you die, then, from the city walls?' Ilessa asked coldly. 'I did not see your brother die. But I was there when your father had his throat opened. Would you have me witness your end too?'

Roaric glared at his mother, then turned on his heel and walked out into the wintry light. For all the harshness of her last question, Jaen could see the tremor in Ilessa's lips and chin as her last son turned his back on her and went back to his warhorse.

*

The two women were together, on the walls of Vaymouth, to watch events unfold. Jaen had argued against it, fearful for Ilessa's heart.

But the Thane's mother had only murmured, 'I need to see. I need to see for myself. I won't have someone else coming to me, bringing me that news.'

So they were on the walls watching when the horns sounded all round the rim of the city. They were there when Vaymouth opened its gates and poured its men, by the thousand, out onto the fields. Warriors and townsfolk, seamen and exiles, all came flooding out in thick dark streams. The noise of their advance reverberated through the stones of those walls. Jaen felt it, in her feet, in her breastbone, the deep rumble of imminent carnage.

The Black Roaders were not unprepared, but nor were they capable of ordered movement. Their companies massed in tardy disarray, some not at all. Bands of horsemen galloped up and down behind their dishevelled lines, as if maddened and disorientated. Campfires, inadvertently kicked apart in the rush for weapons and armour, spread and soon flames were flickering up from tents and from piles of stores.

Jaen stared out as both armies began to come apart almost at once. From either side, while the hosts churned back and forth in confusion, knots of warriors would break free, like swirling bees separating from a greater swarm, and rush forward to throw themselves futilely against their enemy. Jaen had never seen such a conflict before, but she had been wedded to her Blood's greatest warrior for many years, and she knew a little of how battles were meant to be fought. And she knew a good deal of how precious life was, and how reluctantly it should be given up.

This was a new time, though. New rules governed the waging of war and the value of life alike.

The two armies never mustered a coordinated advance; they simply bled into one another as more and more of their numbers flung themselves into the fray. The open ground between the two forces was gradually whittled away, contracting into little islands of stillness in a sea of furious motion, finally disappearing altogether as the waves of strife and death closed over them.

Jaen and Ilessa now gazed out over a single tempestuous form that swayed over the land, surging first here and then there, drifting slowly south and leaving the trampled ground strewn with hundreds of bodies.

'There is my son,' Ilessa said quietly.

She pointed, and Jaen saw Roaric, atop his great horse, leading his Shield in a wild charge through the heart of the battle. They cut a swathe through the vast throng, though whether it was foes or friends who were going down beneath their flashing blades and pounding hoofs it was not possible to tell. On and on they rode, and a multitude of deaths attended their passage.

In time a denser knot of figures took them in its grip, and the waves of that cruel sea lapped ever higher about them, and seemed about to overwhelm them. Jaen could feel Ilessa tensing by her side, and could only wonder at the woman's stubborn, dignified determination to witness her son's fate. It would have been beyond Jaen to stand here and watch Taim fight for his life in this way.

The horsemen were obscured for a few moments, swamped by the throngs of bodies pressing in against them. Then the host thinned itself again, and they could still see Roaric, unhorsed now, fighting with his Shield about him, laying down whole drifts of corpses before them. Set to drown in blood, Jaen thought gloomily. Set to cede dominion over the world to death itself.

And so it went, for a long time. The tides of battle ebbed and flowed; the dead crowded the field, coalescing amongst the grass into a single smooth bruise on the surface of the land. Long after it seemed that the fallen must outnumber the living, an end came. It was a stuttering, hesitant ending, imprecise. In some places on the field warriors found there was no one left to kill. In others the forces of the Black Road began to straggle away, scattering in any and all directions.

Weary cheers went up along the walls. Not from Jaen or Ilessa. The two of them went down and waited inside the city's greatest gate. Roaric's army came trickling back in. The men stumbled and fell; stared about them with wide, uncomprehending eyes. Few were capable of celebration or of responding to the approbation of those who had watched their victory from afar. Several staggered in through the gate and, as if they had been sustained only by the driving imperative to attain that goal, fell in the roadway, dead or unconscious.

At last the Thane returned to his city. He came not on his mighty warhorse, but carried on a litter by his Shield.

Ilessa drew them aside and leaned over her son.

'He took no wound, my lady,' one of the massive warriors carrying the litter said. 'He simply fell, and we found him thus.'

The Thane of the Kilkry Blood laughed and wept at the same time. Tears streamed from his eyes.

'Roaric,' Ilessa whispered. 'Roaric.'

All too clearly Jaen caught the pleading in those words, the all-consuming desire for her son to return to her from whatever place he had become lost in. But he did not respond. His jaw moved, but no words emerged.

'Take him to the Tower,' Ilessa said, defeated. 'Time will heal him, or nothing will.'

Gryvan oc Haig stared in disbelief at the figure kneeling before him.

'At the gate?' he said.

'Yes, sire.' Kale's intonation was typically flat and dispassionate, but even he was regarding Igryn oc Dargannan-Haig with a certain puzzled fascination. 'Trussed and bound, just as you see him.'

'And no one saw how he came to be there?'

'There was a crowd milling about. When it cleared, he remained. With a burlap sack over his head. And a message. A parchment tucked inside his jacket.'

'Message?' Gryvan could feel his anger building. He was heartily sick of surprises, even ones as relatively benign as the unexpected return of something he had thought lost. Each new instance of the unanticipated merely fed his conviction that he was conspired against. Mocked. 'What message?'

'That we should, if we want to know where Igryn oc Dargannan-Haig has been these last few days, consult with our Chancellor.'

Gryvan roared, and swept the wine ewer and goblets from the table at his side. They skittered across the marble floor, spinning and decorating the polished slabs with a spray of red liquid.

'Send for him! I want to see my Shadowhand here now.'

The word reached Gryvan some time later that his Chancellor was indisposed and unable to come to the Moon Palace. The message had been delayed in its journey between the two palaces because the first man dispatched to convey the summons to the Chancellor had been swept up in a running street fight between two very extensive families in the Meddock Ward and been knifed in the heart. Both the contents of the message and the reason for its tardiness infuriated Gryvan. He could assert control over neither his city nor the chief official of his court.

The High Thane went through his palace like a gale. Its disorder, the frantic demeanour of its inhabitants, further stoked up the fire in him. He bellowed at the servants milling pointlessly about in the corridors. He kicked aside the hunting hounds that had somehow got loose in one of the stairwells. The thunder of his rage preceded him through the palace, and all who heard it scattered at his approach.

He found the Bloodheir in his chambers, playing some dicing game with the slatternly girl he had been spending so much time with recently. Gryvan could not remember her name, but he remembered very well that Abeh had forbidden her to enter the Moon Palace.

'Get the whore out of here,' the High Thane growled as he stalked into the room.

Aewult bridled at that. 'There's no—' he began, but Gryvan was in no mood for debate.

'You prefer to stay here rather than in your own palace while the unrest continues, so be it. But while you do, you'll obey our . . . my rules. Get the whore out.'

'Go, Ishbel,' Aewult said grudgingly to her.

When she was gone, Gryvan slumped heavily onto one of the cushioned benches that flanked the fireplace.

'Where's your brother?' he asked wearily.

Aewult smiled bitterly.

'Stravan is . . . indisposed. He found a stock of exceptionally fine Drandar wine this morning. And a number of young ladies eager to share it with him.'

Gryvan shook his head. Stravan was a sot, and a wastrel, and a burden of a son. Unworthy of his distinguished lineage.

'He is not the only one indisposed,' he sighed. 'Get yourself ready. You and I are going to the Palace of Red Stone. There are answers there, and I mean to have them. You might learn something. To have one son fit to succeed me should at least be possible, surely.'

VII

Anyara paced listlessly up and down in front of the fire in her chambers in the Palace of Red Stone. Coinach was seated with his head in his hands.

'We have to go,' the shieldman said. 'Somehow. Anyhow. That was the chance you wanted, the audience with Gryvan. Nothing came of it. We have to get out of Vaymouth. The place is tinder.'

Anyara had never seen him so disturbed. He had killed a man as they returned from the Moon Palace earlier that day. As they left the vast main square – all but deserted now – that adjoined Gryvan's towering home, and started their way down a wide street lined with stalls and shops, the man had run out from an alleyway. Closer to old age than youth, he was dressed as an artisan. Certainly a trained and skilled worker, perhaps even a Craftsman. Yet he wailed as he ran at Anyara's horse, his eyes bulging from their sockets. Coinach was riding on her other side, so he was unable to come between them. The man threw himself up at Anyara before she had a chance to react. Only the fact that he clumsily missed his grip on her arm prevented him from dragging her from the saddle. She tried to slap him away, but he ducked beneath her sweeping arm and scrabbled once more for a hold, this time on her leg.

Coinach landed a stinging blow on her horse's haunch, and it sprang forward startled, carrying her immediately out of reach of her assailant. Coinach had calmly leaned low out of his saddle and killed the man with a single sword stroke to the neck.

He was considerably less calm now.

'The city's not safe,' he said, not for the first time since their return.

Anyara kept pacing, her mind working furiously.

'We can't run away,' she muttered. 'The Chancellor could deliver this city, this Blood, every Blood to the Black Road. If that's what he wants to do.'

'We don't know.' He lifted his head out of his hands.

'I know,' snapped Anyara. 'I've heard him. I've looked into his eyes. He's going to drag us all down into ruin, unless someone stops him.'

'Do you want me to kill him?' Coinach asked dolefully. 'Is that it?'

Anyara stopped and looked at him.

'Would you do it, if I asked you to?'

'Of course,' he said without hesitation. 'But if I did . . . what then?'

There was a soft knocking at the door, followed at once by a tentative, familiar voice: 'My lady?'

'Come in, Eleth,' Anyara called, and the maid entered. That the girl's mood had improved compared with recent days was immediately obvious. There was a renewed energy in her movements, and a bright and alert gleam in her eye. Anyara found this bewildering when the city around them was sinking every day further into chaos.

'You seem much happier,' she said, unable to entirely conceal her confusion and faint suspicion.

'Thank you, yes.' Eleth smiled. She paused, but when she realised that more explanation was expected she added, 'My father was . . . sick. But the sickness has . . . well, it's gone away.'

'If only all sicknesses were so amenable,' Anyara muttered.

'Yes, my lady. The High Thane is here, my lady. He has . . . I was told to say your presence is required.'

'Gryvan?' Anyara said in surprise, raising her eyebrows towards Coinach.

The shieldman rose slowly to his feet, frowning.

'I don't understand,' he said.

'And the Bloodheir, too,' Eleth said.

That thoroughly deflated Anyara's briefly waking hopes. Of all the people she desired to see, or imagined could possibly be of any assistance to her, Aewult nan Haig was the very least and last.

'You shouldn't go,' Coinach said firmly.

Anyara grunted. 'You want me to turn down a summons from the Thane of Thanes, while I'm trapped in the same building with him? Oh, Coinach, I have to go. And it's another chance, isn't it? It might be. We don't know. We'll never know, if I don't try.'

Coinach's face fell, but he said nothing.

'Where's the Chancellor's wife?' Anyara asked Eleth.

'Oh, she's been sent for too, my lady. On her way, I'm sure. If not there already.'

Tara was waiting for Anyara outside the broad double doors of a room Anyara could not recall ever having been inside. They were ornately carved from some exotic dark wood. They smelled of oil, and gleamed.

Tara took Anyara by the arm as she approached. Eleth was dismissed with a silent look.

'Listen to me,' Tara whispered. 'I know what this is. Gryvan's angry, looking for answers. He's only here because Mordyn refused to go to him in the Moon Palace earlier. Listen to me.'

Tara's agitation was unsettling, especially in one normally so entirely in command of the impression she gave.

'Please. Do not lose me my husband, Anyara. That is all I ask of you. Let it be a sickness. A sickness of the mind. Not treachery. Not binding. If you should convince Gryvan of such things, he will have my husband killed. If it's a sickness . . . there might be exile. Imprisonment, perhaps. Not death.'

Anyara did not know what to say. She felt indebted to this woman, and understood something of just how much she treasured her husband. And yet . . . there was more at stake than that here.

Kale pulled the doors open. The lean shieldman stared out at them with chilly indifference, as if he knew none of them.

'You wait out here,' he said levelly to Coinach.

'No,' Coinach said promptly.

Kale smiled then, and it was a strikingly lifeless and troubling sight.

'It is not a request or a suggestion. It is the command of your High Thane.'

Anyara smiled reassuringly at Coinach, though she felt more in need of reassurance herself than of providing it. He turned

reluctantly away and stood with his back against the wall, staring straight ahead. Kale ushered Tara and Anyara inside, and
closed the doors behind them.

The room was high-ceilinged, the walls painted with bright
murals. No windows. One other set of doors, opposite those by
which they had just entered. A single bare table set with six
chairs, at two of which Gryvan oc Haig and his son were seated.

'You must let me provide some refreshment,' Mordyn Jerain
was saying casually. 'Wine, at least.'

'Nothing,' Gryvan snapped.

Mordyn Jerain turned, a transparent pretence at having only
just noticed Anyara and Tara's arrival.

'Ah, here we are.' He smiled. 'Now perhaps we can resolve
this confusion.'

He wore all his old charm, and it fitted him as snugly as a
custom-made glove. Anyara looked at him, and it was like looking at an entirely different person from the one who had given
her the bruise still discolouring her face. Here was someone all
fluid grace and natural warmth.

'Sit, sit,' he said to Anyara, gesturing towards chairs. 'The
High Thane wants to talk with us.'

Watching him warily, Anyara settled into a seat opposite
Gryvan. Tara Jerain, she noticed, was staring at her husband,
rapt. Her face did not seem to be able to decide between unease
and relief, as if she did not trust what her eyes and ears told her.

'You too,' Mordyn said gently to her, and Tara sat at Anyara's
side.

Gryvan, evidently inured to the effects of the man's charm by
long exposure, was glowering at the Shadowhand as he walked
slowly around the table. Aewult looked merely bored, though
he did favour Anyara with a particularly savage glare before he
resumed his studied detachment.

'I want answers,' Gryvan rasped, his hands bunched into fists
on the surface of the table.

'As do we all.' Mordyn nodded. 'And we shall have them, I am sure.'

He paused suddenly in his circuit of the room, and frowned.

'Do you hear something?' he asked of no one in particular. And in the question's wake came the unmistakable sound of raised voices and hurried feet somewhere within the Palace of Red Stone. Then what struck Anyara immediately as the sound of fighting. Her first thought was concern for Coinach, but the disturbance seemed to be coming from the front of the palace, beyond the door through which Gryvan and Aewult had presumably entered, not that at which Coinach stood guard. Tara was rising from her chair, alarmed.

'Wait, wait,' muttered Mordyn, extending a hand. 'It's probably nothing, but let's wait a moment. Let's not rush into anything.'

'I'll see what's happening,' said Aewult, rising, but Gryvan pushed his son back down into his seat.

'Kale,' the High Thane said. 'Find out what it is.'

The brief tumult was already fading, but Gryvan's shieldman obediently turned and went out through the doors behind the High Thane's chair. Mordyn moved round that way, craning his neck as if to peer out as the doors swung shut behind Kale. The Chancellor took hold of the doors to hurry them on their way, and pushed them firmly closed. There was a dull *clack* as some latch fell into place. Anyara frowned at the sound, which seemed out of place. Inappropriate.

Mordyn turned, each of his hands reaching into the opposite sleeve. He withdrew them as he stepped forward, smiling. Anyara saw the gleam of metal, and had a vivid, ghastly memory of a feast night in the Tower of Thrones, and a serving woman leaning close to Lheanor oc Kilkry-Haig. She opened her mouth to cry out.

'How simple,' Mordyn said with satisfaction.

Tara was rising once more from her chair, shock plain on her face. Gryvan twisted round in his chair to see what was happening.

The Chancellor drove one of the long-bladed narrow knives into the back of Aewult's neck, at the base of his skull. The other went in under Gryvan's chin as he turned onto it. As soon as the blades were planted, the Shadowhand was running, darting around the table. He reached the second set of doors before either Tara or Anyara had got free of their hampering chairs.

'Coinach!' Anyara shouted.

The same dull *clack* of wood on wood as Mordyn sealed the doors.

'What have you done?' Tara Jerain gasped, hands rising to her mouth as she looked from her husband to the dead Thane and his son, their blood flooding out over the table.

'Paid some clubmen off the street to stage some distracting little trouble,' Mordyn muttered.

He ran at Anyara, surprisingly fast, and seized her by her shoulders. He threw her violently against the wall and she fell.

'Didn't really think that would work,' she heard the Chancellor saying through the faint ringing in her ears.

She could hear the doors shaking too. Coinach shouting: 'Anyara!'

'Thought I would be dead by now, but it would have been a price worth paying.'

Anyara got unsteadily to her feet. Mordyn had his wife by the throat, was holding her down on the surface of the table. Her mouth was agape.

'I suspected the game was done as soon as I heard you had been to see Gryvan. Knew it beyond doubt when I got his message demanding I go there myself. A pity. I could have done so much more. But this will do. This is enough.'

Tara had her hands about Mordyn's wrists, straining ineffectually to pry them apart.

The door shook once more beneath Coinach's assaults. Anyara looked from the latch holding the door shut to the knife protruding from the back of Aewult's head. And chose the knife.

She leaned across the table and wrenched it free with a sickening crunch. Mordyn looked round at her.

She rushed at him. None of the meagre training she had received from Coinach was needed. Mordyn raised no defence. He merely looked into her eyes as she ran at him, and kept his hands on Tara's throat. Anyara stabbed him in the side, under his arm. She did remember something Coinach had told her then, and punched the knife in and out once, twice more, reaching for the heart. To be certain.

Mordyn fell heavily. Tara did not stir at first, but then lifted herself up groggily, one hand pawing at her neck. Anyara opened the door to admit Coinach. The shieldman came in with sword in hand, his eyes widening in astonishment as he took in the gory scene.

'What happened?' he murmured.

'We have to get out of here,' Anyara said, considerably more calmly than she felt. 'Help me with Tara.'

She tried to put supporting hands under Tara's elbows, but the Chancellor's wife pushed her away. She was staring down at her dead husband.

'Tara,' Anyara said quietly. 'We should go.'

The doors opposite rattled as someone tried to open them.

'We really should go,' Coinach said emphatically.

The doors crashed open under Kale's foot, and the High Thane's shieldman strode in, sword readied. His eyes moved with precision and speed, and settled on Coinach. Kale leaped forward, brushing the corner of the table. His sword came sweeping down. Coinach raised his own, and caught the descending blade and held it there. He brought his knee firmly up into Kale's groin, lifting him momentarily off his feet and staggering him.

Coinach went after him, making two or three rapid slashing cuts. A single slightly misjudged parry and Coinach's blade had skidded off the top of Kale's blocking thrust and into his side. Anyara heard a rib break from the other side of the room.

Kale buckled, and Coinach hit him again, and again as he went down. Once Kale was on the ground, Coinach finished him with a straight thrust to his throat.

He frowned as he sheathed his sword.

'I had heard he was better than that.' He sounded vaguely disappointed.

VIII

Ess'yr scaled a mighty tree and crouched there, far above, in the crook of a branch. Sunlight had cracked the clouds and it spilled in pale abundance down through the boughs, patterning the forest floor with a web of shadows and ponds of light. It warmed the tan hues of Ess'yr's hide jacket. Breathed life and lustre into her hair. Gazing up at her, Orisian squinted into the unfamiliar glare. He had to raise a hand to put a protective shadow over his eyes. How long since he had done that? He could even feel, when a beam of that light fell upon his cheek and his jaw, just a murmur of warmth in it. A whisper, presaging a new season. That heat stirred memories of other years in his skin. The only place it could not penetrate was the thick scar where a White Owl spear had opened his face. That remained cold and dead.

'Can you see anything?' he said. He did not call it out, for though she was high, she would hear him well enough.

'The valley.' Her voice came drifting down from the canopy, as natural as falling leaves. 'I see your valley.'

The land sloped away on either side of them, to north and south. Southwards, sunwards, there was only Anlane, rolling to distant horizons. Northwards – Orisian turned that way now, though he could see nothing through the tangle of tree trunks and branches – northwards lay his homeland.

'How far?' he asked the treetops.

'Tomorrow,' Ess'yr replied. 'Late tomorrow, we could be under an open sky.'

Murmurs passed amongst the warriors gathered at the base of the towering oak. Orisian could not read their tone. It might be anticipation, unease, even unrest. K'rina was seated with her back against the massive bole. Yvane was trying to ease water into her, trickling it out from a skin onto unresponsive lips. Neither was paying attention, of course. They had become almost a world unto themselves, just the two of them, bound together – and separated from the others – by their alloyed blood. It pained Orisian, but he understood it too. At some level, he understood it all too clearly.

He let his gaze ascend once more, tracing the line of the tree trunk up through the great spray of limbs, seeing her there. The dappled shade made her almost seem a part of the tree, or of the forest itself. Had he not known she was there, he would never have detected her. Then she moved, extending a long arm and shifting her weight smoothly so that her leg could come reaching down. She turned and bent her head to look for that next foothold, and for a moment her eyes met Orisian's, and they looked at one another, she above and he below, through the fretwork of branches.

Then she was moving down, as easily as if she descended a stairway. As he watched her, Orisian had a sudden vision of a young girl – Anyara – in another tree, in another time, doing just this, but coming loose and falling, tumbling down, rattling from bough to bough all the way down. He could hear the sickening sound of it, and could feel the shock and lurching fear that had filled his child's breast. Now, in Anlane, he lifted his hand to his mouth to still the very cry he had let slip all those years ago.

But it was Ess'yr, not his sister, who was coming down towards him, and he blinked his way clear of the vivid memory. He anchored himself with the sight of this graceful form moving with utter confidence back to earth. She jumped the last of it, landing lightly on the balls of her feet in front of Orisian. Her knees folded and she sank down onto her haunches, recovered her spear from where she had left it by the tree, and straightened. She wiped her free hand across her upper chest, leaving tiny fragments of loose bark on the hide.

'Late tomorrow,' she said quietly, and he nodded.

The sound of movement some little way ahead, down the dipping northern slope, drew every gaze and had men reaching for their swords, but it was only Taim Narran and the two warriors he had taken with him, struggling free of thick and brittle undergrowth.

'No sign of trouble,' Taim said as he came up towards them. 'Varryn says some White Owl have passed along a trail down at the bottom in the last day or two, but they were moving quickly. And there was some smokesign from a long way to the east. Too far off to be much of a worry yet.'

'We've been lucky,' said Orisian.

From the corner of his eye, he saw the grimace of disgust that flashed across one of the warriors' face. He understood it at once. Eagan had died; had been killed by Orisian himself. No luck attended upon such a journey. How could such a thing have left him so unmarked that he should utter such foolish words? He was ashamed, but bewildered too. For a moment, he was unsure whether he had in truth killed Eagan. It had the quality of delusion, of nightmare, that memory.

'Not so lucky,' said Yvane, still squatting down beside K'rina.

Orisian looked sharply at her, wondering if – as she had sometimes before – she knew the pattern of his thoughts without his needing to say a word. But she was on another track.

'There shouldn't really be any White Owls at all wandering around these parts at this time of year. They should all be cosied away in their winter camps, telling themselves tales and tending their fires. Don't start thinking we've luck in our company. They might be busy hunting each other now, but a spear *a'an* will be just as happy to make our acquaintance if they stumble across us, I'm sure.'

Orisian nodded. Beats of pain were taking hold in his temples. He could feel himself drifting again, something in him trying to separate itself, to sink away and turn to other thoughts, other dreams. The forest around him, even the ground beneath his feet, was beginning to seem unreal and thin. If he reached out, he thought, he might pierce it; put a rent into the world and see what lay beyond it.

He shook himself and began to walk downhill. He was frightened to look into the faces of the men he needed to follow him, fearful of what he might see there.

'Let's cover what ground we can today and tonight,' he said. 'Then tomorrow we'll see. We'll see where we are, and what to do.'

'All right,' Taim was saying briskly behind him. 'You heard. There's nothing to be gained by lingering here.'

For a time, as the day dwindled into dusk, Ess'yr walked alongside him.

'I had forgotten . . . until just now, I had forgotten the first man I killed,' he said softly to her. 'Do you remember? You were there.'

She did not reply, but he could tell from the way she held her head, the way she curbed her stride to match his own, that she would listen, if he talked. It was not easy to do so, for his thoughts grew less clear and less easily herded with every passing hour. But she would listen, and there was no one else he would be so willing to speak to.

'The Tarbain I – we – killed,' he said, 'at the cottage in the Car Criagar. He was the first, and I had almost forgotten what that felt like. How it made me feel. Now, I have killed another man – Eagan, his name was Eagan – and there was almost no burden to it. He was one of my own men, one of my own Blood, and his death had too little weight to it.'

'It was necessary,' Ess'yr said quietly. 'Varryn saw. He told me.'

'Perhaps. I don't know. There's a lot I'm not sure about. It was not something I ever wanted . . . I never wanted to be able to kill men and have it be so . . . light.'

The ground was falling away slowly but steadily beneath their feet. Anlane was gradually diminishing itself around them, yielding pace by pace to the pull of the great valley that lay to the north. It was as if the very shape of the earth conspired to draw them down towards whatever waited by the Glas, in Kan Avor.

'I think of the life I lived once,' Orisian murmured, watching the green grass and the broken, withered leaves, 'before my mother and my brother died, and it's as if I'm on a ship, and that life is an island, falling away behind me. I can't reach it. I can see the sunlight on it; I can hear waves breaking on its shore; I can remember, almost, how good it felt to be there. But I can't reach it. It's further away every day.'

'Where does your ship go?'

'What?'

'This ship you are on. Where does it go?'

'I don't know.'

'All journeys have the same ending.'

'Do they?'

'You call it the Sleeping Dark. We call it *Darlankyn*.'

'I suppose so. I hope not yet, though. Not yet.'

She was quiet for a time, and Orisian fell into the rhythm of his own steps. He could hear – acutely, it seemed to him – the fall of his feet, the rustling of the fallen leaves beneath them, the soft sighing of grass under his heel and against his shin. Yet he heard nothing of Ess'yr. She moved through this place in silence, as if she had no substance. He wondered for a moment, without alarm or distress, whether she might not be an entirely imagined presence, summoned up by his wandering mind. Perhaps the real Ess'yr was somewhere up ahead, hunting and tracking her way through the forest with her breath; perhaps he walked now with the Ess'yr he longed for, not the one who was.

But she spoke again, and she spoke of things his mind could surely not have woven for itself.

'There is some kind of return in every journey, in every life. When the God Who Laughed made my people – all my people, all Kyrinin – he walked across the world and came, at the end, back to the place where he began. There are mountains, in the lands of the Boar clan now: they are *Eltenn Omrhynan*. First and Last, perhaps you would say. They are the knot in the circle of his journey, the beginning and the end. An important place to us. But what he did on the journey was more important. In the shape made he upon the land, he spoke a truth. Endings and beginnings are smaller things than the movement between them, and the manner of it.'

'That sounds like Inurian,' Orisian said, and though once he might have regretted reminding her of her lost lover, now that hardly seemed to matter.

She said nothing at first, and they strode on, side by side, beneath the leaning, leafless trees of Anlane.

Then: 'It does.'

'Do you think of him often?' Orisian asked. 'I do, now.'

'Yes,' she said very softly.

Orisian felt gentle sorrow walking between them, like a friend: not separating them but linking them.

'He would not want us to remember only the ending of him, I suppose,' said Orisian. 'It was the movement that came before that mattered. And the manner of it.'

'Yes,' said Ess'yr again after a few heartbeats, a few paces.

And then she lifted her head and looked towards the sun, and lengthened her stride and moved on ahead of him, returning to

Anlane's embrace. Orisian watched her go this time without any pangs of regret or trepidation. This did not feel – as so many such moments had in the past – like a parting.

IX

Disaster came upon them slowly, revealing itself by increments as it emerged from the shadows and the wilds. It came first in the last dregs of the twilight, in the form of tracks through the mud at the side of a stream, that Varryn leaned close to, and tested with his fingers, and proclaimed half a day old at most. A White Owl family, with children, he said, moving north and west.

It came again, betraying a little more of its shape in the gathering darkness, as the scent of a distant fire that none save Ess'yr or Varryn could detect. None doubted their inhuman senses, though, and all followed the Kyrinin as they bent their course away from the unseen, fearful beacon and led their stumbling, blundering charges through the night-thronged thickets. Some of the warriors muttered mutinously at the unwisdom of traversing wight-haunted lands by nothing more than moonlight, but Orisian could read the urgency and unease taking root in Ess'yr and her brother, and he kept them moving.

They did halt, in time, if only briefly. A taut, restless interlude in which they blindly passed morsels of food from hand to hand to mouth and rubbed aching feet in vain attempts to soothe them. Ess'yr and Varryn went out into the night, of course, remorseless in their suspicious quartering of this untrustworthy ground.

While they were gone, K'rina began to moan softly. It was a troubling sound, like the mournful voice of the darkness itself.

'Keep her quiet,' someone hissed in sibilant anger.

'I'm trying,' Yvane muttered, and though he could not see her clearly, Orisian could hear her slight shifting movements as she reached for K'rina. Whether to comfort her or cover her mouth, he did not know.

'She's unsettled,' Yvane whispered as the other *na'kyrim*'s restlessness diminished. 'Agitated. Feels something or knows something. Because we're getting closer, maybe.'

Ess'yr returned suddenly, as if stepping out from one of the grey tree trunks into their midst. She brought with her another fragment of threat, another traced portion of disaster's outline.

'Someone is killed, far behind us,' she said into Orisian's ear, so close he could feel the warmth of her breath. 'We hear him dying. A Kyrinin. We must move. Death runs through the forest. We must run faster.'

But they could not run, for Anlane would not so easily open itself to humankind, or any kind perhaps. Not in the sombre darkness, not when its soils were soaked with meltwater, its streams swollen. They could only struggle on, none of them – Orisian least of all – knowing whether what lay before or behind them was more deserving of their fear. Ess'yr stayed close, guiding their every pace with inexhaustible patience. For all her efforts, they slipped and tripped and fell. But they kept moving, as if by moving they might hasten the departure of the treacherous darkness and eventually leave the night behind.

Orisian dreamed without sleeping, even as he staggered along, of Inurian, and of Rothe and others. They were formless dreams composed of nothing but the presence of the lost. He dreamed, or thought he did, of Aeglyss. He had no other name to give to that pitiless black fog he imagined drifting through the forest all around him. There was no malice in it, just a cold and bitter accusation of futility that sapped his strength and his will. He could feel not just his legs but his heart and his hope growing sluggish and torpid.

By the time dawn came, he had forgotten its possibility. All but a last, small stubborn part of him had surrendered, and accepted that the night and the forest had consumed all the world, and would be its entirety for ever. When the light came, wan and hesitant, he disbelieved it at first, and thought it only an illusory trick of his failing mind. But it was a true light. It brought no relief, though. Instead it brought a slow nightmare, shuffling in their wake out of the darkness, gathering itself, closing on them.

'We've lost someone,' Taim Narran said grimly.

They stood in bleary, numb assembly beneath a lightning-split oak. The great wound in the tree's trunk was darkened by age, the exposed heartwood softened by rot. A gnarled knoll of rock and earth and thin grass stood nearby, a knuckled clenching of the forest floor.

'Kellach's gone,' said Taim. 'Did no one hear anything? No one see anything?'

There was only a shaking of heads, a casting down of eyes. Taim's anguish was raw, sharpened by his exhaustion. It hurt Orisian to see it. He wanted to tell the warrior not to blame himself, but it would do no good. It was not the kind of guilt Taim could put aside, even when it belonged to his Thane, not him.

One of the warriors was weeping. His comrades watched him. They said nothing, showed nothing: no sympathy, no understanding, no contempt, no judgement. They merely watched, as if tears were now as natural and inevitable a thing as the clouds drifting above them. He did not weep for their lost companion, Orisian knew; he wept for everything. Because there was something rising in him that demanded the shedding of tears. Something that might, before long, demand the shedding of blood.

'We cannot go back,' Ess'yr said flatly.

No one looked at her.

Then Varryn was running down towards them, swinging around the shoulder of that bare knoll. He leaped from a boulder to land lightly at his sister's side, already hissing something to her in the Fox tongue as he hit the ground. Tension sprang into her shoulders.

'The enemy,' she said.

And with nothing more than that, no more warning, there were White Owls amongst them. Figures spilled over the knoll and came rushing down like a loose flock of great pale birds. Orisian had time only to lift his shield and snap his sword free of its scabbard before there was movement and noise all about him, a storm of it. A solid blow on the face of his shield knocked him back a couple of paces, but the Kyrinin who had struck him swept on by. Orisian had a glimpse of wide grey eyes, the dark and swirling *kin'thyn*, a rictus of a mouth. He was not sure the White Owl had even seen him.

The next assuredly did, for a spear darted at Orisian's thigh. He knocked it down and aside and its tip punched into the mossy earth. The Kyrinin who wielded it dropped it and ran on, bounding past the wild flash of a warrior's blade. They had not come to fight, Orisian realised. The White Owls were pouring through the thin rank his men had prepared to meet this supposed charge, not pausing to offer anything more than the most cursory of assaults. In two and threes, they came leaping over the crest of the knoll, sped down its flank and danced their lithe way through the cordon of slow and clumsy humans, and then were gone, plunging back into the forest. It was like the dolphins that breached sometimes in the Glas estuary: emerging for only the briefest of instants into the world of light and air, then gone again, back into the limitless blank ocean.

Not all those making up that bewildered, impotent cordon were human, though. And one of them at least was fast enough, and impassioned enough, to weave a furious dance of his own. In a single sideways glance, Orisian saw Varryn, a fervent smile upon his face, moving with impossible, lethal agility. The Kyrinin flicked out his arm, and his spear punched a neat hole in a White Owl's neck, and was withdrawn before the victim had even begun to stagger. Varryn lunged to his side and caught another on the forehead with the spear's butt, streaking a red split across the white skin; he spun and the spear was suddenly in flight, blurring up the slope and into the stomach of a third descending White Owl.

A flicker in the corner of his eye had Orisian ducking and lurching away from a shadow, but the Kyrinin who cast it was past him and gone in the same moment. He looked after the disappearing woman, and saw Yvane crouching down, her back to him, protective arms enclosing K'rina's hunched form. And Taim Narran standing in front of the two *na'kyrim*, making a wall of his body and sword and shield. The warrior did not reach for any of the White Owls as they sprinted by; he let them pass. He saw Orisian looking at him.

'Get over here,' Taim snapped, and Orisian obeyed instinctively.

He stood at Taim's side, a fraction behind him, and they watched the Kyrinin flowing around and beyond them. In every face that passed Orisian saw the same thing: some strange admixture of panic and confusion and fear. It was so far from the measured composure he associated with Kyrinin that he found it almost repellent.

As suddenly as it had begun, it was over. But Varryn was unwilling to let it end. He sent an arrow skimming between the tree trunks in pursuit of the last of the receding figures, ran forward a few paces and set another to his bowstring, then another. He sped into the dappled forest without a backwards glance.

There were a handful of dead White Owls, and one of Taim's men. A spear was embedded in the warrior's chest, broken off halfway down its length. It must have been almost an accident, Orisian thought, staring down at the youth's corpse. They were not even trying to kill us, and still someone had to die. He knelt and gently closed the open, blank eyes.

Ess'yr climbed to the top of the knoll and crouched there, turning and lifting her head this way and that.

Orisian returned to Yvane and K'rina. They were rising carefully to their feet, the one supported and guided by the other.

'Are you all right?' he asked Yvane.

She looked at him, and for the first time he saw in her eyes the same empty despair that he felt lodged patiently and watchfully at the back of his mind. In Yvane it had come into its full, bleak flowering.

'This can't go on,' she said. 'Did you see them? Did you feel it in them?'

'What?' asked Orisian cautiously.

'Out of their minds. Didn't know who they were, what they were doing. The weight of him, of what he's done, too much for them.'

Orisian nodded, for the want of anything to say.

Yvane swallowed and seemed to recover herself a little.

'The White Owl clan is older than any of your Bloods. It's older than the Kingship that came before, even. There were people who called themselves White Owls when the Whreinin still hunted through these forest, in the Age before this one.'

'When there were still Gods,' Orisian murmured.

'Perhaps. And you see? You see what they have come to? Slaughtering one another like maddened beasts. Running about, senseless. Lost children.'

'It's what we're all coming to, isn't it?' said Orisian quietly. 'We're halfway there already. That's why we have to go on.'

Ess'yr came down from the knoll. There was blood on the tip of her spear, Orisian noted. A glutinous smear of it, already drying.

'We must move,' she said.

The unfamiliar strain in her voice, as much as her words, alarmed Orisian. Her face was as elegantly expressionless as ever, but something was tightening within her.

'More come,' she said.

As if summoned up by that single terse statement, there were cries in the forest. Looping, bounding cries, like the voices of birds. Distant, Orisian thought, but drawing nearer. The sound was unearthly, a disordered, jumbled melody of stretched and falling notes. It could have been Anlane itself, the mind of that vast place, calling out. Or announcing its waking. Announcing its joining of battle.

'They hunt,' Ess'yr said. 'We must go. Now.'

She led them on, moving now with insistent haste that they struggled to match.

'What about Varryn?' Orisian called after her.

'He will find his way,' she told him.

Yet another of the babbling streams that crossed Anlane like veins in its vast body blocked their path. Too wide to leap across, they would have to wade.

Ess'yr paused upon its bank, looking up and down its writhing rocky length.

'In the water,' she said, and stepped into the flow. She turned and began to splash downstream, picking a nimble course between weed-clothed stones.

There was an instant of hesitation amongst those who followed her. Some of the men exchanged doubting, reluctant glances. But those calls were still in the air behind them, bounding through the treetops.

'Hurry,' said Orisian, and went after her.

His boots filled at once with the brutally cold water, as if seized by hands of ice. The current pushed at his heels, piling water up against the back of his legs. Sensation retreated, withdrawing up through his limbs, leaving his feet deadened to all save the dull pain of intense cold. He stumbled, constantly fearful of losing his footing on some slick and slimy stone. Behind him, he could hear the others following. Though in truth he did not know whether they followed him or fled those haunting voices that filled the forest.

The brook led them where it willed, cutting a more or less

northerly course over gently sloping ground. The notion settled upon Orisian that he walked in waters that would soon be part of the Glas. He was carried homeward by some fragment of the single titanic movement that joined stream, and great river, and ocean. This stream down which he laboured might soon be waves lapping at the walls of Castle Kolglas. And with that thought, he realised that he was not moving homeward at all, for his home was gone. Whatever he was returning to, it was not home but something else.

He heard a splash and breathless, gasping curses behind him, and turned. Yvane was struggling to raise K'rina from where she had fallen. Water churned about them. Taim stopped to help, waving the rest of the men on. Orisian waded back against the force of the water, but K'rina was on her feet by the time he reached them.

'Is she all right?' he asked Yvane, but the *na'kyrim* did not hear, or ignored him.

As they moved away from him, a fleeting glimpse of something pale drew his eyes back up the stream. He looked that way, and saw nothing. Only the drooping trees that lined the banks. The water murmuring busily along. Clumps of rushes nodding at its edge.

Then something: a single movement from left to right, as of an indistinct figure passing a distant window. And another. White Owls, he realised, darting across the stream. They were at the furthest limit of sight that the dense forest and the wandering stream's course would permit. The only sound was at his back, as his companions made their sodden way along the bed of the brook. He saw these silent, wan instants of motion as the Kyrinin crossed one by one, and it seemed to be happening in another place entirely, without connection to him.

Until one of them stopped, halfway across, and stared directly at him. Even at that distance, Orisian knew their eyes met. He could envisage precisely that intent grey gaze, and feel its questioning touch upon him. He was already turning as a second figure joined the first, and as a flurry of fluting bird calls came down towards him, riding the cold air that hung above the stream between the overhanging trees.

'They've seen us,' he shouted. 'They're coming.'

The waters were hateful now, thickening about his legs, hampering every desperate surging stride.

'Out of the water!' he shouted, but Ess'yr already had them clambering up onto the bank.

Orisian's feet throbbed as he staggered onto the grass, his sodden, heavy leggings plastered to his skin.

'We need some clear ground,' Taim was muttering. 'Can't win against Kyrinin if we get spread out, scattered amongst the trees.'

Ess'yr was listening intently to the calls cascading through the forest.

'They gather first,' she said.

'Not mad, these ones, then,' said Yvane bleakly. 'They know what they're doing.'

K'rina was leaning against her, shivering. Looking at the frail *na'kyrim*, a wave of weariness and feebleness ran through Orisian. All he had achieved here, following instincts that had seemed so sure and certain, was to deliver them all to a futile death.

Ess'yr was not finished yet, though. She led them on, away from the stream. The warriors followed without urging, their fear rendering them at last pliant. Orisian could see in their slumping shoulders and their gaunt, empty faces that the forest, its rigours, its accumulation of threat, had defeated them and left them willing to cleave to any guide who appeared to grasp its subtle horrors.

So they came to a place where a great oak, its girth the token of its agedness, had created about itself a wide ring of ground untrammelled by briars or shrubs. When in leaf, its sprawling branches must have cast such shade that nothing but moss and the most meagre of grasses would grow there. Pigeons rattled out of its crown. Beneath it, Ess'yr turned and stood. Taim Narran looked about with a frown.

'Not much,' the warrior growled. 'But if it's the best we can do . . .'

'No more time,' Ess'yr said. She leaned on her bow, forcing its notched limb down towards the looped end of the string.

'You two get down,' Taim said to Yvane and K'rina, jabbing the point of his sword groundward. 'Lie flat, and we'll shield you as best we can.'

Yvane sank down onto her haunches. She had to tug at K'rina's arm to bring the other *na'kyrim* down.

'We keep between them and the arrows,' Taim told the remaining warriors. 'And keep as much of ourselves behind our shields as we can. Depending on what sort of mood they're in, they may lose interest if they see arrows aren't going to do the job. Happens sometimes, with Kyrinin.'

Not this time, Orisian thought. No one fights with only half their heart any more. He took his place with the others in that feeble shield wall beside Taim. Just seven of them altogether, each sunk down onto his heels, shrinking himself into a knot of tension behind his shield. They arrayed themselves in half a circle, with the two *na'kyrim* lying at its heart, and behind them the great bulk of the oak. Orisian could smell the wood of his shield, and the dry leather of the grip to which his hand clung with such desperate rigidity. He looked back. Ess'yr was kneeling over Yvane. The Kyrinin's face was a mask of perfect concentration as she brushed the flights of her arrows with careful fingers, seeking flaws. Deciding, perhaps, in which order to let them fly. The very stillness of her features in such moments gave the branching, curving tattoos of her *kin'thyn* an almost painted beauty, Orisian thought. He saw Yvane watching him with narrowed eyes, and he turned back into his shield and flexed his fingers about the hilt of his sword.

'Now,' Ess'yr whispered with no trace of urgency.

And like massive, gale-driven drops of rain striking shutters, the arrows hit the shields. First one, then a second, then a rippling drumbeat of them smacking home. Orisian felt his own shield tremble against his arm. And again, this time spitting fine splinters into his eyes. He blinked and saw the very tip of an arrow protruding from the inner face of the shield.

There was a scraping, and a moaning, and a shifting of bodies. And one of the men was slumping back. Orisian leaned back a little to look towards the sound. The man's lower leg was spitted by an arrow, feathery flights on one side of his calf, bloodied point on the other. Others shuffled clumsily sideways to close the gap he had left. Orisian heard the snap of the arrow's shaft breaking, and the gasp, through gritted teeth, as the man pulled the arrow through his flesh.

Within the rhythm of the arrows on shields, there were now a few duller, deeper notes, as some thudded into the trunk of the huge tree behind them. And another sound joined the chorus: the thrumming of Ess'yr's bowstring as she sent shaft after shaft skimming out just over the tops of the shields in answer.

'Stay down,' Orisian murmured, but he did not think anyone heard him.

A spear rattled off the rim of his shield. He ducked instinctively. Then a deep silence descended. Within its ominous emptiness, a bird – a real bird, this – sang a brief, nervous song some way away. Orisian glanced towards Ess'yr. She was hunched down low, head dipped beneath her shoulders.

'What now?' he whispered.

She shook her head and gave a brief, puzzled shrug of her eyebrows. It was such a human gesture it made Orisian smile.

Taim stretched up a little and peered out. Orisian waited a moment, then did the same. The forest stared back at them, blank and motionless.

'Can't be that easy,' Taim murmured.

The wounded man had torn a strip from the sleeve of his shirt, and was binding it about his leg, grimacing in pain. He fumbled at the knot, his hands blunt and clumsy. Yvane made an irritated noise through her teeth and pulled herself forward on her belly. She slapped the man's hands aside and did his work for him.

Orisian returned his attention to the forest, and strained to untangle the slanting tree trunks, the shifting shadows, the clumps of undergrowth. Nothing. No sign of anything save the silent, constant forest itself, complete and impassive. But he imagined White Owls crouching within that concealing mass, flickering messages to one another on spidery fingers, signalling intent. Taim was right, he was sure. It could not be this easy.

'They're still there?' he asked Ess'yr.

She nodded.

Having completed her ministrations, Yvane slipped back to her place at K'rina's side, brushing hair away from the *na'kyrim's* face. It made Orisian think of Anyara, and he did not know why. He frowned, troubled by that image, which had the texture of memory yet could not, for a moment, find its place in his past. And then it came. It was the echo of Anyara doing just that: brushing their mother's hair aside when it had fallen across her eyes as she lay sick . . . dying . . . in her bed. There had been a sheen of sweat across Lairis' skin, the smell of malady in the air. From amidst the awful cull of the Heart Fever, amidst all its crippling horrors and sorrows, that was what his mind chose to retrieve now. That one quiet moment. A moment of gentleness in the presence of death.

'There,' Taim breathed, and Orisian was wrenched back into the present.

He saw the same thing Taim did. Figures drifting silently back and forth amongst the trees. All the movement was sound-less, patternless, as if in search of an as-yet-unexpressed form. It spread slowly around them, widening its compass, claiming more and more of the forest.

The wounded warrior edged back into line, struggling to keep the weight off his bloody leg. And the movement out there found the form it had been seeking, and ceased. Orisian's heart beat once, twice as he stared out. He held his breath, for everything seemed poised in that narrow span of time upon some brink. Then they came, from all sides, rushing in.

'Up!' shouted Taim as he surged to his feet.

Orisian rose, heard arrows whipping by, saw the Kyrinin running towards him, felt their blind fury like a breeze on his face, and then sight and sound and touch all collapsed into a single impenetrable blur. All existence came to be only the act and the sensation of fighting and struggling.

A White Owl charged straight at him, spear levelled. It glanced off Orisian's shield, and its wielder ran without pause onto the point of his sword, taking it into himself just under his ribs. Orisian's arm gave beneath the weight of that savage merging, and the dying Kyrinin fell against his shoulder. Human and inhuman eyes met for an instant. Orisian saw nothing in those ashen pools. The Kyrinin blinked and slipped to the ground.

Orisian twisted his sword free, fending off another attack with his shield. He hacked about him, battering aside spears and arms that seemed to come reaching in from every side. A hand closed on the upper rim of his shield and began to pull it down and away from him. Taim was suddenly there, cutting at the wrist of the offending arm. Warm flecks of blood hit Orisian's face.

He was dimly aware that he was faster now, more assured than he had been before. His blade moved without the need for conscious thought. It swung and blocked and stabbed according to some instinctual imperative of its own. But still he was no match for the man who had once been Captain of Castle Anduran.

Taim barged through the mass of White Owls. He did not wait for them to come to him, did not give them the time and space to exercise all their speed or dexterity. He ducked this way and that, cutting a gory path across the front of Orisian, and seemed always to be half a moment ahead of any attack that was directed against him. Arrows and the broken stump of a spear adorned the front of his shield like quills, until Taim battered it into the chest and face of a Kyrinin warrior and splintered them against his bones.

Someone fell at Orisian's feet. He glanced down. One of his warriors writhed there, an arrow in his face. The chaos in which Orisian was caught crowded out any response to that sight, and his eyes flicked up again at once. A tall White Owl was bearing down on him, a great club – a knotted branch of long-dead wood – held above her head in both hands. Orisian got his shield up, and the cudgel shattered against it. Fragments of it stung Orisian's brow and scalp. The blow knocked his shield low, almost tore it from his grip, and he swayed back. The woman flung the broken remnant of her weapon at him. He twisted his head out of its tumbling path, but it grazed his cheek. She ran at him and he hammered his sword into her upper arm with all his strength. It went deep, through sleeve and skin and flesh, and knocked her aside.

Beyond her, he saw a young Kyrinin – slighter and younger than he was himself – sitting astride the chest of a dead or dying man, pounding at his wrecked skull with a rock. The sight was transfixing. Orisian watched in stunned awe as the rock rose, flicking gore and blood into the air.

He was almost too late in blocking another spear thrust, and was staggered by it. The spear's tip scraped along the leather belt at his waist. Orisian slashed at his attacker, but the White Owl sprang nimbly back. And looked down, startled, at the other spear that suddenly burst from his own stomach.

Varryn carried his impaled victim a couple of paces forward before driving him down onto the ground. Orisian started to thank him, but saw at once that the Fox was far beyond the reach of any words. Varryn's eyes had a glaze of fierce detachment. He snarled savagely as he hauled at his spear to free it from the back of the White Owl. The blue tattoos on his cheeks were overlaid with streams of blood coursing from a ragged scalp wound. His hair was matted down over his brow.

He hissed as he spun, bringing his spear round in a flashing flat arc and breaking it across the midriff of another closing White Owl. He leaped high and came down on the back of a Kyrinin who was sparring with Taim. Orisian stepped forward. A flicker of movement sensed out of the corner of his eye had him lifting his shield. It caught an arrow out of the air and shook. Orisian looked out towards the youth who had loosed the shaft. The Kyrinin stared back at him, slowly lowering his bow with trembling hands, and then turned on his heel and vanished into the forest.

Orisian turned about. The shadow of the oak tree now fell upon the dead, the dying and the last of the fleeing White Owls. Soft moans and gasped breaths. The stench of blood and spilled guts. Orisian saw a Kyrinin arm extended up, reaching weakly and futilely for the overhanging boughs. He saw Taim Narran on his knees, shield laid flat before him, panting. He saw more than a dozen bodies, and one White Owl limping in a tight, unsteady circle, holding a crippled and ragged arm tight in against her side. She gave out a susurrant whimper. Her eyes were closed. Varryn put an arrow into her neck, and she staggered sideways and then fell.

Varryn turned towards Orisian. The Kyrinin's chest was heaving in a way Orisian had never seen before, from exertion and perhaps from the intensity of the fires that burned within him. Fires that subsided now, for the warrior blinked and blew out his cheeks, stretching the coils of his blue *kin'thyn*, and let his bow hang limply from his hand. His eyes cleared.

Orisian nodded, a gesture of simple acknowledgement, a welcoming back of someone who had been absent, in more ways than one, until that moment. But he realised that the Kyrinin's attention had already found another object. Those eyes focused beyond Orisian, sharpening upon something over his shoulder. Varryn's face went slack, his lips parted. Orisian turned, frowning.

And only then did he grasp the true shape of the disaster that had been closing upon them – upon him – all this time. For Ess'yr lay on her back, hair spread over the grass like a filamentous disc framing her head. She stared up, unblinking, through the branches of the oak tree to the sky above. One hand rested lightly on her breast, the fingertips just barely touching the shaft of the arrow that was sunk deep into her fluttering chest. Her blood was turning the deerskin of her jacket black.

5

Kan Avor

There is a ruin at the heart of the Lannis Blood: Kan Avor, the drowned city where once the Thanes of Gyre ruled, and where the creed of the Black Road was nurtured and tended. It stands now empty and silent, in the cold embrace of still waters and marsh. Birds roost upon its crumbling walls and bats hide in its broken towers.

The people of the Glas Valley treasure this ruin, and all but venerate it. They think it a token of their determination, a glorious symbol of their past triumphs over the Black Road. They imagine that its persistence invigorates them. 'See,' they say to one another. 'See these broken and shackled towers. Here is the fate of our enemies. So strong is our grasp upon this land that we can tame mighty rivers and with them drown the cities of our foes.'

It would have been better to unpick this city: to break it apart, stone from stone, carry away its every timber, plough its streets back into the soft earth until nothing remained. Kan Avor is the constant shadow of the past upon the present. It commemorates not glory but unforgiven and unforgotten hurts. When men venerate the memory of war and strife, and make temples of its relics, and seek to learn from the ruins of yesterday how they should live their lives today, then they have made themselves prisoners of the past, condemned to fight its wars again and again. For few wars are ever truly finished. There is always some remaining vein of bitterness for those who can neither forgive nor forget to mine.

Time works many wonders, but they are not all to be treasured.
It makes shackles out of past triumphs, burdens from victories.
Bonds from memories. And it heals only if those who ride its cur-
rents are willing to be healed.

From *Hallantyr's Sojourn*

I

The Inkallim came to the *na'kyrim* in his ruined, rotting citadel on the floodplain. She came hesitantly, almost stumbling, eyes gritted and reddened by sleeplessness. Though the waters that had once imprisoned this city had retreated, it could never be free of their legacy. So she came with mud on her shoes, the stink of decay and mould on her clothing. And though she was one of the Children of the Hundred, and had been fashioned by those who trained her into a cold and remorseless weapon, imbued with all the certainty of her faith and her capabilities, the world had become wholly inhospitable to certainties. So she came as a supplicant, and for the first time in her hard life there was fear in her as she spoke.

'Aeglyss, can you hear me?'

The *na'kyrim* did not pause in his shuffling, limping, staggering progress around the columned hall. He hauled his cadaverous form on a weaving path amongst and around the pillars, wandering aimless in that sparse forest of stone trees. He walked barefoot, and his split and scabbed feet left prints of pus and blood on the dank floorboards. He moved slowly, and seemed at each and every moment to be on the point of falling.

Yet the air the Inkallim breathed felt alive. It was heavy in her mouth and throat and lungs, full of his power. It pressed upon her chest and her back and shoulders, as if he was not only contained within this shambling and broken body in its stained, ragged gown, but also in the glistening, moist walls and in the space they defined. As if he was everywhere.

She followed him, walking in those bloody footprints.

'Can you hear me?' she asked. 'You must help me. You must hide some of your light, Aeglyss.'

He did not seem to hear her, for though he murmured erratic little whispers, whatever conversation he held was with himself, or with no one. What few words rose loud enough for the Inkallim to hear were in a language she did not know.

'Please,' she said. A word that her lips barely remembered well enough to form. 'Our warriors turn on one another. They forget themselves, their cause, everything. They lie down and do not rise. They lose their minds. There is sickness in every street, every shelter. Fevers claim more each day, and there is barely a healer with enough sense or strength to treat them. Our triumph – the creed's ascendancy – remains incomplete . . .'

He turned suddenly and sharply. His thin gown hung slack from his bony shoulders. The contours of his bones – ribs, hips – showed through its material. He stared at her from deep within the pits his eyes had sunk into. There was blood in those eyes, a fine net of countless broken vessels leaking soft red.

'Who are you?' he asked quietly. His voice cracked and creaked like the stale hinge of a long-forgotten door.

'Shraeve,' she told him. 'Shraeve. You know me.'

'I know everyone,' he grunted. And turned away once more, lurching on in his unsteady circuit of the hall. There were cries rising up from outside, wailing that might be lamentation or simple madness. The Inkallim was not distracted by them. Such sounds – and worse – were common currency now in Kan Avor. The city had found its voice in them. She followed after the *na'kyrim*.

'Shraeve . . .' he whispered. 'Shraeve . . . Shraeve. Yes, the raven. The fierce one, the cold one. Thinks she's so wise, so clever. Not a true friend.'

'You can calm them,' she insisted. 'You must calm them, bring our people back to us. If they will not – cannot – submit themselves to our commands, everything we have gained could yet slip away.'

'There is nothing I can do,' Aeglyss said bluntly, and then halted and looked around him as if puzzled. He frowned in contemplation.

'There must be,' said Shraeve.

He stared at her, and there was a shifting of the shadows about him. He flickered in and out of darkness for a few moments. It pained her eyes, and she clenched them almost shut.

'Must be?' he hissed. 'Don't you think I would, if I could?'

Scourges and daggers filled his voice. She, Banner-captain of the Battle Inkallim, quailed before this feeble, tottering figure.

'Nothing *must* be,' he cried in tones of venom and fire. 'I am only the gate, and the truth enters through me, becomes me, and shapes the world according to its tenets. What we see now is only the true nature of the world, of us all. Nothing more. I cannot prevent it.' He was suddenly speaking softly, so laden with sorrow and regret that those same feelings took hold of Shraeve. 'I cannot close what has been opened. Cannot heal my wounds. Cannot bring them back, none of them. I cannot even tell, any more, where I end and it . . . everything . . . begins. I don't know whether I poisoned it, or it me . . . You can't imagine . . . how I wish . . .'

He sagged against a pillar, then just as quickly gathered himself and lifted his head.

'We discover the truth now. That's the thing. We become what we have always been, at our root. We enter an age of misrule, and I am its herald, its doorkeeper, its lord. Its God.'

'The Black Road is the truth,' Shraeve said. She backed away from him. He waved a dismissive hand in her direction, its flaking raw skin oozing fluid.

'Hate is coming,' he murmured, lifting his gaze towards the

ruptured roof of the hall. 'He is coming. From Glasbridge. Is there . . . is there still a place called Glasbridge?'

'Of course.'

'Oh, he burns brightly. He's the hardest, the purest of you all. Nothing but hate to him, and it's all his own. He takes nothing from me, gives nothing.' The *na'kyrim* sounded strangely joyful, raised up by a perverse pleasure.

'Who?' Shraeve asked. 'Kanin?'

'Kanin. Yes. The brother. There's no flame will forge a keener hatred than the breaking of families. I know that. I learned that. I learned that a long time ago.'

'He's coming here?' Shraeve asked.

He looked at her clearly for the first time then, fully present and aware. He appeared almost surprised to discover that he was not alone, though his sallow features were only briefly troubled.

'You should not spend your energies fighting a chaos that cannot be halted,' he rasped. 'You do not need to worry about such things. Whatever consumes us, will consume our enemies too. There are none left to oppose us, for my Shadowhand does his work well. None except him perhaps. Kanin. He's moving. Drawing near, with hate in his heart and hate all around him, like a cloud. He's done what you say you can't, raven: kept a host at his side, found the will to quell it and guide it. So now we'll see. Who is stronger, the Battle Inkall or a Thane who has no thought in his head save vengeance?'

'Do not let her die.'

'Get out of my way, then,' barked Yvane, pushing Orisian so forcefully that he rocked back on his heels.

She was packing moss around the arrow embedded in Ess'yr's pale flesh. The Kyrinin's throat was trembling with each breath as if it contained beating wings. Her eyes were open but unseeing. Orisian had leaned over her, and looked into them, and found nothing there. No response, no recognition, only vacant grey orbs in which he saw the depths of his own despair.

'Please,' he said now to Yvane, but the *na'kyrim* was not paying any attention to him.

'Where's Varryn?' She looked around, fruitlessly scanning the silent forest. 'I need those herbs before I try to take the arrow out.'

The blood had almost stopped. It had soaked into Ess'yr's jerkin and into the grass beneath her. It had laid down crusted ribbons across the ivory of her exposed breast and shoulder. It had coated Yvane's fingers. The fletching of the arrow, standing almost two hand spans above Ess'yr's chest, twitched in time with her breathing.

'Is she—' Orisian began.

'I don't know,' Yvane shouted without looking at him. She bent down and pressed her ear to that pallid chest. She listened for a moment and then straightened and pushed a finger into Ess'yr's mouth, parting her slack lips.

'She's not breathing blood, as far as I can see or hear,' Yvane said. 'That's good. Where's Varryn?'

'Watch her!' Taim Narran was suddenly shouting.

Orisian twisted round on his haunches, startled by the anger in the Captain's voice. K'rina was staggering away, plunging with surprising speed into the thickets to the north of the spreading oak tree. Taim was already running after her, spitting curses at the man who had been tasked with watching the comatose *na'kyrim*. That man was entirely untouched by Taim's scorn, for he had his head in his hands and was groaning distantly.

Orisian surged to his feet, so clumsily that he lurched sideways and almost fell. He could still see K'rina, struggling with entangling briars. She would not get far, surely. Taim would have her in just a moment or two. He looked down at Ess'yr; felt anew the aridity of his mouth, the impotent tremors starting in his hands. The fear. He knelt down again.

'Keep clear,' Yvane muttered. 'Give me room.'

She tried to feel under Ess'yr's shoulder while holding down the compress of moss with her other hand, but quickly hissed in frustration.

'Lift her up a little,' she told Orisian.

He was afraid to touch Ess'yr. He felt sick at the thought of causing her pain, of doing unwitting harm.

'Lift her shoulder,' Yvane snapped.

He did, and Ess'yr gave a faint, descending sigh. She was still there, at least enough to feel something. Yvane probed at her back, exploring her shoulder blade with firm fingers. Apparently satisfied, she nodded to Orisian, and he let Ess'yr sink back into the grass as gently as he could. She was so light, he thought. So light.

'The head of the arrow's almost through,' Yvane said softly. 'Nicking her shoulder blade, I think, not in it.'

'Is that good?' Orisian asked.

'Maybe. Is any of this good? Arrow has to come out, or she'll die a hard death. Might do anyway. Getting it out's going to be an ugly business.' She shook her head.

Taim Narran returned, a feebly struggling K'rina held tightly in his grasp. Orisian registered them only in the dimmest of ways, for he was shaken by memories of almost visionary intensity and immediacy. Inurian, lying with an arrow buried deep in his back, the strength – the life – draining from him with every breath. The two of them, Kyrinin and *na'kyrim*, lay side by side in his imagination.

'Look at her, look at her,' Yvane was whispering. 'What's a Fox doing here? She should be up there in the Car Criagar, in some *vo'an*. Hunting deer. Tanning hides. They should all be there still. Not dead, not dying.'

She looked up as Taim gently settled K'rina down onto the ground beside them. As Yvane's gaze settled upon her fellow *na'kyrim*, whose expression was entirely blank, almost childlike, her brow furrowed and sadness tugged at the corners of her mouth.

A mist of light rain drifted down through the branches of the oak. It was cold on Orisian's face. He curled his lips into his mouth, sucked that wet breath of the sky from them. Ess'yr's eyes were slowly closing.

'We need shelter,' he said.

Yvane nodded curtly.

K'rina was trying to rise again. Taim Narran pressed her down with a hand upon her shoulder. Orisian looked around. The dead lay all about, some in strangely twisted or contorted poses, other looking as if they had fallen asleep. Of the three Lannis warriors who had survived, two stood staring silently outward, though it was difficult to tell whether they were watchful or simply lost in distraction. The third, the man who had let K'rina slip away from him, was still whimpering into his hands. Lost not in distraction but in the miasma of dismay and despair Orisian could sense thickening just beyond the boundaries of his own thoughts. He saw all this, and found it faintly unreal and distant, as if he viewed it through the translucent gauze of the thinnest curtain.

Varryn came running, spear in one hand, a mass of leaves and stems and bark in the other. He rushed in and dropped to one knee beside his ailing sister; opened his fingers to show his bounty to Yvane. The *na'kyrim* stared at the herbs and then grunted.

'If that's the best we can do,' she said.

'The forest edge is near,' Varryn reported dully. 'Open ground. A Huanin hut. Empty.'

'We should go,' Orisian said at once.

Yvane grimaced. 'She won't move well. We need to get the arrow out first.'

They carried Ess'yr back to the stream down which they had fled earlier. She moaned as they went, lapsing in and out of consciousness. Every agonised sound that escaped her lips rasped on Orisian's ears and made him wince.

At the water's edge they laid her down on her side. Yvane quietly and calmly cut away Ess'yr's jacket with a knife, peeling it back from her shoulder. The *na'kyrim* whispered to Varryn in the language of the Fox as she worked. His expression betrayed no reaction to her words. His gaze never strayed from his sister's face. Orisian turned his head aside, averting his eyes from the blood caking Ess'yr's skin.

He looked back in time to see Yvane setting down a crushed handful of the herbs mixed with moss. She had squeezed it into a neat, flat compress. Then she nodded to Varryn. He took the protruding shaft of the arrow in both hands and snapped it cleanly off, close to the flights. Ess'yr gasped, the pain finding her even in whatever distant, detached place she now resided. Orisian's eyes widened in sudden understanding as Varryn took hold once more of the broken shaft.

'Are you sure?' he asked.

'Be quiet,' Yvane told him. 'This needs doing.'

She rotated and stretched Ess'yr's arm a little, flexing the shoulder blade beneath her pristine skin. And Varryn pushed the arrow deeper. Its point burst bloodily out from Ess'yr's back. She jerked and groaned, but Yvane held her. Varryn moved quickly round behind his sister, took hold of the gory head of the arrow and pulled it, with a single, firm movement, through her body. Rivulets of blood trickled from both new and old wounds.

They washed her with water from the river, working back through the gore to expose and clean the tears in her skin. Orisian had to fight off waves of nausea, and his hands shook as he opened them to let the water he cupped there spill across her breast and shoulder. It was not horror or disgust that had hold of him, but fear. The thought of this woman dying made him feeble. Helpless.

Once the wounds were bandaged, poultices securely strapped in place, Varryn slung his sister over his shoulder and strode away northwards without another word.

'Thank you,' Orisian said to Yvane as she rose, wiping mud from her knees. She did not reply, but went to help K'rina get to her feet.

Taim already had the three warriors moving, following Varryn. He watched Orisian with an unreadable expression.

'Are you all right?' he asked.

Orisian shook his head then shrugged. He did not know the answer to that question, and it seemed entirely unimportant to him.

'We should hurry,' he said, stooping to pick up his shield. 'The White Owls might come back.'

'They'd probably have returned already if they were going to. Some kind of madness in them, to fight as they did. Should have waited for darkness, picked us off one by one. Not the Kyrinin way, running onto swords and shields like that. As if they didn't care any more about their own lives. Perhaps they don't care enough about ours to try again.'

They went in a straggling single line through the fringe of Anlane, moving with less caution now than once they had. It did not take long for the forest to begin to thin. The trees were interspersed with stumps where the tallest and straightest of their brethren had been felled. Soon enough, there were more stumps than standing trees, and they came out at the crest of a long, shallow grassy slope. At its foot was a woodsman's cottage. Its shutters and door hung open. Crows roosting on its roof scattered upwards. Varryn was already halfway down the slope.

Orisian paused there, amongst the last of the saplings, Anlane's outliers. Beyond that cottage, stretching out into the grey veils of soft rain, was the Glas Valley. Flat ground scattered with clumps of trees, dotted here and there with lonely buildings almost lost in the mist. Home. But he felt neither welcomed nor relieved. It had been a kind of desperate hope that brought him here, yet now he could imagine nothing good coming of this return. And still, despite that terrible foreboding, he felt it was where he had to be. If he belonged anywhere, it was here, in this bleak moment; and if there was any purpose he could claim as his own, it awaited him somewhere out there in the mist. In his homeland.

II

Kan Avor dominated the grey skyline like a challenge. Kanin smiled at the sight of its jagged, broken towers, its crumbling sprawl. A great rotten bruise on the earth. His pleasure was not engendered by the city itself, though. It was what it signified that woke his venomous, obsessive desires and promised them fulfilment. In his imagination visions crowded in upon him: an endless succession of different deaths for Aeglyss. He could smell the halfbreed's blood, hear his wails, see his head springing free from the stump of his neck or his stomach split open by a single slash from a sword. He could feel his own hands about the halfbreed's throat, the bones in there cracking and splintering beneath his iron grasp.

Kanin fought to rid himself of these all-consuming imaginings, but could do no more than cordon them off in a part of his mind, so that though he still heard their intoxicating whispers and still felt that unbridled longing for the release their realisation would bring him, he had the space within his skull to think clearly. To do what needed doing.

The main body of his ragged army was streaming ahead of him, struggling through the marsh and mire towards Kan Avor. Lannis folk, most of that vanguard. They spread out as they advanced. Not an army at all, in truth. Just a mob given licence to visit vengeance upon their most hated enemies, blinded for the moment to the truth that they did so in service to another enemy. They would be worthless, Kanin knew, as soon as they met any organised resistance. But they could still serve a purpose, and it was a matter of complete indifference to Kanin whether a single one of them lived to see tomorrow's dawn. As was his own survival, as long as he achieved his goal before death claimed him.

His horse was restless beneath him, eager to follow the rushing figures ahead. He gave the reins a gentle tug, and muttered a soothing word or two to the animal. Sheets of heavier rain swept through, intermittently obscuring Kan Avor's looming form. All the land around the ruined city was turning into a swamp. Kanin did not mind. The mists and rain offered some concealment.

He twisted in the saddle and looked down the neat line of his Shield. Igris was despondent and sullen, rainwater trickling from his hair down over his cheekbones. Behind stood two hundred Black Road warriors, all on foot, all silent and grim-countenanced. This was all that Kanin had managed to retain his hold upon. The rest had rebelled, or disappeared, or gone mad. The Glasbridge they had left when they marched out that dawn was a chaos of warring bands, frenzied killing, hungers of every kind let off their leash.

'We move round to the south,' Kanin told Igris. 'Let those Lannis idiots draw out what they can of the halfbreed's defences.'

Igris stared dolefully after the vast rabble of townsfolk flailing its way across the flat ground, closing slowly on the distant ruins.

'Wake up,' snapped Kanin.

His shieldman stirred himself and nudged his horse into motion. Kanin's Shield led the way, and the rest of the warriors fell into column behind them. Kanin summoned Eska and the other two Hunt Inkallim with a flick of his head. They came, with Eska's three hounds following at their heels. The dogs' fur glistened with moisture, drawn like dew from the air and beaded over their bristly hides.

'I will find the halfbreed,' Kanin said to the Inkallim. 'I will try to kill him. You make your own away. Use whatever confusion we may create to draw near to him. Do nothing to endanger yourselves. Whatever Cannek may have told you, I do not want your aid. I refuse it, unless and until you see me within reach of the halfbreed, and act then only if in doing so you can aid me in striking him down. Do you understand?'

Eska nodded casually.

'Do you consent?' Kanin asked pointedly.

She smiled narrowly. 'I was commanded to preserve your life if I could, Thane. But it is difficult, when the one to be protected is so uninterested in his own continuation. It is our feeling –' she included her silent companions with a brief glance '– that either you or the halfbreed must die. It is evidently not possible for both of you to persist in this world. Therefore, keeping you alive seems to require that we first accomplish his destruction.'

'Good,' grunted Kanin.

Eska shrugged. 'Only sense. And, in any case, I dislike what I have seen of him and of his adherents, and of the kind of world he creates around him. Cannek's judgement of him feels right to me. Perhaps fate will yet validate it, through us.'

'If I fail,' Kanin said as he guided his horse after his marching warriors, 'if I fall, do not be deterred. I am sure the Hooded God, if he still watches over us, finds you more to his liking than me. Fate may yet favour you even if it condemns me.'

'Our feet are upon the Road, Thane,' Eska called after him.

He made no reply, but rode on through the rain.

The slaughter began far out to Kanin's left. He saw it dimly, through the obscuring, pulsing bands of drifting rain. He heard it fitfully, for the air was sluggish and an unwilling messenger.

But it pleased him, for it was a beginning; and once begun, this would flow quickly to its end.

Figures came running out from the grey bulk of Kan Avor, first just a few of them and then more and more until they swarmed across the boggy plain. There were no battle lines drawn up, no planning or preparation. People just emerged from the city and threw themselves at the motley forces advancing upon it. Kanin and his own company watched, but no enemy emerged to oppose their careful skirting of the city's southern edge. The killing and dying was done closer to the river, where the ground was as much water as earth.

Knee-deep in pools, tripped by tussocks of reed and grass, amongst the emergent bones of those who had died on this same field more than a century and a half before, the desperate and deranged flung themselves at each other. They drowned one another in the stagnant waters, fell and were trampled and suffocated in the sucking mud. They beat and tore with swords and fists and cudgels and stones. A few horses churned through the marsh, most of them ridden by ravens of the Battle Inkall, but they were clumsy and ponderous. The rain fell, and washed blood from wounds down into the waterlogged foundations of the valley; cries rose, and screams, into the vaporous clouds.

All of this Kanin saw from a distance, but even across that intervening space he felt the nature of it. He felt its savagery, its mindless, flailing, destructive energy. He felt the yearning it embodied: the hunger to kill and to be killed. He knew it well.

'Turn to the city,' he called out.

Entering Kan Avor, passing between its first shattered buildings and onto its foul streets, was to cross a threshold. Beyond, within, lay a land of the dead and mad, the crippled and ailing. Some of the bodies scattered through the ruins bore the marks of violence – many had been dismembered or were half-eaten – but more were unblemished. Sickness, starvation, exhaustion had made this blighted place their home. Skeletal forms lurked amongst the remains of the city. They stared out from its shadows, coughing and shivering and cowering.

The wet stench was foul: rotting flesh, excrement, burned meat. As Kanin led his company in, the ruins slowly rising about them as if clambering out of the saturated earth, he could hear dogs howling. Rats teemed in the shadows, running in gutters and alleys like streams of dark water. Above, broad-winged birds turned in endless circles, stacked above one another in columns of patient observation.

Soon, even amidst such dereliction, they were having to fight their way. Men and women spilled out from the side streets, came tumbling out from doorways, leaped down from rooftops or the tops of walls. Like animals, starving beasts, they threw themselves at Kanin's company. They came in such numbers and with such ferocious abandon that the column was scattered almost at once. Inchoate carnage spread itself through the ruins, all against all in a frenzy of bloodletting.

Through that violent sea, Kanin ploughed a steady path. He cut away the hands that clung to his saddle and tore at the reins. His horse reared and stamped down, pounding bodies into the sodden dirt, crushing them against ancient cobbles. The street was choked with pushing, surging masses of people. Forests of spears jostled towards him, rattling against one another. The air bristled with missiles of every kind. Stones and tiles and bolts and darts flew like great dark insects. Kanin felt blows on his shield and shoulders and legs, but none seemed to wound him.

And he found himself transported once more into that high, calm place where the demands of battle freed him of all other concerns and burdens. His sword rose and fell, the beat of a martial heart marking out the rhythm of his progress. The faceless horde that milled before and all around him was to him as inanimate and brute a thing as a thicket of tangled undergrowth. He carved his way through it, and its blood painted his boots and his blade and the flanks of his plunging, straining mount. He took no joy in it, for in itself it had no meaning to him. But his body felt more filled with fiery life than it had in a long time, and his mind as light and free.

Ahead, through the rain, he could see the cluster of decapitated towers at the heart of the city. Once the abode, he dimly recognised, of the Thanes of Gyre; once the sanctuary in which the faltering fledgling creed of the Black Road had been protected and nurtured. Without that protection, so much would have been different. Everything would have been different. And those same shattered palaces would not now be the abode of abomination and corruption. Eska had assured him he would find Aeglyss there, lodged in the very centre of this dead place, like a maggot deep in the flesh of a carcass.

The crowds in front of him thinned, and he stabbed his horse's flanks with his heels. It burst forward into an expanse of open ground. Other riders came with him and erupted into that space with wild cries. They rode down the scattering dregs of their opponents, driving spears into backs. Kanin wheeled his horse about, aware that it was breathing badly, perhaps wounded, certainly on the fringes of panic. Igris and a few others of his Shield were emerging from the street. Blood – their own and that of others – was on their faces, in their hair, splattered across their chain vests and leather gauntlets. The drizzle made countless red tears of it, flowing down over them.

Battle still raged behind them and on every side. Screams and the clash of weapons echoed flatly from the stones of the dead city, heavy on the air. Figures struggled back and forth, fell, faltered, died.

'Did you see Eska?' Kanin shouted at Igris.

His shieldman shook his head dumbly. Kanin did not care. He had cast his dice, and in the casting had liberated himself. He looked around at the undulating walls that bordered this grey field of rubble and mud. There were beams of rotten wood sticking out from a heap of stones, split and eroded and draped in rotting plant matter. A dead woman was sitting with her back resting against one of those beams, her head slumped forward onto her chest, her arms laid limply on the ground beside her.

This place, this whole foul city, had been dead for more than a hundred years and dying for longer. Death was drawn to it, and freeing it from its long inundation had only opened the way for ever more mortality and decay and corruption to flow into it and fill its derelict streets. Kanin, for those few transcendent moments as he turned about, was filled with the sudden desire to see everything, every detail of the desolation, and take it all into him. He was, he thought, the avatar of death, returning in fierce splendour to his natural home. Aeglyss was not in truth the lord of this place or of the world that was being born; no, it was Kanin himself, and the slaughter that attended upon him.

The moment, the vision, passed, and he sank back into his saddle. He was still imbued with a desperate excitement, but he was only a man once more. He led his warriors across the rubble and puddles and corpses towards an opening – the stone-formed memory of a street, perhaps, that once ran from this wide square. It carried them deeper, closer to the jagged bulk of palaces and parapets in which all Kanin's desires were now invested.

Like vermin, like swarming vermin, the inhabitants of Kan Avor came clambering and staggering from every side. Kanin and his Shield were beset once more, their horses plunging through a clawing sea of outstretched hands, a rain of stones. His sword arm ached, but his mounting anger drowned out that weary pain. He raged against the capacity of this city to oppose him; to vomit this unending flood of poisoned flesh up from its crevices and alleyways and drains, and batter at him with it.

He was turned about for a moment as his horse faltered in confusion or weakness. He saw two of his men go down, dragged into the gaping maw of the mob and devoured. He saw how few warriors remained at his side and at his back. And his horse slumped down, tried to rise, and failed. The throng closed on him. He was crushed and beaten and choked with the heat and stink of bodies. The light of the muted day was dimmed still further as a dozen hands hauled him from his saddle, and the crowd engulfed him. But he still had his sword and still had strength in his legs.

He rose, and made of his blade and shield a storm. He killed and killed until he was no longer alone; until Igris was there, and others. Until they opened a path of corpses that led on. Deeper.

There were only six of them. Their horses were gone, all dragged down. The rest of the warriors were dead or scattered, fighting their own doomed battles now. Behind them, the entire city seethed with slayers and their victims, their voices and their struggles filling the sky with a single shrill howl.

Kanin ran, and Kan Avor yielded its heart to him. It took him in beneath the cliffs of its greatest edifices, and led him down cobbled streets, past doorways with carved lintels, and eroded statues bedecked in regalia of mud and moss. It took him into its rotten core.

The first of the Battle Inkallim came running alone, quite suddenly, from beneath a cracked archway, a long thin axe held out to her side. Like a dark arrow. Kanin veered towards her, but two of his Shield were closer and faster. They stepped between Thane and raven. And the raven feinted and weaved her darting way inside a sword thrust, and split one of their skulls. The second shieldman cut her across the hamstring, and she staggered but did not lose her grip on the axe. It came free of bone, and swung low and hard into the man's knee, taking his leg from under him, the joint flexing at an impossible angle.

The Inkallim limped another clumsy pace towards Kanin before she fell. He hammered his sword halfway through her neck. Her eyes turned white as they tipped back in their orbits.

'Sire,' Igris shouted.

Kanin turned. Seven more Inkallim, arrayed across the street. They were relaxed, their shoulders loose, their expressions full of calm confidence. Two leaned on spears; others cradled naked swords. Shraeve was there, arms folded across her chest, staring at Kanin.

'Have enough died yet, Thane, to assuage your anger?' she asked him levelly. 'Have you amassed sufficient dead to convince you of your error?'

Igris and the last two of his Shield – one man, one woman – stood in front of Kanin.

Shraeve smiled as they formed that defiant barrier.

'Your forces are somewhat meagre, Thane. If fate's favour is measured in numbers, I think you find yourself condemned.'

Kanin looked back over his shoulder. The way he had come was closed off: thirty or more men and women, warriors and commonfolk and Tarbains. All wild-eyed, half of them bloodied. The rain had stopped, he realised. Blood no longer ran freely, but thickened and crusted on skin.

His hopes became dust. What had seemed so possible now was plain folly. What madness had been upon him that he had thought himself capable of overcoming the fever of an entire world?

'You did not think we would leave him undefended, did you?' Shraeve said.

He stared back at her, and in that stare she evidently found the answer to any and all questions.

'Very well,' she said with a dead smile.

And even as she spoke, two spears were in the air, spinning along shallow arcs. Kanin started forward. So did Igris and the other two of his Shield. Only Kanin and Igris completed more than half a stride, as the spears hit home.

Shraeve did not even move. The six other ravens spread into a half-circle, sinking gently into fighting stances. Kanin and

Igris found themselves back to back, as that half-circle slowly extended itself, reaching to enclose them.

'My feet are on the Road,' Kanin heard his shieldman murmuring. 'My feet are on the Road.'

Kanin bit back his scorn for such futile fidelity. But what did it matter? Death came as it wished, and what rode in its wake only the dead could know. Let those entering its embrace believe what they wished. To die a fool was no worse than to die alone and faithless.

A flurry of blows. The scuffing of feet over the grimy cobbles. A hissing gasp. Kanin did not look round. He could not, for the three Inkallim facing him edged closer, eyeing him with all the focused intent of hounds stalking a stag at bay.

'Igris?' he muttered.

He heard metal on metal. Something – a shield, perhaps – striking the ground. Another muffled impact and then silence.

Igris slumped against Kanin's back. The sudden weight almost made him lose his balance, but he leaned against it. Slowly, the burden slid down his spine into the small of his back, across his thighs. Then it was gone, and Kanin swayed for a moment. He spared only the briefest of instants to look down and see Igris lying there, face down, his head by Kanin's feet. There was blood on his neck and scalp.

Kanin grinned at the nearest of the Inkallim.

'So be it,' he said.

But they backed away. They opened the circle that had held him and fell slowly back into rank across the street, aligning themselves with Shraeve once more. Past her shoulder, past the hilt of her sword, two dozen paces back, at the base of a tall column of curved stonework that could only encase a stairway, a door was opening. Kanin straightened, lowering his sword, letting his shield come back to his side.

And Aeglyss emerged.

III

Aeglyss leaned heavily on Hothyn the White Owl as he advanced out into the street. His head – a simple skull, almost, in its gaunt and fleshless angles – lolled on a limp neck. The plain robe he wore was patterned with brown and red and black stains, the exudates of the wrecked and porous body beneath.

At the sight of him, Kanin was instantly blind to all else, and he sprang forward.

'Be still,' Aeglyss said, like a thunderclap on the damp air.

Kanin staggered to a halt, dizzied. The world spun about him for a moment, a swirling vision of dirty grey stonework and mud and figures that flashed past too quickly to be recognised. He steadied himself. The *na'kyrim* was staring at him, and that gaze was all contempt, all confidence.

Shraeve started to move. Long, languid strides, hands reaching slowly up for the hilts that framed her face. Her eyes were on Kanin, wholly committed to his death. And he could see it quite clearly for himself. He could envisage with the utmost clarity his own graceful execution. She would be like a hawk, composed entirely of speed and power, falling upon him. He would die now on Shraeve's twin blades, and go into the darkness knowing he had failed. He would follow Wain, knowing there would never be an answer to her death.

He knew all this, and the weight of it felt as though it would crush his heart, but still he hefted his sword in his hand and tightened his grip upon the straps of his shield until the leather creaked, and stepped forward to meet her. Perhaps . . . perhaps . . .

'Wait,' said Aeglyss.

Shraeve stopped. She passed from motion into perfect immobility in the blink of an eye. Her gaze remained locked onto Kanin. He found that he had come to a halt too. Two dozen paces separated Thane and raven. Kanin could feel his heart thumping, straining, in his chest. Its beat was the only sound in all the world. A silence descended upon them all, every warrior gathered there at Kan Avor's centre.

Then Aeglyss was edging sideways, his gown trailing through the mud. He moved like an ancient, all brittleness and fragility. But his voice . . . his voice was like the ocean.

'You have done all that you could have done, Bloodheir,' the halfbreed rasped. 'No. Thane. I forget. Or remember too much.'

He coughed and shivered. Blood was trickling from his nose. Hothyn followed him, a watchful, silent attendant.

'You never understood, though. Because there is something in you – this hatred – that deafens you, blinds you, you never grasped what has been happening all around you. You see only the surface of things. But you needed to *feel*, Thane, if you were to understand.'

Aeglyss extended a bony arm, and pressed his hand against a wall. He leaned thus, letting the ruined city take his weight.

'If you could have felt it, you would have understood that this is not something you can undo. Not with all your hatred, all your stubbornness. You are not equal to the task of opposing me, because I am become the world.'

There were cracks in the skin of the halfbreed's naked scalp, Kanin could see. Fissures in him. Failings of the body. But it was not his body that filled the street, coiled like fog around the buildings, streamed out from the stones. It was not in his limbs that his awful strength resided.

'I am become the world,' Aeglyss repeated. His eyes were closed. His eyelids were seeping sores. 'And it would be easy to let you die, for the world is finished with you. But that is not what I want. And the choice is mine to make.'

'No,' said Kanin through gritted teeth. The denial cost him a great effort, for the halfbreed's monumental will had hold of him.

'Yes. You will be what I want you to be, Thane, because that is the nature of things now. Surely you do not imagine you could have come this far, had I not permitted it? I think a thing, and it becomes real. That is what . . . that is how . . . No, no. Things have happened . . . Did I dream them? Scavenge them from the memory of the world? Things I never wanted . . .'

Then something darted from the ruins, some dark fleck of movement that leaped towards the *na'kyrim*. It was too fast to follow, too fleeting for any of them to react. Any of them save the one Kyrinin. In the time it took Kanin to turn his head, Hothyn managed a single surging stride, set his hands on the halfbreed's shoulders, twisted and hauled him aside, and caught the crossbow bolt square in his own back.

The White Owl fell against Aeglyss, and in the manner of that collapse Kanin could see at once that he was dead. Aeglyss swayed for a moment, reaching round to grasp the stub of the quarrel that had buried itself between ribs and deep into the heart beyond, then the Kyrinin's weight was too much for him and he toppled backwards.

The passage of time slowed. Shraeve was pointing. Inkallim were running, homing on the source of that fatal dart. Kanin blinked – it felt glacial and leaden – and looked back to Aeglyss. The *na'kyrim* was pinned beneath Hothyn's corpse, struggling feebly to roll it away. And Kanin moved. One long stride, then another, giant paces that swept him over the silt-packed cobbles. There was nothing save the sight of the halfbreed, down and distracted, and the feel of his own body, the might that coursed through his legs and his shoulders and chest. The world, the future, fate: all of it yielding itself to him and opening itself. He had but to reach out and take hold of what was offered. He ran towards Aeglyss, and his sword was rising, attaining the height from which it would fall, and in falling salve all hurts.

Shraeve hit him from the side, driving her shoulder into his armpit. It felt like a log of hardwood punching into his ribcage, and it knocked him from his feet. She somersaulted away from him and somehow twisted so that she came to rest facing him, crouched on one foot, one knee, hands already up and grasping the hilts of her swords. Kanin tried to get to his feet, but his shield hampered him. He was too slow, he knew. He had seen Shraeve fight; seen her speed.

But the Inkallim was smiling, rising without urgency. Her two swords eased free of their scabbards and she held them out, one on either side, rolling her wrists so that the blades stirred the air in lazy circles.

Kanin's flank where she had hit him protested violently as he lifted himself off the cobblestones. He used sword and shield to lever himself up, and forced himself to straighten, ignoring the cramping pain from his ribs. He wanted to look for Aeglyss, but Shraeve was advancing slowly, that disdainful smile still upon her face.

'Come, then,' Kanin murmured. He would welcome it now, to be freed from the chains of sorrow and failed hopes.

'I killed your sister, Thane,' Shraeve said quietly. 'Not Aeglyss. Me. It was necessary.'

'Necessary. Necessary.' Kanin repeated the word in incomprehension. It had no meaning to him, his mind could not grasp its shape. It bore no relation he could conceive of to Wain. To her death. Yet it filled him with renewed fire. It burned away the dull fog of surrender.

He threw himself at the Inkallim, and heard as he did so, as if from very far away, Aeglyss crying out, 'Don't kill him.'

She was all that he had imagined she would be. A dark and dancing flame, always and inevitably just out of reach. He fought as he never had before, knowing that there was nothing to preserve his strength, or will, or passion. It all came to this.

Shraeve's swords wove fluid webs which he could not penetrate. They notched his shield and struck splinters from its face.

Her body described patterns that he did not recognise, and could not follow or predict. His blunt attacks lagged always an instant behind, though he poured every last measure of his skill and effort into them. His boots scraped and slipped across the uneven surface of the street; hers flowed. She laid open his cheek. She dented the chain links on his breast.

Kanin had never been so wholly present within the moments of a battle. He had never been so fast or so acutely conscious of each movement, each fractional instant. He had never been a better warrior than he was there, facing Shraeve in the decrepit streets of the shattered city, beneath broken towers. And it was not enough. From the first ringing touch of their contending blades, he had understood that it would not be enough.

He cut at her hip. Shraeve blocked the blow. As he pulled his sword arm back to gather the distance for another attempt, he found the point of her second sword pursuing it, lancing diagonally between the two of them towards his elbow. He straightened that retreating arm out and twisted his shoulder back to let Shraeve's lunge take her across him. She turned as she went, showing her back to him. He began to bring his shield sweeping up and around, aiming its rim at the side of her head. A sudden dip and surge and Shraeve was rising, still turning, in the air; moving no longer across him but towards him. Her trailing arm was snapping round. Kanin saw it, read its path, and could do nothing to prevent it.

A dark blur, as of a rock rushing down at him, and the pommel of her sword hit his cheekbone, just in front of his ear. He felt his shield strike Shraeve, but she rolled over it, like an acrobat playing games at a feast. The impact had blinded him. Pain flashed through his skull, as bright and loud as summer lightning. There was a ringing whine in his ears. His legs softened, the knee joints quaking and yawing as he staggered, sinking towards the cobblestones.

Another stunning blow, in the centre of his chest, deadening him. He plunged backwards, blind and deaf. His body was nothing but pain and crushing pressure. He hit a wall or perhaps the ground, the back of his head cracking against stone, and felt consciousness faltering. The beat of his heart slowed and slowed.

'Don't kill him,' he heard the *na'kyrim* saying again as he receded.

*

As soon as the bolt had leaped from her crossbow, Eska was gone. She ducked and scrambled on all fours away from the waist-high stump of wall that had concealed her. Behind her, shouts, pursuit. She did not need to look. Shraeve's ravens – perhaps even Shraeve herself – would be pouring through this labyrinthine rubble in moments. If she had permitted herself the luxury of such feelings, that might have given Eska a certain pleasure. She would, in many ways, welcome the testing of her skills against their cruder abilities. The Battle might benefit from a lesson in humility.

Now, though, it was escape that dominated her thoughts. She had glimpsed, down the path her quarrel had carved through the air towards the *na'kyrim*'s chest, the woodwight's first reflexive movement. He had reacted with an immediacy she would not have thought possible. This was a lesson for her; one she would remember, should she ever be required to hunt his kind. She could not be certain, for certainty would have demanded hesitation, but she guessed that he might even have been sufficiently fast to save the halfbreed. Her sole concern now was to keep herself alive long enough to find out, and if necessary to rectify her failure.

She hauled herself, snake-like, through a hole at the base of a wall. Frost or flood had broken out just enough stones to permit her passage. In the unroofed chamber beyond, the mud was deep. It coated her face and stomach as she slithered into it and sprang upright. There were three corpses here, lying as if asleep against piles of fallen building blocks, wrapped in blankets. They had been alive when she first came this way. Sick, probably dying, but alive. She had seen many such pathetic groupings as she picked her way through Kan Avor's dismal maze. Half the people of the city seemed to be in the grip of one affliction or another. The febrile suffering of these three in particular, she had chosen to end. It would have been intolerable to her to leave them there alive – even if only barely – across her chosen escape route. She paused only long enough to sling her crossbow across her back, roll one of the bodies aside and retrieve her spear from where she had left it, hidden beneath that dead flesh.

She vaulted through what had once been a window, and splashed into the puddle of filthy water beyond. The ruins stretched out before her, the leaning, slumping carcasses of countless houses. She ran into that thicket of stone, more concerned with speed now than concealment. The Battle would come quickly, as was their wont. They seldom submitted themselves to the restraint of subtlety.

It would have been easier had she not been left alone by the unpredictable tumult of Kan Avor. One of her fellow Inkallim she had heard die, overrun by the raving mob that he led away from her. The other had simply disappeared as if the city had opened and folded itself about him.

Even now, the sounds of war hung over Kan Avor like a fell miasma. The fire Kanin oc Horin-Gyre had lit had taken on a life of its own, and Eska could feel for herself the creeping, persuasive seductions of its sole imperative. Its hunger for death and violence gnawed at the edges of her mind, trying to make her its own. There would be few save the dead left here by nightfall.

Against the background murmur of slaughter, she caught a nearer sound: splashing footfalls behind her, the rattle of scabbards on belts. Too close to be ignored. It was not, then, to be easy. Still, she had one ally left to her. She turned in a narrow passageway floored with great square paving stones. The remnant walls that bounded it were high enough and narrow enough to make it ill-suited to swordplay; a spear, though, would work well. As she stood there, settling into a ready stance, she whistled: a long, keening note.

The first of the ravens appeared at the end of the passage, shouted at the sight of her, and came straight at her. He was a big man, and broad. Behind him, she glimpsed one, two more, but his dark mass blocked her sight of them as he closed on her. She read his intent in his eyes and his pace: he would impale himself upon her spear, and keep it there, in his body, while his companions rushed over him to cut her down. Typical of the Battle. And likely to undo her, Eska judged. She whistled again, still louder.

The Battle Inkallim was almost on her. She dipped into a crouch, bracing herself. The force of his charge onto her spear shook down through its shaft into her hands. She resisted only enough to be certain that mortal damage was done, and to hear the roaring, gasping bursting of the air out from his lungs, and then she dropped the spear, turned and ran.

She could hear them coming after her, stamping over their dying fellow. But she could hear something else now, ahead of her rather than behind, and it was a sound that might yet save her.

The hound came into the narrow gullet of constricting rubble at a pounding gallop, teeth already bared in a spittle-ornamented snarl, its massive shoulders pumping, its back flexing as it strained for every fragment of speed its frame could give. It came with fury, for that was what her call had demanded of it. This was the last of them – the others had died clearing her path in through the outskirts – and it was the best, for she had chosen to preserve it for just such a moment as this.

She hurdled the beast as it bounded towards her, and it flowed beneath her without faltering. It had eyes only for those following in her wake. She landed and spun on her heels, already shrugging the crossbow free from her back. She watched the great dog fling itself up at the throat of the leading Inkallim, even as her hands dragged back the bow's string, as her fingers went to the quiver of bolts at her belt and plucked one out. Dog and raven went down, thrashing in a confusion of limbs. They battered themselves, both of them, against the stonework, against the ground. The kicking of the Inkallim's legs, and the thick, desperate cries, told her the hound's teeth had found a grip.

The second of the ravens could not pass the flailing combatants. He hacked at them instead, raining ferocious indiscriminate blows down. His blade opened the dog's haunch, broke its hip, skinned its shoulder, and still it fought and shook its massive head, tearing at flesh. The woman beneath it had stopped struggling. The last of the Inkallim set both hands on the hilt of his sword and raised it before him, point down. He plunged it into the hound's body, just behind its neck, and the animal gave a gurgling whimper and went limp.

The man looked up then, sword still buried deep in the dog, and his eyes met Eska's. She was sighting down the line of the quarrel. She saw his recognition of his fate. He tensed to withdraw his blade. She freed the bolt, and it was in his chest, and he fell silently back. His sword stood there, erect. It had gone through the dog and into the dead woman beneath.

IV

The cottage smelled of abandonment. The outside, the winter, had seeped into its fabric, softened it and made it no longer habitation but incipient ruin. There were browned leaves on the floor, blown in through open windows. Dark stains tracked the invasive waters that had found their way in through an unmended roof. It was cold and empty in the way only a place that had long lacked a fire in its hearth, and voices around its table, could be.

Orisian ran his fingers over the carved bowls that were still neatly stacked on a shelf and the bottles draped with cobwebs. The detritus of lives now lost or driven off. There were no bodies, at least. Orisian could remember all too clearly another woodsman's cottage, on the slopes of the Car Criagar, where a good deal of blood had been spilled. That place had smelled much worse.

Ess'yr lay on a low, hard bed. Orisian saw in her something entirely new: a fragile vulnerability. Pangs of a powerful emotion swept through him, but it was no simple thing. He felt it acutely, but could not fully understand it. Guilt, longing, fear. All those things and perhaps more.

'Can I get you something?' he asked softly, not wanting to rouse K'rina from her torpor on the other side of the room. 'Water? Food?'

'Nothing,' Ess'yr whispered.

He sat on the edge of the bed; felt the lightest of contact between the small of his back and her thigh. She appeared to be on the brink of sleep or unconsciousness. Her eyes, as she looked up into his face, would lose their focus now and again, and drift, then return to him and be sharp and clear once more. Even her intricate tattoos, the token of the lives she had taken, seemed to have lost some of their colour and faded a little into the pallor of her skin.

'You would never have been here if you had not found me that night,' Orisian said. 'Winterbirth.'

He could see in her eyes that she heard him, and understood him, but she said nothing. If she felt pain, she did not show it. Now, as ever, she drew upon reserves of calm and composure he had seen in no one else, calm that exceeded the capacity of the world to assail it. It was, he suddenly realised, something precious beyond limit to him: that there should be someone near at hand who had within them that imperturbable strength, that resilient self-possession and balance. Someone, he thought, who had found that core of grace and peace and persistence that he had unknowingly been seeking himself since the Heart Fever stole the better part of his life away.

Inurian had had it in some measure. Ess'yr had it in abundance. Orisian looked at her and saw . . . he saw another world, another life. In those sculpted features and their unutterable grace he saw a world that should have been. One in which there had been no deaths, no Heart Fever even; in which there was still laughter, and companionship, and a lightness of spirit. He was not sure whether he was a part of that world he glimpsed. He did not know whether, in it, he would have found her. He did not even know whether what he saw came from within her, or within him, or from somewhere else entirely. But it was, despite that, utterly beautiful to him. It was filled with light, and that light shone in her alabaster skin, and in her eyes, and in her fine, frail lips.

He reached out carefully, and touched her. As he had imagined doing so often. He laid his fingertips on the curve of her chin, and felt a gossamer strand of her gleaming hair brush the back of his hand. Through his fingers he felt her warmth, and it seemed to him that that was a part of the light too. He leaned towards her, sinking as if towards a dream.

And her hand was on his chest, gentle but firm. The slightest roll of her head took her skin away from his fingers. He felt the pressure of her hand on his breastbone. It was not urgent, not hard, but it was calmly insistent. She slowly pushed him back and lifted his face away from hers.

'No,' she said, soft as the movement of a feather, and the light receded. What he had seen, that place, that possibility he had caught a distant sight of, faded. He felt alone and reduced. But he nodded, just once.

Ess'yr let her arm fall back to her side. She closed her eyes. Orisian rose from the bed and walked away. He could remember the light, just. He could remember how it had made him feel. But not what it contained. Not precisely what it was that might have been.

Outside the cottage he found a colourless world, desolate. The stumps of felled trees. The cold prickle of drizzle on the air. A muffled, sluggish silence.

Yvane was sitting on a stump not far away. She was picking dried berries from a clay pot she must have found somewhere inside, placing them one by one into her mouth. She watched Orisian as he emerged and stood blinking up at the featureless clouds. He turned away from her. There was a path beaten into the grass. He followed it to the side of a tiny stream running in a narrow cut between concealing clumps of grass and rushes. He knelt down and scooped searingly cold water over his face. It ran from his chin and bubbled on his lips as he breathed through it.

He sat there and looked back towards the cabin. It looked lifeless, even now. It looked as though it belonged to the brooding forest that waited just a little way up the slope. Yvane was walking towards him, still eating those berries as she came. He ignored her, and stared at the timber walls, the slanting roof, the collapsed woodshed, as if the cottage and its contents were a mystery he might unravel by examination; as if it held a secret truth. But his mind was empty. For the first time in days – weeks – there was a hollow silence in him. Nothing.

'She will probably live, if the wound stays clean,' Yvane said, looking down at him. 'If she's tended.'

He nodded but said nothing. The *na'kyrim* offered him the little pot and the last of the wizened fruits it contained. He waved it away.

'If Varryn finds the medicines he's out looking for now,' Yvane added. 'It's not the best of seasons for it—'

'She will live,' Orisian interrupted her.

Yvane sniffed. 'Probably.' She lifted the pot and tipped its contents into her mouth.

'She will,' Orisian said.

Yvane bent and raised a handful of water to her lips.

'I hope you're right,' she said, after she had swallowed it down.

Movement at the door of the cottage drew Orisian's attention. K'rina came hesitantly out into the damp, stumbling, her arms folded across her chest. She made her way northwards over the dark grass. Yvane saw Orisian was looking that way, and turned to follow his gaze. She sighed.

'I'll . . .' the *na'kyrim* began, but Orisian shook his head.

'No need. See?'

Taim and one of the warriors were coming, returning from their foray out into the fogs and rains of the valley. They trudged steadily and slowly up towards the cabin, adjusting their path without a break in stride to intercept K'rina's weaving course. Orisian and Yvane watched the two burly men close on the oblivious *na'kyrim* and gather her up, turn her about and ease her back towards the bed she had risen from. They were gentle, as if they shepherded a sick child, or a simple one.

'Before we left Highfast, I spoke with Eshenna about K'rina,' Yvane said.

Orisian stood up. The movement dizzied him.

'She was a kind and gentle woman, from the sound if it,' Yvane went on. 'Too kind and gentle, perhaps. She cared for Aeglyss, back there in Dyrkyrnon, when no one else would.'

'Don't, Yvane.'

'No, you should hear this. Why not? She made good fish traps, apparently. And knew the best places to put them. She caught a lot of fish. She used to sing to the children. Old Huanin songs. Her parents were—'

'Yvane . . .'

'Why don't you want to know?'

Orisian could have left her, walked away from her and taken refuge in the cottage. But something in him would not permit that. Something chose to face her. They were both quite calm. For once, there was not the slightest trace of argument between them.

'Because it's not knowledge I can do anything with,' he said to her.

'Her parents . . . Ah, I can't remember their names. Eshenna told me, but it's so hard to keep things clear now.' Yvane rubbed her cheek wearily. 'But it doesn't matter. The point is that she had parents, they gave her life. She was a child once, and grew, and lived and thought and hoped and wanted. All of that wasn't for this. Not be made into . . . this. To be used.'

'I know. She had a life. I know that. She didn't deserve any of this. But how many of our lives turn out the way we hope they will? *Na'kyrim*, Huanin, Kyrinin. We none of us deserved any of this, did we?'

'It's her love for Aeglyss . . . Whatever's been done to her, it's hung on the hook of her love for him. She's the moth to his flame, or maybe it's the other way round now. But it started with love.'

'It's too late for this, Yvane. This is where we are. There's no going back, no unpicking what's brought us here.'

'You're taking her to her death.'

'We don't know that,' Orisian snapped. 'Unless you know more than you've told me, we can't be sure. Do you? Have you kept something from me?'

Yvane returned his gaze sternly.

'I know nothing more than you,' she said. 'But don't pretend you understand less than you do.'

'I might have led us all to our deaths. All of us, Yvane. We could all die. Every one of us. Do you want to know the name of every man's parents? What about Ess'yr? Shall we drag her from her bed, demand that she shares with us her family, her life? I don't know the name of her mother or her father. I don't know where she was born, where she has been. I don't know . . . Shall we . . .'

He faltered, suddenly becoming aware of how his voice was rising. There was a dampness on his face and when he touched a fingertip to it, he was surprised to discover that he was weeping.

'She will live,' Yvane said quietly.

'I . . .' Orisian mumbled, hearing the words as if someone else spoke them, 'I . . . was born in Castle Kolglas. I learned how to hawk with my sister and my brother, along the shore. My mother sang. It was the greatest happiness . . . It was like joy when she sang. Her name was Lairis. My father's name was Kennet. And my brother's . . . my brother's name was Fariel.'

He shook his head.

'We die,' he said. 'We all die. Known or unknown, mourned or unmourned. All that we are, and all that we have been, passes. We all come to that same end, and it's neither just nor deserved nor glorious. You don't need me to tell you that, Yvane. And you know as well as I do, better than I do, that all of this – Aeglyss, everything – all of it has to stop, somehow. If it doesn't . . . if it doesn't we're all lost.'

A brief fire in her eyes – the heat of anger – and sudden venom in her voice. 'And it's always *na'kyrim*, isn't it, who pay the price? Every convulsion, every war, whatever its cause, it's *na'kyrim* who get crushed in the middle of it. Too strange, too different . . . too feared . . .'

She lifted a hand to her brow, wincing in pain or distress.

'I'm sorry,' she muttered. 'I'm sorry. It's . . . I lose track of myself . . . I can't tell what's his, what's mine. There's so much hurt to draw on. Or perhaps it draws on me, on all of us. But I know . . . I do know. She's all we – you – have. There's nothing else to set against what he's become.'

'Then why? Why fight against it? Why make it hard?'

'It should be hard, don't you think?' she said at once, with just a hint of that old combative note. All her own that, none of it borrowed from the Shared. 'That's all that's changed, now that Aeglyss has loosed his poison in the Shared: it's made it easy. It's taken away everything that should be there, all the restraints and hesitations and sympathies. It's freed us all to surrender to the darkest of our instincts, the most painful of our memories. And I don't want it to be so easy.'

She lifted her hands as if to beg for his understanding, but then let them sink back.

'He's made of the Shared, the whole, something that separates us all, turns us inwards, and leaves us with nothing for company but our anger or grief or fear or hate. The one thing that binds and unites us, and he used it to divide us. He made us alone.'

Her voice fell as she spoke. She seemed suddenly so much older and more fragile than ever before that Orisian almost reached out to take her hands. Yet comfort felt like a lie to him. It had no place here or anywhere. And perhaps that was of Aeglyss' making as well, but even if so it made the bleak thought no less certain, no less tenaciously rooted in his mind.

'You stay here, with Ess'yr,' he said. 'There's nothing more you can do. I'll . . . I'll take K'rina. No, not take her; I will only follow where she leads now, Yvane. I'll force nothing on her, just keep her safe, as the Anain who fashioned her can no longer do. Justly or unjustly, the need – the desire – is in her. All I will do is give her the protection she needs to fulfil it. If that is a cruelty, and cold . . . I don't know. It seems to me that it's the smallest of the cruelties that lie ahead down other paths any of us – all of us – might follow.'

'Do you know where we are?' Orisian asked Taim softly as they stood together in the doorway of the cottage.

The warrior frowned out at the landscape slowly emerging from the thinning mists. A heavy dusk was gathering, settling itself across the dank, still valley, but in this last slow hour of the day it was yet possible to see some way over the grassland and the fields. A solitary owl – not white but pale like sand – was ghosting its way through the murk. There was no other movement. No sound.

'I've an idea,' he said. 'South of Grive. Kan Avor can't be more than a day's walk, if that's what you're thinking.'

'It is. But it'll be a night's walk.' Orisian grunted. 'We've become creatures of darkness. I fear daylight more than the shadows now. And there's no time to wait, in any case.'

Taim glanced back into the gloomy interior of the hut. Yvane was crouched at Ess'yr's bedside, applying a fresh poultice of the herbs Varryn had brought back from the forest. The Kyrinin himself stood behind her, watching every movement with a dark intensity on his face.

'She can't travel any further,' Taim said.

'No. Yvane will stay with her, tend her. It's . . . it's probably for the best in any case. I wouldn't want her . . . either of them . . .'

Orisian let the sentence fade away. It was a fruitless thought. All thoughts seemed fruitless, defeated by the unfathomable obscurity of the future. It was as if an endless bank of sea fog lay across his path, impenetrable to foresight. He found he did not fear it, though. He almost welcomed it, for the promise of release it offered. Its dark, unknowable embrace could be no more harsh, no more painful, than that of the present or of his memories.

'Owinn is the only one left, I think,' said Taim. He nodded towards the young warrior seated on a tree stump, methodically cleaning the blade of his sword with a handful of wet grass. 'The other two haven't returned. We may have lost them. Or they've lost themselves.'

'Is he . . .?' Orisian was unsure how to ask the question, but Taim understood anyway.

'He seems calm. Untouched. Can't be certain, of course. Nothing seems certain any more. But so far I've seen nothing in him to make me fear for him.'

'He can stay, then. Guard them. I would go alone, Taim, if I thought I could. I'd take no one but K'rina. But if we find trouble . . .'

'I know,' Taim said levelly. 'I wouldn't stay, even if you commanded me to.'

'I'm sorry,' Orisian said. 'I truly am.'

Taim smiled. There was great weariness in it, yet Orisian was struck by how easily it seemed to come to the warrior's lips. There was nothing forced or pretended about it.

'Enough sorrow already,' Taim murmured. 'It mends nothing. Now we just see what happens.'

Orisian went to stand over Ess'yr. Yvane had moved away, crushing roots with the heel of her hand on the scored, frayed surface of an old table. Varryn remained, though, looking down at his sister. He stared at her with such concentration, with so knitted a brow and such narrow eyes, that it seemed he might almost imagine he could heal her grave wound by strength of will alone.

Ess'yr herself was awake; conscious, if only distantly so. Her eyelids were heavy.

'We will have to leave you here,' Orisian said to her. He did not bend towards her or reach for her, or do anything to close the distance between them. There was no bridge to lay across that gap now. He knew that. He could never draw any nearer to her than this, never know any more of her than what he already did. It was a terrible loss to him, that fading away into nothing of possibility. He could not even say whether he was capable of bearing it, for the burdens on his heart no longer differentiated themselves one from the other. They merely pressed down, a single, slow pressure that one day, he knew, would become insupportable in its collective weight.

It took her a moment or two to focus on his face. He wondered what she saw but could read nothing in her gaze.

'Taim and I will take K'rina a little further. As close as we can to wherever it is she wants to go. Tonight.'

At first he was not sure she could even hear him. Her lips, her eyes, remained motionless and placid. But then she moistened those lips with the tip of her tongue.

'Go well,' she whispered.

He nodded. It seemed wholly insufficient, yet there was nothing more in him to say. Nothing that the sadness within him would permit to rise to his lips, at least. To leave now would be to leave an ocean of words unuttered; to attempt to make words of the ocean would do nothing to drain it. He turned away.

'I think Inurian would find it good, what you do,' he heard Ess'yr say in that frail voice. 'He would find it wise.'

'I hope so.'

He felt a powerful need to be outside, free of the confinement of that cottage. The rain might be gone, the mists cleared, but the cold air of the descending night still bore enough moisture to make its touch soft and fresh. He closed his eyes and lifted his face towards the sky.

He did not know how long he stood thus. No thoughts, none of the turbulence that had grown so familiar, troubled him. He simply stood, face uplifted, until the softest of movements at his side drew him back.

'My sister . . .' said Varryn, uncharacteristically subdued and hesitant '. . . my sister asks that I go with you.'

Orisian frowned.

'Stay,' he said. 'Watch over her. She may need you.'

Conflicting emotions disturbed Varryn's smooth features, like the shadows of the roiling clouds passing overhead. It was a momentary perturbation; he set his jaw firmly, pushed his chin out a fraction.

'No,' the Kyrinin said. 'I will go with you.'

'Why?' Orisian asked, but Varryn had already turned and was ducking his head under the cabin's lintel.

Orisian stared after him briefly. Then the sound of that owl, calling its melancholy notes out across the valley, drew him back to the soft night. There was nothing to see. Darkness had all but engulfed the land now. And when Orisian looked out into it, he saw not so much the absence of light as the absence of everything. A waiting void.

V

The dead came down the River Vay, drifting in lazy fleets, turning in the current. They bumped along the hulls of the barges and ran up onto the mudbanks where the river's bends robbed the waters of their force. Seagulls came up from the sea, sculling across the sky, flocking down to loiter around any grounded corpse and wait for it to be opened by dogs. There were the corpses of men and women and children from the masterless villages on the Vaywater; Kyrinin corpses from the river's distant marshy headwaters, where the Snake had fallen into strife with the Taral-Haig Marchlords; corpses from the vast flat cattle lands north of Drandar, where nobles long settled in wary peace now openly feuded, and Heron Kyrinin crossed the river to prey on the displaced or undefended.

In Hoke, capital of the Thaneless Dargannan Blood, half the city burned while its garrison of Haig warriors was besieged in its barracks. Those men too burned, in time. Along the shore, a Dornach ship landed raiders who razed a village and then fell to fighting amongst themselves over the loot.

In the Far Dyne Hills, west of Dun Aygll, where once Kings mined for precious metals and woodsmen mined timber from forests they thought inexhaustible, gangs of youths hunted tithe-collectors. Punitive bands of warriors – Haig men and

Ayth men alike – hunted youths and their families. Wandering companies of Black Road scavengers and pillagers roamed the bare hillsides, brutally aimless in their destruction. Many villagers, despairing of all order, drove their flocks south into the immense vale of the Blackwater River, where the lowlanders defended their lands with ambushes and pit traps.

Far beyond the Vale of Stones, in the still snow-cloaked lands of the Black Road, Battle Inkallim – few of them now but ferocious still – warred with the High Thane's companies. Townsfolk rose on one side or the other. One night, when the moon was stark and full, warriors broke into the Sanctuary of the Lore, dragged many of its youngest Inkallim out into the snow and killed them beneath the watchful pine trees.

In Dyrkyrnon – secret Dyrkyrnon, secluded by both choice and by the trackless wetlands in which it nestled – *na'kyrim* walked in fear of the Shared, of shadows in the mind, of each other. Some became deranged and fled into the marshes, there to drown or die on the spears of the increasingly untrusting Heron clan. Some lapsed into uncommunicative despair and began to waste slowly away. One tore her own eyes out and plunged a fish knife into her own neck.

The world reeled and staggered, and with the rising and setting of each sun it descended deeper into the morass from which it could not pull free. And though the days grew longer, as winter withdrew slowly into the north, it seemed to all its inhabitants that there was a diminishing of light, an overthrowing of it by ever more profound darkness.

*

Anyara watched Coinach's face. In the dim light of a single candle he was trying to slip some heavy thread through the eye of a huge needle. His intense concentration, and the not infrequent winces of frustration, amused her. She turned her attention back to the pot of broth simmering over a low fire. It smelled tolerable if not good. It would be warming at least, and there would be enough left to be reheated at dawn tomorrow, to fortify themselves against the long and likely uncomfortable journey that awaited them.

The cottage was cramped but secure and dry. They had no idea whose it was. Tara Jerain had simply told them they would be met at a certain place on the road towards the docks outside Vaymouth and provided with shelter. And so they had been. Tara was, as had become clear, a resourceful and knowledgeable woman. She had provided them with horses and suitably worn and moth-eaten clothing to conceal their status. She had found them the Tal Dyreen captain who meant to run the first ship into Kolkyre, now that the blockade of that city was at the very least unlikely to be strictly enforced and quite probably abandoned altogether. Anyara could think of nowhere else to go. She wanted to be as close to the Glas Valley as she could, and to be amongst at least a few of the people of her own Blood. The dangers of the journey and the destination, such as they were, seemed to her no greater than remaining in Vaymouth.

The city was lit by fires every night, as competing factions fought blindly, wildly for control. The slightest rumour, of any kind, was enough to send vengeful mobs raging through the streets. No one knew who ruled. Stravan oc Haig, notionally Thane since the death of his father and elder brother, had not been seen for days. Dead of a pox, some said; poisoned by his mad mother, claimed others. Merely drunk and asleep, most insisted.

It was no place to be, especially for those present at the death of Chancellor, High Thane and Bloodheir. Tara had assiduously spread word that Kale had been the killer: a Hunt Inkallim incredibly waiting all these years for the most opportune moment. It was impossible to say how many believed such a wild tale. But Lheanor had died in his Tower of Thrones at the hand of an ageing woman, and in such a world who was to say what might happen?

Tara had not spoken a word to Anyara about what had happened. The vacant look that was often in her eyes, her subdued manner, the shaking that often took hold of her hands, so violent she could not hold a cup steady, all suggested its effects. But she would not speak of it, and Anyara had not forced her.

There was a shuffling outside the door, and Coinach at once dropped the still-unthreaded needle and reached for his sword. Then a tapping and a whisper.

'My lady, it's Torcaill. Your brother sent me.'

Coinach was still cautious as he opened the door just a fraction and peered out into the night, but he saw a face he knew, and the tension fell out of his frame.

'There were three of us, but the other two . . .' Torcaill looked ashen, even in the yellow light of the candle. Like a man who had been without food or sleep for days on end. His clothing was filthy and frayed.

'It was difficult,' he said. 'And when I reached Vaymouth, I heard you'd been in the Chancellor's palace. I went there, and his wife . . . Tara, is it? She told me where to find you. Once I had convinced her I was who I claimed to be, and that wasn't easy. Is it true . . . what they say happened?'

'It depends what you've heard,' muttered Coinach.

'We'll tell you soon enough,' Anyara said. 'Orisian sent you? Where is he? How is he?'

She could hear the impatience in her own voice, but it was only excitement, eagerness, and it pleased her. She revelled in it.

'I have a message from him,' Torcaill said, and proffered a canvas tube.

Anyara took it and unfurled the parchment from within. She leaned closer to the candle to read it. The handwriting was crude and a little clumsy. Her brother had never been the most gifted with a quill.

She read it quickly, thinking she would read it again more slowly once she had its gist. But a single reading was enough for her. She put it aside. The parchment, so long trained to the shape of that tube, rolled itself up again and hid the words.

Anyara felt she might cry and blinked into the embers of the fire a few times. But tears did not come. They were not quite ready. She found, after a few moments, that she was embracing Coinach instead.

VI

Shraeve brought Kanin up from the fetid, half-flooded cellar into which he had been cast. His hands had been bound behind him long enough for all sensation to have leaked out of them. She pushed him along a echoing hallway where silt was caked at the base of the walls. There were other Inkallim there, he was dimly aware, just two or three of them. They stared at him but said nothing.

He was propelled roughly out into the street, and almost fell. He winced at the assault of the light, for feeble as it was, it seemed garish after the gloom of his prison. His discomfort was brief, for Shraeve steered him in through the doorway to the spiralling stair that led up to the halfbreed's lair. The steps were worn and uneven, the walls rough and coated with mould and webs.

Kanin offered no resistance. He consisted of nothing but hate, and it filled him so completely that it choked any coherent thought. It was a greedy, many-hued hate that made no distinction between Aeglyss, Shraeve, himself. Of all its indiscriminate barbs, the sharpest were perhaps those turned inward. He loathed his failure, his weakness.

He emerged into the hall at the top of the stairs, and heard Aeglyss before he saw him.

'Cut his bonds.'

'He might still be dangerous,' Shraeve said behind him.

'You think so? Cut his bonds in any case.'

The Inkallim sawed at the cords about his wrists with a knife. When the bindings fell away, the blood rushing back into his hands was agonising. He barely noticed the pain, consumed instead by the immediate notion of spinning about and attacking Shraeve. But the Inkallim pushed him violently forward before the cut cords had even hit the ground, and he staggered some way down the length of the hall and fell to his knees.

'Stand up,' the halfbreed said.

Kanin's body did so, a little clumsily, without his mind even having the time to consider refusal. He looked at the *na'kyrim*, sitting there on his stone slab bench, and saw only the roughest, most approximate, imitation of a living man: hairless, suppurating, cadaverous. Pathetically small, too feeble to move. But the shadows around and behind him seemed to have a life of their own. And the eyes that fixed themselves upon Kanin, though bloody and sickly, still carried a vile intensity.

'You must do something,' Shraeve said as she moved to stand beside one of the columns lining the hall, level with Kanin. 'There are only three or four of us left fit to fight. The rest are dead or sick, or fallen away into madness or stupor. The whole city – the whole valley – is full of nothing but the dead and the dying. Those not yet too weak from disease or hunger . . . all turn against all. There is no order.'

Aeglyss did not move. His eyes did not stray from Kanin's.

'We have no armies left,' Shraeve said, more strident. 'There are none to command, and none willing to listen to any command. If you do not cure this sickness that afflicts—'

'She doubts me now,' Aeglyss said quietly to Kanin. 'Even her. No. No. She doubts herself, her judgement. She wonders if she made a mistake.'

'That is not true,' Shraeve said at once.

'Liar.' Said without a trace of emotion, as if it were a word without the slightest weight. 'She thought I would serve her ends. Be a sword in her hand and make her the champion of her creed. As you, your father, thought I would serve your ambitions, and then be cast aside. Now, too late, she wonders what she has unleashed upon the world. She wonders what has become of the great armies fortified by my will she thought would carry her triumphant across all the world. Well, the day of armies is past. The world is conquered by other means now.'

Shraeve shifted her weight, took a single stride forward.

'Be still,' Aeglyss said sharply.

The Inkallim did as she was commanded. Still, the *na'kyrim* had not so much as glanced at her.

'You don't imagine I cared what became of any of them, do you?' he murmured to Kanin. 'The White Owls? You, your cause? Never. None of it. I only . . . I only cared to be a part of it all. To be a part. But none of you would have me. And now look. You will become a part of me, instead. I am become . . . all of it. Everything.'

'Nothing,' rasped Kanin.

'You don't believe that.' There was perhaps a bitter smile stretching Aeglyss' bleeding lips. 'You, more than most, see a little of it, I think. Not all, of course. You don't understand. None could . . . not even me. All that has happened, is happening, to me . . . I don't understand it.'

'This is a waste of time,' Shraeve said. 'We must—'

'Quiet,' whispered Aeglyss, and the word contained such vast insistence that Kanin felt his own throat constricting, and felt fear momentarily gnawing at the edges of his hatred.

'You made this happen, Thane,' Aeglyss said to him.

'No,' growled Kanin.

'Yes. Nobody but you. I served you and your family loyally. I did what was asked of me, brought your army to the gates of your enemy's city. Yet you turned your back on me. You made me a liar in the eyes of the White Owls. Because of that, because of your treachery, I was taken to the Stone. I was broken and remade. So should I thank you for your betrayal, for turning me into what I now am? Should I praise your mindless loathing of me, since it has made me into . . . into this? Or should I kill you for it? Should I make you suffer as I have suffered, as all the meek and the different and the outcasts have suffered?'

Kanin wanted to fling himself at the foul vision of decay slumped on the bench before him, but his legs would not obey him. They were dead things beneath him, barely able to support his own weight.

'I tried to do myself again what was done to me on the Breaking Stone, you know,' Aeglyss murmured. 'I thought I might be able to control it, if I . . . I tried to . . . grow. It did not work. I am already all that is possible.'

He grunted out a strangled laugh.

'There, Thane. You have made me all that is possible. And it's not enough. Mind and body cannot sustain what I have become. Not without breaking, without crumbling. I can make slaves of Shadowhands and the sisters of Thanes. I can master the Anain, make myself lord of the Shared, make myself the very thought at the core of the world. Yet I cannot control it. I cannot make that thought sharp and neat, cannot choose how it ebbs and flows. Soon I will be gone, lost in the very storms I have created, and only that thought – that storm – will remain, for ever. I will have reshaped the world in my image, and the world shall be as I have made it, unto its very end. Yet I cannot even mend my own flesh.'

'Perhaps,' said Kanin, 'you know in your black heart that the only thing that could mend you is death.'

Aeglyss stared at him without speaking. Those eyes held Kanin, stabbed him, picked him apart. There was not the slightest movement in the *na'kyrim*'s crippled frame, yet Kanin felt the violent energies seeping out of him.

'There is truly nothing in you, save that one desire,' Aeglyss croaked. He sounded both fascinated and puzzled. 'You are unlike any of them, even the Children of the Hundred, in your purity. There is nothing to you now other than hate. Of me, of yourself. And at the heart of it all, the longing to see me dead. As if that will cure you.'

Kanin could say no more. The halfbreed had him in some intangible grip that was wholly irresistible.

'But if it was true . . .' Aeglyss whispered '. . . if it was true. I do not know what would become of me, if you had your wish. You could kill the body, perhaps . . . but . . . I do not know any more. I do not know if you can stop this . . . this . . .'

He coughed and shook. Dropped his head for a moment, and freed Kanin from that oppressive gaze, but not from the bonds of his attention. Then he looked up again and smiled the smile of a dying man.

'Do it then,' he said.

Kanin did not move. Aeglyss looked sideways towards Shraeve, moving his eyes but not his head.

'You will not raise a hand against this man,' the halfbreed rasped. 'I forbid it.'

Shraeve's resistance to the command was obvious. But so was its immense force. Kanin could feel it weighing down upon him, and he was not even its object. The Inkallim's face twitched as internal wars raged between her instincts and the halfbreed's indomitable will. There could only ever be one outcome.

'You hear me?' Aeglyss asked her. 'You understand?'

Shraeve nodded once, the muscles and tendons in her neck taut, her teeth clenched.

'Good.' The *na'kyrim's* eyes drifted back, took a moment or two to find and settle upon Kanin once more. 'Here is your moment then, Thane. Here it is. You can set both of us free now. Do as your heart dictates.'

And with that last word, Kanin was set free. Vigour surged through his arms and his legs. Every fragment of doubt or despair that lurked within him melted away before the single bright truth that he stood now in the sole moment of any consequence in his life. And that he was capable; he was potent. He could – would – forge precious meaning from the base metal of all that had gone before.

There was no one here but him and Aeglyss. There were no walls about them, no sky above, for the entirety of existence was composed of the two of them: the decrepit halfbreed, croaking and wheezing, and the man who had come through war, through years, through a lifetime, to kill him.

Kanin walked forward. Each stride felt vast, consuming immense distances as it bore him closer and closer to the feeble figure awaiting him. Aeglyss was lifting his head slowly. He was expectant, unresisting. Kanin could have laughed with joy. He opened his hands, feeling the limitless power they contained. He looked into the halfbreed's eyes as he descended upon him, and saw nothing there: no colour, no life, no awareness.

Now, Kanin knew, now there will be peace. Now I will be made whole again.

His hands were on the halfbreed's throat. As so often in his dreams, in all his bitter longings, he had become the bearer of death: a raven sweeping down from a God's throne to bestow endings and darkness and punishment. He felt bone beneath his fingers, and cartilage and wasted muscles that offered no resistance. He squeezed. Felt that fragile neck yielding.

And then his mind was opened, and he was inundated. He was caught up in a torrential flow that parted him from his body, made of him a cloud that was tugged and torn and stretched across an intolerable expanse of . . . everything.

He was on a great stone, crucified there, with lances of fire driven through his wrists and into the rock, overwhelming agony burning in him. He was running, fleeing through dense forests of trees that reached out for him, and he could hear and smell and taste the wolfenkind who ran alongside him, just out of sight, their animal voices taunting him with promises of a savage death. He was a King, riding a ship in a younger world, closing on a sandy shore. A child watching a Kyrinin army in malachite armour marching through the streets of a white city. He was rocking on the deep currents, looking up towards the surface of the sea, watching the light fracturing and dancing down through the waves.

He chased Wain through the rocks. It was summer. They were young. He could not catch her, for she was the faster, the nimbler, but still he chased, drawn onwards by the sound of her laughter shivering around the boulders. She let him catch her before long. No game could hold her interest for long. She was standing, staring back the way they had come, with a serious expression on her child's face.

Behind them, below them, Castle Hakkan was spread over the mountainside. The sunlight somehow softened it and made it look almost warm.

'You will be Thane one day,' Wain said gravely.

'What?' Kanin asked. He wanted laughter and pursuit, not stern conversation.

'You will be Thane, and I will be a Thane's sister.'

He pushed her, but she was not to be so easily forced back into levity.

'And we'll be great warriors,' she said firmly to him, fixing him with that steely gaze that their father found so amusing.

'Great warriors!' Kanin cried in agreement, engaged by the idea.

'And we'll fight wars. We'll fight wars at the end of the world, in the Kall. We'll be the best, the bravest of all.'

'Both of us.' Kanin grinned. 'Great warriors.' And he was so sure of it, back then. He could see the whole of his life laid out ahead, him and Wain marching into it side by side. The two of them, lit by the sun, illuminating the world with their own fierce light.

Kanin looked down. In his small hands – so smooth, so delicate – he had a stick. He was clasping it, wrapping his fingers
around it, trying inexplicably to crush it.

'I asked you once for forgiveness.'

The voice was inside Kanin. He was suddenly nothing more
than a thought adrift in shadow. And that other thought, the
one to which the voice belonged, was with him, entwined about
him, wrapping him in its coils.

'That was a mistake,' it said. Kanin existed only when it
spoke. Between the words he was nothing. Absence. 'I did not
understand then. Now I know better. There can be no forgiveness. What I have done, what has been done to me, what I have
become . . . it is all beyond forgiveness, or blame, or guilt, or
judgement. I am the Shared . . . consumed by it, consuming it.
Which . . .'

The voice faltered, and Kanin remembered himself a little.

'Which of us can say what is right or wrong? Such things . . .
There is no meaning to it. Not when we are all but different
aspects of a single thought in a single vast mind.'

No, Kanin thought, not knowing what it was he denied.

'I am the mind of the world,' the voice whispered into him, and
now it was jagged with anguish, with a pleading cadence. 'Too
much. I don't know what's . . . I have forgotten what is madness
and what sanity. But you can free me from this. Perhaps.'

Kanin sucked in a great stinging breath and looked down at
Aeglyss' blistered and bleeding face. Wounds opened up there
even now, the skin parting as if sliced by an invisible knife. Thin
blood was trickling down over Kanin's hands where they still
held the halfbreed's neck in their grip. But his fingers were as
iron, heavy and inert. Kanin could not compel them to close any
further, could not even feel them.

Aeglyss' eyes were closed. Kanin could smell the foul sores
that pockmarked his brow and scalp. It was the stench of a
plague pit.

The halfbreed's throat was half crushed, but still he spoke. Those split and scabbed lips barely moved, yet the voice was clear and crisp in Kanin's ears.

'Show me, Thane. If I am mad, if I am a disease, a mistake, show me. I will not yield. I cannot. It will not permit that, what is in me. But you can overcome it, if that is what the world requires.'

Kanin willed his hands to extinguish the life they held. They were deaf to his mind's commands. He stared down at them, and wept in frustration and cried out in rage.

Aeglyss slowly lifted his own hands and set them about Kanin's wrists.

'Now,' the halfbreed whispered. 'Now. If not now, then never.'

Kanin had no answer. His arms were dead weights, unyoked from his will. He could feel the wall of denial, of resistance, rising up before him as Aeglyss gathered his strength. A gloom was settling about him, a clot of dead air, greyed and fibrous. He could not breathe.

'Never, then,' Aeglyss hissed.

Kanin cried out in pain as his hands were slowly but irresistibly forced apart. The *na'kyrim*'s thin arms had an impossible strength in them, and Kanin had nothing with which to oppose it.

'Kneel down,' Aeglyss commanded, and Kanin did.

With perverse gentleness, Aeglyss released his wrists, but before Kanin's arms could fall back to his sides, the halfbreed delicately took hold of his hands. There was a terrible intimacy in it. Kanin could feel those long fingers pressing into his palms; he could feel a thumb resting lightly on the back of each of his hands.

'I am so tired,' Aeglyss said sorrowfully. Then, so fiercely that Kanin felt the words as daggers in his chest and stomach: 'You failed me. Again. You failed me. What is in you . . . not strong enough.' His voice was fragmentary. Something in his neck was broken or displaced.

Kanin shook his head. Failure was too small a word for this. The enormity of his fall was overpowering. Crippling.

'I am so tired,' Aeglyss rattled. It sounded like the shifting of cartilaginous rubble in his throat.

The slightest beat of pressure; the halfbreed's thumbs pressing down a fraction harder. Kanin's hands crumpled. He heard the breaking of every bone like a flock of argumentative birds swirling about his head. He felt every rupture like a point of cold, coruscating fire. He screamed as tendons split, joints were twisted apart. Bones split and split again, splintering into smaller and smaller fragments. He felt the debris within his hands being pulped, and the pain was so vast and unendurable that he fell away towards oblivion.

But Aeglyss would not allow that escape. Kanin's consciousness was embraced by that of the halfbreed, and borne up by it, and thrust back into the world of limitless suffering. Kanin looked up at the *na'kyrim's* ruined face. Aeglyss was opening and closing his mouth like a man choking. No sound but inarticulate croaks emerged. Kanin heard more, though, within his head.

'Stay with me, Thane. I am not done yet. Not done with the world. You made me. You will be my witness.'

Aeglyss released Kanin's hands and the Thane roared in stupefied agony as they hung limp from his wrists, bloated bags of blood and fragmentary wreckage.

'You should have killed me a long time ago,' said the air, and the boards beneath Kanin's knees, and the pitted stone of the columns, and the darkness crowding across his vision, all speaking with the voice of the halfbreed. 'Now it's too late. For all of us.'

VII

K'rina walked as if in a daze, blundering through the night in an erratic, wayward fashion. She stumbled across the rough fields, veering aside from ditches only at the last moment, sometimes splashing down into them without pause and hauling herself up and out the other side. When the occasional stand of sallow and alder loomed suddenly out of the darkness, she would barge her way through it, showing no sign that she was even aware of the branches snagging her clothes or scratching her face.

Taim followed as steadily as he could, never more than half a dozen strides behind the *na'kyrim*. Her unpredictable and uncompromising course made it difficult, as did his determined efforts to keep equally close to Orisian. The Thane matched K'rina's path and pace out to her left. Somewhere on the right, further ahead, was Varryn, but the Kyrinin stayed in the darkness and Taim had seen no hint of him for some time.

Though K'rina was the unwitting, unconscious guide, it was for Orisian that Taim reserved the greater portion of his attention. Taim stumbled many times, in some dip or rut in the ground, because he strove to keep the young man in sight.

He could not tell whether it was this constant battle with his senses and with the night, or the simple all-consuming nature of his concern for Orisian's safety, but Taim felt a rare calm in him. For all the aching of his leg – the thigh muscle still tormented by the memory of that bone-studded club – and the constant enervating anticipation of some sudden assault, he found himself untroubled by distraction, from either within or without. His mind followed a strangely placid course, even as his body struggled on through the lightless, treacherous fields.

It was simplicity that gave him this clarity. He accepted but a single task upon his shoulders now: to bring Orisian safe out of this. It mattered not at all what lay ahead, or what familial longings remained lodged in his heart, or what fears circled him – dark possibilities riding raven wings – and tried to colonise his imagination. All these were things he had no time or space for. They all foundered against the great wall of his need to preserve the life of his Thane. In the singular and absolute primacy of that task he had come perhaps to the purest expression of his self and his history. That he should have come to it as he might well be entering upon the very threshold of his own death did not trouble him. Indeed, it seemed fitting. Taim was content.

Birds erupted now and again from thickets or from the reeds fringing ditches, whirring low away into the darkness. They were the least alarming of the night's surprises, for strange and unsettling sights and sounds became ever more frequent as they moved further out into the Glas Valley.

The rotund carcass of a cow was suddenly there, in the middle of a bare expanse of ploughed earth. As they passed it by, that bulging form was revealed as grim illusion, for the innards had been hollowed out: the animal's ribs and the dried, tight hide they supported encased nothing but a great cavity. Following K'rina across a shallow ditch, Taim found something that was both resistant and yielding beneath his foot. He looked down and saw the white and puffy skin of an eyeless corpse, lambent in the faint moonlight, just beneath the surface of the water.

Hoofbeats drummed their way along some track far out to the right. Taim closed up on Orisian. They slowed a little, Orisian catching hold of K'rina's trailing sleeve to hold her back, and the sound came pounding closer. Too fast, Taim thought. No rider with any wit would go at such speed without light to see by. And when the great brown horse blurred past them, it was indeed riderless, though saddled and with stirrups flailing at its flanks.

Not long after, Varryn abruptly appeared in K'rina's path and brought her to a halt. He nodded wordlessly ahead. It took time, for it would reveal itself from the corner of an eye, not when he looked directly at it, but soon enough Taim found the dimmest, feeblest tinge of a campfire out there in the blackness. They led K'rina on a wide looping detour, and it was the Kyrinin who decided when they had put sufficient ground between them and the distant flames to let her move freely again, in accordance with whatever mute instinct drove her.

Once there was laughter. It drifted to them from the west, clear but thin. It was a despairing, straining laughter, like the cry of some forlorn animal, closer cousin to misery than joy. It rose and fell, and lost its shape and dwindled away.

For a time Taim was sure he could hear Orisian mumbling to himself. He could not see his Thane's lips so could not be certain, and the sound was far too soft for any words to reach him. It worried him, for Orisian had seemed in the last few days to be on the brink of some entirely solitary, personal desolation. Like a man clinging to a branch at the river's edge, half in the current and half out of it, his strength failing, the pull of the water growing.

They halted at last, and took cover in a drainage channel that ran close to a burned-out farmhouse. The water was not as deep as it should have been – the channel was blocked somewhere, perhaps by rubble or a slide of earth – but still it came up over the tops of their boots as they crouched there watching the first grey light of dawn leach into the eastern sky. Taim had to hold K'rina down to prevent her from clambering to her feet and going blindly on. He did it as gently as he could, and she was far too slight and weakened to resist him.

They had not spoken one to another all through the night. The silence had become embedded. Taim was taken by surprise when Orisian broke it.

'Why?' he asked Varryn softly.

That this was a return to some unfinished matter between them was plain. At first he doubted whether the Kyrinin would respond. The answer came, though, as perhaps it would not have done but for that long night the three of them had spent together in this hostile land.

'Because she asked me,' Varryn said. 'Because I was not there when she took the wound. If I was there, perhaps she would not have been wounded, but a . . . a burning was in me. I was lost to myself, lost in the hunting of the enemy. A thing that can make such a madness . . . it should stop. It should end.'

The quiet wrapped itself about them again, and Taim let his eyes close. He had become accustomed to exhaustion, inured in part to its crippling effects, but it was heavy now.

'Because a good man died to win this woman for you,' Varryn said unexpectedly. 'He would run with you now, if he lived. I run for him. Because I saw Anain die. I saw trees made dust. The man who can do this . . . he will make the ground upon which we walk a dead thing. He will shape clouds out of fear and hide the sun, and we will walk in shadows. It would be a good thing to kill him. Are these reasons enough?'

'Yes,' whispered Orisian after a while. 'It's enough.'

Taim opened his eyes in time to see Kan Avor emerging from the night. Its low grey mass lay across the valley like a granite mountain that had collapsed in on itself. Tendrils of smoke ascended from the ruins towards the light seeping over it from the east. Clouds of black birds climbed from their roosts, and even here, even at this distance, Taim could hear them calling: a raucous, fierce greeting of the new day.

*

'I thought they would be everywhere,' Orisian muttered as he stared out over the lip of that muddy ditch. He shifted a little to take his weight off a stone in the bank that dug into his hip. 'I suppose I imagined there would be armies here, the whole valley an armed camp. But it's . . . it's a wasteland.'

Taim grunted. 'We've seen what happened elsewhere. And to the White Owls, and to us. If there are armies here, it looks like it'll be armies of the dead, and the mad.'

Orisian glanced up towards the dim sky.

'It won't be properly light for a while yet. We might reach the ruins, don't you think? Without being seen?'

Neither Taim nor Varryn made any reply. Both warriors

stared out across the level plain towards the hulking mass of Kan Avor. When Orisian looked, he saw no movement, no sign of life save those few thin columns of smoke rising from the ruins, but he was prepared to await the verdict of more experienced eyes.

He feared the consequences if they judged it necessary to await the return of night, though. The darkness brought entirely too much with it now. What was the working of utter exhaustion upon him, and what the corrupting influence of Aeglyss and the Shared, he did not know. But whatever the cause, he dreaded the prospect of yet more black hours in which he would be hunted by his own mind.

He had heard the voices of the dead: Inurian, his father, Rothe, others he did not even recognise yet had known to be shaped without living breath. He had felt waves of wretched dismay breaking over him. For a time – no dream this, something sharper, more potent – he had found himself no longer trudging through the fields but curled in the corner of his childhood bedchamber in Castle Kolglas. Folded in there, bunched into a ball, with his arms covering his head, too terrified to open his eyes. He remembered hope but did not feel it. It might take but one more night to extinguish even that slender memory of it.

'The woman could go alone now,' Varryn said quietly. 'It is not so far, if this dead city is the end of her journey.'

'No,' Orisian said. 'Whoever is in there, sitting around those fires . . . she'll blunder into them.'

Taim laid a soft hand over K'rina's mouth to stifle a murmur.

'If we can make it to cover before the sun's in the sky, before the cold's relented enough to get people moving . . .' he muttered without enthusiasm. 'I like our chances no better if we try to hide out here'

They went on, stumbling on feet deadened by the cold water. Orisian felt desperately exposed, yet his spirits rose. He was liberated from the suffocating, haunted darkness. Even the grim transformation of his homeland that the advancing daylight revealed could not entirely restore the despair that had been riding his back.

They trod on land that should, at this time of year, have been submerged beneath the reflective pools of the Glas Water. Now it was a great sprawl of black, almost liquid mud, dead reed and debris. There were rotted timbers that had been in the water's grip for decades; the skeletal hull of a little boat abandoned by some fisherman or fowler years ago; even, in places, the shrunken, withered remains of fish that had been stranded by the receding flood, and must have been hidden from scavengers by snow.

Once, as they struggled across that wasted expanse in the gloomy dawn, there was a figure, far away across the mire: some lone wanderer, stumbling and lurching and falling as they did themselves. Too far away to be a threat. Yet Orisian could not help but stare as he splashed through one slick after another of black water. There was something in that lone, tiny figure that held him. He found himself thinking – believing – that it was him; that he was watching himself, from this great distance, and seeing himself as he truly was.

K'rina led them closer and closer to the ruined city, and soon enough Orisian could distinguish the outlines of what had once been individual buildings. That was when they started to find bodies. Some of them were half-buried in the soft earth, some lying in pools. Some were old, picked at by animals, decaying; most were fresh, their features not yet marred, the dried blood not yet washed by rain from their wounds. There were discarded weapons strewn amongst them and here and there the corpse of a horse.

The city rose out of the marsh stealthily. First a few shaped stones, barely visible amongst the rushes. Then a stretch of wall that appeared from the sodden earth and sank back into it within a few paces. Then a stretch of paved road, then the suggestion of a house in a straight-sided pattern of rubble. Then they were amongst it, and Kan Avor showed itself to them.

Sullen dogs staring at them appraisingly as they passed. Rats a dark ripple over the ground as they scattered from a corpse at the sound of Orisian's footsteps. A campfire giving out one of those faint pillars of smoke that they had seen from out in the valley, but abandoned. No one to tend it or relish its warmth.

The dead. Lying in drifts along a street where some cruel battle had recently been fought out. Beneath a crowd of crows that rose sluggishly from their feast when disturbed, but went no further than the nearest uneven remnant of a wall, and settled there in a patient black line. The dead. Clustered around the ashes of an extinct fire, still wrapped in sleeping blankets.

And the living. A woman, haggard without being old, sitting alone in the ruin of a courtyard. She rose when she saw them and came feebly towards them, but fell and could not rise again. Orisian was not sure whether it had been desperation or anger he had seen on her face.

A little cluster of the sick, at the base of a flight of foreshortened stairs that ascended towards some destination long lost. They coughed and sweated and shivered, and embraced one another, and watched Orisian and the others without hope, interest, or appeal.

Varryn turned and hissed a soft warning, but too late. A handful of warriors emerged ahead of them, coming round a corner and halting, staring towards them in confusion.

'Hold onto K'rina,' Taim said at once.

Orisian did so, clamping her thin wrist in one hand and pulling her towards the shelter of a shapeless pile of rubble. She struggled against him, driven by a fiercer, stronger desire than ever before to continue on.

One of the Black Roaders was loading her crossbow. The others – spearmen – charged. Varryn calmly plucked an arrow from his quiver. He raised his bow, loosed the arrow in a single fluid, rapid movement. The woman with the crossbow fell dead even as she was lifting it to her shoulder.

Taim walked out to meet the three charging spearmen. One of them was growling as he ran. Taim flicked the outstretched spear of the first aside with his sword, and crouched to put his shield into the man's knees. The helpless, hapless Black Roader, undone by his own reckless pace, was sent cartwheeling right over Taim, landing hard on arms and head in the middle of the street.

Taim surged up and sideways, one spear thrust missing him entirely, the other deflected upwards by his shield. He cut the second man down as he ran past. The third found Varryn coming to meet him, and slowed a touch to level his spear once more. Orisian could not even follow what happened, for the Kyrinin was ruthlessly fast. A blur of spears, the crack of wood against wood and then against skull, and a single lunging stab in and out again. Varryn was already walking over to kill the man Taim had first tumbled as his opponent looked down in surprise at the blood spreading across his stomach, let his spear fall, and sat clumsily down on the cobblestones, pressing both hands against his belly.

'We need the worst, the most tangled and confused of the ruins,' said Taim as he sheathed his sword. 'The harder the going, the less likely we are to be seen or to stumble across trouble.'

Orisian nodded. K'rina was still pulling against him. It seemed, though, that she did not understand what it was that restrained her. She did not look at him, merely strained against his grip like a sheep snagged on some thorn bush. When he followed the line of her gaze, it led him to the dark knot of taller, more massive ruins in the city's heart. That was where she wanted to go. That was where whatever called so insistently to her would be found.

VIII

Kanin rose feebly through oceans of pain. He was made of it, and inhabited it. The light he ascended towards hurt him. The hard stone he began to feel beneath him woke aches in his muscles. And his hands . . . his hands gathered into them all that ocean through which he swam. They were like fire.

He moaned as he forced open his crusted eyes. The pain of his maimed hands was beyond anything he could have conceived of. There was nothing else save that searing, pounding, crippling torment. All that he saw and heard came to him through the howl of agony, rendered all but senseless by its journey.

Shraeve was standing before Aeglyss. Saying something, angry. The *na'kyrim* simply stared at her.

Shraeve shouted at him. Kanin could not make out what she was saying. Her anger could not penetrate his pain. But then, though his lips did not move, Aeglyss spoke, and Kanin could hear his words, for they were of the same stuff as his pain, and thus within him. A part of him.

'The Shadowhand is dead. I can't remember . . . did I tell you that? He died. And was glad of it. I tasted him as he faded into . . . into the Shared. Into me. No, it doesn't matter. He served his purpose. He did what I required of him.

'As did you, my fierce raven, until this . . . this doubt entered into you. What happened? Is it too bright for you, this light you have helped to reveal? I tell you there is no more need for armies or for wars, that the victory is already won. But you don't understand. You don't hear. Very well. Very well.'

Something else amongst Kanin's pain then. A flow, a gathering of force. Shraeve had gone down onto her knees. One hand reached impotently towards Aeglyss, the other fumbled at the hilt of one of her swords.

'I knew you would turn against me eventually,' Kanin heard

the great voice say, almost sad. 'The last of them, perhaps, but in the end . . . the same. But I can heal you of this betrayal, Shraeve. The Shadowhand is gone . . . that fragment of my will I lodged in his mind is returned to me. I can give it to you, and bind us closer than ever before. I can give you back that faith you have lost.'

Shraeve was sitting back on her heels, her spine arching, her head tipping back. Her arms fell limp at her sides. Her mouth was open, and though Kanin could hear nothing from her, he thought she might be screaming.

'Yes . . .' the halfbreed's voice whispered in the bones of Kanin's skull. 'You don't have to leave me yet. Never. You'll stay at my side. Can you see, Thane? Do you see? This is what your sister submitted herself to. She became a part of me, as she could never have been a part of you.'

Kanin fainted away at that moment, but the refuge of insensibility was fleeting. He was called back, dragged back into that foul hall of pain and cruelty and horrors. Aeglyss had not moved. Shraeve was striding towards the door. Kanin knew – or was shown – that the Inkallim was no longer as she had been. Though he saw two people before him, there was but a single will.

'We might need her yet, Thane,' the monster murmured inside him. 'There is an . . . intent. Somewhere near. Intent. Not fierce, not burning, but clear. Becoming clear. I feel it but cannot find it. We will see. You and I. We will see.'

*

Never had Eska moved with such care and precision. A near-lifetime of training, of submission to the strictures and teachings of the Hunt, went into her every delicate step over the loose rubble. She judged every fall of her foot with minute attention; assessed and refined her balance constantly. She passed across the treacherous territory of Kan Avor as silently and slowly as would a cat suspecting the presence of an unprepared mouse.

She did not return to her previous vantage point. To do so would be absurdly reckless, and though her emotions were running high, they were not yet so incapacitating as to rob her of all sense. She found instead a more distant but well concealed perch. There was an empty courtyard that must once have been colonnaded, for there were the stumps of columns, like a line of dead trees. Set into its furthest wall were shelved alcoves in which she guessed statues once had stood. Those statues were long gone, and Eska crouched in place of one of them, half her own height above the ground. She was in shadow there and confident none but the most acute of eyes would uncover her.

From that secluded nook she could gaze out across the ruined court and through a gap in the opposite wall – originally a window perhaps, but now roughened into a ragged hole – into the street beyond. Thirty paces up that street, in her line of sight, two Battle Inkallim stood outside the door from which she had seen the halfbreed emerge to confront Kanin oc Horin-Gyre. The door, she assumed, behind which the *na'kyrim* now lurked, somewhere in the crumbling palace. She meant to put an end to him – was determined upon it as she had been upon no other task in her life – but would do so meticulously. Carefully. And that required the removal of those who would protect him.

She had seen no sign of other Inkallim on her approach to this hiding place. Had seen in fact hardly anyone who was not obviously sick in body or mind or both. The whole city had declined into a kind of demented lassitude. Whatever unnatural pall of corruption lay over the place – and she could feel it herself, feeding the turbulent emotions within her – had defeated and destroyed all save a handful of its inhabitants.

She set one bolt down on the ledge at her feet. Held another between her teeth while she cocked the bow. Everything was done slowly, with small movements. She had nothing and no one to fall back on this time. There could be no mistakes.

She took aim. She visualised the flight of the bolt, its dipping flight across the courtyard, through the window, out into the light and on into flesh. It was clear in her mind's eye. The man she had taken as her target was looking away, talking to his companion. She exhaled, waited for a single heartbeat and released the bowstring. As soon as it was gone, she knew it was a good kill. If the man did not make some sudden, unexpected move, he was dead.

She lowered the crossbow and levered its string back into place. She did not watch the first bolt's flight as she reached for the next, but she listened attentively and was rewarded with the thud of its strike and the cry of surprise that greeted it. She raised the reloaded bow and settled herself for the second time.

One of the Inkallim was down, moving fitfully and, she could tell from those movements, hopelessly. The second was running down the line of her aim. He was good, she acknowledged. Alert and fast. She fixed her eyes on his chest, just off centre, and exhaled.

The Inkallim veered abruptly out of sight. She could hear him for a moment, but then even that clue was taken away. She dropped lightly to the ground. Her spear rested against the wall by the alcove, but she left it where it was for now. If he got close enough for her to need a spear, she would most likely be in fatal trouble anyway.

She strained her senses, reaching out to gather in any traitorous sound or glimpse that might offer itself. Nothing came. She turned slowly, crossbow poised. Nothing. She waited.

The Inkallim came rushing from behind her. She heard his boots on the stone slabs. She spun and looked into his eyes, and the crossbow trembled in her hands as it loosed its cargo. The bolt knocked the raven off his feet. Eska puffed out her cheeks.

She caught dark movement at the very edge of her field of

vision. Turned. And saw Shraeve sprinting towards her. The door on the far side of the street stood open. Shraeve was running for the hole in the wall that separated them. There was no time for another bolt. Eska reached blindly for her spear.

Shraeve leaped, bent her head down, folded her knees up into her chest, and came flashing through the ragged window. Eska had her spear in her hand and was running before the raven hit the ground. She ran not for the open door, but for the ruins. Her only chance, she knew, would be if she could rid herself of Shraeve.

Eska had always been fast, even by the standards of the Hunt. Shraeve matched her, though. Eska could measure in the sound of the raven's pounding feet the ebbing away of her hopes. She cut into alleyways, vaulted fallen walls, swept over tumbled stones lying like scree against the face of a building. And Shraeve drew gradually closer.

Eska burst upon a band of ragged people struggling over the corpse of a dog. They were pulling it this way and that, snarling at one another. They looked up and let the carcass fall. To her they were made of stone. She weaved her path through them without breaking stride, heard their cries like low moans falling from her back. She heard too their more strident cries as Shraeve ploughed through them, and the sound of impacts and bodies falling.

Eska asked her legs for more and found they had but little to give her. The slightest lengthening of her stride. That was all. She still held her crossbow in one hand, her spear in the other. They hampered her and grew steadily heavier. A passageway spat her out into open ground: a wide square speckled with pale bodies from which birds rose and dogs retreated at her sudden appearance.

She turned, out in the open, chest heaving, lungs burning, to face Shraeve. Who slowed as she came near, lapsing into a casual walk and then coming to a halt. She had not even drawn her swords. She stood there empty-handed, and regarded Eska with narrow, dispassionate eyes.

'My feet are on the Road,' Eska said breathlessly, and flung the crossbow.

She darted forward in its wake, both hands set firmly on her spear. Shraeve dodged the spinning bow with ease and reached for her swords. By the time Eska closed with her, the blades were free but still high. It looked like a trap to Eska, who could see the shaft of her spear shattering beneath downward blows. At the last moment she snatched the blade of the spear aside and brought the butt round in a low sweep towards Shraeve's knee. The raven danced back out of reach.

Shraeve rushed forward behind that failed attack, but Eska, retreating, managed to spin the spear in her hands in time to level its tip and fend off the charge. They circled one another. Eska placed her feet carefully, mistrusting the uneven ground. She never let her attention stray from Shraeve, though. She did not expect this to last long.

'You have betrayed the faith,' she said, in the slender hope of winning some minor advantage by distracting the raven. But Shraeve did not even blink. She might as well have been deaf.

Eska caught the slight dip in Shraeve's hips. It gave the merest instant of warning. Shraeve surged forward. Eska stabbed. Shraeve crossed her swords beneath the spear and snapped them up. Eska watched the shaft of her spear caught in the intersection of those two rising blades, lifted by them, its barbed point guided harmlessly over Shraeve's shoulder. She tried to whip it back, prepare for another lunge, but it was too late. Shraeve somehow parted her swords in such a way that one pushed the spear out high and wide as the other came low and flat for Eska's belly. It was smoother and neater and faster than anything Eska had ever seen.

She twisted desperately, but still the blade sliced across her lower back. She felt it cutting her. And still Shraeve was moving. Inside the spear now, she pivoted on her leading foot and kicked Eska in the stomach.

Eska staggered. Bile burned up her throat and she gagged. Her spear was torn from her hands. Her heels met a block of stone and she fell. The back of her head hit another hard angle as she landed, and pain encircled her skull.

She grimaced up and saw Shraeve standing over her, swords already returning to their sheaths. Eska tried to roll onto her hands and knees, but her wounded back cramped and the searing pain locked her in place. Shraeve picked up the barbed spear. She held it over Eska's stomach. Drew it back in preparation for the final strike.

Then suddenly lifted her head, and turned it to one side, frowning. As if she caught some summons on the air. Eska could hear nothing. But Shraeve straightened, shook her head once. Eska tried to roll aside again, and this time she mastered her body's protests. She began to move just as Shraeve, almost absently, punched the spear down.

It went through Eska's side. She heard its point grating on the stones beneath her, felt her blood following it. She gasped and took hold of the spear's shaft with one hand. Through eyes almost shut by pain, she saw Shraeve turning away, running back towards the centre of Kan Avor.

IX

They crawled through the wreckage of Kan Avor like cautious rats picking over the carcass of a whale. Were it not for K'rina, it would have been easy to lose track of where they were and where they were heading. Every time taller walls or buildings closed about them, Orisian lost all sense of direction. K'rina knew, though. Always and instinctively. She would have scrambled recklessly and eagerly, as fast as she could go, through the ruins if they had let her.

It fell to Orisian to restrain her, for Taim and Varryn spent their entire concentration upon scouring the way ahead for any hint of danger. There was little. One man – a warrior from one of the Black Road Bloods – they found trying to light a fire with a pathetic pile of damp sticks. Varryn killed him quietly. Other than that, the only movement they detected was distant.

Orisian was struggling with a mounting pain inside his head: not in the bone but deep, in the place where his thoughts dwelled. It came and went, but each time it retreated it returned stronger and sharper. There was whispering as well, but that he was becoming accustomed to. The competing tasks of preventing K'rina from rushing on ahead and traversing the derelict terrain safely and quietly himself were demanding enough to keep him from slipping entirely into the diffuse besieging despair and anger he felt all about him.

He had the strange sense that they were falling, not advancing. Some great pit was drawing them into itself. Yet of all the feelings clamouring for his attention, fear was the least of them. He had somehow moved beyond the reach of that particular assailant. Perhaps he was simply too tired, in all possible ways, to succumb. The utter desolation of Kan Avor, the physical and mental destitution of those they had found alive here, the weight of the dead upon the city: all of this seemed to be murmuring to him that it was too late. Whatever happened, a wound had been delivered to the world that could never be quite healed. Too much had been broken for it ever to be restored to its former state.

Still he went on. And if he detected an increasingly wild edge to Varryn's movement and gaze, he chose to ignore it. If he thought he saw Taim's shoulders sinking gradually lower, and a grim, sombre intensity taking hold of the warrior, he said nothing. Kan

Avor had them all in its grip, and it could only be endured, not escaped.

K'rina led them, in the bleak afternoon light, to a street over which the greatest of Kan Avor's surviving edifices loomed. It might have been a palace in the lost days of the Gyre Blood's dominion. It had the stubs of towers still adorning its upper reaches, and faded carvings in its stonework. Blank and empty windows looked out from high in its walls over the grey ruins.

The *na'kyrim* almost tore free of Orisian's grasp as they crouched behind a low wall, staring at the open door opposite them. He had to take a firm hold of her shoulders with both hands to keep her from running out into the street and bolting for that door. She hissed in frustration and tried to shake him loose.

'Leads to a stairway,' Taim murmured.

'Is that an Inkallim?' Orisian asked, staring at the corpse slumped against the base of the wall just outside the doorway.

'I think so.'

'Not long dead,' Varryn observed. His tone was tense, as if his jaw and lips and tongue were becoming too stiff to easily move.

'I'll take a look,' Taim said. 'Wait for my sign.'

He advanced cautiously into the street, looking up and down its length. He edged closer to the doorway, pausing to lean tentatively down towards the fallen Inkallim, searching for any movement in his chest.

Satisfied, Taim leaned through the open door. After a brief, tense wait, he withdrew and gestured towards Orisian. Varryn moved at once, eager to throw off his enforced immobility. Orisian followed more slowly, K'rina bucking in his grasp.

'Seems deserted,' Taim whispered as they gathered by the doorway. 'Can't hear anything. Perhaps they're all dead.'

'Not all of them,' Orisian said. 'Not him. You can feel that he's not dead, can't you?'

Taim nodded tightly.

'Whatever K'rina wants, it's in here,' said Orisian. 'He's in here.'

'Someone,' Varryn hissed.

'Where?' demanded Taim.

The Kyrinin nodded towards the end of the street, already reaching for an arrow. As he did so, an Inkallim emerged. She was tall, and ran with long, easy strides. Her black hair was tied back. She carried two swords, held loose at her side, slightly splayed ahead of her. She betrayed no surprise at their presence, but increased her pace and came racing towards them.

Varryn's arrow sprang out to meet her. She swayed, and it skimmed past her arm. Orisian was astonished.

'Get into the stairwell,' snapped Taim.

She was coming still faster. Varryn snatched another arrow from his quiver and sent it darting for her chest. Again the Inkallim dipped and twisted in mid-stride, but she was closer now, with less time to react. The arrow smacked into her shoulder and stayed there. She barely faltered.

'Keep her out of here, if you can,' Orisian said to Taim. He yielded at last to K'rina's silent demands, and let the *na'kyrim* drag him into and up the stairwell. She climbed quickly, and he followed, one hand on her trailing wrist, the other clumsily drawing his sword. He scraped it against the confining wall of the spiral.

His head was spinning. He felt as if he was fighting against a raging headwind as he climbed those rough steps. Some great pressure leaned against him. It was nothing conscious, nothing directed, just the immense weight of whatever he drew near. Now, too late, he felt fear taking hold of him. Whether it was his, or someone else's, he did not know, but it tightened and tightened.

At the head of the stairway was a plain wooden door. Orisian pulled K'rina aside just as she reached out for it. He leaned close, listening intently. He could hear nothing, in part because there was a throbbing bellow building within his head. He closed his eyes for a moment and fought back the terror that made him want to sink down onto the ancient stone and curl up there; fought the empty certainty of his own impotence that flooded into him; fought the sapping weariness that made granite of his arms and legs.

He fought against all this but could not defeat it. Could not entirely hold it back. But nor was he defeated by it. He slowly pushed the door open and led the suddenly calm and compliant K'rina inside.

The daylight coming in through the windows and through the holes in the collapsing roof was not strong enough to dispel every shadow from the hall. The rows of pillars that ran the length of the chamber on either side laid faint dark bars down across the floorboards. There was a musty, damp smell.

Some way down the hall, slumped against the foot of a pillar, was a man Orisian did not at first recognise. He took in his haggard features, his battered chain mail. It was difficult to tell whether the man was alive or dead, awake or asleep. But his face was familiar. Orisian's gaze dropped to the man's hands, resting in his lap. They were thick, like fat, overfilled waterskins. And black and blue and yellow with damage. The fingers lay at odd, ungainly angles. Orisian looked back to the man's face and frowned. It was the Horin-Gyre Bloodheir, he realised. The man who had hunted him through the streets of Koldihrve, who had tried and failed to kill him there in the Vale of Tears.

Orisian took a hesitant step into the room. The old soft floorboards creaked beneath his boots. He glanced at K'rina, puzzled by an abrupt change in her demeanour. She was staring down the hall, her grey eyes entirely absorbed in whatever she saw there.

Orisian peered into the gloom that filled the far end of the chamber. He thought he could see, pale and indistinct, some small, sunken figure sitting there. Unmoving. Corpse-like.

'Who are you?' a vast and sullen voice asked inside his mind.

*

Taim barely had time to ready himself before the Inkallim was upon them. He lifted his shield across his chest. Saw Varryn set both hands on his bow and draw it back like a club. Then she was there, and leaping high into the space between them. Taim thought she meant perhaps to fling herself beyond them in an attempt the reach the doorway they blocked, but even as the expectation formed, he saw that it was wrong.

Both blades lashed down towards him, clattering against his shield with unexpected force and driving him backwards. Her right leg kicked out at Varryn. The Kyrinin was fast enough to crash his bow into her thigh; not fast enough to avoid the lunging foot that hammered into the base of his throat and sent him staggering into the wall. Taim heard the crack of his head against the stonework quite clearly. Varryn slumped down.

The Inkallim landed with perfect balance and poise. She flicked a single glance at the stunned Kyrinin, then fixed her gaze on Taim. As she did so, though, one blade reached back towards Varryn.

Taim roared and rushed at her, shield foremost, sword held back for a stabbing thrust. The Inkallim drifted out of his path with absurd ease and casually cut open his upper arm as she did so. But he had put her out of reach of Varryn, for now at least.

She rose out of her fighting stance and took a few leisurely steps sideways. They carried her a little closer to the door. Taim backed towards it. Varryn was not stirring. There was no way Taim could defend both stairway and Kyrinin without quickly losing one or both. Suffused with sharp guilt, he chose the stairway, and hoped that the Inkallim cared more for that than she did for finishing an unconscious foe.

'I saw you once before, I think,' he said to her. 'In a snow-storm, at Glasbridge.'

'Did you?' She seemed entirely uninterested. 'Stand aside.'

'I can't do that. My Thane commanded me to hold this stair.'

'That boy who was with you? He's nothing.'

'He is my Thane.'

Her lip curled in disdain. She reached up and hooked a single finger over the shaft of the arrow still embedded in her shoulder. With the most fleeting of grimaces, she snapped it off, leaving just a split stub protruding from her flesh. Taim considered attacking her in that moment of distraction, but in truth it was no distraction at all, for her eyes never left him, her balance never wavered.

She let the broken arrow fall and sprang forward in a flurry of whirling blades, belabouring his shield, ringing against his own sword. His defence was desperate. This raven was astonishingly fast and precise. She nicked his thigh. Almost had his eye; would have done, had he not read the sudden change in her blade's course at the last possible moment and jerked back.

She paused as he retreated into the doorway itself.

'You're too late,' he said, hoping to keep her attention upon him and away from Varryn.

She glared at him but made no reply. She moistened her lips. There was a constant shiver running down Taim's neck and spine, a kernel of pain building behind his eyes, a flutter of bitter hopelessness in his heart. None of this he believed to be truly his, and he set himself against it. But it would not release him entirely. It sapped his strength and his will.

His mind reached for hope, for inspiration. Its harvest was meagre. There was perhaps the faintest suggestion that the arrow hampered her movements. If so, that would only grow worse if he could live long enough to give it the chance. And there was the stairway. He edged back into the shadows at the foot of the spiral of steps. She needed space to get the best from

those fearsome swords and from her speed. Above her, with
shield between them, he would have a chance. To delay her, if
nothing else. But only if she came after him.

'You cannot reach him,' he said as he reached back to set his
foot on the first of the steps.

She smiled then, the malevolent smirk of a wolf.

'You think not?' she said, and ran at him.

*

Orisian could not answer the question that had been put to him.
The depth and resonant power of the voice that had asked it
stunned him, and made him for a moment stand quite still, letting his sword and shield hang down.

'You mean me harm.' The voice rang like the mightiest, most
sombre of bells. 'That I can feel, can know. But it's a cold kind
of . . . regret. It doesn't burn in you as it did in the others.'

Orisian gathered himself, almost groaning at the effort it
took to shake off the deadening pain and the weight of the fell
mind that pressed down upon his own. K'rina was walking very
slowly forward, taking tiny steps. That roused Orisian enough
to get his own, leaden body moving. He forced himself ahead of
the *na'kyrim*.

'Who is that with you?' the voice asked him. 'I can't see. My
eyes . . . Can't find anything . . . What? You've brought some
empty vessel with you? A body with no mind, no thought, no
life in it?'

Orisian advanced, each halting stride a struggle. He could
hear Kanin muttering something, but did not look. He kept his
gaze fixed on the *na'kyrim*, who slowly became clear amidst the
shadows as Orisian drew nearer.

He thought at first that Aeglyss must be dead. A naked, hairless, scabrous head on a lopsided and bruised neck. The face,
what little Orisian could see of it, marred by a score of tiny
wounds and blisters and blemishes. Streaked with blood. Fragile
shoulders, the bony points of them showing through the gown.

That gown itself, foully decorated with stains. The hands, one lying atop the other in Aeglyss' lap, so wasted that Orisian could see every bone through the skin. Each finger ending in an open sore where the nail should have been.

The whole entirely withered and wretched and unmoving. Yet he was not dead, for Orisian heard him, and could feel his seething will all around. It ran dark, intrusive fingers over Orisian's thoughts. This was the home and heart of all that poisoned the world and the Shared. Orisian recognised the teeming mass of unfettered emotion that clawed at him, could almost see it as a boiling black cloud that filled the hall and flooded out through the windows, rushing in great spreading columns out into the sky, blanketing the world. The anger and the bitter hatred, the self-loathing, the fear. It was all here, in its first and simplest form.

'Why do I catch the scent of Anain?'

The doubt, the almost childish puzzlement in those words, was so acute it made Orisian sigh in distant pain. He was losing himself beneath the onslaught of this formless, purposeless power. If he did not act, he would be unable to do so at all.

He lurched forward, sword raised.

'No,' the voice told him. 'Kneel.'

And his sword slipped from his numb fingers, and his knees buckled and he went down heavily. He shrugged his arm free of the shield and it fell away from him.

'Who are you?' This time Orisian did not think the question was for him. 'I can't see you. Why can't I see you?'

K'rina was shuffling closer to Aeglyss.

And then, quite suddenly: 'Aeglyss,' K'rina said. 'It's me. It's K'rina. I came for you.'

She had a beautiful voice. Light, and fine, and easy.

Orisian could feel Aeglyss' confusion. It was so powerful, it became his, and he stared, uncomprehending, at K'rina as if he was seeing her for the first time. She stood straight, head held up. Alive and present. He felt a subtle transformation taking place inside him, inside everything. That confusion and the anger that underlay it was shifting, changing its shape. Those first emotions did not disappear, but a . . . joy was merging itself with them.

'K'rina?'

'I came for you, my son. My foster son. I felt your pain and knew I had to come.'

'Yes.' Orisian thought his skull might burst at the vigour in that single word.

'I am here for you.' K'rina smiled, stretching her arms out towards Aeglyss. 'Come. We can be together.'

'Yes.' Again, it was exultant, rising, roaring upwards. 'Let me see.'

Orisian felt all that force and power that swirled about him gathering itself, drawing itself in to coalesce around that one smiling woman, and within her. K'rina shook. She rocked from toe to heel. Her arms jerked. Her mouth opened.

There was a sudden lessening, a dampening of the cacophony raging inside Orisian. He rose to his feet, fighting back surges of nausea. He recovered his sword. When he straightened, testing the weight of the sword in his hand, K'rina had turned towards him and was staring at him.

'What?' she said through taut lips, but the voice was not truly hers now. It quivered with Aeglyss' power, with his strident tone. 'No.'

The snapped denial was like a blow in the face. Orisian closed his eyes and shook his head to try to clear it.

'No,' he heard again, and the sound rang around the hall, setting echoes of fear and anger running across the stone.

The anger found a home in Orisian, and burned in him and blurred his vision. Amidst that fierce seizure he knew what needed to happen. What needed to be done. He advanced towards K'rina.

'No,' cried Aeglyss yet again in K'rina's voice.

'I'm sorry,' gasped Orisian through the waves of crushing fury
that broke over him. He could feel blood running from his nose.
There was liquid beading in his eyes, and he did not know
whether that was blood as well or tears. He took another heavy
pace closer to K'rina.

She moved suddenly, tottering on rigid legs towards him,
toppling as if to fall at his feet. She was reaching for him, those
delicate white hands splayed, coming towards his face. Aeglyss,
Orisian shouted silently at himself. It is Aeglyss. Only him.

They were in each other's embrace then, clasped together.
K'rina's hands closed themselves on Orisian's head. His free
hand settled on her waist, just firm enough to feel her hip
bone. With his other hand he drove his sword through her
midriff.

As steel entered flesh, so those fingers laid on his scalp suddenly tightened and pressed down, and Orisian was flung
tumbling and scattering and attenuating out of his body.

He was there, with Aeglyss, inside the howling nothingness
that was K'rina. Orisian was but a collection of thoughts pulled
this way and that by the raging tempest. That tempest was both
Aeglyss and what had awaited him here within the shell of the
woman who had once been his loving guardian. Two vast powers
contended, the one striving to drag itself back and up towards
the waking world of surfaces and light and substance; the other
flailing at the first, raking it, dragging it, entwining it, struggling to contain it and haul it away, down into the bottomless
void beneath.

K'rina was cage and she was trap. There was nothing of her
here, not the most tenuous echo or memory of who she had been
or what she consisted of. Her body had been mere vessel for
older, vaster powers. Orisian could feel himself coming apart,
unable to shape coherent thought amidst such titanic expression
of unbridled potencies.

Aeglyss – the maelstrom that was his rage and desire – was in the grip of the immense will of the Anain. Their furious struggle, a storm fit to encompass worlds, threw off gouts of raw sensation that tore holes in the fabric of Orisian's consciousness, and left fragments of themselves drifting through his faltering thoughts.

He felt rasping tendrils of briar wrapped around his naked limbs, gouging great troughs into his flesh. He felt writhing tendrils forcing themselves into his mouth and into his throat, piercing him, growing into him. He felt clouds of leaves brushing over his skin; heard the creaking of ancient, mindful timber; tasted loam.

He was Aeglyss lying shivering in the snow, folded into the arms of his dead mother, feeling himself dying piece by piece of grief and fear. He was Aeglyss crucified upon the Breaking Stone, enduring the agonising revelation of possibility, feeling in the core of his being the immeasurable, unbounded wonder of the Shared opening itself to him and filling him like a flood bursting through a holed dyke.

He glimpsed, for a flashing, searing instant, the workings of the Anain mind, the many-in-one immensity of its slow movement through the insubstantial world within a world that was the Shared. He glimpsed their longing to silence the raucous, poisonous chaos Aeglyss inflicted; their deep and diffuse dismay at the suffering, the deformation, he brought to all the countless minds woven into the web of the Shared; their fear of him. And their cold and cruel calculation in taking the only living being he loved and snuffing her out of existence like the most trivial of flames on a candle, hollowing her out and making of her a snare for the monster loosed in the Shared.

Wave after wave of experience and awareness burned through Orisian, and each left him thinner than the last, each carried away some portion of his being. But then something changed, and what was rushing up towards him, blanking out all else in the enormity of its power, was no mere fragment, no glimpse. It was Aeglyss, his entirety.

And Orisian was suddenly back in his own body, standing in the hall in Kan Avor with K'rina's hands pressed to his scalp, his sword in her stomach. Her eyes – black eyes, lightless – staring into his own. He could feel Aeglyss raging towards him, feel the buffeting of his approach and the purity of his deranged anger. He could not move. Those fingers crushing against his skull were like steel claws. His own muscles were lifeless and limp, unresponsive to his terror.

He understood. Aeglyss could not be killed with sword, or knife, or fire. No bodily harm could silence him as long as he could reach into the Shared, for that was where the essence of him dwelled now. He would be unending, and a part of him would reside, for ever, in every and any mind. Unless he could be contained in this *na'kyrim*'s body as it died. Unless the Anain could hold him there while Orisian's blade stilled its heart. Some part of the Anain would die with him, for the prison they had made of K'rina could not be escaped, even by its makers; but Aeglyss would cease, and be gone from the world and from the Shared.

But now Aeglyss was ascending again. He was boiling up to the surface and pouring himself into Orisian.

'Yield to me,' Aeglyss howled. 'Open yourself to me. Become a part of me.'

Blood ran thickly over Orisian's lips now. He could taste it. He could feel it inside his ears, trickling out and down his neck. K'rina's fingers were white-hot bars against his bone. He could feel himself collapsing beneath their impossible strength.

'No,' he thought.

'I will give you life,' Aeglyss roared. 'Let me in.'

Orisian was diminishing, like mist exposed to the morning's glare. He could still feel his pain, but he was moving slowly away from it. He could observe it from beyond its crippling weight. He could hear and feel the Anain rising in Aeglyss' wake. They climbed from the deeps, reaching for him.

All the corruption of the Shared that Aeglyss had begun was now removed from it, locked with the *na'kyrim*'s mind inside K'rina. He poured it into Orisian. Every bitterness, every resentment, every hatred and fear and jealousy ran through him in place of blood, in place of the air in his lungs. Its coruscating intensity eroded him.

Out of it, though, out of that dark and misshapen memory of the Shared, he could find one thing. One choice. He could remember Lairis, and Fariel, and Kennet. Inurian and Rothe. He could smell his mother's hair, and hear the golden music of her voice. He could see Fariel, standing silhouetted against the sun. He could embrace his sorrow at the loss of those who had gone before and without him.

'Release me,' commanded Aeglyss. 'Give yourself to me.'

K'rina's hands crushed in against his skull. Orisian could hear crackings, ruptures. The splitting and collapsing of bone. Light was flaring in his eyes. It would end if he but yielded. The Anain were there, enfolding Aeglyss. But the *na'kyrim* was flooding into Orisian, forcing his way between the last resistant strands of thought.

Such agonies resounded in Orisian's head that he was blind and deaf and dumb. He felt hollow breakage in his temples, the back of his skull.

No. He did not speak it. He simply chose. And reached towards the beloved dead. As they faded, and he faded, he could feel Aeglyss falling away. Into the smothering Anain. Into the eternal, perfect cage of K'rina. Aeglyss screamed in impotent ire. And fell. And he faded, just as Orisian did. He faltered, just as Orisian did. He ceased.

*

The Inkallim came on and up. She lacked the room for elegant and deceptive swings in the tight confines of the stairwell, but still she was fast, and in her hands those swords could stab and probe with all the speed of daggers. Again and again, a rain of blows aimed at his chest and shoulders would draw Taim's shield up, and then she would somehow have changed her grip on a sword and it was lancing down towards his feet. Each time he had to yield another step, and together they climbed, in that fierce dance, slowly towards whatever lay above.

At length, inevitably, Taim was too slow, and she laid a deep cut through the side of his boot into his calf. He felt the blood at once, even as he was steadying himself. His strength was flowing out, through that and his other wounds. He could not hope to sustain this effort for long. Already, he was breathing hard, and his shield was beginning to feel heavy on his arm. If he permitted this struggle to continue, he would die, and so would Orisian.

There would be, he knew, no more than a hint of an opening, so that was all he sought. When it came, he was not even confident it was so much as a hint. She was moving up and forward, both blades lunging up but a little way behind the rising of her body. His feet were as they had to be, his back heel braced against the riser of the next step. The natural flow of his weight was taking him forward. He launched himself, flung himself as high and hard as he could, aiming to pass over her shoulder. And he let his sword fall, for he needed his hand.

He made a club of his shield and punched it into her shoulder, driving the stub of the arrow still deeper into flesh. He reached for the strapping that held her scabbards crossways on her back with his free hand, locked his fingers under it, and rolled himself over her, surrendering his body to the plummeting fall beyond. Her twin swords darted up more quickly than he had expected, and he felt another slicing pain across his leg, but his weight had hit her by then, and he was falling into the open spiral of the stairwell beyond her, and taking her with him.

They fell entwined, clattering and flailing their way down. Taim felt a finger breaking as his hand was twisted free from its grip on the strapping, a blinding blow on his cheekbone that split the skin, bruises being hammered into his legs and flanks by the steps and the walls. His shield almost broke his nose. He could hear metal clanging off the stonework.

The final impact was punishing. Taim landed on his side, with his shield beneath him. A searing pain made him think for a moment he had snapped a bone in the arm pinned under him; there was no sound of breakage, though. He sucked in a chestful of air, lifting his dazed head and looking blearily about for the Inkallim. She was lying on her front beside him, blood streaming from a gash in her forehead. He could not see her swords. Her eyes were already blinking open, staring out at him through the blood coursing over them and through the lashes.

Taim's body was a welter of small agonies and expansive aches. It screamed and spasmed in protest as he willed it to move. The Inkallim planted her hands and pushed herself up. Taim caught the hiss of pain as she did so, and took heart from it. He struggled to get his knees under him so that he could rise. The Inkallim was halfway up, but her injured shoulder, with that arrowhead buried deep inside it, buckled and dipped, and had her swaying.

Taim hit her backhanded across the mouth with the ball of his gloved fist. She rolled onto her side, into the base of the wall. Taim staggered to his feet, but lost his balance and had to put out a hand to stop himself falling back onto the stairs. A sudden stave of fire impaled his thigh, and he looked down to find her fingers clawing into the wound she had put there earlier. It was her weaker arm, for with her good one she was hauling herself upright, scraping herself up against the wall.

Taim howled, and hammered the edge of his shield down on her extended shoulder. Her bloody fingers were ripped free from his leg. Taim thought he heard something snapping or tearing in the shoulder joint. He whipped the shield back up and hit her in the face with it. She slumped. He hit her again and again, putting all his weight behind the shield, pounding it at her head until he felt her skull break.

Chest heaving, propped against the wall on one straight arm, trembling, he shook the shield free. It rolled out into the street, spun a wobbling circle there and fell flat. Taim took one short look at the dead Inkallim and climbed the steps. Each small rise felt like torment, and he had to hold on to the walls to keep himself from falling. He found his sword halfway up. His broken finger was in his sword hand, so he had to hold it in the other. The hilt felt thick there, clumsy and unfamiliar.

He found an open door at the top of the stairs and stumbled into a hall. His feet were loud on the rotten floorboards, but there was none there able to react. He walked heavily forward to where K'rina and Orisian lay together in some strange embrace, in the centre of the hall. Orisian's sword had transfixed the *na'kyrim*.

A twisted, tortured strand of sound drew Taim's attention to one of the pillars. A battered, dishevelled man was slumped there, with dead ruins for hands. Taim did not recognise him. He was laughing, but it was a sick, choking kind of laughter. He was staring down towards the far end of the hall.

Taim looked that way, and saw perched on a low stone bench, a small, pale cadaver. It looked almost as if someone had arranged it there: set the hands together neatly in its lap, placed the bare, blistered, decaying feet side by side, perfectly aligned. It was a frail thing. A sad, pathetic thing.

And then Taim realised it was not dead. Its chest shivered with faint breath. He walked slowly towards it. It did not move save for that tremor in its ribcage. It made no sound save for the rustle in and out of fresh and spent air. Taim stood over it. His mind was clear, he realised. For the first time in . . . weeks, perhaps, there was a flawless unity: he was whole, and entire, and only himself. He heard nothing save the slow, calm turning of his own thoughts. He felt nothing save weariness and sadness.

He put a hand under the horror's chin and lifted its face. It was ravaged by disease and injury. But the eyes were open. Taim looked into them. They were full of blood, only the smallest flecks of their original slaty grey showing through here and there. And they were empty. Utterly unresponsive.

Taim ran his sword through the centre of that fluttering chest. There was almost no resistance. It was like cutting through parchment. The corpse fell sideways and lay there on the bench. Taim turned away and walked back to stand over Orisian. The man propped against the pillar was still laughing, though it was softer, fading slowly. He was looking at Taim now, watching him with an unreadable expression.

Taim wondered briefly whether to kill him. But he did not know who he was, or what he deserved. His injuries would surely put an end to him soon enough. And, most powerfully of all, Taim had had enough of killing. He sheathed his sword and went down on one knee.

Taim raised his dead Thane in his arms, and bore the body away from that hall. He was surprised at how light it was.

X

Winter's end came amidst a series of damp days, with cloud and winds that ran boisterously up the Glas Valley. Some few eager trees brought forth the very first tender leaves of the new season, as luminously green as the most radiant of gems. White blushes of delicate flowers spread through the forest floor. Birds rediscovered their songs.

This resurgence went uncelebrated, even by those for whom this movement of the world out of slumber and into renewed wakefulness would normally be cause for festivity. There had in past years been garlands of the earliest flowers worn by the girls, flocks of sheep or cattle driven through the streets of towns with all the children running alongside and feasting, of course.

Few hearts were light enough for such things this year. Many were fearful, bewildered. Some were still engaged in the business of bloodshed. Some were waiting, still hoping, for certainty that the awful shadow beneath which they had suffered, and to which they had lost a precious fraction of themselves, had truly lifted. And some were yet making hard journeys toward unknown futures.

Eska of the Hunt and Kanin oc Horin-Gyre descended into the lands of the Horin Blood down an old, long-disused drover's road. He leaned on her, for he was still weak and seldom had the strength to walk unaided for very far.

That he had any strength at all was a source of no little surprise to Eska. She had thought him to be doomed when she found him in the hall in Kan Avor, slumped on the floor close to the wasted corpse of Aeglyss and that of another *na'kyrim*, a woman Eska did not recognise.

The Thane's hands had been black with corruption. Useless appendages already, she suspected, rotting on the inside. She had cut them off and sealed the stumps with fire. It was necessary, but she had expected such treatment to kill him. As it transpired, Kanin was more resilient than she had imagined. He had not died then, and she was beginning to believe that he would not be dying soon.

The long walk through the mountains had been brutal, for she had kept them well clear of the Vale of Stones, disinclined to follow what she adjudged was likely to be a dangerous, if much easier, path. The flood of the faithful that had come south across the Vale was now reversed, but in different form. Now, it was a trickle, a meagre, desultory flow of broken and lost people. Most of those Eska had seen were dazed, so defeated by the memory of what they had seen and felt and done that they made themselves easy victims of the vengeful people of the Glas Valley. There were even fewer of those than there were survivors of the Black Road army, but their anger burned the brighter, and they hunted the retreating companies mercilessly.

So Eska had chosen a rougher, narrower trail, winding its way through higher valleys and around colder peaks. There had been bad weather and driving winds, but Kanin had not succumbed. Nor had she, and her own wound was no small burden. It had been a prolonged and agonising business extracting her own barbed spear from her flank. She had made several unsuccessful attempts at breaking the shaft, and pulling it through her body before she achieved it, and in the course of her struggles had several times been rendered senseless by the pain. She still could not walk without considerable suffering, and bending or stretching or twisting were entirely beyond her.

The weight of Kanin oc Horin-Gyre across her shoulders made it worse. But she said nothing.

The Thane had said no more than a few words to her all through their long march. He talked sometimes in his troubled sleep, but it was seldom comprehensible. When they rested, he would simply sit and stare out across the blasted snowscape. Silent. Lost in memory, or imagining, or thought. Sometimes he would look down at the blunt, bandaged stumps of his wrists. If he despaired at the sight of his maiming, he hid it well.

And now they at last descended. There was still snow, but it was melting quickly. On the lower slopes Eska could see people moving, and further down the valley a little village. Distantly, she could hear the lowing of cattle cooped up in some shed.

'It's done, then,' she said to Kanin.

And to her surprise he took his arm away from her shoulders and slumped down into the snow and sat there weeping. His face crumpled as thoroughly as would that of any distraught child. Eska stood at a respectful distance and waited. It took a long time.

When he was emptied of it, he looked across to her and lifted his arms from his knees.

'Do you think a man can still be Thane, with . . .' He could not finish the question.

Eska shrugged.

'I do not know. I saw a man once, in Kan Dredar, who had lost his hand. To a bear, I think. He had a carver make him a wooden one. It was crude. Of little use, and he could not wear it all the time for it rubbed his . . . skin raw. But he looked whole.'

'Ha. I would settle for that. To look whole. If I had my hands, still all I would hope for was to look whole. Some wounds never close up, no matter how carefully they are tended. But a man need not be whole to be Thane. Come, help me up. Let us see what welcome awaits us.'

*

Anyara stood with Ilessa oc Kilkry on the quayside of Kolglas, watching the crew ready the ship. They worked in silence. The crowd assembled all along the harbour watched in silence. The seagulls wheeled overhead, screeching.

'I am grateful that you came,' Anyara said to the older woman.

'Of course. Our Bloods spring from the same root. And now, it seems, we are greatly in your debt. Your brother's debt. Of course I came.'

Anyara smiled and nodded her thanks. There was a faint warmth in the sun on her face. It felt like an entirely new thing: a sensation she had never before experienced in all her life. As if it were a new kind of warmth in a new world.

'You must have a great many demands upon your time, though,' she said. 'And it cannot have been an easy journey.'

'Are any journeys easy now? And there is too little time, no matter where I am, how hard I labour. Repairs. Rebuilding.

Finding food for the unhomed and the orphaned. The Tal Dyreens bring shiploads of grain and require us to empty our treasury in exchange for it. The Black Road still lurks in distant corners of our lands. We will be fighting bandits for years, I think. Many fled into the Vare Waste, many beyond the Karkyre Peaks, where by all rumours' account they are not welcomed by what remains of the White Owls. Not welcomed at all.'

'And Highfast?'

'It might be again as it was once was. Perhaps. There are some prepared to try. A few. There was a message from one of them – a man called Hammarn – for the *na'kyrim* . . . for Yvane. I gave it to her last night. It seemed to please her, though it was difficult to be sure.'

Anyara looked along the quayside a little way. Someone was moving through the crowd, handing out oatmeal biscuits and offering ale. It seemed a strange fragment of normality amidst so much that felt unreal. Impossible.

'Your son . . .?' she asked quietly.

Dismay perturbed Ilessa's features, just briefly. She mastered herself.

'Unchanged. Roaric is lost to us, I fear. He moves and breathes, and speaks even at times. But his sense has fled him. He is Thane, but . . . but the reins must stay in my hands. For as long as I can hold them.'

'I'm sorry.'

'Sorry. Yes. It will not be easy for either of us, I think. The Bloods are not accustomed to the rule of a woman.'

Anyara grunted. 'To say the least of it. They will accustom themselves to it in time. But not yet: every day I am asked when I intend to marry and put a Thane on the throne beside me.'

'You should,' Ilessa said, too quickly, too forcefully. It was gentler when she repeated it: 'You should. Not to please others, not to silence doubters. Because you will not want to be alone. Not for long. Do not make yourself alone.'

'No,' murmured Anyara. And then asked, 'What do you suppose will happen?'

'We can't know that. We will have to wait and see. And hope we meet it well.'

The crowd at the far end of the harbour shifted and parted, and a small group came through. Yvane, and Coinach, and Taim Narran with his arm about his wife Jaen. That was a good sight, those two in such an embrace. It made Anyara smile. The first time she had smiled today. She was still smiling as her eyes met Coinach's, and his own lips caught the warmth and reflected it.

'My lady,' her shieldman said, dipping his head respectfully as they drew near.

He took such pleasure in flouting her command to call her by her name. It was a game between them now. A gentle, affectionate game.

Yvane looked the most despondent of all of them. Her gaze was on the lidded clay vase Anyara clutched to her breast. Anyara tightened her grip on the vessel.

'It will soon be done,' she said to the *na'kyrim*, and Yvane nodded sadly.

'They look to be ready, my lady,' Taim said.

Anyara turned to the long, low boat. The oarsmen were at their posts. The helmsman stood at the tiller. That smile was gone already, but it could not have survived this moment in any case.

'Let's go then,' she said.

Taim hugged his wife, and kissed her forehead, and whispered in her ear. She touched her hand to his cheek and backed away. The rest of them descended into the corpse-ship.

The oarsmen edged it slowly out of the harbour. Castle Kolglas, standing on its rocky outpost amidst the waves, watched them pass; and Anyara watched it, awash with memories, with regrets and sorrow. The place was still empty, still a ruin. She did not know when – or if – it would be habitable once more.

There was a rare, light wind from the south today, and Anyara was glad of that, for she wanted this outward journey to be a quick one. Once beyond the harbour's embrace, the single square sail was soon raised, and it flapped and creaked and then caught the wind and tightened, and the prow of the ship began to punch its way through the waves, out into the Glas Estuary.

Anyara sat alone on a bench, with that vase held tight, and closed her eyes. She surrendered herself to the sound of the sea on the hull, the voices of the seagulls that escorted them, the sun on her face. It was not peace, but there was a secret stillness in those sensations she could draw upon.

Dimly, she could hear Taim talking with Ilessa oc Kilkry behind her. Their voices were low.

'And Haig?' Taim was asking.

Ilessa snorted. 'Chaos, from what I hear. They lost thousands in the battles, and now they're fighting Dornach and Dargannan in the south. It's going badly, evidently. Not that anyone seems to know who is giving the orders. One day I'm told it's the Crafts, the next someone says Stravan has turned up and taken the throne. Whoever it is, they're in no position to try to drag Kilkry and Lannis back under their yoke.'

'Perhaps there's no Haig Blood left at all,' Taim mused.

'There's Abeh. But they say she lost her mind when her husband was killed, and hasn't recovered. Foul woman. I'd not wish such . . . horrors on anyone, but she . . . no, not even her perhaps. What about the Black Road?'

'Oh, it's . . .' Anyara could hear Taim's shrug. 'Mystifying. We had a message from Ragnor oc Gyre himself – meant for Gryvan, but we took it – pledging immediate peace, lasting peace. We questioned the messenger, sent one or two scouts north across the Vale ourselves, and it's as if the madness hasn't ended up there, as far as we can tell. The Inkallim have been all but destroyed, but whatever's left of them is fighting Ragnor, along with half his own people. Horin-Gyre seems to be the only Blood that hasn't taken up arms against one of the others.'

'Well, it gives us time, at least.'

'It does. But I leave as much of the plotting as I can to others now. I've hung up my sword. There's a new Captain in Castle Anduran: Torcaill. He's . . .'

Anyara let the voices fade from her awareness. Time. There was never enough of that.

They stepped onto The Grave. A wind-scoured, bare isle beneath the rugged headland of Dol Harigaig. Anyara could feel the spray from the waves breaking along the island's western shore. The wind cast her hair across her face.

It was called Il Dromnone first, and people said it was the body of a fallen giant. It became The Grave during the Heart Fever, when the harboursides of Kolglas and Glasbridge filled every day with bodies wrapped in cerements, and the corpse-ships ploughed back and forth with cruel regularity. Lairis and Fariel had come here. Now she had brought Orisian to join them, certain in her heart that it was what he would have chosen.

She cradled the clay pot containing his ashes in her arms as she walked over The Grave's uneven, slick rocks. Taim had carried Orisian out of Kan Avor through a day and long night, without stopping, to a cottage on the edge of Anlane where others waited. They had built a pyre amongst tree stumps, looking out over the valley, and consigned him to the flames. Afterwards, Anyara knew – though the *na'kyrim* would not speak of it – Yvane had gone back into Kan Avor with Taim. And what, she wondered, must it have cost the warrior to return to that place, having once escaped it? They had gone back and found K'rina's body, and buried it out in the marshlands by the River Glas.

But Anyara had not been there, for any of it. Now she would mourn in her way. Yvane, Coinach and Taim stood by the boat on flat rocks. She walked away from them, going alone across the naked isle, buffeted by the wind, tasting the sea on her lips. When she came to what she thought was the highest point in The Grave's low emergence above the waves, she stopped and stood, and savoured for a moment this wild and free place. The wind was bringing tears to her eyes. It was not grief. Not yet.

She held the urn in both hands and lifted it up, showed it to that little group gathered back at the water's edge. Then she turned and showed it to two more watchers.

High up, on the precipitous slope above the cliffs of Dol Harigaig, two pale and distant figures stood. They were too far away for Anyara to see clearly, but she knew that Varryn and Ess'yr had eyes much sharper than her own. She was not sure, but she thought one at least of them raised an arm in acknowledgement of her gesture.

Anyara hugged the urn to her and knelt down. She did cry then, briefly. She folded herself over that hard clay vase, and was angry, and sad, and frightened. She let those feelings go, on the wind; imagined them tumbling and skimming away over the foaming crests of the waves into the north.

She took the lid from the urn, and let the wind take her brother's ashes too.

'Forgiven,' she whispered as she watched it clouding away, dusting itself over the rocks, spinning on gusts into the sky.

'Forgiven, of course. But there was nothing to forgive.'

As the corpse-ship readied itself to depart from The Grave, a small rowboat was lowered noisily over the side. Yvane climbed down into it, and a single oarsman – the strongest of the crew. He flailed his way across the waves and the wind to a narrow gravel beach nestled among gigantic black boulders on the southern flank of Dol Harigaig. He drove his tiny craft up onto that beach, the pebbles hissing as the keel ploughed into them.

Yvane clambered out, ungainly but dry-shod, thanked the man

and walked towards Ess'yr and Varryn, who had descended to meet her. No words were exchanged between *na'kyrim* and Kyrinin. They climbed together up onto the high ground, going slowly and carefully over first a winding trail made by wild goats, and then on the damp, slick turf of the headland. Ess'yr moved easily, though one arm was still bound up in a tight sling.

They walked for a long time along the Car Anagais that formed the steep northern shore of the estuary, skirting the tree line as they went. The land was empty, for the Fox were much reduced, and no *vo'an* remained south of the Vale of Tears. Perhaps in future years. Perhaps.

Late on the second day, as the greater ramparts of the Car Criagar came into sight ahead of them, they turned northward, and began the long descent through hills and wooded vales towards the Dihrve Valley.

They parted then. Yvane and Varryn went on ahead to find a place to camp for the night. Ess'yr went down to the thickets along the side of a narrow, gurgling stream. She found there a stand of willow, and cut a stem. She chose a good one, straight and healthy, on the brink of giving forth its fresh, dagger-shaped leaves. She trimmed its cut base to make the wound clean and neat. Then she pushed it into the soft, moist earth close to the bank of the stream. She opened the hole it had made by rolling her wrist, swaying the stake round in widening circles, and then withdrew it and laid it flat on the ground.

From under her belt she brought a folded scrap of deerhide. As she could work with only one hand, she had to put it down on a fallen log in order to open it out and take hold of the knotted cord it contained. She knelt and gently lowered the cord into the hole the willow stake had made. Her long fingers carefully pressed it in deep, to make sure it was settled and secure there. She paused, head bowed, in reflection for a few moments.

Ess'yr rose, and planted the staff of willow over the cord. She firmed it into place with her foot and stepped back. The willow stood tall and perfectly erect. She nodded once to it, respectfully, turned and walked away. To find her brother and the *na'kyrim*. To join them beside a fire, and eat and rest and anticipate the coming of a new season.

Epilogue

Anyara

With all my heart, I would be with you now. I try not to fear for you. I remind myself that you were always the stronger of us. Even when there were three of us, I think perhaps you were the strongest, though I did not understand it until later.

Rothe died. Torcaill can tell you how and why, if you want to know. We are the last of home now, you and I, the last of Kolglas. I look around me, and I see familiar faces, but I miss those I knew in Kolglas.

I want more than anything to walk with you through the market in Kolglas again, and to go hawking with you along its shore, and to steal warm bread from its kitchens. That is what I mean to do. It is what I hope to do. But that may not be how this ends. I do not know if I can make any difference in any of this, but I think I see at least the outline of something that perhaps needs to be done. And I choose to try to do it.

You do not deserve the burden, but there is no one else. If I am gone, I leave to your care our Blood and our home.

I think now, looking back, that we all die, little by little, as each of those we love departs before us. Forgive me, sister, if I have gone before you.

Orisian

The Passage of Time

The First Age

Began when the Gods made the world and put the One Race in it to inhabit it.

Ended when the One Race rose up against the Gods and was destroyed.

The Second Age

Began when the Gods made the Five Races: Huanin, Kyrinin, Whreinin, Saolin and Anain.

The Huanin and Kyrinin made war upon the Whreinin and destroyed that race, and were thereafter named the Tainted Races for their sin, and forfeited the love of the Gods.

Ended when the Gods departed from the world.

The Third Age

Began with the absence of the Gods, and with chaos.

Year

280 The Adravane and Aygll Kingships arose

398 Marain the Stonemason began the construction of Highfast, at the behest of the Aygll King

451 The Alsire Kingship arose, and the era of the Three Kingships began

775 The three Huanin Kingships united against the Kyrinin clans and the War of the Tainted began

787 Tarcene, the Aygll King, was bound, his mind enslaved, by the *na'kyrim* Orlane; his own daughter, in despair, killed him

788 Tane, the Kyrinin's Shining City, was captured by the Huanin armies, the Deep Rove was raised by the Anain, and the War of the Tainted ended

792 Morvain's Revolt, a rising against the faltering Aygll Kingship, culminated in a failed siege of Highfast

793 The last Aygll monarch – Lerr, the Boy King – was slain at In'Vay, and the era of the Three Kingships ended; Aygll lands descended into chaos and the Storm Years began

847 The Bloods – Kilkry, Haig, Gyre, Ayth and Taral – were founded in Aygll lands, and Kulkain oc Kilkry became the first Thane of Thanes; the end of the Storm Years

849 Kulkain oc Kilkry bade Lorryn the *na'kyrim* establish at Highfast a library for the preservation of learning and knowledge

852 The last Alsire King was slain, and the first King of the Dornach line took his throne in Evaness

922 The Black Road heresy arose in Kilvale; Amanath the Fisherwoman, its originator, was executed and the creed outlawed by the Bloods

939 Avann oc Gyre-Kilkry, Thane of the Gyre Blood, adopted the creed of the Black Road

940 Civil war broke out amongst the Kilkry Bloods, between the adherents of the Black Road and those opposed to the creed

942 Following their defeat in battle at Kan Avor, the Gyre Blood and all adherents of the Black Road were exiled beyond the

Vale of Stones, and founded there the Bloods of the Black Road: Gyre, Horin, Gaven, Wyn and Fane

945 The Lore and Battle Inkalls were founded by the Bloods of the Black Road

948 The last attempt by the Kilkry Bloods to crush the fledgling Bloods of the Black Road in the north ended in failure; their armies retired south of the Vale of Stones and the fortification of Tanwrye began

959 The Hunt Inkall was founded by the Bloods of the Black Road

973 The Lannis Blood was founded, in reward for Sirian Lannis dar Kilkry's defeat of the invading forces of the Black Road at Kolglas

997 Haig replaced Kilkry as first amongst the True Bloods

1052 The Dargannan Blood was founded

1069 The Lannis-Haig Blood defeated Horin-Gyre in the Battle of the Stone Vale, near Tanwrye

1070 Tavan oc Lannis-Haig died, and his son Croesan succeeded him as Thane of the Lannis Blood

1097 The Lannis-Haig Blood was afflicted by the Heart Fever, which killed almost one in six

1102 The Dargannan Blood rebelled against the authority of Haig, and Gryvan oc Haig, Thane of Thanes, summoned the armies of the True Bloods to march against them

Cast of Characters

The True Bloods

Haig
Lannis-Haig
Kilkry-Haig
Dargannan-Haig
Ayth-Haig
Taral-Haig

Haig Blood

Gryvan oc Haig	The High Thane, Thane of Thanes
Abeh oc Haig	Gryvan's wife
Aewult nan Haig	Gryvan's first son, the Bloodheir
Stravan nan Haig	Gryvan's second son
Ishbel	Aewult's companion
Kale	Gryvan's bodyguard and Captain of his Shield
Mordyn Jerain, the Shadowhand	Chancellor of the Haig Blood, a Tal Dyreen
Tara Jerain	The Chancellor's wife
Eleth	A maid in Mordyn Jerain's palace
Torquentine	A man in Vaymouth
Magrayn	A woman in Vaymouth, Torquentine's doorkeeper
Lammain	Craftmaster of the Goldsmiths
Lagair Haldyn	Gryvan's Steward in Kolkyre

Lannis-Haig Blood

Orisian oc Lannis-Haig		The Thane
Anyara nan Lannis-Haig		Orisian's sister
Taim Narran		Captain of Castle Anduran
Jaen		Taim's wife
Coinach		Anyara's shieldman
Torcaill		A warrior
The Dead:	Kennet	Orisian's father, killed at Kolglas
	Lairis	Orisian's mother, died of the Heart Fever
	Fariel	Orisian's elder brother, died of the Heart Fever
	Croesan	The late Thane, Orisian's uncle, killed at Anduran
	Naradin	Croesan's son, killed at Anduran
	Eilan	Naradin's wife, killed at Anduran
	Inurian	Kennet's *na'kyrim* counsellor, killed at Sarn's Leap
	Rothe	Orisian's shieldman, killed in the Veiled Woods

Kilkry-Haig Blood

Roaric oc Kalkry-Haig		The Thane, second son of Lheanor
Ilessa oc Kilkry-Haig		Roaric's mother, widow of Lheanor
Herraic		Lheanor's cousin, Captain of the Highfast garrison
Erval		Captain of the Ive Guard
The Dead:	Lheanor	The late Thane, killed by the Hunt Inkall
	Gerain	Lheanor's first son, killed in battle at Grive

Dargannan-Haig Blood

Igryn oc Dargannan-Haig	Former Thane, now blinded and imprisoned at Vaymouth

The Bloods Of The Black Road

Gyre
Horin-Gyre
Gaven-Gyre
Wyn-Gyre
Fane-Gyre
and the Inkallim

Gyre Blood

Ragnor oc Gyre		The High Thane, Thane of Thanes
The Dead:	Temegrin	Third Captain of the High Thane's armies, killed by Aeglyss at Kan Avor

Horin-Gyre Blood

Kanin oc Horin-Gyre		The Thane
Vana oc Horin-Gyre		Mother to Kanin and Wain, widow of Angain
Igris		Kanin's shieldman
The Dead:	Angain	The late Thane, died in his bed
	Wain	Kanin's sister, killed at Kan Avor

Inkallim

Theor		First of the Lore Inkall
Nyve		First of the Battle Inkall
Avenn		First of the Hunt Inkall
Goedellin		Inner Servant of the Lore Inkall, emissary of Theor
Shraeve		Banner-captain and field commander of the Battle Inkall
Cannek		A Hunt Inkallim
Eska		A Hunt Inkallim
The Dead:	Fiallic	Former Banner-captain of the Battle Inkall, killed by Shraeve

Others

Huanin
Kyrinin
Na'kyrim

Huanin

Alem T'anarch	Ambassador of the Dornach Kingship to the Haig Blood

Kyrinin

Ess'yr	A woman of the Fox clan
Varryn	Ess'yr's brother
Hothyn	Son of the White Owl Voice, now companion of Aeglyss

Na'kyrim

Yvane		A *na'kyrim* in the company of Orisian
Eshenna		A *na'kyrim* from Highfast, now in the company of Orisian
Hammarn		A *na'kyrim* from Koldihrve, now in Highfast
Amonyn		A *na'kyrim* in Highfast, lover of Cerys
Olyn		A *na'kyrim* in Highfast, Keeper of Crows
K'rina		A *na'kyrim* from Dyrkyrnon, once foster mother to Aeglyss
Aeglyss		A *na'kyrim* who survived the Breaking Stone of the White Owls
The Dead:	Cerys	The Elect of Highfast, killed there by Aeglyss
	Tyn	The Dreamer in Highfast, killed there by Aeglyss
	Bannain	A *na'kyrim* in Highfast, killed there by Aeglyss